Open Your Eyes

by

Jann Rowland

One Good Sonnet Publishing

This is a work of fiction, based on the works of Jane Austen. All of the characters and events portrayed in this novel are products of Jane Austen's original novel, the author's imagination, or are used fictitiously.

OPEN YOUR EYES

Copyright © 2014 Jann Rowland

Published by One Good Sonnet Publishing

All rights reserved.

ISBN: 0992000033
ISBN-13: 978-0992000035

To my family who have, as always, shown
their unconditional love and encouragement.

ACKNOWLEDGEMENTS

Particular thanks and recognition to a
Remarkably supportive family who
Incite my passion for writing,
Demonstrate absolute support, and
Encourage me to follow my dreams.

&

Proofing help, as always, my partner Lelia, who
Reads my broken
English, provides suggestions,
Justifies my efforts, and
Understands and shares my passion.
Double thanks to all who
Indicate
Continual support and
Encouragement of every kind. Your assistance is appreciated.

"Some time or other he *will* be—but it shall not be by *me*. Till I can forget his father, I can never defy or expose *him*."

Mr. Wickham, Pride & Prejudice, Chapter 16

Chapter I

*I*t is a commonly understood truth that pleasant young men in possession of fine and pleasing manners have no trouble making themselves agreeable to single young women.

However, it should also be understood that not all young men have the best intentions when recommending themselves to others. Sometimes, in the course of general conversation, a choice of words, a phrase which perhaps should not have been spoken at all, can at times induce a young lady to obtain a much greater knowledge than a young man had intended or wanted, assuming that such a lady is astute enough to discover the meaning behind the words which were spoken. In some cases, when a young man has harmful or untrue statements to impart, he may even contradict what he has previously said if he does not take great care in remaining consistent.

Such was the situation in which Elizabeth Bennet found herself one fateful evening in her Aunt Phillips's parlor.

Were Elizabeth to be honest with herself, she would be forced to confess that she appreciated Mr. Wickham's words concerning the man she loved to detest—Mr. Fitzwilliam Darcy. The man had had the gall to offend her on the night of their first meeting and had subsequently proceeded to reinforce her estimation of his proud and haughty ways, his selfish disdain for others, and his perceived superiority over everyone with whom he came in contact.

And if she had not already thought him to be disagreeable, her time at Netherfield would have sealed the matter. His performance there—his ill-concealed superiority, especially concerning the matter of his faults or lack thereof—had more than convinced her that Mr. Darcy was a man who thought himself so much better than the world around him. He was undoubtedly intelligent, but this intelligence only magnified his pride, conceit, and the meanness of his opinions concerning those whose situations in life did not equal his own.

Thus, when Mr. Wickham related his claim that Mr. Darcy had denied him of his godfather's chosen reward, suddenly Elizabeth felt she had proof that Mr. Darcy's faults included not only appalling manners, but also unchristian behavior. Indeed, if he could behave in such a manner toward a young man with whom he had been raised, how much crueler might he be to the world at large?

Elizabeth had to acknowledge that her decided opinion of Mr. Darcy meant she was taking Mr. Wickham's story in eagerly, being overcome with an almost fervent glee—mixed with outrage at Mr. Darcy's audacity—at hearing this proof.

But then Mr. Wickham had spoken those fatal words in response to her fervently stated opinion that Mr. Darcy should be publicly disgraced for his actions, telling her: "Some time or other he *will* be—but it shall not be by *me*. Till I can forget his father, I can never defy or expose *him*."

Elizabeth rolled the words around in her head, thinking that perhaps she had mistaken Mr. Wickham's meaning. Had he instead been suggesting some other conviction? Or perhaps he had misspoken and inferred something wholly unintended?

No, there could be no mistake. According to Mr. Wickham, he could never expose the master of Pemberley, as he had too much respect for the man's father. And if that was so, then why had he shared his intelligence with her, an acquaintance of only a few hours? What could he mean by it?

"Miss Bennet?"

The sound of Mr. Wickham's voice pulled Elizabeth from her reverie, and she peered up at him, noting the half frown which had come over his face.

"Oh, please forgive me, Mr. Wickham," blurted Elizabeth, not knowing what to say. "I believe I allowed my mind to wander."

She was now not as interested in continuing this conversation as she had previously been—his contradiction of his own words made her suspicious of his designs, and she wondered whether his cheerful and agreeable manners were an affectation to hide whatever he truly was from others. Though she was still confused and upset over the realization, what she wished for most was a respite in which she could examine their interactions and his words in a more thorough manner. Only then could she more fully discern for herself whether this man could be trusted.

"I had not thought I had lost the ability to hold the attention of a lady, but it appears I was mistaken." declared Mr. Wickham, his tone light and playful.

No doubt he intended his words in jest, but Elizabeth took just enough warning in them to determine that *if* his confidences were false and *if* his manners were a mask to hide the real man, it might not be prudent to openly acknowledge her understanding of his duplicity. If he was truly attempting to deceive her, then the character defects necessary to defame another man without scruple, almost certainly hid *other* character defects of a potentially more serious nature. So Elizabeth, calling on her own social prowess, fell back on what she knew best—she teased him.

"Oh, I do not know that I would say that, Mr. Wickham," said she, giving him an arch look. "I assure you that I consider you every bit the diverting conversation partner."

Mr. Wickham laughed, his good humor apparently restored. "I am very glad to hear it, Miss Bennet. I must own that I have never before met such a charming young lady with whom I have been able to converse with so easily despite such a short acquaintance. I am very much looking forward to knowing you better."

Had Elizabeth missed the contradiction of his own words, she might very well have also missed the salacious gleam in his eyes and the way they raked over her form. Feeling suddenly uncomfortable in his presence, Elizabeth was forced to acknowledge that his company had lost much of its allure. His flattery was as thick and sweet as honey, and his charming smile now seemed false—a mask donned to mislead others. Elizabeth still determined to think on the subject at a later date, but at that moment, she was resolved not to fall for his false flattery!

Still, there was small talk to be made, and until Elizabeth felt she could extricate herself from his company, she had little choice but to affect a friendly and engaging mien. Serious contemplation would come later.

So she sat in his company, speaking with him, laughing at his witty repartee, and sharing a little of herself with him, if only to keep him unsuspicious of her feelings, and as their conversation progressed, she began to feel ever more confident that her suspicions were correct. Invariably, as their discourse progressed, Mr. Wickham attempted to turn the conversation back to Mr. Darcy and to wax poetic upon the wrongs done to him by that gentleman. Though Elizabeth almost ground her teeth together in frustration, she listened, commiserated, and showed the proper amount of outrage and empathy, all the while trying to turn the conversation to other subjects. The problem was that the man did not seem to have much to say of anything else. Of literature, he was perfectly indifferent; of the topics of politics and the current situation of the war with the French tyrant, he seemed to have little real knowledge. There seemed to be, in truth, little for them to discuss on an intellectual level.

He flattered well and said pleasing words for the purpose of enlarging her vanity, but it become quickly evident that he was all charm and little substance, though Elizabeth suspected that had she been taken in by his manners and missed the contradiction of his words, she might very well have fallen under his spell. As it was, the effect of his flattery was quite different from what he undoubtedly intended, as it informed her that she had best be wary in this man's presence; he was not a man to be trusted. It was a very relieved Elizabeth who finally surrendered his company to Lydia, who had cajoled Mary into playing so they could dance.

The following days were spent in introspection as Elizabeth attempted to puzzle through the problem of the two gentlemen from Derbyshire. So extreme was her distraction that it was remarked upon by all the members of her family—her mother with vexation, her younger sisters with amusement, and her father and Jane with concern. She assured them all that she was very well, and she claimed she was merely distracted by a few things which had been on her mind.

Much though she would have liked to share her suppositions with Jane, she decided against it after much thought. The intelligence imposed upon her by Mr. Wickham was in such question that she felt she could not take the chance of exposing it to anyone for fear that it could create unsubstantiated rumors about Mr. Darcy. Besides, Jane would have insisted that there was some great misunderstanding and that neither young man was to blame. Elizabeth, who knew that the world was a much harsher place, could not bear to force such unhappy conclusions upon her beloved sister, especially when they were all based on suspicion and innuendo.

In regard to the gentleman from Derbyshire, she was forced to consider him more than she had ever been disposed to do before. She was conscious of the fact that her poor opinion of Mr. Darcy had been formed on the strength of his one rude statement the night of their first meeting. Every subsequent interaction between them—at least from her side—had been colored by that single event.

Elizabeth was forced to revisit her opinion of him. She had branded him as having the worst sort of pride and conceit, but given what she knew of his station in life, she now had to acknowledge that though excessive pride was indeed a defect, he *did* have much of which to be proud. Other than that, she was forced to conclude that she had nothing with which to accuse him—nothing in his manners or character suggested evil or immoral tendencies, and his behavior after their initial introduction had been impeccable, if a little aloof. In fact, everything she had witnessed of him suggested that far from being a *bad* man, he was in fact a very upstanding one.

Did he consider himself to be above his company? Elizabeth had to acknowledge that he likely did, if his behavior was anything to go by. But though he perhaps did espouse such feelings, his manners certainly did not reach the level of the supercilious and barely concealed contempt which the Bingley sisters had so frequently displayed. And unlike them, with his connections to an earl and his possession of a great estate, not to mention his own obvious intelligence and bearing, he actually had some reason to feel superior. By contrast, the other members of the Bingley party had little in comparison to excuse their putting on airs. Their wealth—though undoubtedly considerable—was still tainted by the stench of trade, and as a result, Caroline Bingley and Louisa Hurst possessed a much higher opinion of their position in society than they had any right.

Furthermore, Elizabeth realized that the fact of Mr. Darcy's friendship with someone such as Mr. Bingley was also a mark in the man's favor. Many men of his station would no doubt feel a man such as Mr. Bingley to be completely beneath him and would behave with condescension, if they recognized such an acquaintance at all. Mr. Darcy, however, appeared to treat Mr. Bingley as a close friend and confidant. This in turn suggested that perhaps his reticence in company was not entirely that of a perceived sense of superiority. That he was an intelligent man was not in question, but why such an intelligent and worldly man would be so reserved was beyond Elizabeth's ability to understand. All she knew was that he did not necessarily appear to be as conceited as she had at first thought.

As for Mr. Wickham, Elizabeth felt that she had not spent enough time in his company to form any real opinion. They had only shared the one true conversation at her Aunt Phillips's gathering, and because the weather had turned wet following that day, there had not been a lot of contact with others of the neighborhood or the officers of the militia since. Of course, this was in keeping with Elizabeth's introspective state. She welcomed the opportunity for thought and the distance from the two gentlemen the rain afforded.

Mr. Wickham was certainly handsome—at least as handsome as the master of Pemberley, though his light cheerfulness was a stark contrast to Mr. Darcy's dark and serious mien. His mode of address was most certainly gentlemanly, his manners engaging, and Elizabeth thought that his conversation would be deemed interesting and effortless on first impression. Of course, as Elizabeth also took into account his preference for speaking of his supposed woes at the hands of the Darcy family, not to mention the lack of substance in anything he said, his manners were decidedly less pleasing than they had been initially. As Elizabeth had noted during her aunt's party, he seemed little disposed to speak of anything else. And of course, Elizabeth had not missed the way he had leered at her . . . .

The other memory which intruded upon her consciousness was the meeting between the two on that dusty road in Meryton. That the men had been surprised to see each other was unmistakable, but their individual reactions were perhaps more telling. Whereas Mr. Darcy had seemed angry to see Mr. Wickham, the other man had shown a distinct level of distress upon noticing his erstwhile companion. And though Elizabeth could not be certain, subsequent thought on the subject had led her to the conclusion that whatever had happened between them, it was Mr. Wickham who had reacted in such a way as to suggest that the presence of the other man was a cause for consternation rather than the reverse. If her perception was indeed the truth, it dealt a further blow to Mr. Wickham's claims of ill-use. The matter certainly did not do him any favors.

Many times during those days, Elizabeth found herself frustrated enough that she thought to apply to Mr. Darcy for his side of the affair. After all, Mr. Wickham had already seen fit to extend his version of their dealings, so should Mr. Darcy not be allowed the same courtesy?

But then the thought of Mr. Darcy's imperious gaze directed upon her with *even more* displeasure than was already his wont made her realize what an impertinence he would consider such an application to be. There was certainly no reason for him to share such matters with a mere country lass, regardless of what his childhood companion had seen fit to impart. Speaking to Mr. Darcy on the subject was out of the question.

In the end, Elizabeth decided that she was rather tired of thinking of *all* young men from the north, and she resolved to extend nothing beyond the barest of civility and courtesy to *both* Mr. Darcy and Mr. Wickham. It was for the best, after all—one was too far above her in his own eyes, while the other other's eyes seemed to harbor secrets and lies. She would ignore them both.

Chapter II

The days after Aunt Phillips's card party saw a distinct cooling in Mr. Collins's ardor for Elizabeth. So preoccupied was she that she had hardly noticed the withdrawal of his attentions until it had been brought to her attention by a most unlikely source.

Now, it must be said that Elizabeth had no proof in the matter, as Mrs. Bennet had not raised the subject within the range of her hearing, but knowing how fixated her mother was upon securing Mr. Bingley for Jane, Elizabeth was quite certain that if Mr. Collins had shown any interest whatsoever in Jane, she would have warned the man off immediately. But as Elizabeth had no known prospects herself, it would be an easy thing for her mother to put *her* forward as a potential marriage partner. Thus, it seemed likely that Mrs. Bennet had given her tacit—if not overt—support to his suit, as Mr. Collins had begun to pay her his attentions within a day of arriving at Longbourn.

Unfortunately for Mr. Collins—and perhaps fortunately for Elizabeth—the parson had not a subtle bone in his body. *He* likely considered his suit to be cleverly done, filled with the *delicate compliments* of which he had boasted upon his arrival. But the manner in which he chose to sit by her, regaling tales of his patroness; the way he accompanied her on the walk to Meryton the day they had met Mr. Wickham, though his frame was not such as was meant for walking;

the way he attempted to flatter her with that oily smirk of his, acting as if she should be hanging on his every word—all these things proved beyond a shadow of a doubt that he considered her to be the companion of his future life. In the privacy of her mind, Elizabeth could not imagine anything more repulsive than to be married to William Collins, though an overly prideful Mr. Darcy might come close. But as she was now completely uncertain of her perception of Mr. Darcy's character, she could not even state that with a surety.

Elizabeth had always tried to be polite to Mr. Collins—much as she wished to tell him outright of her disinterest—but her politeness had only served to spur him on. It was not in her to be purposefully rude to someone, especially when that person was a guest in her father's house, so she had suffered in silence, consoling herself with the knowledge that should he ever come to the point and ask her, she could safely refuse him, knowing that Mr. Bennet would never make her marry a man for whom he himself had no respect. Her mother would make a fuss about it, of course, but in the end, she would be forced to capitulate.

Of particular import to Mr. Collins's suit was the delivery of the invitation to the ball at Netherfield. Though perhaps simply dispatching the invitation with a servant might have been sufficient— which Elizabeth suspected had been done with the other families in the area—Mr. Bingley instead delivered the invitation for the inhabitants of Longbourn in person. Elizabeth, despite her distraction, could not help but understand the compliment he paid to Jane for such attention. And even if Elizabeth had missed such a thing, Mrs. Bennet was not about to let anyone forget that *she* considered it to be a tribute to her eldest daughter.

Fortunately for Elizabeth's peace of mind, Mr. Darcy did not accompany Mr. Bingley in delivering the invitation—at that point in her ruminations, Elizabeth was still uncertain of whether she wished to see Mr. Darcy at all.

After being announced to the room, Mr. Bingley entered with a jovial smile. On his heels, Miss Bingley entered the drawing-room, her nose upturned as if the entire house was permeated with the foulest stench. Elizabeth considered it to be rather ironic—while the Bennets were not wealthy, they were an established gentle family; the Bingleys, on the other hand, possessed wealth which was tainted by its having been made in trade. Of course Miss Bingley would never own to such a thing, but it was the truth nonetheless, and it exposed Miss Bingley's behavior for the pretentious nonsense that it was.

"Mrs. Bennet!" greeted Mr. Bingley as he strode forward and bowed. "How do you do?"

Mrs. Bennet beamed and thanked him for visiting, and the visitors sat down, Mr. Bingley with a contented air which became even more pronounced when he looked at Jane, who blushed in response. Miss Bingley never lost her own air of superiority, though her eyes narrowed at the evidence of her brother's preference.

Pleasantries were exchanged for the next few moments, though soon Mr. Bingley was speaking with Jane exclusively, as was his wont. In another part of the room, Mrs. Bennet had cornered Miss Bingley and was now conversing with her as though they were old friends. The very sight required Elizabeth to stifle a chuckle.

After about a quarter of an hour spent in this attitude, Mr. Bingley broke off his conversation with Jane—whose color, Elizabeth noticed, was rather higher than it had been before—and addressed the room.

"Mrs. Bennet," said he, "we have come today with a specific purpose in mind. My sister and I would like to invite you—all of your family, of course—to a ball to be held at Netherfield on the twenty-sixth of November."

With a flourish, he produced a card tied up in ribbons which he presented to Mrs. Bennet with a smile.

"Oh, Mr. Bingley, I am sure we should be quite happy to attend!" enthused the Bennet matron. "How good of you to invite us!"

"I am sure we shall be very happy to have you attend," replied Mr. Bingley, an effortless air of good cheer evident in his manners. He continued after a moment, but while his words were directed at the room, his eyes had returned to Jane. "A ball would not be the same without your presence.

"In fact," continued he, a smile tugging at the corners of his mouth, "the delivery of the invitation, though important, was not my only reason for visiting today. Miss Bennet, since I am assured that no other man has had the opportunity to apply for your hand, I feel confident in requesting your favor for the opening set. Will you oblige me?"

Jane colored, and her eyes dropped to the floor—Jane always had been surprised to be singled out, whereas Elizabeth had always expected it for her—but she was able to respond with tolerable coherence that she would be very happy to cede those dances to Mr. Bingley.

"Excellent!" enthused Mr. Bingley, and though he had not appeared to be in any doubt of the success of his request, he nevertheless smiled and began to speak with Mrs. Bennet, thereby allowing Jane the opportunity to collect herself.

It was some minutes later, after Mr. Bingley had once again been speaking with Jane, when his sister, with some testiness, reminded him that they had other appointments that day. They departed soon afterward, but only once Mr. Bingley had unabashedly stated how much he was looking forward to welcoming them to Netherfield. In the end, Miss Bingley almost dragged him from the room in her haste to escape.

Of course, there was one bit of news that Mr. Bingley dropped just before he left. It seemed that he had issued a general invitation to the officers of the militia regiment to attend the ball, a circumstance which was greeted with enthusiasm and no little silliness by Kitty and Lydia. While Elizabeth would have preferred that they had been excluded, she knew that it would not have been proper for Mr. Bingley to have done so. The prospect of dancing with Mr. Wickham slightly worried her, for the fact that he had singled her out as the one to hear his sordid tale seemed to suggest that he had developed an interest in her during their short conversation. She was almost certain that she would be unable to avoid his unwanted attention—not if she wished to dance with anyone else at the ball.

Still, the situation could not be altered at her whim. Whatever Mr. Wickham's intentions, he could hardly do anything in the middle of a ballroom with the entire neighborhood to witness, so as long as she was careful, Elizabeth was confident she would come to no harm.

The mere thought caused Elizabeth to shake her head in wonder at the direction her thoughts had taken her. The man had told her improper stories, it was true, but in her flights of fancy, she was now imagining him to be intent on harming her! Surely there was no cause for such alarm. As such, she put all worries about the ball behind her. Unfortunately, thoughts of Mr. Wickham, Mr. Darcy, and the stories she had been told could not be suppressed so easily.

The truly pertinent events with respect to Mr. Collins's deflected attentions happened after their Netherfield neighbors departed. The ladies were ensconced in the parlor with Mr. Collins—Mr. Bennet having escaped to his bookroom as soon as he could contrive a good reason for doing so—and the discussion centered on the invitation to the ball. Lydia and Kitty were, of course, all aflutter with excitement for the upcoming amusement, with Lydia loudly taking credit for inducing Mr. Bingley to keep his promise. Jane appeared to be pondering the time she would be in company with Mr. Bingley, if her dreamy expression was any indication, while Mr. Collins and Mrs. Bennet spoke of Mr. Collins's attendance and expectations for the evening. Elizabeth would have had to be a simpleton to have missed the less than subtle prompts Mrs. Bennet was directing at Mr. Collins in order to induce him to secure Elizabeth's first set. Mr. Collins, uncharacteristically, was somewhat reticent, and though he did look at Elizabeth more than perhaps would otherwise be warranted, no invitation was forthcoming.

Finally, her mother, frustrated with Mr. Collins's continuing reluctance, addressed Elizabeth directly:

"Lizzy, surely you are anticipating the ball, are you not?"

Elizabeth, once again having slipped into her thoughts, started for a moment before assuring her mother that the prospect of a night in company at Netherfield was by no means disagreeable.

"But Lizzy, surely *you* have some specific *expectations* for the evening, do you not?" The fact that Mrs. Bennet's words were accompanied a significant wink in Mr. Collins's direction was not lost on Elizabeth. However, she determined to ignore the hint.

"No more than usual, Mama. As you know I do enjoy dancing, and as such, Mr. Bingley's ball is an opportunity for amusement and the opportunity to take pleasure in the company of all our neighbors. I cannot imagine any further anticipation to which you may be referring."

Mrs. Bennet's eyes narrowed, and she gazed at her daughter with obvious displeasure. However, for once choosing a more subtle method of getting what she wanted, she turned and addressed Mr. Collins once again.

"Your own attendance must bring you great pleasure, Mr. Collins."

"Yes, indeed," allowed the obsequious parson.

"It is very fortunate that you have a bishop who is agreeable to your partaking in such amusements."

"Indeed it is," agreed Mr. Collins with a bow. "My bishop is a very amiable and understanding man. However, I truly believe that the proposed amusement is harmless and in keeping with the office of a clergyman. The man giving the ball is honorable and upstanding, and I seriously doubt that there is any evil tendency involved. And I do so love to dance myself—I hope that I will be favored with the hands of . . . many agreeable young ladies for the evening."

Elizabeth was not truly paying attention to his long-winded discourse, but she was aware that she did not wish to spend any more time than necessary in his company, and moreover, she did not wish to allow him the opportunity at this juncture to begin his dancing aspirations by securing *her* hand for a set.

"Then I am very happy for you, Mr. Collins," said Elizabeth, as she rose to her feet. "There are many times in life when one must be necessarily focused on more serious matters, so it is a wonderful opportunity to be able to indulge in some amusement. I am sure you will have a lovely evening at Netherfield."

Then Elizabeth announced her intention to retire to her room to rest, as she had had little sleep the previous night. As she walked from the room, she felt the force of her mother's displeased gaze upon her back, but she chose to ignore it—it was best that Mr. Collins lose his ardor and her mother give up this doomed attempt to pair her with her cousin before they were both disappointed.

The next day brought a deluge which was to last until the day of the Netherfield ball. Under normal circumstances, Elizabeth might have been vexed at the thought of being denied her favorite activity of walking the country paths so close to the onset of winter, where her walks would be denied for the most part until spring. In this instance, however, Elizabeth chose to regard the matter with a philosophical bent, recognizing that the cessation of her cousin's attentions meant that she could in some measure enjoy the comfort of her home without any worry of being imposed upon by an entirely unwanted suitor.

On the few infrequent occasions when the rain did cease for a time, Elizabeth availed herself of the paths in the back garden closest to the house, and on one of those occasions, she found herself in the company of her sisters as well as Mr. Collins. Mrs. Bennet had determined that it would be best for the younger members of the family to gain some fresh air while the opportunity presented itself. Whether her mother specifically meant for Elizabeth to walk with Mr. Collins, she was uncertain, but as Elizabeth was still preoccupied, he was soon found to be walking with Mary, exchanging observations about some religious text with which they were both familiar. Jane chose to walk by herself a few paces behind Mary and the parson, though she did not appear to be taking part in their conversation. Elizabeth wandered by herself for a short time, but soon she found herself accosted by Lydia.

"Lizzy!" hissed Lydia as she fell into step by Elizabeth's side. "Whatever are you doing to poor Mr. Collins?"

Elizabeth regarded her youngest sister with a blank look. "*Poor Mr. Collins?*" echoed she. "I am sure I have not the faintest idea of what you are talking about."

Lydia glanced back at the parson and her middle sister and then took Elizabeth's arm, directing her toward a nearby bench which was largely dried from the deluge. Elizabeth noticed Mr. Collins's eyes following them, and she thought for a moment that he would approach, but he must have decided that the conversation was much more interesting, for he kept walking along Mary's side.

Once they had progressed out of earshot, Lydia turned to Elizabeth and let out a loud giggle which was imitated by Kitty, who had approached from Elizabeth's other side.

"Your impersonation of Mary these past days has been very impressive, Lizzy," stated Kitty. "Perhaps you should share your weighty thoughts with the rest of the family."

Elizabeth regarded her second youngest sister as if she were daft. "Impersonation of Mary? Of what are you speaking?"

"We all thought that Mary was the one who was above earthly concerns," broke in Lydia. "But lately, your contemplation of the heavens has quite perplexed us all."

Flushing, Elizabeth looked down. Until that moment, she had not thought that her introspection had been quite so obvious to her family. But if Kitty and Lydia—the two sisters most likely to be immersed in their own concerns—had noticed her distraction, then it was equally obvious that everyone else in the family had as well. That still did not explain Lydia's first comment.

"I may have been a little . . . thoughtful lately," said Elizabeth, ignoring Lydia's snort of amusement, "but I am quite sure that I have not the faintest idea of what you are talking about in regard to Mr. Collins."

Lydia and Kitty exchanged another giggle. "So you have not noticed that Mr. Collins appears to be less . . . eager in his pursuit of you?"

"Has his conversation not lessened these past few days?" prompted Kitty.

"I am quite certain that Mr. Collins's conversation is so abundant that one may safely attend to only one word in three and never repine the loss of the other two," said Elizabeth. "So if I am hearing less from our voluble relation, then I can only be thankful that he has given me less to ignore."

All three sisters laughed heartily at this jest. Once their mirth had subsided, Lydia continued:

"Well, your new method of dealing with Mr. Collins appears to have much greater effect than your last. You may not have noticed in the midst of your thoughts, but Mr. Collins is much less likely to importune you with his opinions than he was previously. In fact,

Mama is beside herself. He appears to be withdrawing his attentions, and you know what that will do to her nerves."

"I am afraid that while I have compassion for my mother's nerves, that does not extend to marrying Mr. Collins in order to settle them," was Elizabeth's irreverent reply.

Both of her younger sisters sniggered at her words, but they were not to be turned aside so easily.

"Mr. Collins has become downright reticent in your company, Lizzy," said Kitty. "Did you not notice how Mama was attempting to induce him to request your first set for the ball at Netherfield?"

Elizabeth shrugged. "I had noticed that he did not seem inclined to ask. For that, I am profoundly grateful, I assure you."

"I am certain we are all grateful," said Lydia with an indelicate snort, "as he has not seen fit to ask *any of us* yet! But that is exactly the point; when Mr. Collins arrived, did you ever believe he would be reticent about *anything?*"

Frowning, Elizabeth peered across the gardens to where Mr. Collins was still walking with Mary. Now that Lydia had mentioned it, she found this change decidedly odd. The man was loquacious and in love with the sound of his voice—restrained was hardly the word she would ever use to describe him.

But that was exactly what he had been in the past few days, just as Kitty and Lydia had said. His reserve had made its appearance in the days since her encounter with Mr. Wickham and her subsequent distraction on account of Mr. Wickham's grievances against Mr. Darcy. There was only one explanation for why he had suddenly withdrawn his amorous intentions, and the very thought of it caused Elizabeth to break out in laughter.

"I suppose I have discovered the secret to inducing Mr. Collins to desist," said she with a beaming smile.

"Oh, do tell," urged Kitty.

"Yes, we should both love to know it," said Lydia, "so that we may do the same should he turn his attentions to us."

Elizabeth smiled at her younger sisters, thinking that they were much more pleasant when they were speaking in confidence rather than running amok, drawing attention to themselves with their loud voices, and mortifying her with their behavior.

"I have tried to be politely distant," said Elizabeth. "I have also tried to hint that I am not interested and that I would prefer he would pursue someone else, but he never seems to take the hint. In fact, it appears to spur him on.

"But it seems as if all that was required was to act distracted and ignore him. I dare say his vanity is unable to withstand such treatment. Therefore, if you find yourself in need of dissuading Mr. Collins's attentions, simply take no notice of him, and he shall go away."

Once again, Elizabeth's younger sisters erupted in giggles, drawing the eyes of the object of their mirth. But though he seemed to disapprove of their behavior, he chose to ignore it in favor of his conversation with Mary. Of Jane, there was no sign—she had evidently decided to return to the house.

"But why have you been so distracted lately?"

Elizabeth turned to Kitty to reply when Lydia let out a snort and said in a mischievous tone:

"By my reckoning, it stems from our meeting that handsome new officer, Mr. Wickham."

Elizabeth turned to Lydia with an admonishing glare, but Lydia just waved her off.

"I know what you will say, Lizzy," said she, "and therefore I shall keep my opinion to myself. But Mr. Wickham is frightfully handsome, and should you be preoccupied with thoughts of *him,* I could not find fault with you."

Biting her lower lip, Elizabeth regarded her younger sisters. She had come to the resolution that she would not share Mr. Wickham's story with anyone. Unfortunately, Lydia and Kitty were still very young, still very impressionable, and at risk of being completely under the power of a man with pretty manners and a handsome face, especially if the man was dressed in regimentals. If Mr. Wickham was what Elizabeth had begun to suspect he was, were Lydia and Kitty—as featherbrained as they were—not the most in danger of falling prey to his wiles?

Surely something of a warning could safely be imparted to her sisters, could it not? And was it not much more dangerous to keep any hint of his suspected improprieties from them? They might not listen to her—indeed, that outcome was perhaps as likely as not—but at least with the knowledge in the backs of their minds, they might be somewhat forearmed should the man try anything improper.

"I *have* been thinking about Mr. Wickham," acknowledged Elizabeth. "However, it is not his manners or his mien which have occupied my thoughts."

"If it has not been either of those, then I should like to know what you have been thinking of," said Lydia.

Glancing around and ensuring that Mr. Collins was nowhere near enough to overhear, Elizabeth looked closely at her younger sisters.

"Mr. Wickham's gentlemanly manners are visible for all to see. However, I am not certain that they are a reflection of the true man."

Lydia and Kitty both appeared to be nonplussed at Elizabeth's statement. "What do you mean, Lizzy?" asked Lydia.

"Mr. Wickham imparted some information to me about himself and his past," replied Elizabeth, "but I am not certain he spoke the truth. For one thing, he contradicted himself when he spoke, and for another, he attempted to defame another man with his words. And this happened during the first real conversation I ever had with the man!"

"Who did he speak badly of, Lizzy?" asked Kitty.

"You are such a simpleton sometimes," interjected Lydia with a huff. "Even if Mr. Wickham has never confided in me as he has in Lizzy, given their reactions to one another on the street when we met Mr. Wickham, I should say that Mr. Darcy and Mr. Wickham are already acquainted. Besides, it seems to be accepted in Meryton that they have a previous acquaintance."

Elizabeth peered sharply at Lydia, ignoring for the moment that her sister seemed to be more perceptive than she would previously have suspected. "What have you heard?"

"Nothing more than that—and much less than you have yourself, I presume. But come now, Lizzy; of what did Mr. Wickham accuse Mr. Darcy?"

Shaking her head, Elizabeth answered, "No, Lydia, I shall not share any of it. As I said, it was a most improper communication, delivered as it was to an acquaintance of less than a day, and it was substantiated only by the assertions of the one who delivered it. I shall not repeat any of the words Mr. Wickham said, as I am convinced that it is at best exaggeration or, at worst, outright falsehood!"

"How can you be certain, Lizzy?" asked Kitty.

"I cannot," replied Elizabeth. "But given the fact that Mr. Wickham related his story to me and then in the next breath assured me that he would never expose Mr. Darcy's behavior, Mr. Wickham's statement appears to be disingenuous at best. I did not like the gleam in his eye when he spoke of Mr. Darcy, nor did I like the way he assumed that I would give credence to his tales of ill use. I suggest that we all take great care in pronouncing judgment based on unsubstantiated claims."

"Ugh!" cried Lydia. "Now you even *sound* like Mary!"

"I am sorry if I am offending your sensibilities," said Elizabeth with a smile, "but I believe it to be true."

"But Mr. Wickham is so handsome!" Lydia's voice had by this time almost approached a wail, and Elizabeth, wary of attracting Mr.

Collins's attention, knew that she needed to have a long overdue talk with her sisters.

"He is handsome," said Elizabeth in a soothing tone. "But if you think about it objectively, so is Mr. Darcy."

"But Mr. Darcy is so severe," interjected Kitty. "Mr. Wickham is *nothing* like Mr. Darcy."

"No, I dare say he is not," agreed Elizabeth. "But you must both understand," said she, pausing to look at both of her sisters, "a pleasing countenance coupled with pretty manners may hide the sort of character which is very much darker than you might suspect."

Obviously curious at her sister's meaning, Lydia tilted her head to the side. "What do you mean, Lizzy?"

With a sigh, Elizabeth regarded her younger sisters, thinking of Mary as well. None of the three was slow of thought or lacking in comprehension, but they were all sadly lacking in knowledge about the proper behavior of a young lady in society, though the issue was less pronounced in Mary. Elizabeth knew that it was in part due to a mother who was of mean understanding herself, yet it was also due to Lydia's naturally high-spirited manners and Kitty's tendency to follow Lydia in everything thing she did. As for Mary, the tendency of others to refer to her as the plain Bennet daughter had led her to retreat somewhat from the world, and the experience had not done her manners any good.

Life was especially difficult for Kitty and Mary. Jane, serene and beautiful, was beloved by both of her parents, and Elizabeth and Lydia, for different reasons, were their father's and mother's favorite children respectively. As a result, Kitty and Mary were sometimes the forgotten children. Mary handled her situation by trying to attain accomplishments in order to receive the praise she craved, while Kitty emulated Lydia, hoping to gain her mother's approval.

But they were not beyond aid, if they could only be made to understand certain truths about their class. Content as she was with the society of her eldest sister and father, Elizabeth had despaired of them and focused on her own concerns, though she felt mortified more often than not by their behavior. Perhaps she had been mistaken in taking a passive role—perhaps it was time to be more active and serve as a mentor to her younger sisters. They could not become much worse, she decided, so there was nothing to be lost.

"Lydia, Kitty," began Elizabeth, looking alternately at each of her younger sisters, "do you remember Emma Whitaker?"

Kitty crinkled her brow in thought. "You mean the girl who married that man from Bedfordshire after being caught in a scandalous situation?"

"The very one."

"Oh, do tell more," interrupted Lydia with a gleam in her eye. "When did this happen?"

Elizabeth glared at her youngest sister. "While I would not normally forward gossip, I think that the events are instructional in this instance. Emma is a lively young woman who is several years my senior. She was well-liked by all, and she was deemed to be engaging, intelligent, and demure, and no one could find fault with her.

"Now, although I do not know exactly what occurred between Emma and Mr. Standish, I do know that we were all surprised to hear that they were found in a compromising position. And though I cannot state anything with a surety, there have been whispers since then that Emma engineered the event in order to entrap Mr. Standish into marriage."

"How scandalous!" exclaimed Lydia, who appeared to enjoy the shameful gossip.

"Indeed," replied Elizabeth. "Now, I can firmly state that Emma, much like Mr. Wickham, was well regarded and deemed to be a proper young woman by everyone with whom she came into contact. But *if* she did attempt to trap Mr. Standish for the purpose of making him marry her, it puts her character in a very different light altogether."

Kitty appeared to be puzzled. "But Lizzy, you said you do not know for certain that she has done this. Why would you bring it up then?"

"Because the situation is similar," said Elizabeth. "I cannot tell you for certain that Emma did this. But the fact that she was found in a compromising position at all calls her character into question. I do not in general hold with society in gossiping and ruining a person's reputation based on suspicion, but a person's behavior is often much more important than their words—one's true character will often come out through actions, regardless of how one may try to hide it.

"In the matter of Mr. Wickham, I found him to be completely charming, with impeccable manners and an engaging way of speaking. However, certain comments he made during the course of our conversation induced me to question his motives. And if I found it necessary to question his motives, then it almost certainly casts aspersions on his character, for some of the things of which he spoke were not communications he should be making to an acquaintance of such short duration.

"This is why I state that you cannot necessarily judge a person based on their countenance or on their manners, and this goes for Mr. Darcy as well as Mr. Wickham."

"Lizzy!" cried Lydia. "Are you starting to soften toward Mr. Darcy, the man who called you 'not handsome enough?'"

"Perhaps a little," acknowledged Elizabeth. "He was still very wrong to say something such as that in a crowded assembly room. But I have been forced recently to reexamine my interactions with Mr. Darcy, and I must truthfully state that I know no particular evil of him. He is, without a doubt, somewhat prideful and arrogant. However, in my subsequent dealings with him, I must say that his manners have been scrupulously proper."

Kitty looked on with a shrewd eye. "Mr. Wickham must have said something particular to induce you into this much introspection."

"Indeed, he did, Kitty," replied Elizabeth. "But I shall not share any more. I believe that I have done enough myself in defaming Mr. Darcy's character, though I should have kept my own counsel in the matter of his slight. I shall not spread further stories, especially ones which I believe to be the grossest of falsehoods."

"It is a complicated business," said Kitty with a little distress. "How are you to ever know if someone is telling the truth?"

"You cannot with any surety. To be safe, it is best to withhold judgment, but also to withhold your trust until someone has been proven to be honorable. That holds true not only for a casual acquaintance, but also for any man whom you may regard as a potential marriage partner."

"It does not signify," said Lydia, waving her hand airily. "I shall marry an officer anyway, and I am certain they are all trustworthy. They are members of His Majesty's army, are they not?"

Elizabeth affixed Lydia with a frown, wondering if she had heard anything that had been said. "So you are determined to marry an officer?"

"Have you any doubt?" demanded Lydia.

"I suppose not," was Elizabeth's reply. She affected nonchalance, thinking that her ambivalent manner might give greater weight to her words and help Lydia see that there may be a flaw in her plan. "In that case, I wish you well. It is not an easy life, from what I understand. That you wish to give up a life of easiness for one of work and economizing speaks very well to your character, I am sure."

Elizabeth made to rise, but she was arrested by Lydia's loudly spoken, "Whatever can you mean?"

Glancing back, Elizabeth saw that Lydia, though taken aback by

Elizabeth's statement, was not as of yet truly concerned. Elizabeth meant to make her so.

"Why, you must know that an officer in the militia is not wealthy man, Lydia. I dare say that most below a certain rank would not be able to afford a wife, and if he could manage it, then he would have to be very careful with his resources."

As Elizabeth continued to speak, Lydia's eyebrows rose to the point where they were almost covered by her hair. Again, Lydia was not a stupid girl, but she had never been taught to think critically or focus on serious issues.

"But . . . but . . ." stammered Lydia.

"But what, Lydia?" asked Elizabeth. "Surely you must know this."

Suppressing a chuckle at Lydia's uncomprehending stare, Elizabeth turned to her, intent upon illumining her on the realities of the future she was contemplating.

"Listen to me—both of you. You are aware that our father is not a rich man, and yet he is able to provide for us quite comfortably. But you must understand that the difference between even a modest land owner and an officer in the militia is quite large. Our father earns about two thousand per year from Longbourn, but even a captain has only a fraction of that amount at his disposal.

"You must think of what that life would entail if you were married to a military man. You would have no servants—or perhaps no more than one or two—to do the work for you; you would have to do everything yourself. There would be very little pocket allowance for you to buy clothes or bonnets; while clothes are a necessity, you would need to make them last longer and buy materials which are not nearly as fine as that to which you are accustomed. Another consideration is that the life of a soldier would almost certainly require you to be mobile. Take our militia company, for example. The militia never settles in one place for long—they must move to wherever the regiment is ordered. You could have no long-lasting friendships, as you would only be in a certain place for a short time."

"But what about balls and parties and all the events that go along with being an officer?" cried Lydia.

"Yes, an officer is expected to have a place in society," replied Elizabeth. "But there is a lot more to being a soldier than attending balls and the like. They have their duties to fulfill, and those must necessarily take precedence over society."

Lydia appeared to be on the point of wanting to cry, and though Elizabeth did not like to see her sister so distressed, she knew that someone needed to acquaint her with the reality of the situation.

"Listen to me, Liddy, Kitty," soothed Elizabeth. "I know you think that officers are wonderful men who lead exciting lives, but you are only seeing very little of what their lives truly consist." Elizabeth watched her sisters, noting that they were listening intently to what she was saying. Perhaps there was hope for them yet. "If you truly loved an officer and had faith that he could provide for you, then there would be nothing wrong with marrying him."

"You are talking about a man like Colonel Forster, are you not, Lizzy?" interjected Kitty.

"The colonel does seem to be a good man," agreed Elizabeth. "But he is of higher consequence than any of the other officers because of his rank. But not all officers are necessarily cut from the same cloth as Colonel Forster. Given what I have experienced with Mr. Wickham, I suspect that his character is truly different from the colonel's."

Once Elizabeth had said her piece, neither of her sisters said anything for a long moment. In the past, Elizabeth would have expected them to discount her words entirely, laughing them off or accusing her of not understanding the true state of things. That they were at least thinking was a very good sign.

"Then we should look for an estate owner?" ventured Kitty hesitantly after a few moments.

"I cannot tell you what you should be looking for," said Elizabeth in reply. "It is up to you to decide what you want in life. You might be very happy as an officer's wife, and I could not gainsay you if that is what you decide. For that matter, there are many men of many different professions who are all good and proper and able to provide for you and love you admirably.

"But I want you to understand what you will be committing yourself to. And regardless of what you wish for in a marriage partner, you must understand that a man expects a demure and proper woman, not one who runs amok without the slightest thought toward propriety."

Elizabeth could see both of her sisters start at her words, and she wondered for a moment if she had been too blunt. But bluntness was required—her sisters were beyond the point of listening to anything else.

"Are you saying we are too . . . too . . . loud?" asked Kitty with a stammer.

"You are both a little too exuberant at times," answered Elizabeth. "With such behavior, you run the risk of attracting the wrong sort of man." Elizabeth smiled. "I hate to sound like Mary again, but what she says is true. None of us have much in the way of dowry and connections — we have little more than our charms to recommend us. A good man of society desires all of these things, and it may make finding a marriage partner difficult. But if a man cannot have our virtue and the assurance that we will not embarrass him, any personal feelings he may possess will not be enough. We must be proper if we are ever to find husbands, because we do not have anything else to tempt a man."

Knowing she had made an impression upon them — both Lydia and Kitty were appearing somewhat introspective, which was decidedly not normal for either — Elizabeth smiled to herself, thinking that she would allow them to ruminate on her words before offering more counsel. It was at that moment, however, that the heavens opened up, and rain began pelting them. Abandoning all ladylike behavior, the three rose from the bench and fairly ran toward the house, laughing like children once they had attained shelter. A few moments later, they were all hustled up to their rooms for a change in clothes, and Elizabeth was left alone to her reflections. It had been a very good talk with her two youngest sisters, one which she had not had in quite some time. They still had a long road before them, but it was a start.

It was the next day when the situation between Elizabeth and Mr. Collins finally came to a head — or more correctly, when Mrs. Bennet decided she had had enough of Elizabeth's behavior toward the parson.

"Lizzy!" hissed Mrs. Bennet when Elizabeth descended the stairs. "I would speak with you child."

Sighing, Elizabeth allowed herself to be guided to the dining room, which was deserted at that time of the day. After Elizabeth sat at her mother's request, Mrs. Bennet peered at her with some exasperation and then spoke:

"What do you mean by ignoring Mr. Collins, Lizzy?"

"I am certain I do not understand your meaning, Mama," said Elizabeth. "I have given Mr. Collins no more and no less attention than I ever have."

"And I assure you that you have been most inattentive, Lizzy. Mr. Collins has paid a considerable amount of notice to you and may be close to declaring himself, but your distraction has blunted his enthusiasm."

"Oh, Mama, I do not wish for Mr. Collins's attentions. Let him direct his interest to another, more welcoming recipient."

Mrs. Bennet sniffed in distain. "Well, if that was your purpose, then you have succeeded admirably. After witnessing your woolgathering this past few days, he appeared disinclined to continue his courtship of you. Luckily, your sister Mary's discourse was enough to draw him in, and he was induced to ask her for the honor of her first set at the Netherfield ball. Had you given him any encouragement, he assuredly would have requested *your* hand for those sets."

Elizabeth could not mask her astonishment and delight. "That is very good for Mary, Mama! She does hold him in some esteem, and she is but rarely asked to stand up for the first set. I am happy that she will be able to partake in the amusement."

"Do you delight in ruining your chances for matrimony, Lizzy?" demanded a thoroughly displeased Mrs. Bennet. "You must give Mr. Collins more encouragement if you are to secure his interest. A man will not come to a resolution without *some indication* that you welcome his advances, you know. What shall become of you if you do not persuade him?"

Suppressing a sigh at her mother's single-minded obtuseness, Elizabeth thought cynically that Mr. Collins had apparently been willing to be encouraged by nothing more than her coldly polite responses to his inanities. Surely he was a man who was completely capable of bestowing—and transferring!—his attentions without a hint of a lady's assistance! Deciding that it was time to forever put an end to Mrs. Bennet's hopes for her and Mr. Collins, Elizabeth thought of how she could answer her mother and convince her to cease her attempts to promote the match. The answer, of course, had been provided by her sister's fortuitous—but not completely unsurprising—diversion of Mr. Collins's attention.

"Mama, I have already told you I do not welcome Mr. Collins's attentions, and I must tell you know that I have not solicited them in any way. If Mary *does* welcome them, then why should I stand in her way?"

"Whatever can you mean, child?" demanded Mrs. Bennet. "What does Mary have to do with the matter?"

"Only this, Mama," answered Elizabeth. "If she welcomes his attentions, why should you direct him to me? Would you interfere with Mary's happiness, and put me in the situation of having to refuse a man I could not in good conscience accept?"

While Mrs. Bennet's eyes widened at the thought of Elizabeth actually *refusing* an offer of marriage, Elizabeth also understood the calculating gleam which appeared in her eyes. Elizabeth knew that regardless of the fact that her mother had always considered her second daughter to be a little wild, Mrs. Bennet had always considered Mary Bennet to be the most problematic when it came to assuring a good match. That Mrs. Bennet thought this was due to Mary's relative plainness was more than evident considering her frequent effusions on the subject. However, Elizabeth had always felt sorry for Mary—she certainly could a pleasant girl if she tried, and Elizabeth had always felt that Mary's physical deficiencies could be overcome with more flattering dresses and a change in the severe bun which was her most frequently chosen hairstyle.

"You believe Mary likes Mr. Collins?" asked Mrs. Bennet.

"I am not privy to Mary's thoughts, Mama," responded Elizabeth. "However, I can tell you that she appears to find his company less irksome than the rest of your daughters do."

"But what of your future and the future of this family, Lizzy?" said Mrs. Bennet, a significant whine entering her voice. "I had counted upon you marrying Mr. Collins and ensuring our ability to keep our home when your father leaves us. You *must* do your duty and accept Mr. Collins!"

"Mama!" said Elizabeth in a stern tone. "I shall certainly do no such thing. I would be miserable with Mr. Collins for a husband; surely you must see that!"

Mrs. Bennet blushed, and her gaze fell to the floor. "I suppose he is a trifle . . ."

"Servile?" interjected Elizabeth. "Or perhaps he is a little stupid? Over-impressed with his own importance? He is all of these things, Mama. He is certainly not a bad man, but I could never live a life with a partner whom I did not at least respect. You know that my father would support me in this; I would never accept Mr. Collins's proposal, and he would be offended by my refusal to marry him and would not consider any of my sisters after I rejected him.

"And you should think very hard on which of your daughters most suits him, Mama. I could certainly marry a parson if I was truly in love with him, but can you really see me as the wife to Mr. Collins? Does Mary not suit him so much better than I?"

The gleam of understanding once again entered her mother's eye, allowing Elizabeth to reflect that she had won the point with her arguments. She was relieved by the lifting of a weight that she had not truly known existed.

"You are certain of Mary's interest?" queried Mrs. Bennet.

"I am certain of nothing, Mama. All I can tell you is that she does not appear to *dislike* his presence, which is something you could not say about your *other daughters*. For any further specifics, I suggest you apply to Mary for her opinion."

"Oh, there is no need for that," said Mrs. Bennet, her manner already distracted by plans and machinations. "Yes, I believe Mary will do nicely. In fact, Mary is far less stubborn and far more malleable than you are. I am certain she can be persuaded to do her duty."

"Mama, before you marry her off to Mr. Collins or anyone else, I would suggest you ask for her opinion on the matter. I do not imagine she would appreciate being a pawn in some Machiavellian marriage game merely to ensure our family's comfort."

"Lizzy!" cried Mrs. Bennet. "This is most certainly not a game! You must understand how important this is for us—how precarious our position is."

"I do, Mama," soothed Elizabeth. "I understand our position precisely, I assure you. However, you must understand that people do not appreciate having their lives decided for them without their consultation. And besides, I believe that if you were to apply to Mary for her opinion on the subject, you would not be disappointed. Mary's sense of duty is such that I believe that she would feel bound to honor your wishes and marry Mr. Collins to save our family. I believe she does feel some inclination toward him, so you should not be disappointed. Ask her, Mama."

Mrs. Bennet was silent for several moments, her expression containing far more understanding and compassion than Elizabeth had ever before felt from her mother.

"You are speaking of Mary, but referring to your situation, are you not?" said she at length, surprising Elizabeth with her perceptiveness. "*You* would not have appreciated Mr. Collins making his addresses toward you merely on the strength of my recommendation."

"No, Mama, I would not have," confirmed Elizabeth. "But you should not worry about me—the situation would have been uncomfortable for us all, but I am not one to allow others to determine my fate. I would have refused him, Papa would have supported me, and you would likely have been offended. But eventually, the furor would have blown over, and we would have been as we ever were."

Leaning forward, Mrs. Bennet took Elizabeth's hand and looked her in the eye. "But Lizzy, you *do* wish to marry, do you not?"

"Of course I do," replied Elizabeth. "But I intend to take great care in choosing a man to be my husband. You know enough of my disposition to realize that I would be miserable if I were to choose awry. I must have a man who I will love and respect—nothing else will do."

"I suppose you are correct at that," mused her mother. "But shall you find a man in this neighborhood? I boasted to Mr. Darcy of our four and twenty families," she said, laughing at the thought, "but that is truly a small company in which to find a husband."

"I dare say I shall not find a husband in Meryton, Mama."

"Then we must see our Jane married to Mr. Bingley. That way you shall have access into greater society and shall gain the opportunity to meet someone who you can respect."

Elizabeth laughed. "Oh, so now you would pair me with Mr. Bingley's friends? Whom shall I choose? Perhaps Mr. Darcy—he is rich and very handsome, after all."

"How can you be so tiresome as to suggest such a thing, Lizzy?" demanded Mrs. Bennet, though her mouth had curved into a slight smile. "Mr. Darcy appears far too high and mighty for the likes of the Bennets of Hertfordshire!"

"Indeed, he is, Mama," agreed Elizabeth. "Mr. Darcy certainly has enough pride for us all. But I believe I should warn you, Mama—I have had reason to reexamine my interactions with Mr. Darcy, and I believe that we may have misjudged him to a certain extent."

The return of her flighty and emotional mother was amusing as Mrs. Bennet said with a sniff of disdain: "I am sure you believe that, Lizzy, but I shall endeavor to think of the man exactly as I have before. He is very proud and disagreeable and truly vain to think himself above his company, and if I were you, I should not forgive him of his abominable slight so easily. But as he is a friend of Mr. Bingley's, I shall keep my thoughts to myself and attempt to be civil.

"And I would recommend you do the same," continued Mrs. Bennet, rising to her feet. "After all, he is a great friend of Mr. Bingley's and certainly must exert some influence with his friend. Displease him, and you may find it difficult to meet other rich men with whom Mr. Bingley *and* Mr. Darcy must *both* associate. We cannot have that—not if you are to find a suitable husband."

Elizabeth decided there was no response to her mother's words. "You are very right, Mama. I will take your suggestion under advisement."

"Very well," replied Mrs. Bennet, and after a few more moments of comments and advice, all of which Elizabeth intended to ignore, she left, presumably to corner Mary regarding the attentions of one

William Collins.

It was fortunate that she had had this conversation with her mother, Elizabeth reflected. Though she was confident that she never would have been required to marry the parson, she also knew that her refusal would have caused an upheaval which would have permeated the house for weeks.

Chapter III

*I*t proved remarkably easy to redirect Mr. Collins's attentions to Mary, though Elizabeth privately suspected this might have had something to do with the fact that he was already inclined to give up his previous preference anyway. A short discussion with Mrs. Bennet about how Mary was eminently suitable to be the wife of a cleric, and Mr. Collins was paying his attentions to Mary as assiduously as he had previously been directing them at Elizabeth.

Mrs. Bennet once again surprised Elizabeth by following her advice and speaking with Mary concerning the matter of Mr. Collins. Furthermore, Mrs. Bennet actually *listened* to Mary and allowed her daughter to voice her opinion on the matter. Of course, it did not hurt at all that Mary showed no inclination to oppose her mother in this matter, seeming to be content to allow Mr. Collins to pay his addresses to her in any way he saw fit. All in all, Elizabeth found her relationship with her mother had improved, as Mrs. Bennet was effusive in her praise of Elizabeth for showing the greatness of mind to understand her sister's preferences.

Mary also benefited from the attentions of Mr. Collins. Though she had always possessed an upright moral compass, Mary's way of expressing herself in moral platitudes and passages from Fordyce's sermons had often hidden that fact. Gaining the attentions of a man, though he could be as pompous and tiresome as Mary herself had been known to be, seemed to settle her to a certain extent, and her stodgy comments on morality came with less frequency and less gravitas than they had been known to in the past.

The middle Bennet daughter also benefited from being the focus of Mrs. Bennet's attentions by virtue of the fact that she now had a suitor of sorts. With Jane and Elizabeth's assistance, she was able to shed, to a certain degree, the label of "plainest Bennet sister." As Elizabeth was of a size with her, it was no great matter to take one of Elizabeth's dresses and alter it to fit Mary, her unofficial courtship with Mr. Collins giving her reason to dress up in a manner she had never cared to before. Mary would, therefore, willingly wear something far finer to the ball at Netherfield than was her normal wont. The sisters also spent hours in Mary's room, trying out more flattering hair styles. The results were pleasant to them all, and Elizabeth was gratified to see that her prediction about Mary's looks to be proven correct. By the time the day of the ball arrived, Mary's transformation had been completed, and if she still could not match her sisters in pure physical beauty, she could at least be termed as pretty in her own right.

It was thus that the Bennet family made its way to Netherfield on the night of November the twenty-sixth for the ball. The atmosphere inside the family carriage was far more subdued than the trip to any previous engagement for the past several years had been. The youngest Bennets were for a change well-behaved, their ears, no doubt, still ringing with the facts Elizabeth had shared with them. They had both been quieter than was their wont, and though Elizabeth could still see signs of over-exuberance and a blindness to propriety, she was philosophical in thinking that they were not likely to change overnight.

Netherfield took on the appearance of a fairy castle that evening. The house and its environs were decorated with lanterns spaced evenly along the length of the drive to the front entrance, while flickering candlelight and tantalizing hints of color spilled through the windows, accompanied by elegant strains of music wafting out into the night. If Elizabeth let go of her imagination, she could almost see soaring battlements rising up over the house and hear the hearty welcome from the lord and lady of the land to all their guests.

It was a quirk of fate, perhaps, but as Elizabeth descended from the carriage, she happened to look up at the house and witnessed Mr. Darcy looking down on them with all the intensity she had come to expect from him. And though she would have tried to discount the possibility, she had to acknowledge that *she* was specifically the one who had caught his eye, a fact made abundantly clear when she met his gaze and dipped her head, prompting a nod in response. She looked away, wondering what the man's game was. Could he be interested in her particularly?

Immediately, Elizabeth brushed her fanciful sentiments aside—as her mother had said, the Bennets of Hertfordshire were of a sphere far too low for a man such as Mr. Darcy. Turning her attention to the entranceway, Elizabeth was impressed by what she saw before her. The decorations were tastefully done—royal blue and silver being the predominant colors—and the atmosphere created was slightly romantic in feel due to the dim lighting and prelude music drifting over the assembling revelers. Though Elizabeth would have liked to suppose that the romantic feel was due to her sister Jane's progressing courtship with Mr. Bingley, she rather thought that Caroline Bingley had planned the evening in the hope of forwarding her attempts to ensnare Mr. Darcy. Regardless of her intentions, Miss Bingley *did* know how to plan a successful event—Elizabeth doubted the entire production would have been amiss in the midst of the London season.

The Bennet family moved sedately through the greeting line, the youngest two performing admirably under the watchful eye of their eldest siblings. The whole family was greeted with the affability she had come to expect from Mr. Bingley, the same contrived cheerfulness from his sisters, and the unsurprising disinterestedness of Mr. Hurst. Of Mr. Darcy, there was no sign; he had obviously felt there was no need to receive Mr. Bingley's guests since he was, after all, merely a guest himself.

Elizabeth, though she would be loath to own it, peered through the assembled, looking for any sign of the two men who she wished to avoid. She would not be intimidated and induced to flee from before them, but that did not mean she was insensible of the very great benefit of simple avoidance.

Kitty and Lydia soon made their way away from the family, and though their energetic spirits were once again rising as they approached the ballroom, they were still quiet enough that Elizabeth could notice some improvement. They immediately approached two of their officer friends—Mr. Sanderson and Mr. Denny—and after greeting them with credible decorum, they moved into the ballroom. Mary was escorted by Mr. Collins—causing Elizabeth to shudder with relief at having escaped his attentions—while Jane's hand was soon on Mr. Bingley's arm as he led her into the ballroom.

As she was about to follow them, Elizabeth was stopped by the sound of a gentleman addressing her, putting an end to all her thoughts of evading her fate.

"Miss Bennet! I am truly delighted to see you. You are looking remarkably well this evening."

Suppressing a sigh, Elizabeth turned and curtseyed. "I thank you, Mr. Wickham," said she. "I must say you are looking rather dashing yourself."

"You mean this old thing?" asked he, gesturing toward his impeccably pressed scarlet jacket. "It is nothing, I assure you."

His gallantry and flirtation were already beginning to grate upon Elizabeth's nerves, and she inclined her head and attempted to enter after the other guests. "The ball is about to start, Mr. Wickham. I believe I should follow my family."

"Indeed, you are correct," said Mr. Wickham quickly. "But if you will allow me, I should be vastly pleased to escort the most beautiful lady present into the ballroom."

"Then do not let me keep you a moment longer, Mr. Wickham," responded Elizabeth. "You should hurry to the side of this wondrous creature to whom you refer."

It was impossible to miss the exaggerated gallantry and penetrating look which accompanied Mr. Wickham's reply. "I assure you, Miss Bennet, that I have no need to search elsewhere for such a creature. Ah, the ball appears to be about to start," continued he, while extending his arm to her. "Shall we?"

Seeing no other way to avoid his company without being rude, Elizabeth accepted. She rested her hand on his arm as lightly as she was able, hoping to escape his presence as soon as she could.

The interior of the ballroom was decorated as splendidly as the rest of the manor, but Elizabeth was preoccupied with the necessity of escaping from Mr. Wickham's presence. She had barely begun the attempt when Mr. Wickham turned to her and spoke:

"Miss Bennet, if you are not engaged for the first set, I would be pleased if you would accept my hand for those dances."

Inwardly cursing over the man's inability — or unwillingness — to see her disinterest, Elizabeth was forced to accept his invitation, lest she be forced to sit out for a considerable portion of the evening's entertainment.

The music started, and the partners took to the floor. While she found Mr. Wickham's presence and company increasingly offensive, Elizabeth could not but acknowledge that he was a capable and graceful dancer.

The initial moments of the dance were passed in silence, Elizabeth feigning concentration on the steps while Mr. Wickham regarded her earnestly. His attention seemed to be a little excessive, and though she attempted to keep her countenance, Elizabeth could not help but wonder at his thoughts. Had he seen something of her behavior which had helped him see her suspicion of his motives?

At length, just when Elizabeth had started to become accustomed to his silence — and indulged in a hope it would continue indefinitely — he spoke, drawing her attention to the other side of the ballroom.

"It would seem, Miss Bennet, that we have drawn the attention of a particular gentleman."

Elizabeth's eyes followed the direction of his accompanying nod, and she saw Mr. Darcy standing to the side of the dancing company. On his face was affixed the most fearsome scowl she had ever beheld, and the object of his displeasure appeared to be none other than herself and Mr. Wickham.

She turned back to her partner, just catching the insolent smirk the man directed at Mr. Darcy.

"He appears to be most discontented, does he not, Miss Bennet?" was Mr. Wickham's flippant comment.

Elizabeth shrugged her shoulders in a dismissive manner. "Perhaps. I know not how to interpret Mr. Darcy's facial expressions, as he often seems to regard the rest of the world in such a manner."

"Well said, indeed, Miss Bennet!" exclaimed Mr. Wickham with a sardonic smirk.

They separated due to the dance, allowing Elizabeth to compose herself for the final steps of their time together. If Mr. Wickham meant to bring up the subject of Mr. Darcy's offenses against himself, he would be disappointed, for Elizabeth was in no mood to indulge him. She was therefore surprised by Mr. Wickham's sortie when they had joined together again.

"Darcy still watches us, Miss Bennet." His sneering nod in Mr. Darcy's direction was ignored. "It is almost as though he believes he has some proprietary claim upon you. You have no relationship with him, have you?"

Shocked by Mr. Wickham's audacity, Elizabeth directed the full force of her displeasure at him. "That is an impertinent question, and I shall not dignify it with an answer."

"Come now, Miss Bennet," said Mr. Wickham with a laugh. "You shall make me jealous indeed, and I should dearly love to know if I have a rival for your affections. Do you not see that you make yourself appear guilty by not answering? Surely there is no reason to hide it if you *do* have a deeper relationship with the inestimable Mr. Darcy. Catching the very *rich and influential* master of Pemberley would be quite the feather in your cap, after all."

He grinned and bowed to her as the dance ended, putting a hand over his heart in mock gallantry. "I swear I shall not tell a soul of your secret."

Now Elizabeth, attuned as she had been to the man's mood throughout the entire dance, felt a frisson of unease pass through her. He undoubtedly intended for his words to be taken in a light-hearted manner, but Elizabeth found she could not do so. His expression when he spoke betrayed a kernel of intense interest, not to mention a sense of discontent at what she assumed was the thought of her preference for his mortal enemy.

But Elizabeth was not about to play his game. Not only had he completely deserted propriety with his insolent questions, but her anger at his presumption had been aroused. To suggest that she was *guilty* of anything—even should she be attached to Mr. Darcy, strange though the thought seemed—was an arrogance which not even Mr. Darcy could match. And the insinuation that she would attach herself to a man merely for his fortune and position in the world left her offended and wishing to put this man firmly in his place.

As Mr. Wickham took her hand and led her from the floor, he watched her expectantly. Elizabeth wasted no time in informing him of her displeasure.

"Mr. Wickham, I shall not speak of such a matter, and I beg for you to drop the subject. The state of my relationship with *anyone* is a matter which is of absolutely no concern to you. You are completely unconnected with me, Mr. Wickham, and therefore, I must insist that you cease this line of questioning immediately."

Mr. Wickham's expression became affronted. "No connection, Miss Bennet? Do you discount our friendship so easily?"

"*What friendship*, Mr. Wickham?" demanded Elizabeth. "By my account, we have met exactly three times—all within the last week, I might add—and had two conversations, one of which was filled with impertinences and improper innuendos. I do not know with what sort of woman you usually consort, but I assure you that I am not the kind of woman who is willing to be treated in so familiar a manner on so short an acquaintance as you have today."

"In that case, I must apologize, Miss Bennet," said Mr. Wickham formally, his manner and expression cold. "I assure you that I meant no harm."

"Apology accepted, Mr. Wickham," replied Elizabeth, inclining her head. "Now, if you will excuse me, I believe I should like to have a word with Miss Lucas."

Giving a stiff bow, Mr. Wickham retreated, and though he was attempting to control his temper, Elizabeth felt that she could see in his carriage a barely concealed rage. She shivered, certain now that she had glimpsed the true man behind the façade.

Yet though she now had more reason than ever to question Mr. Wickham's motives concerning Mr. Darcy, she still had no true desire to know the actuality of the matter between the two gentlemen. Both men had offended her, and she found herself disinclined to have any further contact with either of them.

Putting thoughts of both men from her mind, Elizabeth greeted Charlotte warmly and stood for the next several moments with her friend, speaking of various doings in their lives since they had last seen one another. Slowly, Elizabeth was able to shed the dreary thoughts which had been plaguing her for the past week, and she felt her brightness of spirits return. Despite the efforts of the two young men, she would not allow the pleasure she took in a ball to be ruined!

For the next hour, Elizabeth was able to lose herself in the enjoyment of Mr. Bingley's ball. The food and drink was excellent, the company engaging and happy, and when she looked upon Jane's shining countenance, Elizabeth felt that the magic of the evening was doing its work. And since Elizabeth was not as a rule inclined toward gloomy thoughts, the ball provided a perfect atmosphere in which to lose herself to a diversion while improving her perspective dramatically. She had even managed to avoid dancing with Mr. Collins!

Though Elizabeth had been too caught up in fending off Mr. Wickham's advances to notice, a giggling Lydia had informed her that Mr. Collins had misstepped several times and had run into another dancer twice during the first set. Elizabeth laughed quietly with her youngest sister, gently admonished her to not allow her amusement to become loud or vulgar, and left to search for her middle sister.

Surprisingly—or perhaps unsurprisingly—Mary was unconcerned about Mr. Collins's fiasco. A clergyman was, by virtue of his position, unlikely to be required to dance with any great frequency, after all, and the lack of skill on the dance floor was not a large deficiency. Besides, if it truly became a problem, it was one which could be fixed with a little time and patience.

Happy that her sister was taking such a positive approach to the situation, Elizabeth complimented her and, seeing Mr. Collin's approach, swiftly retreated, having no desire to put herself in his company.

She had just finished dancing with Sir William's eldest son—a pleasant young lad of two and twenty summers—when she was startled by the approach of one of the young men whom she had been endeavoring to avoid.

"Miss Bennet," intoned Mr. Darcy with a sharp bow. "If you are not otherwise engaged, would you do me the honor of standing up for the next with me?"

Never before had Elizabeth wished that she had already been asked to dance as she did at this moment! However, knowing she had no real choice but to accept, she allowed in a gracious but distant voice that she was not engaged and would be honored to stand up with him. Mr. Darcy repeated his perfunctory bow and stepped away, allowing Elizabeth to resume her conversation with Charlotte.

"Eliza, I am all astonishment," exclaimed Charlotte. "The forbidding Mr. Darcy has actually deigned to ask one of the locals to dance."

"Indeed, he has, Charlotte," replied Elizabeth with a sigh.

Charlotte affixed her with a stern gaze. "Now, Elizabeth, you do not mean to offend Mr. Darcy, do you? You should consider that he pays you a great compliment by singling you out like this—after all, he has danced with no one who was not previously a member of his party since he came to the neighborhood."

"Come now, Charlotte," said Elizabeth, laughing. "You cannot seriously think that I mean to insult Mr. Darcy."

"I am not so certain, Eliza. You *have* been very vocal in your dislike for the gentleman."

Rolling her eyes, Elizabeth affixed a stern gaze upon her friend. "Regardless of my feelings, I would never willfully offend someone of my acquaintance, Charlotte. It is true that I do not seek Mr. Darcy's attentions, but *I do* know how to behave with the proper decorum."

"That is good to hear, Elizabeth. But I still believe that Mr. Darcy has paid a great deal of attention to you since he arrived—the man's eyes rarely leave you, for heaven's sake! If he can be induced to pay you the compliment of a dance, he may be able to be persuaded to pay you an even greater compliment, thereby securing your family's future and that of your future children."

"Surely you have jumped from a single dance to matrimony in the blink of an eye," cried Elizabeth.

"Many marriages have been founded on less," insisted Charlotte.

"Oh, yes, indeed. But those marriages were nothing more than business transactions, with fortune and connections on both sides. I have none of these things.

"Besides," continued Elizabeth, when Charlotte would have spoken again, "I know not what to think about Mr. Darcy—or his compatriot from the north—and I shall endeavor to leave both of them to their own devices while hoping they leave me to mine."

Charlotte's expression was all puzzlement. "I am sorry, Eliza, but I have not the pleasure of understanding you. To whom do you refer?"

"Oh, I am sorry, Charlotte! I have not shared the particulars with you. You have perhaps heard of the new officer in the militia—a Mr. Wickham?"

"Yes, indeed," responded Charlotte with a laugh. "I believe your youngest sisters have waxed poetic on the subject of Mr. Wickham and how it was so unfair that he should single you out for the first dance."

Elizabeth shook her head—though she had thought her observations about Mr. Wickham had been heard and accepted by her youngest sisters, apparently the effects of a pleasing countenance and a gentlemanly address held more attraction than she had hoped.

"In fact," continued Charlotte, startling Elizabeth from her reflections, "if I am not very much mistaken, I believe the man is watching you at this very moment."

Her friend's observation was indeed correct—as Elizabeth followed Charlotte's eyes across the room, she noticed that Mr. Wickham *was* watching her, an absent frown of concentration etched upon his features. When he noticed Elizabeth looking at him, he nodded his head slightly in her direction. Elizabeth could only wonder what the man was about. He had to have some inclination that she did not wish to discuss his misfortunes—her set-down concerning his impertinence as they left the dance floor had been pointed, after all, and could not be otherwise interpreted. Why was he so intent upon procuring *her* good opinion? Elizabeth could not imagine his purpose, but she heartily wished he would pay attention to someone else.

At that moment, the music for the next set began, and Elizabeth, observing that Mr. Darcy was even now approaching, leaned forward and whispered to Charlotte that she would explain everything later. She then allowed her hand to be taken by the gentleman, and they made their way to the dance floor.

Chapter IV

ancing with Mr. Darcy, Elizabeth mused, was no onerous task—the man was light on his feet, he executed the dance steps precisely and with grace, and he was not unpleasant to look upon. No, dancing with Mr. Darcy was not distasteful; indeed, she felt that had she met the gentleman under different circumstances—had his behavior been more polite and pleasing—then a dance with him might in fact be quite enjoyable. How different would matters have progressed had he held his tongue, or even better, had he followed his friend's advice and danced with her?

Likely not much different, she thought to herself. He *was*, after all, still a very proud individual, and though she might have thought better of him from the start, she could not imagine that he would have sought her attention any more than he already had. And his constant contemplation of her, Elizabeth had noticed, appeared to be accompanied by an almost unconscious air of disapproval, one which only appeared to reinforce the unkind comment he had made about her. Surely Charlotte was seeing far too much into his attention.

A part of her whispered what she had considered earlier that week—that Mr. Darcy was not at his best in a ballroom—but now that she was faced with the reality of the man, she thought her previous ruminations were not the whole of the story, though they may have contained a germ of truth. No, she was certain Charlotte could not be correct in her estimation of Mr. Darcy's regard—every circumstance confirmed Elizabeth's opinion, regardless of his solicitation of her hand for a dance.

The first few moments of their time together were accomplished in silence, not that Elizabeth would have expected anything less from the taciturn man. However, eventually, he surprised her by opening his mouth and commenting:

"You seem to be enjoying the ball immensely, Miss Bennet."

Elizabeth masked her surprise at his statement. "I am indeed, Mr. Darcy. I do love to move in company, and I am inclined to dance whenever the occasion permits it.

"I believe *you also* may be enjoying yourself more than you have during similar events in the past," continued she after she had considered the matter for several moments. Though she had determined that she did not care to know him better, her natural curiosity was overcoming her previous decision, and she decided that this could be her only opportunity to draw him out.

"Perhaps," allowed Mr. Darcy. "Though I believe you know that I do not, as a rule, enjoy dancing, I can be persuaded to take enjoyment given the right inducement."

If Elizabeth had been surprised before, she was all astonishment now. "Do you mean to tell me that you have found an inducement here in our poor country?"

His piercing stare was a little unnerving. "Indeed, I do."

"Mr. Darcy, I assure you there is no need to flatter me—I already feel the honor of being singled out by you intensely, I assure you."

"And I do not flatter on a whim, Miss Bennet, and I ask that you refrain from responding in kind—surely you are above such artifice. I have the pleasure of dancing with a singular young lady who is not impressed by my fortune or connections and does not praise me for the purpose of exciting my attention or attempting to entrap me with pretty words, fluttering eyelashes, and falsely presented attachment. Please be assured that I take great pleasure in your company, and I intend no insincerity."

Feeling a little discomposed, Elizabeth was silent, attempting to digest this new information. She had known of Mr. Darcy's riches and his importance, but she had never considered what an object of interest—or an object of prey!—he must have been to every available young woman of society. To a man of his position, what must it be like to be forever hearing of his wealth and status rather than his person?

Was *that* the reason for his reticence?

"In that case, I thank you for the compliment, Mr. Darcy," responded Elizabeth once their movements had brought them close enough again for discourse.

A light smile graced his face, leading Elizabeth to reflect that he truly should spend more time smiling—it transformed his face when he did so!

"You are quite welcome," answered Mr. Darcy.

They moved through the steps in silence for some time, Elizabeth contemplating the meaning of his words and wondering at his praise. Though perhaps it suggested that he was not truly so displeased with her as she had thought, she still could not imagine he had as much interest as Charlotte had averred he did. What a truly difficult man he was to understand!

They continued through the dance steps, weaving their way down the line, until they had joined together again. As Mr. Darcy clasped her hand, he peered thoughtfully at her and spoke again:

"You appear to be a popular partner, Miss Bennet. When I determined to request your company for a set, I was concerned that you would not have one available to grant to me."

"I flatter myself that I rarely have to sit down unless gentlemen are scarce," replied Elizabeth, wondering if he would catch her hint at the night of their first meeting.

He did not—or if he did, he hid it well. "Still, it is a credit to you, I believe, for if a woman is not handsome or not accomplished at the dance, men would not solicit her hand regardless of the relative numbers of each sex in attendance."

"I believe you are correct, Mr. Darcy, though I wish that the rules of society were not quite so strict. After all, a woman must wait for a man to ask for her hand to dance, and if she is not sought after, she may forced to spend the majority of the evening sitting and watching others partake in the amusement."

Elizabeth glanced at Mary almost involuntarily, noting how she was standing by the side of the dance floor with the ever-voluble Mr. Collins. When she looked back at Mr. Darcy, Elizabeth idly wondered if he caught the significance of the look. It was likely, as he was a perceptive man. He gave no outward reaction, however, and she continued:

"Furthermore, a woman must suffer through a set with a disagreeable partner and swallow her objections to him, or else she must sit out the rest of the evening."

"Indeed, I believe you are correct," said Mr. Darcy. "And I cannot but agree with you that this is very unfair to young ladies."

They separated due to the steps, weaving their way around the dancers. When they had rejoined in the middle of the line, Mr. Darcy said:

"Has your experience this evening been satisfactory?"

Elizabeth peered at him, wondering what he meant to learn through his line of inquiry. She was not certain she wished to answer his question, but she preferred to be honest.

"For the most part, it has. I have stood up with young men I have known most of my life, although my first partner is a new acquaintance. *He* at least wishes to enter into a friendship with me, it seems."

As soon as the words left her mouth, Elizabeth knew she should have held her tongue—she had, after all, resolved on remaining ignorant of the true state of affairs between the two young men. Upon hearing her statement, Mr. Darcy's countenance immediately darkened, and though he kept control over his expression, Elizabeth had the distinct impression that he wished he could indulge in a scowl.

"Mr. Wickham indeed possesses the ability to make himself truly agreeable, obtaining friends wherever he may go," said Mr. Darcy quietly. "However, inevitably, when those friends become aware of his true character, the only friendships he manages to retain are with those people who are most like him in character."

"Are you warning me against Mr. Wickham, sir?" demanded Elizabeth, speaking in a low voice and completely setting aside her previous decision.

"I most certainly am."

"Of what do you have to accuse him, then? I assure you he was most specific in his own accusations toward you."

If Mr. Darcy's countenance had been stern before, it was downright intimidating now. "He told you his *tale of woe* in the middle of a dance at a ball?" was his incredulous demand.

"No, Mr. Darcy, I apologize for misleading you. His communications were made to me the night we first met him in Meryton—the day you came upon us in the street. It was at a small card party my aunt in Meryton had hosted where the officers were invited."

The full force of his displeasure was blunted, although Mr. Darcy still appeared to be highly offended. As they continued to move through the dance, Elizabeth warily kept her eyes on him, watching as he attempted to master his temper and calm himself. They were even now entering the final steps of the dance, and Elizabeth longed for it to be over, so she could escape from this man.

"And did you believe his assertions, Miss Bennet?" asked Mr. Darcy as their hands joined together one final time.

Elizabeth colored and dropped her gaze to the floor. "I will own his tale *did* take me in for a time, Mr. Darcy, but then I considered his contradictions and the impropriety of his addressing such subjects with a new acquaintance such as myself. It was then that I began to distrust him. I assure you, his performance during our set did not do him any credit, nor did it inspire any further belief on my part."

The music came to an end, and Elizabeth curtseyed while Mr. Darcy bowed. Mr. Darcy stepped forward to grasp her hand, and he led her from the floor, his face an expressionless mask of concentration.

At length, when they had departed the floor, Mr. Darcy turned to her abruptly and addressed her:

"Miss Bennet, are you engaged for the next set?"

Astonished, Elizabeth could only gaze at him, wondering at his motive. "I do not believe it would be proper to dance *two sets in a row*, Mr. Darcy—we would incite the most violent gossip amongst those of the neighborhood. Not even Mr. Bingley has paid as much attention to my sister as this."

After a sharp glance in Mr. Bingley's direction, Mr. Darcy turned his attention back on Elizabeth. "I am not asking you for another dance, Miss Bennet. But I believe that as Mr. Wickham has attempted to impose himself upon you and discredit me, it behooves me to answer his charges and ensure that you understand exactly what kind of man he is. It would only take a few moments of your time, and we would be back for the following set, if you would indulge me."

Elizabeth was torn. Her curiosity was urging her to accept his offer, while her determination not to be caught up in a feud between the two men urged the opposite. In the end, it was his earnest look which made up her mind—that and the fact that the clues he had already imparted to her suggested that there was much more to Mr. Wickham than he had betrayed to the neighborhood. If he truly was as bad a man as Mr. Darcy seemed to be indicating, it was only prudent for her to obtain as much information as she could for the purpose of protecting herself and her family.

"Very well, Mr. Darcy. I am at your disposal. However, I do not necessarily believe that a ballroom, where anyone could overhear us, is the proper location for such a discussion."

"Shall we take a turn about the terrace then?" inquired Mr. Darcy. "We shall have a modicum of privacy and yet be in full view, thereby protecting your reputation."

They made their way to the doors at Elizabeth's assent, and after she had gathered her wrap, they exited out onto the large terrace situated at the rear of the house. There was a chill in the night air, but it was not excessively cold—it was more bracing to a hardy soul such as Elizabeth. The sky was mercifully clear after days of steady rain, and the stars were brightly twinkling overhead. In all, the locale was subdued, with few others present, and though the strains of music and the dull rumble of conversation and music persisted at the back of her consciousness, Elizabeth found it quiet and comfortable and perfect for a private discourse.

Stepping away from the entrance, Elizabeth and Mr. Darcy made their way to the balustrade overlooking the formal gardens at the rear of the house, stopping at a location which was slightly separate from the few others who had escaped the ballroom. Leaning against the railing, Elizabeth turned her attention to her companion with an upraised eyebrow. Mr. Darcy chuckled at the sight and shook his head, clearly diverted by her manner.

"I thank you for your indulgence in this matter, Miss Bennet, and I compliment you for your powers of discernment—Wickham is a practiced deceiver and well able to charm those who would otherwise see through him."

Mr. Darcy turned abruptly and began pacing agitatedly in front of her, his face a mask of concentration. He continued in this attitude for some moments before he appeared to come to a decision, and then turning, he directed his attention back to her.

"Miss Bennet, I fear that the account I am about to disclose to you will be somewhat . . . difficult for me, and I beg you to allow me to finish my discourse before you ask any questions. I mean to tell you everything, but I do not know if I am able to continue should you disturb me. I must also insist upon your secrecy in what I am about to tell you—there is more at stake in this matter than Wickham's misdeeds."

Whatever she had been expecting, Elizabeth was certain it was not this heartfelt request. She immediately assured him that she would allow him to complete his narrative before interrupting and would keep his confidence. She then listened to his tale with growing astonishment.

"I can assure you, Miss Bennet, that I am likely able to recite Mr.

Wickham's charges toward me almost verbatim—as you might suspect, this is not the first time I have been required to refute his words against me. However, in the interest of time, I shall endeavor to impart to you the *true* history between us, knowing as I do that this communication will completely refute his claims. I will also tell you that I am able to produce documents and witnesses which will prove my assertions, and I am willing to do so, should you require additional evidence."

Elizabeth murmured her acceptance and allowed him to continue.

"I suppose Mr. Wickham has already informed you that we grew up together at my estate at Pemberley. My father was an excellent man, and he had a very close friend and supremely competent steward in Mr. Wickham's father. Old Mr. Wickham fulfilled his position at the estate with very great proficiency and honor, and my father relied heavily on his competence and judgment. It is truly unfortunate that George Wickham did not follow in his father's footsteps, or else he might very well have been *my* steward.

"Wickham and I did indeed play together, primarily alone, as there were very few others of our age in the area. He was also known to my cousins, who were often at Pemberley for the summers. Regardless of our familiarity, however, I could never have called us 'close companions.' As a child, he tended to be the first to break the rules and cause mischief—although I am certain you understand that as young boys, none of us were angels—and that problem simply seemed to grow as the years passed. When we attained the age at which we were to attend school, however, his habits appeared to become unrestrained, a situation which coincided with our removal from the watchful eyes of our fathers when we attended school together. I could not help but notice his lack of morals and his vicious tendencies, both in his insatiable thirst for the gaming tables and his predilections toward those of the fairer sex. Add to that the debts he left behind when he finally quit the village of Lambton, and you will no doubt have an accurate assessment of Wickham's character."

Elizabeth shivered at that last revelation, her mind filled with thoughts of Mr. Wickham's words and actions and the uneasiness she had felt when under his scrutiny. Had Mr. Wickham had been paying her so much attention because he intended her to be his next conquest? She shuddered at the thought.

Mr. Darcy had not finished relating his tale, however, and as he continued, she was forced to listen, anxious for what he would reveal. "My father, however, was very attached to Mr. Wickham, and knowing of his regard, I chose not to illuminate him as to the extent of Mr. Wickham's depravity, which was a decision I shall regret all of my days. In particular, upon his death—which occurred a few months after old Mr. Wickham's—my father recommended in his will that should Wickham be so inclined, a valuable living should be made available to him upon the incumbent's death, assuming of course that Mr. Wickham had already taken orders.

"You should not be surprised, then, that given what I knew of his vices, I considered Mr. Wickham most unsuited to caring after the spiritual needs of the local parish. I believe that I may have searched high and low and failed to discover a candidate more ill-suited to become a clergyman than Mr. Wickham. As a result, I was most relieved when Mr. Wickham informed me soon after my father's death that he was not inclined to pursue the church as a career. As he would not prosper from the living, he approached me in the hope of being compensated in another manner, as stipulated in my father's will. I trust you will understand when I say I was happy to grant him his request, though I knew that the money he demanded would soon pass from his control. I nearly laughed in his face when he assured me he had every intention of studying the law; I seriously doubt he had ever even opened a book the entire time he was enrolled at Cambridge—the idea of him actually applying himself to become an attorney seemed ludicrous."

Mr. Darcy turned and peered at her, yet his expression was strangely gentle. "Can I assume Mr. Wickham told you that I refused him the living in defiance of my father's wishes?"

At Elizabeth's nod, he continued with a sardonic smile. "Mr. Wickham's stories of his misfortunes are nothing if not predictable. I *did* in fact refuse the living, Miss Bennet, but it was after he had already resigned all claims to it and had been compensated accordingly. After he received the money, he left Pemberley and appeared to drop his acquaintance with me, which I was happy to allow happen, considering how ill I truly thought of him by that time. I did not hear from him again until the man who had held the living passed away. Once he heard of the vacancy—I can only assume he still had friends who kept him informed of the happenings in the area—he wrote once again to secure the living, telling me that his study of the law had not turned out well and that he was now resolved upon devoting his life to God. If he had told me such in person, I *would* have laughed at him. You see, Miss Bennet, I had kept track of his movements and his doings, and I was certain that my expectations for the money I had given him were fulfilled—by this time, he was penniless and likely even owed gaming debts which he could not pay.

"I rejected his request, but he was not deterred; indeed, he persisted in his requests, becoming more and more insistent and angry, until I appointed another to the position. He then wrote me a final letter which was most abusive and insulting, and I do not suppose he exercised any restraint in blackening my name to any who would listen. After that, all appearance of acquaintance between us was dropped. Feeling that we were now irreconcilably estranged, I stopped keeping track of him—another mistake I now regret."

At this point, Mr. Darcy became extremely agitated and resumed his restless pacing. Whatever he felt he now needed to impart seemed to be something which gave him true pain. Not wishing him to relive some great tragedy which had befallen him at the hands of his unscrupulous former friend, Elizabeth stepped forward and placed her hand upon his arm, causing him to stop and gaze down at her.

"Mr. Darcy, I beseech you—if the next part of your narrative gives you this much pain, I beg you not to speak of it at all. I believe every particular of what you have related to me, and I fully comprehend the danger of paying any heed to this man. It would not do for me to pry into your personal life. Please, sir, shall we not return to the house?"

A shiver accompanied her declaration, and she realized that the night had begun to feel cold while she had listened to him speak. Or perhaps it was the coldness which was spreading through her entire being at the realization of how close she had come to being taken in by Mr. Wickham.

Mr. Darcy, it appeared, noticed her tremble. He regarded her with an inscrutable expression on his face, and then he pulled his jacket from his frame and settled it about her shoulders.

"I apologize, Miss Bennet. It was very thoughtless of me to have neglected to consider your discomfort. However, I do wish to continue my narration, if you will indulge me; I would have you truly understand what sort of man George Wickham is so you may take the appropriate measures to protect yourself. Please, will you allow me?"

Though she would have preferred to leave the matter at what she already knew, Elizabeth could only nod her head in acquiescence. Mr. Darcy was so earnest and his manner so pleading that she felt she could deny him nothing. How had he altered from proud and disagreeable to irresistible in so short a time?

"I thank you, Miss Bennet," stated Mr. Darcy, once again taking up his narrative. "As I said, I received the final letter from Mr. Wickham approximately two years ago, and I foolishly thought that I had heard the last from him. How wrong I was."

He stopped and reflected, clearly trying to find the words to impart the information he deemed so critical.

"I underestimated Mr. Wickham, Miss Bennet," said Mr. Darcy at length. "Or at least, I underestimated his need to fuel his habits with fortune and the lengths to which he was willing to go to obtain it. In fact, I believe that Mr. Wickham expected my father to bestow upon him a gentleman's income upon his death—perhaps one of the lesser estates—as he had been treated much like a son all his life. What Mr. Wickham never understood was that my father was above all a creature of duty; he never would have broken up the Darcy holdings in such a manner for anyone other than a second son.

"Regardless of my speculation, I saw nothing of Mr. Wickham again until this past summer, when he once again imposed himself upon my consciousness under extremely painful circumstances which I wish I could expunge from my own memory."

Mr. Darcy took a deep breath then, fixing his gaze upon Elizabeth; then he continued his story:

"This past summer, Mr. Wickham imposed himself upon a . . . a young woman of my acquaintance. He persuaded her to fancy herself in love with him and consent to an elopement. He flattered her, professing a longstanding affection for her, and I can only conjecture that he was able to achieve this because she had known him as a young child and because her guardians, never fathoming the fact that Mr. Wickham might attempt to use her in this manner, had left her memories of him unsullied. Of course, Mr. Wickham's primary object was her fortune, which is substantial. I can only suppose that the thought of hurting me added to his inducement on account of my connection with the young woman. Whatever his motives were, he was very nearly successful in persuading her to marry him, he was foiled, however, when the young lady confessed the affair to one of her guardians only days in advance of the intended elopement. Mr. Wickham immediately fled, but not before ensuring she knew in the most pointed terms possible that her money was the only reason he had paid his addresses to her and that he doubted *anyone* would marry such a colorless, mousy little thing without such an inducement."

Mr. Darcy's eyes were fairly glowing with indignation as he detailed the event, prompting Elizabeth to step forward and put her hand upon his arm once again. Gratefully, he smiled at her and took a deep, calming breath.

"Her reputation and her future were thus saved," continued Mr. Darcy. "But though Mr. Wickham's attempt was foiled, her spirits have been depressed since the event, for she blames herself for falling for the charms of that black-hearted villain.

"Now, I would have you understand, Miss Bennet, that I do not consider to bear the entire blame for the affair herself, and her guardians have had difficulty in using the incident as a tool for learning, rather than simply a reason for her to feel shame. On the one hand, Mr. Wickham is a practiced liar and well able to charm a young woman who had no reason to suspect him of duplicity and avarice. On the other, despite her tender years, she *did* behave foolishly. She must amend her behavior — and soon! — or she shall not survive the shark-infested waters of London, where a potential fortune-hunter lurks around every corner."

He stopped and gazed at her with a very serious expression on his face. "This is the extent of my narrative, Miss Bennet, and I thank you for listening to it with so much care and concern. I could not live with myself if Wickham were to use another young woman so ill as he has my . . . acquaintance."

Elizabeth swallowed, on one level wishing she was still ignorant of these matters, while on another feeling grateful that Mr. Darcy had put her on her guard. This had truly been difficult for him, and she fully felt the compliment of his trust. And though Mr. Darcy had not explicitly identified the young lady Wickham had attempted to seduce, Elizabeth could not help wonder if the girl was his sister. Still, it would not do to voice such a thing to him — it was not as though it was any of her concern, after all.

"I thank you, Mr. Darcy. I suspected Mr. Wickham of duplicity, but I certainly had not thought him to be this bad."

He bowed in response, and Elizabeth continued.

"Luckily, I think his interest in me shall not be of long duration. After all, I do not possess the fortune which would lure him, as your acquaintance did. He should forget me in due time and move on to some other more wealthy target."

Frowning, Mr. Darcy spoke again.

"With all due respect, Miss Bennet, I do not believe you are considering the matter through the eyes of a scoundrel such as he. Perhaps he may lose interest if his intention is to make a purchase. Your supposition does *not* hold true if he is attempting to . . .." Mr. Darcy paused for a moment, clearly trying to discover a way to continue in a polite way, given the very improper nature of the discussion. Finally, he shrugged and looked at her. "He may simply to intending to try out the merchandise."

Horrified, Elizabeth gazed at Mr. Darcy. "You think Mr. Wickham has targeted me for such a purpose?"

"Unfortunately, I have not witnessed him in your company enough to truly determine his motives. It may be that he simply wished to blacken my name as is his wont, attempting to make use of your trusting nature to make his stories of woe known to the neighborhood. However, he could very well have some other purpose in mind. You are more than handsome enough to tempt him, and if he were to succeed, you would not be the first young woman he defiled."

Though in other circumstances Elizabeth would have been amused by Mr. Darcy's words—so very like the comment she had heard the night of their first acquaintance—the seriousness of the matter stopped her from making sport with him. The gravity in his expression did not encourage levity either.

"You must also understand, Miss Bennet," resumed Mr. Darcy, "that Mr. Wickham will dare almost anything if he feels it will do me harm. As you have already apprehended, I do not usually pay attention to any young lady, and the fact of my asking you to dance tonight must certainly have garnered his attention, particularly when coupled with our present tête-à-tête. If he discerns any interest in you on my part, he may try to hurt me *through you*."

"Then why have you involved me?" exclaimed an exasperated Elizabeth.

"Because, Miss Bennet, I deemed the risks of ignorance of his true nature to be greater than the risk of his attempting something to spite me. Now that you have the information you require, you may take steps to defend yourself—steps which you may not have taken had you remained in ignorance of these events.

"And besides," was his quiet statement after a moment's reflection, "I *do* find that you intrigue me, and I am becoming increasingly loath to conceal it."

Elizabeth colored, wondering if this was the confirmation of Charlotte's opinion of his regard. Still, *this* was the opportunity she needed to turn the conversation onto less serious matters.

"So am I to understand that now you *do* find me handsome enough to tempt you?"

The intensity of his gaze was almost overwhelming. "More than tempting, I assure you. And I will not make excuses, but please allow me to apologize for the churlish remark which you obviously overheard me speak the night of the assembly. I regret making it. I should have held my tongue and actually looked at you before pronouncing such an obviously false and rude statement."

Elizabeth felt her head spinning as her tenaciously held beliefs of this man were completely washed away. She needed to think further on the matter, knowing that despite all of her ruminations from past few days, she had very quickly gone from a very poor opinion of the man to . . . something more positive. It was all too much to take in at once, and Elizabeth desperately wished for some distance which she could use to further examine her feelings and the information he had imparted to her.

"Apology accepted, Mr. Darcy," said she, determining to avoid the import of his words until she could more fully contemplate it. "I do not doubt your honor or the truth of the things you have told me, and I fully believe your account. However, I think we have been speaking long enough; we shall start making the gossips of Meryton curious if we linger any longer, and I beg you to allow me more time to consider *all* you have told me."

Mr. Darcy bowed and held out his arm. "I agree, Miss Bennet. Shall we enter the house again?"

Agreeing immediately, Elizabeth reached out and took his arm. With all he had given her to consider, she would have liked to find a quiet place to do so. Unfortunately, a ballroom was not exactly an ideal location for quiet reflection.

Chapter V

When they entered the ballroom, Elizabeth relinquished Mr. Darcy's jacket to him with a polite thanks, and Mr. Darcy responded with a bow and a serious look. They then separated, Elizabeth moving to the refreshment tables for a much-needed glass of punch as Mr. Darcy exited the room for a few moments. Though Elizabeth would have wished to follow his example and slip off to the library or some other occupied room, she knew she had best take part once again in the festivities—Mr. Darcy, with his reputation for taciturnity, could escape with impunity, but Elizabeth was well-known in the community for being a social creature. It would not do to invite unwanted questions and speculation.

The first thing she apprehended upon her return was the fact that her conversation with Mr. Darcy had not gone unnoticed. Besides the somewhat angry and intense glare from Mr. Wickham and the unfriendly expression etched on Miss Bingley's face, there were looks of curiosity directed at her from many of her friends and neighbors. Particularly, her mother bustled up to her and, taking her aside, instantly demanded to know what she was about. Not for the first time, Elizabeth wished her mother possessed a little more sense of subtlety; her conversation with Mr. Darcy would be highlighted by her mother approaching her in such a manner rather than the reverse.

"Lizzy!" hissed she, for once keeping her tone low. "I demand to know what you are thinking. I know you wish to find a husband like your sisters, but did we not agree that Mr. Darcy was not worthy of your time?"

"Mama," soothed Elizabeth, "I am not attempting to secure Mr. Darcy."

At her mother's skeptical look, Elizabeth continued:

"Mr. Darcy had some knowledge which he wished to impart to me. That was the reason for my discussion with him."

"Then why do it in clear sight of all our friends? You merely invite speculation into your intentions."

"Would we not invite more speculation and outright rumors if we were discovered speaking alone? Neither Mr. Darcy nor I wished to have such a thing happen—*that* is why we spoke where everyone could see us. This way no hint of impropriety could be levied against us."

Partially mollified, Mrs. Bennet gazed at her daughter for a few moments before speaking. "Lizzy, I have tried to do my best for you and your sisters, but you have always been the stubborn one, intent upon going your own way. As such, I shall not attempt to direct you.

"I would, however, request you clarify a small matter for me. Your discussions with Mr. Darcy—have you changed your opinion of him?"

"To a large extent, yes, I have, Mama."

"And what is your purpose?" asked Mrs. Bennet with a certain studied nonchalance.

Amused at her mother's transparency, Elizabeth stifled a laugh. "Should you not be asking Mr. Darcy what his intentions are, Mama?"

"Oh, you delight in vexing me!" exclaimed Mrs. Bennet.

Placing a placatory hand upon her mother's arm, Elizabeth tried immediately to calm her. "I am sorry, Mama. I believe you have nothing to worry about, as I suspect your comments about Mr. Darcy were entirely accurate. He had some information to relate to me—that is all. I do not doubt that he has no intentions toward me whatsoever."

Though her air was somewhat disappointed—Mr. Darcy *was* a wealthy man, after all—Mrs. Bennet smiled and nodded. Their conversation ended very quickly after that.

For some time, Elizabeth attempted to immerse herself back into the festivities of the evening. It would not do, after all, to allow those of the neighborhood to see just how affected she was by Mr. Darcy's discourse. The speculation must already be working its way through the room, and she had no wish to throw fuel on the fire.

But though her *intent* was to busy herself and drive from her mind the communications she had received from Mr. Darcy, the *actuality* was that her mind stubbornly returned to his words whenever she was not distracted by something else. Her conversation, she thought, was largely lacking its playful and outgoing quality, and though none of her dance partners commented upon her unusual behavior, she caught more than one glance of puzzlement in her direction.

Elizabeth could not imagine that the information she had received was anything but the absolute truth. Not only had the communication concerned private matters of which he would normally not wish to speak—particularly those regarding his young acquaintance!—but they also filled in the gaps which she now knew existed in Mr. Wickham's story. And though perhaps she might have seen these gaps earlier if she had been more discerning, Elizabeth fancied that Mr. Wickham's dissembling had been so cleverly done that detection would have been difficult, if not impossible. If not for Mr. Wickham's error, she could have blithely continued to trust him, thereby making a colossal—and perhaps dangerous—mistake in judgment.

Before hearing Mr. Darcy's words, Elizabeth would likely have thought that the truth would have been somewhere in between the two men's accounts, as was usually the case in a dispute of this type. However, now that she was in possession of the facts, Elizabeth knew that the truth of the matter rendered Mr. Darcy blameless in the entire affair and painted Mr. Wickham as the blackest of villains.

Of Mr. Wickham, she saw much, but she paid little attention to him. His burning gaze and slightly frowning mien gave her to understand that he was not happy that she had spent time with his enemy, but Elizabeth could not find it in herself to care. Now that she was aware of his character, she would give him no further notice and would see to it that her entire family understood exactly the kind of man he was. He did not approach, and she ignored him—*that* was truly the best outcome for the course of the evening.

As she moved through company, she often discovered Mr. Darcy's gaze upon her as was his wont. But whereas she had always thought him to be watching her to criticize, now she believed there appeared to be a more thoughtful quality to his scrutiny than she had noticed in the past. What was especially surprising to Elizabeth was that Mr. Darcy appeared to be somewhat more open than he had previously been in company, and he even danced a few times with some of the local ladies, though he never did stand up for two sets in a row. When she noticed the first lady he chose, Charlotte Lucas, being led to the floor, it had been all Elizabeth could do not to gape in surprise. Her eyes narrowed as she caught his gaze, and he smiled back at her. She wondered at his purpose. Could he be seeking to lessen the speculation about *her* by dancing with other young ladies, or had he seen something of his behavior in her words about his reluctance to engage in social niceties? Was he attempting to inject a little civility in his manner?

Whatever his motives, she could see that his actions were having an effect upon the gathered revelers. He had been branded as the most proud and arrogant sort of man by those of the neighborhood, and his mere willingness to dance with their own young ladies had already begun to soften the attitude against him and deflect some of the attention from herself. Elizabeth was relieved to see it, for it only confirmed what she had seen earlier—Mr. Darcy was not nearly as proud or above his company as Elizabeth had initially suspected. After all, he *had* informed her of his background with Mr. Wickham, and she could not think that a man such as she had thought him to be would have deigned to make such private communications.

It was nearing the supper hour when Elizabeth received her next shock—or perhaps a series of shocks might be more accurate. She had left to enter the retiring room for a few moments, and the next dance had already begun by the time she returned. Seeing her father sitting in a corner with a glass of punch in his hand, she stepped forward, intending to speak with him before the next dance began.

"Ah, Lizzy," greeted Mr. Bennet as she approached. "I see you have managed to gain a bit of a reprieve from the dance floor."

Elizabeth raised an eyebrow at her father. "Contrary to the belief of my youngest sisters, I do not feel the need to have a partner for *every* dance. Missing a set on occasion is hardly a trial."

Laughing, her father motioned to a seat next to him. "I see that your sense has not departed you. Though I did wonder for a time—your very public display with Mr. Darcy did not go unnoticed, you know."

There was a questioning quality in Mr. Bennet's voice, and it gave Elizabeth to understand that her father wished to be assured that she had not been imposed upon by Mr. Darcy.

"Better that than to be caught by some society gossip in a secluded place," replied Elizabeth in a nonchalant tone which was designed to ease his concern. "Mr. Darcy had something he wished to say, and the ballroom was not the place for him to say it."

"Nothing too serious, I hope," said Mr. Bennet. From his tone and the way his eyes roamed back over the dancers, it was obvious that his interest was waning with the confirmation that nothing untoward had happened. But whether it was truly something "serious," Elizabeth was not able to determine. Despite her resolution to make her family aware of Mr. Wickham's true character, she would need to think more on the matter before she was prepared to speak with her father.

"I am somewhat surprised that he singled *you* out," continued her father after a brief pause. "Am I now to understand that he *does* consider you handsome enough to be tempted?"

"Perhaps I am not so beneath his notice as he originally stated," said Elizabeth in like fashion. "But I am sure that he can have no designs on me. He is, after all, descended from an earl, and as such, I doubt I can tempt him with my fortune or my connections."

Mr. Bennet chuckled. "I should think that you are far too sensible to allow that to deter you, my dear. If he cannot be tempted, then you should indeed continue on with him quite charmingly. A young lady such as yourself enjoys being crossed in love, and as Mr. Bingley seems determined to do the honorable thing with your sister, perhaps you can divert yourself by inducing Mr. Darcy to jilt you. I am certain he would do the job credibly."

Smiling, Elizabeth declared that she was not of a mind to be jilted, and then she bid her father farewell and made her way toward the dance floor. There she was arrested with the sight of Mr. Darcy dancing with her sister Mary! Elizabeth almost gaped in astonishment, and when Mr. Darcy noticed her watching, the man actually winked at her. Mary herself, who did not notice the wink, appeared to be quite bemused at having such a handsome and important man pay attention to her, though there appeared to be no further emotion than enjoyment in her countenance. Clearly, Mr. Darcy must have caught her glance at Mary earlier in the evening and proceeded to make certain Mary took some pleasure in the evening. Even for Mary, experiencing the obsequious attentions of Mr. Collins could not induce any such feeling as *enjoyment*.

As for Mr. Collins, he stood to the side of the room watching Mary and Mr. Darcy, the expression on his face warring between awe at the fact that such an important man as Mr. Darcy was paying attention to the young woman he had singled out and consternation that *another* was paying attention to her at all. Elizabeth chuckled at the sight, for surely there was no more ridiculous man on the face of the earth than Mr. Collins.

"Miss Bennet," intoned a stiff voice from behind her.

Startled, Elizabeth spun around and came face to face with the stern and unhappy visage of Mr. Wickham.

Gathering her wits—and her courage—Elizabeth favored the man with the barest hint of a curtsey and murmured a greeting. Apparently, this did nothing to appease Mr. Wickham, as his expression became even darker.

"I see that you are enjoying yourself."

"Is that not what one does at a ball, Mr. Wickham?"

"It depends upon the circumstances and the *company*, does it not?"

Elizabeth did not miss the emphasis in Mr. Wickham's words, but she decided that as he had appeared unhappy ever since she had left his company, perhaps it would be better to feign misunderstanding and attempt to deflect him.

"The company *is* pleasant, Mr. Wickham. After all, I have known these people my entire life. You, as a newcomer, would of course lack the ties of long acquaintance and affection with those present, but I certainly do not."

His eyes bored into her, and Elizabeth instantly recognized his displeasure at her attempt to obfuscate.

"You have not known Darcy for long," was his accusation.

"Indeed, I have not," agreed Elizabeth. "But I must own that upon further acquaintance he improves."

Mr. Wickham snorted with disdain. "Darcy lacks the social skills to recommend himself to anyone but those of his own consequence—among those of the highest circles, his money is all that counts. With anyone else, his manners and pride prevent him from bothering to take the time to be agreeable. You have not already forgotten our conversation from the previous evening, have you?"

"And what would that conversation be, Mr. Wickham?" demanded Elizabeth. She was not inclined to play these games with him any longer. The man was completely impertinent and insolent, and she wished to have nothing further to do with him!

"You know very well of what I speak! How can you still converse with the man and dance with him, given what I have told you of his offenses to me? Have you no compassion whatsoever? Or perhaps it is his fortune which draws you."

Incensed, Elizabeth allowed the full measure of her indignation to show in the glare she directed at him. "I assure you, Mr. Wickham, that Mr. Darcy's wealth or lack thereof concerns me far less than the content of his character, and of that, I am assured there is nothing wanting."

"Oh, so now you are disposed to enjoy the misfortunes of others?"

"I assure you, sir, that I am willing and able to condole with those who have suffered misfortune. But I will not do so when no such person exists."

Mr. Wickham drew himself up to his full height. His eyes flashed with anger, and his expression was truly forbidding and intimidating . . . and much different from the pleasant mask he usually donned.

"I knew that Darcy would get to you," hissed he. "What makes you think that his account of our dealings is any more believable than my own?"

"You give him far too much credit, sir," said Elizabeth, gathering her courage. "You betrayed to me yourself — with your own words — exactly what sort of man you are."

Saying nothing, Mr. Wickham appeared to assume the force of his displeased gaze would cow her into submission, but she would give him no such satisfaction. "Perchance, Mr. Wickham, you are accustomed to sharing your tale of woe with insipid young ladies who are blinded by your affected manners and charming countenance, but I assure you that I am not such a woman. I was not taken in by your account, nor did I miss the impropriety of your address and the contradiction of your words. Now I suggest you go and ply your trade with some more gullible soul, as I do not wish to be imposed upon any further in the matter of your injuries — real or imagined — at the hands of Mr. Darcy or anyone else!"

"Miss Bennet!"

Her name, loudly spoken, startled her, and Elizabeth glanced to the side to see Mr. Darcy standing and watching them, though his attention was mostly upon Mr. Wickham, the hardness of his countenance testifying to the state of his displeasure. During her confrontation with Mr. Wickham, the set had ended, and the couples were removing themselves from the floor. To Mr. Darcy's side, Mary stood, gazing at Mr. Wickham with wary eyes, and back beyond them, her father stood watching them as well, an expression of concentration and worry incongruously plastered upon his face. Obviously, from the surreptitious glances being directed at them from some of the other attendees, her confrontation with Mr. Wickham had not gone unnoticed.

"I believe you promised the next set to me, Miss Bennet," said Mr. Darcy as he regarded her with a gentle smile. But when his eyes moved to Mr. Wickham, who was now watching with undisguised anger, his gaze turned hard and flinty once again. Clearly, this newest episode had increased the animosity between the two men.

Grateful for the opportunity to escape the unpleasant confrontation, Elizabeth bestowed a welcoming smile upon Mr. Darcy. "I thank you,

Mr. Darcy—I had quite forgotten."

Elizabeth directed the barest of nods to Mr. Wickham and then turned and moved to Mr. Darcy's side, murmuring a few words to Mary before her sister moved away to seek her suitor. Mr. Darcy, however, did not remove his gaze from Mr. Wickham's countenance. He stepped forward and said something in a low voice to the man before spearing him with a final glare. Mr. Darcy then turned and approached Elizabeth, offering his arm to her. She took it and thankfully followed his lead away from the lieutenant, noticing at the same time that her father was watching them closely. He gave her a pointed look which she well understood—one which demanded an explanation of the event he had just witnessed—and then she was swept away to the dance floor.

The music started, and Elizabeth began the dances steps by rote, thankful that Mr. Darcy was quiet, allowing her to regain her composure. She doubted that Mr. Wickham would have tried anything in front of the entire neighborhood, but the man's manner had been intimidating. Her initial resolution to not alert him of her knowledge of his perfidy had been correct. Yet now it was no longer hidden from him.

The question was: now that Mr. Wickham was aware of her knowledge, what would he do about it? Would he step back and avoid her, or would he continue as he had that evening in an effort to intimidate her? She could not claim to understand Mr. Wickham well enough to be certain, but she knew who did.

Focusing her attention on her companion, Elizabeth noted that they had already completed more than half the set. Mr. Darcy was silently dancing, but he was keeping a close eye upon her while watching the rest of the hall. She felt warm at the thought of his care and attention, wondering what had caused the change.

Elizabeth allowed herself a small glance about the area, but Mr. Wickham—the object of her clandestine search—was not to be seen.

"I do believe Mr. Wickham has left the ballroom, Miss Bennet," said Mr. Darcy in a quiet voice, forcing her attention back to him. "I cannot say whether he has left the premises or can be found somewhere else, but he is not in the immediate vicinity."

Elizabeth smiled in response. "I thank you for your timely intervention, sir," she said in a quiet voice, mindful of those surrounding them. "And I think even more for your vigilance."

"It was my pleasure, Miss Bennet," responded Mr. Darcy in the same low tone, and with the barest hint of a smile. "I had witnessed his interest in you the entire evening, but since our time out on the balcony, the turn of his countenance and the intensity with which he watches you has filled me with concern."

"And beyond the obvious, to what do you attribute his interest?"

Mr. Darcy shrugged and clasped her hand as they made their way past one another. "Anything from light flirtation to other, more nefarious objectives." Mr. Darcy paused and glanced around, noting the positions of the other dancers. He apparently saw nothing to concern him, as he continued speaking, though in the same low tone, "It certainly can be nothing good, given my knowledge of his habits, but I truly cannot say that he meant you harm."

A blush suffused Elizabeth's face. "I see you have anticipated my apprehension, Mr. Darcy."

"It was not difficult to deduce, I dare say. Mr. Wickham, as I have stated, is possessed of very agreeable manners which are wont to garner him friends wherever he may go. He rarely allows himself to slip in the company of those whom he wishes to impress, and it is only after he has wreaked havoc and departed that he is known for what he truly is. But when his temper is aroused, as our interactions here tonight seem to have done, he can be mercurial and difficult to predict."

"However, Miss Bennet," resumed Mr. Darcy when they met again after a separation due to the dance, "though he is immoral and has many vices, I personally have never known him to be violent. He may, perhaps, have an unhealthy interest in you at present, but given your ability to defend yourself, I suspect you have little to fear from him. He will undoubtedly grow tired of watching you eventually and move on to some other unsuspecting mark."

Though she was relieved that Mr. Darcy did not believe her to be in any danger from his old playmate, Elizabeth still felt a certain disquiet regarding Mr. Darcy's last statement. To the best of her knowledge, Mr. Wickham had been accepted by the community with open arms — could she truly allow the man to reside in the area without making her friends and neighbors aware of the danger he presented? What if he were to run up debts in Meryton as he had done in the past? From Mr. Darcy's account, she felt that the amount of debt Mr. Wickham had left behind had been substantial, and she was well aware of the fact that if the amount was enough, it had the potential to ruin the town's economy.

And what of Mr. Wickham's other proclivities? With Mr. Darcy's hints toward Mr. Wickham's attentions to young ladies, could she truly allow a predator to prowl in their midst without giving warning? And what of her unsuspecting and flirtatious younger sisters? Elizabeth had seen some small improvement in their demeanors since she had explained certain realities to them, but she knew they were in no way changed in essentials from the young women they had been merely a week previously. Would not Mr. Wickham find them easy targets? No, it was in every way unconscionable to neglect to do her duty to her neighbors and her family. The trick was to find a way to persuade Mr. Darcy of the rightness of her conviction.

The music ended, and Elizabeth allowed Mr. Darcy to take her hand and lead her from the dance floor. What astonished her was the sound of the bell announcing that supper was about to be served. She had had no notion that she had just danced the supper dance with Mr. Darcy!

Surreptitiously, Elizabeth glanced about, taking in the mood of her neighbors. Though none of them were overt about it, a few people did glance in her direction and then begin to whisper to their neighbors. It appeared that her *second dance*—no less than the supper set!—with Mr. Darcy had completely eclipsed the murmuring over her very public argument with Mr. Wickham. This all paled in comparison to the haughty and disdainful glare which was even now being directed at her by the hostess.

Cheeks burning with mortification, Elizabeth determined that she must do something to spare Mr. Darcy the speculation of the neighborhood. After all, he had only danced with her again to rescue her from the attentions of the nefarious officer. She was grateful, and as such, she must make it up to him.

Elizabeth dared a quick look at her partner and found him regarding her with a bemused expression upon his face.

"It appears, Miss Bennet, that we have just danced the supper set." He motioned toward the dining tables with a smile. "Shall we?"

Smiling back at him, Elizabeth attempted to remove her hand from his grasp, only to find that he was holding it tightly, with an apparent reluctance to relinquish it. Not wishing to make a scene, Elizabeth did not struggle.

"Mr. Darcy, I thank you for your information and your protection against Mr. Wickham. However, I know you were only acting for my benefit when you escorted me to the dance floor. I shall not hold you to the convention of partnering me for supper if you do not wish to do so."

She was therefore astonished with Mr. Darcy's answer. "On the contrary, Miss Bennet, I shall not hear of anything else. I am much anticipating the opportunity to further our acquaintance."

Not knowing how to respond to this declaration, which was far from what she would have expected from him, Elizabeth allowed herself nothing more than a small smile and a nod of acceptance.

Chapter VI

Though perhaps a dispassionate observer might have felt that the surprises of the evening were now complete, it appeared that fate had other plans.

Seated beside Mr. Darcy at dinner, Elizabeth was in a perplexed state, wondering how her perfectly ordered world had gone so far astray. Mr. Darcy had turned out to be far more complex and much more amiable than she could have dreamed possible. And though he was not skilled with making small talk, he was most decidedly skilled in speaking about subjects of far more substance than the state of the roads or the recent weather.

As they sat down, Elizabeth found herself drawn to the ready way in which he began to speak. They spoke of literature primarily, comparing their thoughts and feelings about great works, sharing many of the same favorites, such as Donne, Shakespeare, and Milton. And though they often disagreed about the things which they had both read, Mr. Darcy was always polite and attentive when he listened to her opinion. In fact, he seemed genuinely interested in what she had to say, and though he often argued his own viewpoints, he never disparaged hers, and he always acknowledged it when she made a particularly fine argument. In short, he did not speak down to her as was the attitude she had often observed in a man toward a woman—

Mr. Collins, stupid as he was, definitely came to mind!—and was eager to hear her out in whatever subject she deigned to speak.

Furthermore, she found his views and opinions to be far more liberal and progressive than she had ever expected. She had always known his mode and manner of speech to be beyond reproach, and when he expressed himself—particularly concerning subjects where he possessed a strong view or intimate knowledge—it was with confidence and intelligence. He truly had plenty to say which was worth hearing; it was not something she would have expected.

Their other main conversation topic—his estate in Derbyshire and the places he had seen during his lifetime—was most captivating to Elizabeth, who had always wished to see more of the world. Though he allowed the beauty of the vistas he had seen in Hertfordshire, he maintained his love for the county of his youth, something with which Elizabeth could not find fault. He told her stories of his visits to the peak district—which was just a short distance from his home—and the beauties of the lake country, where his family owned a small lodge. He had traveled the kingdom extensively and had seen many places over the course of his life. And his description of the things he had done and the places he had seen were fascinating and colorful, so by the end of their conversation, Elizabeth felt she had almost visited them herself.

The one thing he had not had the opportunity to do was to complete the rite of passage for all wealthy young men—the grand tour of the continent. He confided to her that his father had died shortly after he completed his schooling at Cambridge, and as it had been necessary to assume the responsibility of caring for his estate, Mr. Darcy's journey had been canceled. It was his one great regret, Elizabeth discovered, and it was one thing he intended to eventually remedy—his plans included travel to the continent when he finally married as a wedding gift to his wife. Whoever she may be, Elizabeth felt more than ever before that she would be a fortunate woman.

Nagging at the back of her consciousness, however, was Elizabeth's resolution concerning Mr. Wickham. Somehow she must convince Mr. Darcy that the people of Meryton must be told of the scoundrel's ways in some fashion. She had allowed herself to become caught up in his conversation, but she knew that before the end of the meal, she would need to broach the subject with him.

But Mr. Darcy, always perceptive, had apparently already noticed her momentary silence after their animated conversation wound down. "Miss Bennet, is there something which you wish to say?"

Blushing, Elizabeth ducked her head, wondering at this man's ability to read her. "I am sorry, Mr. Darcy, but indeed there is."

"I highly doubt it is anything for which you must apologize, Miss Bennet. By all means, may I know what is troubling you?"

Elizabeth bit her lip and gathered her thoughts, uncertain as to how Mr. Darcy would take her application. Quietly, so as not to be heard by anyone nearby, she said to him: "Mr. Darcy, I am simply wondering to what extent I should make the people of the area aware of Mr. Wickham's true character."

His gaze pierced her with its intensity. "You think there is some danger?"

"You said yourself that he was not a man to be trusted, Mr. Darcy," snapped Elizabeth, her ire excited by his lack of vision in this matter. "It appears that Mr. Wickham has already begun to ingratiate himself into the neighborhood, and more than one young lady appears to be enamored of him."

Elizabeth did not make a specific reference to her younger sisters, but she knew there was no need to. Mr. Darcy had seen for himself the less than ladylike behavior of her younger sisters.

When her eyes shifted back to Mr. Darcy, he was regarding her with a pensive expression on his face. "I am sure you are correct, Miss Bennet," allowed he. "I tend to ignore Mr. Wickham as nothing more than bad business, but I can see where that would allow him to continue with his habits without check."

"I would not wish for him to impose himself upon our small community, Mr. Darcy. At the very least, the tradesmen and those families with young daughters must be warned."

"I agree, Miss Bennet," said Mr. Darcy, inclining his head. "Do you have any suggestion as to how this may be accomplished?"

In truth, this was not something of which she had thought—all of her energy had been bent toward convincing him of the necessity of making Mr. Wickham's bad conduct known. Though Mr. Darcy was well to do and well connected, his influence in Meryton was limited by the short time he had spent in the area as the guest of Mr. Bingley. It would, unfortunately, end up being a matter of Mr. Darcy's word against Mr. Wickham's.

Of more immediate import, perhaps, was the fact that the prevailing opinion of Mr. Darcy in the area was not at all positive, in part due to his own actions, but in part due to the story of his slight against her. The thought caused Elizabeth no small measure of shame at how she had misjudged him. This would be so much simpler if she had moderated her sense of outrage and contained her dissemination of the event!

It was clear that unless Mr. Darcy was able to produce the proof to which he had earlier alluded, he would need someone known and respected in the neighborhood to support him, lest he be branded as a vindictive deceiver. And though she was determined to protect the community, in no way did she wish for Mr. Darcy to give up his privacy or put his acquaintance at risk. They should be able to accomplish their purpose without his having to give up either.

Elizabeth focused once again on her companion, who was waiting patiently for her to speak. "I feel, Mr. Darcy, that the best thing to do would be to inform my father of these transactions and allow him to inform the rest of the community."

It appeared that Mr. Darcy immediately understood the thrust of her suggestion. "The testimony of an esteemed member of the local populace would be much better received than would my own."

"I believe so, Mr. Darcy," said Elizabeth, saying nothing of his reputation in Meryton—there would be time enough to consider this at a later date. If he was to stay in the area for any length of time, she would have to give some thought as to how to reform his character in the eyes of the townsfolk.

"In that case, Miss Bennet, will your father be available tomorrow morning?"

Elizabeth nodded. "I should think so, sir, but perhaps it would be better if I were to prepare him for your visit. He has already witnessed our interactions tonight, and he will expect some explanation. If you come to Longbourn about mid morning, the small delay will allow me to speak to him first."

A nod was her response. "I will bow to your superior knowledge of your father."

They lapsed into silence for some time. Elizabeth attempted to scrutinize him unobtrusively, but she was unable to discern his thoughts. Though she had to confess she certainly did not think ill of him, the truth was that she was not sure *what* to think of him. What she had thought and what appeared to be the reality were now completely different, and she was uncertain how to reconcile them.

"It seems, Miss Bennet, that I am unable to hold your attention."

He was regarding her with a half smile on his face and a slightly teasing glint in his eye.

Elizabeth laughed. "I assure you, Mr. Darcy, that I was merely engaged in considering our discussion. And you should know that the last time such words were spoken to me, I was in the company of your enemy."

Any sting her words might have delivered was allayed by Elizabeth's teasing manner, and Mr. Darcy only raised an eyebrow in response. "So I actually have something in common with that scoundrel besides the location in which we were reared? What, may I ask, was your response?"

"I had just begun to question his tale of his misfortunes when he said those very words. I was uncertain of what he was capable, so I laughed and teased him and attempted to deflect him to other, more palatable subjects."

"A very prudent course, Miss Bennet."

The continuance of this discussion was interrupted by the entrance of Elizabeth's youngest and silliest sister. Lydia, who had been reasonably composed and well-behaved that evening, had finally, it appeared, reverted back to her previous ways. She was dancing through the crowd, holding Mr. Denny's saber over her head and laughing at his attempts to recover it.

Elizabeth half rose from her seat, intent upon preserving some of her family's dignity, when her father—who it appeared had seen her movement—stood himself and approached Lydia, his face alight with amusement at his youngest daughter's antics. He stopped Lydia in the center of the room and, without saying a word, divested her of the saber. Once it had been returned to its proper owner, he escorted Lydia from the room, ignoring her loud protests.

Once order had been restored, Elizabeth resumed her seat, her cheeks flushed with embarrassment at what Mr. Darcy had just witnessed.

"Mr. Darcy, I must apologize for my sister."

"On the contrary, Miss Bennet, I believe your sister's behavior has nothing to do with you. You have never conducted yourself with anything but the utmost of decorum."

Glancing up, Elizabeth was startled to witness on his face a look of compassion and commiseration mixed with disapproval for the actions of her youngest sister.

"And truly, I believe that with a little effort, your sister's behavior could be corrected—after all, much of her disposition is merely the exuberance of youth. She is not so far gone, I think."

"I have tried to change her ways, but thus far, my success has been limited. She is, at least, aware of the fact that not all men in red coats are trustworthy, regardless of how handsome they may appear to be."

The hint was received and understood by Mr. Darcy, and he

nodded while saying, "Yes, and I believe that your father has handled the situation in the appropriate manner. He removed her from the room with as little fuss as the situation allowed and conducted her to another location to deliver his reprimand without embarrassing her further. While I have not yet been blessed with children of my own, I, too, have a sister for whom I am responsible, and although she is very shy and I have never had to cope with such a situation, I understand the proper method of rebuke. I am impressed with your father's actions."

Elizabeth was grateful for his words, but she still worried for her family's respectability. She directed a quick glance at Jane and Mr. Bingley — who now appeared to be deep in conversation again — noting that Mr. Bingley's sisters stood to one side of the room whispering fiercely to one another. *Those two* were certainly no friends to the attachment between Jane and the gentleman.

"I just would not wish for Lydia's behavior — or that of anyone else in my family, for that matter — to interfere with Jane's happiness."

Mr. Darcy visibly started. "Your sister's happiness?" queried he. "Are you speaking of an attachment between your sister and my friend?"

"Indeed, I am," was Elizabeth's quizzical reply. "Can you doubt their feelings?"

Turning to consider them with a frown, Mr. Darcy was silent for several moments before he turned back to her. "I have indeed seen the partiality on Mr. Bingley's side, but I have seen him in love many times before and thought this to be another of his infatuations."

"Are you saying he is not constant?" demanded Elizabeth, concerned for her sister's tender heart should Mr. Bingley turn out to be someone with nothing more than a handsome mien and a shallow personality.

"No, Miss Bennet — Bingley would never cruelly toy with your sister's affections. But his attention is easily turned by a pretty face, and he invariably loses interest when he discovers that his interest is only returned in direct proportion to the size of his pocketbook or that the lady cannot speak two words of substance together beyond the latest fashions."

"I assure you, Mr. Darcy," said Elizabeth frostily, "that my sister is neither of those. Though little displayed, her feelings are fervent and true, and she and I have always determined to marry for only the deepest love."

"Then I commend you for your principles and congratulate your sister. As I said, I had thought that he was merely infatuated with your sister, but your information puts a new light on the situation. The returned affection of an intelligent woman is all I believe that my friend wants, and I am certain that once he understands your sister possesses those feelings, he will be lost."

"You are nothing like I expected," blurted Elizabeth. She then felt a certain consternation for having said such a thing aloud. Blushing, she stared down at the hands in her lap, not missing the startled expression that came over his face before she broke eye contact.

"And what did you expect?"

Still fidgeting, Elizabeth wondered how she could possibly recover from this faux pas.

"I had not expected your compassion or your attention, Mr. Darcy," said Elizabeth very carefully. "I had thought you did not hold me in much esteem."

Mr. Darcy started at this information. "Truly?" queried he, his voice and expression betraying his incredulousness. "How can you possibly believe that I can hold you in anything but the highest regard?"

Dumbfounded, Elizabeth stared at him. "The highest regard?" she echoed, the question sounding somewhat stupid, even to her own ears.

"Miss Bennet, have you missed the fact that out of all the ladies here tonight, I first asked you to dance? What about the manner in which I can barely take my eyes off of you, even for an instant? Then there is the fact that I shared my history with you this evening. Did that not give you some indication of my regard?"

Elizabeth did not know where to look or how to feel. Here was this man all but declaring himself to her, and she had detected no indication of his purpose. How could she have judged him so poorly?

"I had thought you looked on me to find fault," murmured Elizabeth, somewhat weakly.

An amused smile stole over his face, and he reached forward and grasped her hand. "Miss Bennet, though our previous discussion at Netherfield illustrated quite well the fact that no one is perfect, believe me when I say that I can find no fault when I look at you. Quite the contrary, in fact."

Blushing, Elizabeth glanced down, no longer able to keep her eyes on him due to the intensity of his gaze boring into her.

"Perhaps I was not always so overt in my admiration, but I believe that I should rectify that oversight immediately. I very much like what I see in you, Miss Bennet. Your compassionate, caring nature; your liveliness and vivacity; your ability to stand up for yourself and make your opinions known—I cannot imagine that I could have resisted your appeal, even if I were inclined to make the attempt."

He paused for a moment, as if weighing something in his mind, before he appeared to square his shoulders. "My friend is to return to town tomorrow to complete some business he has neglected," said he, watching her intently, "but I assure you that I have no such engagement. I believe we have already agreed that I shall call on your father tomorrow regarding the matter of Mr. Wickham. But I should very much like . . ."

Mr. Darcy trailed off, and for a moment, he appeared to be less than the confident and composed master of Pemberley. His hesitation only lasted a brief instant and then he fixed his ever-serious gaze on her, and the corners of his mouth lifted slightly.

"Well, shall we take this one step at a time?" asked he. "When I visit your father tomorrow, I believe that you will be present, will you not?"

In a day full of surprises, *this* was perhaps the greatest of them all. That Mr. Darcy looked on her with such interest and affection was not something which Elizabeth had ever imagined—it appeared that Charlotte was correct in her opinion of the man.

Feeling a little overwhelmed, Elizabeth could only nod, to which Mr. Darcy's smile became even larger still.

"In that case, I believe I should very much like to see you again. We have spoken of several interesting topics, and I would like to continue those conversations if you would permit it."

"I agree, Mr. Darcy," said Elizabeth, her face warming due to his words. Mr. Darcy had made no declarations to her, but somehow she knew that for a man as reticent as Mr. Darcy, his words were tantamount to an announcement of his intentions.

But Elizabeth, never one to allow herself to be intimidated, gathered her courage and looked him in the eyes. "I would like that very much, Mr. Darcy," said she.

The smile which came over his face was the brightest she had ever seen on his countenance, and she marveled that she was the recipient and the author of that smile. Though she could not imagine what the future held, she was certain that the possibilities which now existed were, without a doubt, far more pleasurable and bright than she had previously thought.

Knowing that the supper hour was now concluded and hearing the opening strains of music, Elizabeth stood in order to move into the ballroom, for she was engaged for the first set after supper with one of the local men. However, as she curtsied to Mr. Darcy, a thought occurred to her. She tilted her head to one side and regarded him seriously.

"I must allow that I am curious, Mr. Darcy—what did you say to Mr. Wickham after you interrupted our argument?"

His answering grin was positively feral. "I merely told him that you were under my protection and that he would leave you and your entire family alone if he valued his freedom."

At Elizabeth's questioning look, he continued: "I purchased and still hold the receipts of his debts in Lambton. They are enough to see him in debtor's prison for many years. He knows me too well to think that I would not be serious in my threat."

"Was that not a little presumptuous, Mr. Darcy?"

"Perhaps," agreed he, though there was no remorse whatsoever in his manner or his countenance. "But you must understand, Miss Bennet—I know my own mind, and I know what I want. Perhaps I was uncertain of your regard, but I was confident after our discussion that you were not *indifferent* toward me. I had hoped that I could persuade you."

"No, I have never been indifferent," agreed Elizabeth. "And I thank you for your care and protection."

After acknowledging his bow, Elizabeth moved away from him. For the first time that evening, she felt completely at ease and content.

Chapter VII

One might expect the day after a ball to be one of lethargy and ease, but for Elizabeth Bennet, it was not to be so. The events of the previous evening were much on her mind, particularly those confidences shared by Mr. Darcy. Thus, though the lateness of the hour when they had finally returned to Longbourn had rendered her exhausted, thoughts and ruminations kept her awake for part of the night and then woke her earlier the next morning than she would have preferred. She attempted to ignore them, but they were not to be suppressed. Therefore, she finally succumbed to the lure of the day and rose from her bed later than was her wont, though it was much earlier than she would have preferred.

The day was to bring more events, she knew, and potentially more surprises. Mr. Darcy was to speak with her father, after all, and Elizabeth would need to prepare Mr. Bennet for the information which Mr. Darcy could impart. Her father would also wish to hear her account of her disagreement with Mr. Wickham. Though Mr. Bennet was somewhat lackadaisical in his duties toward his family, he was not one who would tolerate improper advances and thinly veiled threats toward any of his daughters. At the very least, Colonel Forster would likely hear of his lieutenant's behavior, if he had not already.

Surprisingly, however, Mr. Bennet was not the first to demand

Elizabeth's presence or her time that morning—that honor, if it could be termed to be such, was extended by the other male relation in residence.

Elizabeth had just completed a turn around the gardens, the extended paths about the countryside she preferred being largely inaccessible due to the recent deluge of rain, when she entered the house in order to break her fast. She was surprised to see Mr. Collins in the dining room, as the parson—surprisingly for one of his vocation—had never seemed to be one who was particularly active in the morning.

"My dear cousin Elizabeth," intoned Mr. Collins as he rose and bowed upon her entering the room.

Something about his posture and expression told Elizabeth that he had something to say. And even more, Elizabeth was certain that she would not appreciate his opinions, whatever they were. It was almost enough to make her reconsider taking breakfast, at least until such time as he should choose to vacate the dining room. But to retreat now when she had already entered the room would be rude, so she favored him with a weak smile, meant to discourage him from conversation, and sat at the table. Of course, she knew that nothing short of gagging him would prevent him from having his say, and she was proven correct by the words which issued forth before she had even settled into her seat.

"My dear cousin," said he, "I feel it incumbent upon me by not only our close connection, but also because of my position as a clergyman—and furthermore as the parson of the honorable Lady Catherin de Bourgh—to discuss your behavior last night at Mr. Bingley's ball."

Elizabeth was nonplussed. While her discussions with Mr. Darcy had not been precisely a common occurrence, the precautions they had taken to remain in full sight of the company had ensured that there was nothing improper about them. Furthermore, Mr. Collins's reference to Lady Catherine suggested that she would disapprove, though it could be nothing more than the parson's penchant for referring to the lady as if she were the queen herself.

In this instance, Elizabeth decided that directness was required; it was not for Mr. Collins to reprimand her for her behavior, after all. "I am sure I do not understand to what you refer, Mr. Collins," replied she. "I believe that *my father* found no fault in the way I conducted myself last night, and I am assured that I did nothing more or less than I have done at any other ball."

She sat down at the table, intentionally ignoring the man, and picked up a piece of bread, filling it with her favorite preserves. Simple fare had been provided that morning, as it was the family's habit to rise at disparate times after a late night at a society event.

"On the contrary, my dear cousin," replied Mr. Collins, "I am certain you are unaware of the grievous trial your behavior would inflict upon Lady Catherine and of how rightly she would have been offended if she had been there to witness it herself. But that does not make the offense any less grievous. An ignorance of the law cannot be used as a defense, after all."

"Mr. Collins," said Elizabeth, suppressing a sigh, "as I have never so much as met Lady Catherine, I know of no possible manner in which I could have offended her. I assure you, sir, that nothing I did or said was intended as a slight against your patroness. Therefore, you may rest assured that whatever has caused you to take exception was never meant to be taken in such a way. Now, if you please, I would very much like to finish breaking my fast."

Her entreaty did nothing to prevent Mr. Collins from his purpose—in fact, the light of fanaticism appeared to shine more brightly in his eyes, much as usually occurred when he spoke of his patroness. "That is why I must illuminate you to . . . certain facts, so that you may correct those perceptions which may have been erroneously created by your interactions with Mr. Darcy last night. Indeed, you are to be grievously pitied, as I suspect that expectations which can never be filled might have been excited by Mr. Darcy's attentions to you. I can only conjecture that such an illustrious man would be considered to be quite a catch for your family, though I am persuaded that Mr. Darcy is far too noble and good to have created such attentions deliberately. I am equally assured that he could never be serious in turning his interest on one such as you, for although you are lovely and amiable, you cannot claim the kind of lineage or fortune one such as Mr. Darcy would expect in a woman.

"For you see, my dear cousin," continued Mr. Collins, not allowing her to reply to any of his ridiculous assertions, "I have it on very good authority that Mr. Darcy is in fact engaged to his cousin and the daughter of my patroness, Miss Anne de Bourgh. I believe that I am correct in apprehending that Mr. Darcy and Miss de Bourgh are eminently suitable for one another and are thus intended by the unanimous voices of *everyone* in their family."

The first part of Mr. Collins's speech was insulting—certainly, Mr. Darcy was a wealthy man who possessed an ancestry of which to boast, but to state that Elizabeth was his inferior in such a manner was tactless at best and downright rude at worst. But all thought of such things fled Elizabeth's mind when Mr. Collins referred to an engagement. For a moment, Elizabeth felt such a sense of loss as she had never expected to feel when confronted with such intelligence.

Then reason reasserted itself. Elizabeth *had* indeed discovered something very worthy of praise in Mr. Darcy, but she was by no means in love with the gentleman.

Even more importantly, Elizabeth knew that Mr. Darcy was not a man to raise unwarranted expectations, and he was certainly no bigamist. If he *was* engaged, then she knew that he would not declare any interest in Elizabeth, even in the most oblique manner. The only explanation was that he *did not* consider himself to be honor bound to marry his cousin, and whatever Mr. Collins had heard, it likely did not constitute reality to any degree. Either way, Elizabeth was not about to believe anything about Mr. Darcy which was not substantiated by her own observation and the man's own words—she had nearly been tripped up once by her own prejudice, and she was not about to allow herself to succumb to such accounts again.

The matter having been settled in her own mind, Elizabeth turned her attention back to her cousin. Mr. Collins, completely insensible to the fact that Elizabeth had been paying him no attention whatsoever, had continued to expound upon this supposed engagement of Mr. Darcy's, though given the snippets she had caught here and there, he was engaged in nothing more than extolling the virtues of Miss de Bourgh and, to a greater extent, Lady Catherine. Thus, when he moved on to his next topic of conversation, Elizabeth was not only insulted by his words, but aghast at the man's utter lack of sense.

"Therefore, you must apprehend, my dear cousin, that there is no way you can hope to compete with Miss de Bourgh in any fashion, and you must give up this design to induce Mr. Darcy to propose to you. I can assure you that it will never happen."

"I assure you, Mr. Collins, that I do not mean to keep Mr. Darcy from fulfilling his family obligations."

Mr. Collins peered at her, and though he appeared to be somewhat appeased, he continued:

"I fear that this whole episode is my fault in some manner."

"There is no fault to be had," exclaimed Elizabeth, wondering what the man was about now. "There is nothing for you to fear, so I entreat you to drop the subject."

"And yet you danced with Mr. Darcy twice last night," insisted Mr. Collins. "*And* you were seen to be conversing with him for quite a length of time."

"All of that was initiated by Mr. Darcy," stated Elizabeth in a clipped tone. By now, she was beginning to tire of Mr. Collins's rattling on and was seriously considering quitting the room.

"At your provocation, I am sure," said Mr. Collins with a wave of his hand. "I am not unaware of the stratagems to which a young lady will resort in order to tempt a man's notice."

"Mr. Collins," said Elizabeth, by this time about ready to strangle the parson to keep him quiet, "I was in no way attempting to capture Mr. Darcy's attention. As a woman, I am at the mercy of the man who asks me to dance—I must either consent or refuse and miss much of the amusement. As I do so love to dance, it takes extraordinary circumstances to induce me to refuse a man's request, even if I quite despise him. The circumstances you fear do not exist, and I must beg to you importune me no further."

Standing, Elizabeth made to leave the room, only to pause when Mr. Collins also stood and his voice arrested her once again.

"Perhaps if I had not withdrawn my attentions, you would not have been desperate enough lure Mr. Darcy into your influence. However, that is something that may be rectified, my dear cousin, if you are inclined to acquire a husband."

Surely he was not saying what she *thought* he was saying, Elizabeth reasoned, though with much consternation.

"It was upon you that I focused almost as soon as I entered the house, dear cousin," said Mr. Collins, confirming Elizabeth's worst fear. "It is, therefore, no trouble at all for me to redirect my addresses back to you."

"And what of Mary?" demanded Elizabeth.

"Your sister is a good sort of girl," replied Mr. Collins with a negligent wave of his hand. "But she is perhaps not what I had hoped to find in the partner of my future life. Her piety *is* pleasing, of course, but I am a man, and as such, I also appreciate other . . . attractions, which, quite honestly, your sister does not possess."

Though Elizabeth could not have missed the meaning of his words, the leer with which he favored her rendered any question moot. Incensed, Elizabeth put her hands on her hips and regarded him coldly.

"You would redirect your attentions back to me after giving them to Mary? It is not proper, sir. You have excited her anticipation—engaged your honor, I dare say."

"She shall recover, I am sure."

Once again, Mr. Collins's flippancy was raising Elizabeth's ire, and she was not in the mood to mince words with him.

"Her recovery or lack thereof is not the point, Mr. Collins." Though the man was oblivious, even he must have detected the chill in her voice. "It is not proper to shift one's affections on the whim of the moment. It makes one appear to be inconstant and fickle."

"I am sure that as a clergyman, I am much more aware of what is proper, my dear cousin," said Mr. Collins, his condescending tone once again grating on her, completely incongruous in one as devoid of sense as her cousin. "And I assure you that I mean no impropriety. It is obvious that I should never have attempted to redirect my affections. It is a misstep I shall rectify forthwith."

"No, you shall not, Mr. Collins," said Elizabeth.

Her words brought the parson up short, and he stopped and stared at her, perhaps taking notice of her words for the first time that morning. He had been so intent upon making his point that Elizabeth was certain he had heard no more than one word in three which she had spoken to him. *How the tables have turned,* Elizabeth thought with some wryness.

"I shall not accept any addresses from you, Mr. Collins," continued Elizabeth. "I beg you not to waste your breath on such an endeavor, as you shall not be successful."

"But your father—"

"I am my father's favorite daughter, Mr. Collins," snapped Elizabeth. "I assure you that he will not sanction any engagement to which I have not agreed myself."

A hint of understanding appeared in Mr. Collins's stupid visage, and he paused for a moment, allowing Elizabeth to make sure he knew exactly what awaited him if he persisted in this mad design.

"You will not gain my acceptance, and if you continue on in this fashion, you will offend Mary, and she will not have you either. You will then be left without a bride when you are required to return to Hunsford. Take care, Mr. Collins—do not do anything rash.

"Now, if you will, I believe that I have finished breaking my fast. I shall return to my room."

With that, Elizabeth turned on her heel and strode from the room. But it appeared that Mr. Collins would not allow her to depart without obtaining the final word in the matter.

"I can see your behavior and your lack of proper respect and feminine manners are in no way suitable for me in my position, so I shall not press you further," said he, following her from the room. "But let me advise you once again not to interfere in the matter of Mr.

Darcy's engagement with Miss de Bourgh. Such willful disregard of the proper respect for Lady Catherine's wishes can only harm your future prospects."

Though Elizabeth would disabuse him of his misconception, she decided that she had already done so several times, and once more would not penetrate his understanding any more than the previous attempts. She therefore ignored him and made her way up the stairs, leaving him watching her from the hall. Of Mr. Collins's brand of foolishness, a little went a very long way. His departure from the neighborhood could not come soon enough.

The expected summons to her father's bookroom came half an hour later. Elizabeth had considered going to her father and speaking with him immediately, considering how put out she was by the parson's words that morning. Elizabeth was incensed by his utter lack of anything resembling propriety, not to mention his insensibility to anything but his own selfish concerns and his insistence on spouting off whatever his harpy of a patroness put in his head. Beyond that, she seriously considered making Mary aware of the conversation she had had with him this morning, as she would not wish to see a sister married to such a buffoon. After some thought on the matter, she decided to leave it be—she would not introduce further discord into the house, and Mary seemed able to tolerate him to a certain degree. Elizabeth could certainly hint at the idea that she did not think that Mr. Collins was a good match for her sister, but anything beyond that must be Mary's decision.

Having resolved such matters, Elizabeth descended the stairs and made her way to the door to her father's room, entering when he gave his consent. The room was warmed by a cheery fire, and the smell of books and ledgers intruded on her senses, giving it the homey feel with which she had always associated this particular room. She had always felt safe in here.

"Elizabeth, come in," said he by way of greeting.

As Elizabeth took a seat in one of the chairs in front of the desk, she felt her father's gaze upon her.

"I believe you have something to relate to me, my dear," said Mr. Bennet after a moment of silence. "Your conversation with Mr. Wickham was disturbing. Did he importune you improperly?"

"Mr. Wickham has been importuning me improperly since I first made his acquaintance, I dare say," replied Elizabeth.

Her father peered at her closely, but aside from a slight tightening of his countenance, there was no further reaction. Elizabeth knew that her father was well enough acquainted with her ways that if anything truly improper had occurred, she would have come to him. As he was confident in her character, he simply waited for her to elucidate her statement, something which she would not demur.

"Nothing improper of a *physical nature* has occurred, Papa, as I am sure you well know. But though the *gentleman* has never attempted to impose upon me in such a manner, I dare say that he has never said a proper word to me in any conversation I have had with him."

"Well, now," said Mr. Bennet, his earlier concern turning to bemusement. "It seems that you have a tale to tell me. Can I assume then that this 'improper conversation' to which you refer was not one which is used to entice a young woman to do things she ought not?"

Elizabeth colored and looked down. "Nothing of *that nature*, Papa, though I must say that I have no idea of what his intentions consisted. I believe, unfortunately, that Mr. Wickham has taken an interest in me, though whether that suggests a more malevolent interest or simply a desire to use me to blacken Mr. Darcy's name, I cannot say."

"Ah, yes, the other actor in yesterday's drama," replied Mr. Bennet. "I believe that we exchanged some words about your rather visible conversation with the gentleman from Derbyshire, but I believe that I have not yet heard the specifics. Would you care to enlighten me?"

"I believe Mr. Darcy will be performing that office himself, Papa."

A raised eyebrow met Elizabeth's declaration. "The great Mr. Darcy is condescending to come and visit *me?*"

"Yes, he is," replied Elizabeth. She looked on her father with a stern eye and continued:

"I beseech you not to attempt to make sport with Mr. Darcy. He is not witless like Mr. Collins and shall instantly understand the thrust of whatever you say to him. Besides, he has intelligence about the aforementioned Mr. Wickham, and it would behoove you to listen to him."

Mr. Bennet regarded her with some amusement. "I never doubted for a moment that Mr. Darcy is an intelligent man. After all, he seems to understand that *you* are to be valued, and as such, he can only be commended." Her father paused for a moment and looked at her with some speculation. "Can I conjecture that Mr. Wickham's communications were connected with Mr. Darcy in some way?"

"Not only connected with Mr. Darcy," replied Elizabeth, "but he accused Mr. Darcy of some rather infamous behavior. I shall not recite the specifics—I believe it better that you hear the account from Mr.

Darcy directly. But I assume that it has not escaped your attention that for Mr. Wickham to make such accusations to so new an acquaintance is improper in the extreme."

A nod was the only answer she received on the subject of Mr. Wickham. After assuring her that he was eager to hear Mr. Darcy's account, Mr. Bennet once again focused on another part of the matter.

"It seems, my dear, that you have relinquished your former opinion of Mr. Darcy for one more positive. I am inclined to ask for an accounting of so material a change."

Once again, Elizabeth colored and looked down. Oh, had her previously stated opinions of the gentleman only been more temperate! The accounting of her change of heart would have been much easier to bear.

"I have largely, Papa. You must own that most of my previous antipathy was due to what happened at the assembly."

"Ah, yes, the infamous slight. Have you forgiven him so easily? Or have you found that your vanity is less than you imagined?"

Elizabeth smiled at her father's gentle teasing. "He apologized for his words, Papa. And regardless, Mr. Wickham's communications forced me to reconsider all that I knew of Mr. Darcy, and I realized that other than that unfortunate comment, I knew no evil of him."

"The source of your distraction," said Mr. Bennet with a knowing nod.

"Yes, sir."

"Well, well, then," said her father with an amused grin. "I shall look very much forward to hearing Mr. Darcy's accounting of this Mr. Wickham. Given your words," said he, spearing Elizabeth with a pointed look, "I expect that this Mr. Wickham is not someone who we would wish to admit into our little community so easily. Am I incorrect?"

"No, you are not, sir," said Elizabeth quietly.

Chapter VIII

$\mathcal{M}$r. Darcy arrived at Longbourn a little later that morning—had he been any earlier, it might have been considered somewhat impolite. Elizabeth, who had been watching for his appearance, noted as he rode down the drive to the front of the house that Mr. Darcy's comments about his horses were not merely the rumblings of a man who affected knowledge of a subject in order to impress an acquaintance. He sat on his horse with the ease of one accustomed to time in the saddle, and his horse was tall and clearly of excellent quality. And when he dismounted, while his motions were not flamboyant, they were easy and effortless.

Afraid of being seen watching him from the parlor window, Elizabeth moved to a nearby sofa and indicated to her mother that they had a visitor. Of course, the knowledge of the identity of said visitor would under normal circumstances have caused Mrs. Bennet to flutter around the room in anticipation—Mr. Darcy was single and handsome and, perhaps most importantly, in possession of a fine fortune, after all. But the Bennet matron, rather than reacting in such a matter, instead received the intelligence with narrowed eyes and a rather expressionless mask, one which impressed Elizabeth, as she had never known her mother to hide her emotions. Unless Elizabeth missed her guess, her mother also looked at her with some speculation, but in the end, she chose to say nothing—Elizabeth had already disabused her of the notion that Mr. Darcy had any interest in her, after all, and she appeared to accept her daughter's assurances on the matter.

Mr. Collins was another matter altogether. After their conversation that morning, Elizabeth's cousin had not bothered to initiate any further words with her, which suited her very well indeed. He had, however, continued to watch her, though whether his scrutiny meant that he did not quite trust her, that he was still considering how to resume his attentions to her, or something else entirely, Elizabeth could not say. Disgusted as she was with the man's attitude, Elizabeth was certain that she did not care. But the announcement of Mr. Darcy to the room did nothing for Mr. Collins's temperament—he started at the sound of the gentleman's name and then peered at Elizabeth with some suspicion, as if Elizabeth could cause Mr. Darcy to appear of her own accord.

Mr. Darcy entered the room and greeted its occupants, doing so in a more amiable fashion than Elizabeth had ever before witnessed in his manner. He first addressed Mrs. Bennet, greeting her and complimenting her on the comfort of the parlor—and perhaps lessening the matron's antipathy ever so slightly—and then spoke to the rest of the room, meaning Jane, Elizabeth, and Mr. Collins, as none of the youngest Bennets had as yet made an appearance that morning. It was perhaps a trick of the light or Elizabeth's overly developed imagination, but she fancied that his eyes rested upon her longer than anyone else in the room. She could not quite suppress a frisson of excitement that such a thought engendered.

Elizabeth and Jane stood and curtseyed in response to his bow, and Elizabeth specifically welcomed him, thanking him for calling upon them that morning.

"It is no trouble, Miss Elizabeth," said he, no doubt understanding that their agreement that he should call from the previous evening should not be referenced at this time.

"Still, it is a kindness after so late a night," replied Elizabeth. "And let me take this opportunity to thank you for the wonderful entertainment last night."

"Yes, indeed!" chimed in Mrs. Bennet. "Such elegant arrangements and such fine musicians. I dare say Mr. Bingley's ball was the highlight of the past twelvemonth, Mr. Darcy."

"Please pass our regards on to Mr. Bingley when you next see him," said Elizabeth before her mother could begin a long-winded soliloquy about the splendors of the previous evening. As it was, Mrs. Bennet's raptures were much more restrained than usual, undoubtedly due to the fact that it was *Mr. Darcy* in her parlor.

"I shall do so directly when he returns," promised Mr. Darcy. "Which actually brings me to another reason for my visit this morning."

He stepped forward and, placing a hand in the inner pocket of his coat, removed a letter and handed it to Jane, who looked it with some surprise.

"I noticed this on the mail tray this morning as I was leaving, and I decided to take the liberty of delivering it myself. I believe, Miss Bennet, it is from Miss Bingley."

Hesitantly, Jane stretched out her hand and accepted the letter, thanking Mr. Darcy as she accepted it. She glanced briefly at the letter before she made to put it in a pocket of her dress, when Mr. Darcy interrupted her once again.

"Please do not hesitate to read it on my account, Miss Bennet. I am sure that your mother and Miss Elizabeth are well able to entertain me while you are otherwise engaged."

Though Jane was again surprised at his words, she thanked him and, turning to the side, she opened the letter and began to read. Mr. Darcy smiled down at her and then chose to sit on a chair situated a little to Elizabeth's left and across a small table from Mrs. Bennet. Her mother was regarding Mr. Darcy with an expression of some suspicion—a look which was equally directed toward Elizabeth—but she did not say anything further. In fact, though Elizabeth thought to begin the conversation, she did not have the chance to do so, because as soon as Mr. Darcy took his seat, Mr. Collins, who had taken a chair nearby, began to speak.

"Mr. Darcy," began he, "I find I must thank you for your great condescension in calling this morning on my humble cousin and his family. Indeed, you are to be praised for your goodness and nobility, as the scion of an earl, such as yourself, is rarely to be seen in the parlors of minor gentry. I commend you, sir, for your condescension and your amiability. It puts me greatly in mind of your noble aunt, Lady Catherine de Bourgh, whom I have the greatest fortune to call my patroness."

As silly and obsequious as Mr. Collins's long-winded greeting was, Elizabeth was not surprised to see Mr. Darcy turn an upraised eyebrow on the parson. "I assure you, sir, that I do not consider myself above the average land owner, regardless of my pedigree or the state of my holdings."

"And that speaks very well to your character, sir," replied Mr. Collins with a deferential nod of his head. "I think it not unlikely that most young men of your situation would feel—and be completely justified in doing so—that they were completely above those of less desirable means. It brings to mind the affability and condescension of your noble aunt, Lady Catherine, unsurprising as you are so intimately connected with the great lady."

"There are landowners similar to the Bennets in my own neighborhood in Derbyshire. The Bennets are a good family, and I like to think that I number them among my friends."

Such a statement, even though he had been much more amiable and open the previous night, was still somewhat of a surprise to Elizabeth. It seemed that Mr. Darcy was truly trying to make a good impression, as he was well aware of the fact that his previous one had not been precisely favorable. But though he *had* been more amiable, Elizabeth knew that the man still possessed a healthy measure of pride—was this a change, or was she seeing the man for the first time? She determined to watch him closely, which was even more important because he had shown interest in her particularly.

Mr. Collins, on the other hand, was somewhat nonplussed by Mr. Darcy's statement, and for a few moments, he said nothing further, likely perplexed that Mr. Darcy was not treating him in quite the same fashion as Lady Catherine did.

Finally, however, Mr. Collins said: "As you know, Mr. Darcy, I am your aunt's parson, and I have recently been in her presence. I am therefore in the happy position of being able to inform you that her ladyship—and your fair betrothed, Miss Anne de Bourgh—were in the best of health no more than ten days ago."

At this, Mr. Darcy turned his full attention on the parson, and the fact of his displeasure was easy to observe in his frown and the way he peered at Mr. Collins as if the parson was nothing more than an annoying insect waiting to be squashed. It was also clear that Mr. Collins felt it, too, as he nervously began to mop his face, and he could not quite meet Mr. Darcy's gaze.

"I am not engaged to my cousin, Mr. Collins," was Mr. Darcy's short reply.

Mr. Collins looked up at Mr. Darcy, aghast that anyone would dare to contradict the words of his esteemed patroness. "But Mr. Darcy . . ." sputtered he. "Your fair cousin . . . your esteemed aunt . . . they both are quite set on the match. According to Lady Catherine herself, the union has been planned since you were in your cradles. Surely you cannot renege upon such a longstanding arrangement.

"Besides, Miss de Bough is of such a wonderful and obliging temperament that it is clear that she is the very essence of what you require in a wife. Surely you can see that."

"On the contrary," said Mr. Darcy, "regardless of what my aunt may say, no such formal arrangement exists. She has been clear about *her desire* to have me as a son, but Anne and I have jointly decided that we do not suit each other and do not wish to marry."

Mr. Collins's open mouth, through which no words issued, appeared to indicate his utter lack of understanding. If it had not already been clear that the man had no room in his head for anything other than the words spoken by his patroness, that moment would have removed all doubt.

But Mr. Darcy, apparently seeing that he had managed to quell the parson's words, seemed to decide that further discussion on the matter would not only be imprudent, but also improper, and he directed the subject back to more mundane topics.

They conversed on desultory topics for the next several moments until Mr. Darcy directed a comment at Jane.

"I hope your letter brought good tidings of your friends," said he in an easy manner.

But underneath his complacent demeanor, Elizabeth thought she was able to detect a measure of something else in his manner. He almost seemed to be expecting something, though what it was, Elizabeth could not imagine.

A glance at Jane, and Elizabeth was suddenly concerned for her sister — Jane's color had all but left her face, and though she was as collected as ever, Elizabeth, who knew her sister better than most, thought she detected an air of sadness. What had the letter said?

Though it appeared as if it was an effort, Jane squared her shoulders and turned to Mr. Darcy. "Miss Bingley writes to say that she and the Hursts have left for London, and she does not expect that they will return for some time."

"Did she?" asked Mr. Darcy.

Elizabeth, who had never had any great opinion of the sisters, almost gasped aloud. Mr. Darcy had confirmed that Mr. Bingley was to depart that morning, but he had been clear that Mr. Bingley was to return four or five days hence. His own continued residence in the neighborhood seemed to bear that out. But did Mr. Bingley's sisters intend to try to persuade him differently?

"That is most curious indeed, Miss Bennet, for I have it on good authority—that of my friend himself!—that he means to be in London for but a few days and that the only reason why he went at all was because he was obliged to due to some business which could not be put off."

Jane brightened slightly at Mr. Darcy's words. "But Mr. Darcy, Miss Bingley is most specific in her statement that they will not return. Has there been some misunderstanding?"

"If there has been," said Mr. Darcy, his tone kindly and gentle, "it has been on Miss Bingley's side. Indeed, as Bingley told me that he is quite content in Hertfordshire and that he considers the company to be most pleasing, I doubt that anything short of an invasion by the French could keep him away.

"Trust me, Miss Bennet—in five days, Bingley will be back. I am here waiting for him."

Even self-effacing Jane could not mistake the import of Mr. Darcy's words. She colored slightly and thanked him for this intelligence. For the rest of Mr. Darcy's visit, Jane sat to the side with a slight smile on her face, and though she contributed little, it was clear that she approved of Mr. Darcy most heartily. Elizabeth could not say that she could in any way disapprove herself.

When approximately fifteen minutes had passed, Mr. Darcy changed the subject, indicating his desire to speak with Mr. Bennet.

"I should like to call on Mr. Bennet on a matter of some import, if I may," said he, much to Mrs. Bennet's surprise.

"Call on Mr. Bennet?" repeated Mrs. Bennet, clearly not understanding why Mr. Darcy would need to see her husband.

"Yes," was Mr. Darcy's simple reply. "I have business to discuss with your husband that I had best not delay."

Though it was clear that Mrs. Bennet was afire with curiosity, she, for once, restrained her natural tendency to demand an accounting. Instead, she turned to Elizabeth and said: "Lizzy, please show Mr. Darcy to your father's bookroom."

"Please come with me, Mr. Darcy," said Elizabeth, eager to escape the parlor for a few moments. She knew that she would be facing an inquisition when she returned. She did, after all, have a healthy respect for her mother's instincts regarding the interest any man held in one of the Bennet girls, and Mrs. Bennet's mind would no doubt be racing now with thoughts of pin money, fine carriages, and expensive jewelry.

For that matter, it appeared that Mr. Collins was thinking along those same lines, as he had turned his gaze to Elizabeth with some suspicion. Between the two of them, Elizabeth was certain to be faced with many questions when she returned.

Standing, Elizabeth led Mr. Darcy from the room and out into the hall. The door to her father's bookroom was closed, and as Elizabeth wished for a bit of privacy, she made certain the door to the parlor was also closed before she turned to the man who had followed her.

"Mr. Darcy," said she, albeit a little nervously, "you have my thanks for the assurances you provided to my sister. She is too angelic—she would have claimed that it was all a misunderstanding and that she had deceived herself as to the extent of Mr. Bingley's regard for her. Thank you for saving her this pain."

"It is you she has to thank," averred Mr. Darcy as he favored her with a slight smile. "You made me aware of her regard when it was not easy for one not intimately acquainted with her to see it. When I saw that Bingley's sisters were conspiring this morning, I knew that they would try to convince her of their brother's disinterest. I could not allow her to suffer."

"I would have though they would have tried to convince you to partake in their scheme," said Elizabeth with an arch look.

"Who is saying they did not?" was Mr. Darcy's reply.

They laughed together quietly for a moment before Elizabeth turned a pleased smile on him. "I thank you all the same, no matter how it came about.

"But what shall you do?" asked Elizabeth. "I assume Miss Bingley has closed Netherfield with the intention of not returning?"

"Bingley and I spoke of this possibility," was the reply. "He assured me that he was happy to allow me to stay until his return. Thus, when I informed Miss Bingley of my intentions and told her that her brother knew that I would remain, she was forced to abandon the house without closing it.

"Besides," continued he, "Mr. Hurst was not inclined to make a journey to London only to return but a few days hence. He has also stayed—only Bingley's sisters have made the journey this morning."

"You will not be able to entertain," said Elizabeth, with an amused smile. "But I think it likely that the peace and quiet will suit you quite well."

"My dear Miss Bennet," replied he, "I am sure that I shall find all the amusement I require at Longbourn. And if this matter concerning Wickham does not consume the rest of my time here, then I am sure my trusty horse is as eager for exercise as I am myself."

Elizabeth could only smile at his statement. But wary of Mr. Collins and her mother, both of whom were likely awaiting her return with no small amount of eagerness—or so she assumed—Elizabeth gestured toward her father's sanctuary and knocked on the door.

"Mr. Darcy is here to see you, Papa," said Elizabeth after she opened the door.

"Indeed, he is," replied Mr. Bennet, rising to his feet and greeting Mr. Darcy with a bow. "Thank you for seeing him to my door, Elizabeth."

Curtseying, Elizabeth left the room, closing the door behind her.

Of course, her return to the parlor began a most frustrating time for Elizabeth. No sooner had she entered the room than her mother began plying her with questions, heedless of the fact that Mr. Collins was looking at her through suspicious eyes.

"Lizzy, I must own that I had not expected Mr. Darcy to visit us this morning," said Mrs. Bennet. "Nor any other morning, I should say."

"I must agree with you, madam," said Mr. Collins. "Though Mr. Darcy is the very picture of obliging manners and civility, I would not have thought that he would deign to visit a family such as yours."

That statement apparently struck one of Mrs. Bennet's nerves, as she turned to Mr. Collins with a frown on her face.

"I dare say that Mr. Darcy is not so high and mighty that he should not associate with the Bennets of Longbourn," was her prim reply. Of course, this was a complete contradiction of her words to Elizabeth only a few days before, though Elizabeth was sensible enough not to point that fact out to her mother.

"It is very good of him to call, though," continued Mrs. Bennet, blithely speaking over Mr. Collins, who had attempted to once again interject his own opinion. "And he said he has business with your father, though I am sure I do not know what it could be."

This less than subtle attempt to wheedle from Elizabeth the reason for Mr. Darcy's request to speak with her father went ignored.

"I am afraid I cannot say," said Elizabeth. And it was only the truth—though she was aware of the reason for his visit, she really could not say at that time what precisely they were discussing. Until Mr. Darcy and Mr. Bennet had decided between them what should be done, it would serve no purpose to inform Mrs. Bennet of the truth of their discussion. Besides, once her mother knew, the entirety of Meryton and its environs would also know within the day.

"It is nothing out of the common way, I am sure," said Mr. Collins, finally able to have his say. "It is the practice of great men such as Mr. Darcy to condescend to provide assistance to those within the sphere of their influence. I am certain that Mr. Darcy has come to provide whatever assistance he may render to your father."

"Mr. Bennet has been the master of Longbourn almost as long as Mr. Darcy has been alive," said Mrs. Bennet in a prim tone. "I am sure that if there is any advice being dispensed, then it is likely coming from my husband."

Mr. Collins appeared aghast at the very thought, but Elizabeth, deciding that no good would come of continuing the discussion in that vein, changed the subject, making an observation about the ball the previous night, thus drawing her mother into further conversation on the matter. In time, they were joined by Elizabeth's two youngest sisters, though Mary had yet to make an appearance. That was odd, Elizabeth decided, as Mary was normally not one to lounge in her bed regardless of the previous night's activity, and she rarely appeared after Kitty and Lydia regardless.

But though the conversation was deflected to another topic, Mrs. Bennet and Mr. Collins were not to be so easily denied. One or both of them inevitably attempted to steer the conversation back to Mr. Darcy and the reason for his visit, with Mrs. Bennet invariably declaring that he must have some *particular* reason for visiting, while Mr. Collins adamantly claimed that Mr. Darcy must only be there for some innocuous purpose.

Needless to say that within a quarter hour of escorting Mr. Darcy to her father's bookroom, Elizabeth began to long for the quiet of the paths around her home or, failing that, the solitude of her bedchamber. At the very least, she wished that she had stayed in her father's bookroom and participated in the discussion. At least that way she would not have been subjected to this ludicrous dance her mother and Mr. Collins had forced upon her.

Chapter IX

*I*n actuality, Elizabeth was only required to spend about thirty minutes in the company of her mother and Mr. Collins, but the unfortunate fact was that it seemed almost like an eternity. Not only was her mother's conversation not especially interesting to Elizabeth—Mrs. Bennet was not, after all, the most riveting conversationalist, and most of her words on this morning centered around her expectations for her daughters' future marriage felicity— but Mr. Collins and his grave pronouncements were more than usually tiresome. And even further, Mr. Collins took to stating at great length that there was some misunderstanding—surely Mr. Darcy *could not* mean to offend his aunt and cousin by not doing his duty!—and his conversation that morning consisted of detailing his expectations of Lady Catherine's dream being realized, though it was interspersed with what he considered to be veiled remarks warning Elizabeth away from the great man. By the time that thirty minutes had elapsed, Elizabeth had progressed from merely wanting to be out of the man's company to being desperate to quit the room.

Of course, the fact that her father and Mr. Darcy were undoubtedly discussing *her* as well as the situation with Mr. Wickham did not help her impatience. The man had chosen her as his vessel for defaming Mr. Darcy, and though she preferred not to think of what his motivations might have been, Elizabeth was determined that he would not be allowed to have his way in this matter. The people of Meryton must be protected.

Thus, when the summons came to join the men in her father's bookroom, Elizabeth could only be grateful for the opportunity to escape.

Unfortunately, the summons was also a reason for consternation for the aforementioned Mr. Collins, as he, undoubtedly fearing that she had been hiding a secret engagement, sought to once more prevent the ignominy, though in his ineffectual way.

"My dear cousin," said he when Elizabeth rose to quit the room, "you cannot possibly be . . . This . . . this is highly improper, indeed. You cannot think to . . . to set aside all propriety in this fashion!"

"I was not aware that there was any impropriety inherent in the situation, Mr. Collins," replied Elizabeth airily. "I have been summoned to my father's bookroom, which has happened not infrequently in the past. What could be improper about that?"

"But . . . but . . ." Mr. Collins trailed off and stared at her, equal parts horror and suspicion evident in his countenance. He finally swallowed hard and mastered himself. "My dear cousin, surely you cannot mean to enter into an agreement which has not been properly sanctioned. I appeal to your goodness, your sense of your own worth, and even your duty. Do not do this! Nothing but humiliation awaits you if you persist."

"Of what is Mr. Collins speaking, Lizzy?" demanded Mrs. Bennet. And then she turned a flinty glare on the person of the pompous parson. "And you, sir. Are you suggesting that my daughter is not good enough for the likes of Mr. Darcy?"

"Mr. Darcy is a member of an old, titled, and wealthy family, madam," replied Mr. Collins stiffly. "Your family is all that is good, but you must understand that your situation can in no way compare with Mr. Darcy's. He is destined for much greater things, I assure you."

"Then it is well that I am merely summoned to my father's bookroom," said Elizabeth. "As I said before, Mr. Collins, my father calling for my presence is not an unusual occurrence. I suggest you do not read any more into the situation."

At that, Elizabeth walked from the room, ignoring her mother's flinty glare directed at the parson and Mr. Collins's sputtering attempts to respond to her words. She stopped outside the door to her father's office to gather her composure—though she had affected nonchalance in the presence of the parson, she was in reality quite vexed with him.

Mr. Collins could try the patience of a corpse!

A moment later, she had entered her father's study. Both men looked up from the desk where they had been sitting in earnest conversation and greeted her, though they regarded her with questioning looks. Apparently, her color was still up due to her piqued feelings with regard to Mr. Collins.

Deciding to ignore the unspoken question for the moment, Elizabeth greeted them and said: "You called for me?"

"It was actually Mr. Darcy who suggested that I send for you, Elizabeth," said her father. "Please have a seat."

Once Elizabeth had sat in the other chair, Mr. Darcy took up the conversation. "Miss Bennet, I have spoken to your father about Mr. Wickham, and he has agreed that we must do something to curb his tendencies in Meryton."

Mr. Bennet harrumphed, a most incongruous scowl affixed on his face. "If you know of this Mr. Wickham from Mr. Darcy, then you will know of his proclivities. A man like that could do considerable damage if he was allowed to continue to run up tabs with every tradesman in town. And that does not even consider the harm he could do to the reputations of unsuspecting young girls."

"Kitty and Lydia particularly would be in danger from his machinations," added Elizabeth.

"Yes, Lizzy," replied Mr. Bennet with a wave of his hand. "We cannot have that, so we must do something."

"Which is why we called for you," said Mr. Darcy, clearly ignoring the byplay between father and daughter. "Mr. Bennet and I have agreed that we shall go to Meryton and ask around town about Mr. Wickham's activities with the merchants there. If Mr. Wickham, as I suspect, has been up to his usual habits, then we will take our findings to Colonel Forster. But of more immediate concern is your family and the other families of the area."

Elizabeth gazed at him shrewdly. "Can I assume that you would like me to assist in disseminating the information to the area?"

"You know your mother, Lizzy," said Mr. Bennet with a laugh. "If you tell her of Mr. Wickham's bad behavior, it will be all over the town within a day."

Elizabeth looked at Mr. Darcy with an upraised eyebrow. "You mean for me to tell my mother of your account of Mr. Wickham?"

Mr. Darcy nodded. "Tell your whole family, Miss Bennet, so your younger sisters will be forearmed with knowledge that will protect them as well.

"As for the rest of the community, I am prepared to make the same communication to them as I did to you, with proof as to the debts Mr. Wickham has run up, which I have sent for from my London attorney. This testimony will, of course, be backed up by your father."

With a stern expression, Mr. Bennet regarded Mr. Darcy. "I shall not allow you to take too much upon yourself, young man. You have provided the warning—you must allow us to bear the burden of ensuring the scoundrel does not prosper here."

Mr. Darcy bowed, though it was clear that he was determined to do as much as he could as well. Knowing that there was nothing further to say on the matter, Elizabeth glanced back at Mr. Darcy.

"But your young acquaintance . . . Her reputation must be protected."

"As long as I do not reveal her identity, then she shall be protected," said Mr. Darcy. "Feel free to explain everything I told you to your family, Miss Bennet."

Though Elizabeth still had reservations, she agreed and allowed the matter to drop.

"You will leave immediately?"

"Very shortly," responded her father. "I shall be along directly. Darcy, if you will wait with Elizabeth in the parlor, we can leave in no more than a quarter of an hour."

Agreeing, Mr. Darcy stood and allowed Elizabeth to lead him from the room. However, once she closed the door to her father's study and heard the droning proclamations of Mr. Collins echoing from the parlor, Elizabeth decided that she did not wish to return there and subject Mr. Darcy to his silliness. Instead, she motioned toward the front hall and began walking.

"Unless I have become completely lost, I believe the parlor is in the opposite direction?" queried Mr. Darcy.

A quick glance at his face showed an amusement which stood out on his normally sober countenance.

"I believe a short walk in the garden would be agreeable, Mr. Darcy. The air in the parlor is a little close at the moment."

"Then lead on, Miss Bennet," said Mr. Darcy, clearly amused at her words.

Once she had collected her pelisse and gloves from one of the maids and Mr. Darcy had also received his outer garments, she led him outside and around to the gardens on the opposite side of the house from the parlor, deciding they should be safe for a short time from the meddlesome parson there. After all, Mr. Darcy had only obliquely stated his interest thus far — she did not want Mr. Collins to scare him off before she was able to become better acquainted with his character.

"A delightful area," commented Mr. Darcy as they slowed and began walking through the gardens.

As it was late November, nothing of substance was growing in the garden any longer, the plants having been killed by the persistent frost. Still, there had not yet been any snow that year, so while the air was crisp, Elizabeth found it to be pleasant, and the remains of the summer blooms bespoke of the vibrancy which would exist had the season been more favorable. Trees lined the edges of the gardens, and though they were bereft of their summer mantle, they were still tall and majestic, soaring over the area like some protective titans, keeping the estate safe until the coming spring.

"I confess I love our little patch of garden," said Elizabeth with a smile. "In the summer, we grow lavender, roses, chrysanthemums, rhododendrons, and other flowers. Jane particularly likes rose water, though I find myself partial to lavender."

"I can see that you love to be among nature."

"I must confess I do," said Elizabeth. "I walk outside as often as I can, and Jane and I care for these gardens in the summer, though my younger sisters also help us."

"And your purpose for bringing me out here was to show me the environs of your home?"

Elizabeth turned to him, noting his slight smile and the amusement which shone in his eyes. She returned his smile with one of her own.

"I rather thought that you would be more comfortable out here," confessed Elizabeth. "And my father shall be with us soon, and then you shall be gone."

"That is true. But do not think that you need to protect me from the likes of Mr. Collins."

With a wry grin, Elizabeth turned her attention fully upon her companion. "Who said I wished to protect you?"

Chuckling, Mr. Darcy stopped and directed Elizabeth toward a nearby bench. They sat there, taking in the fineness of the day in companionable silence for a few moments. The birds, those hardier souls that did not seek warmer climes for the winter, were chirping their gay songs, adding a feeling of brightness to what was otherwise a dreary day. The sun, though it had made a brief appearance earlier that morning, had now hidden its face behind a high layer of clouds which, though they did not appear to contain any rain, still darkened the landscape more than Elizabeth would have preferred. Regardless of the fact that the sun was not shining, it was the perfect day for a walk in the gardens with an amiable companion. And Elizabeth was surprised at the thought, as only a week before she could not have imagined thinking of Mr. Darcy in so agreeable a manner.

But before she could consider the matter further, Mr. Darcy spoke once again.

"Perhaps 'protect' is not the correct word, Miss Bennet," said he. "But I must tell you that I have visited my aunt, Lady Catherine de Bourgh, every spring since I became master of my own estate. And I can tell you that I am well accustomed to the type of man my aunt prefers to have as her parson."

"Oh?" asked Elizabeth, amused at his recitation of his aunt.

Mr. Darcy raised an eyebrow in response. "Come, Miss Bennet—I am well aware of the fact that you are a very intelligent woman. Surely you must have suspected it yourself."

"I should prefer not to speak ill of your aunt, Mr. Darcy. We are only just now becoming truly acquainted, and I should not wish to offend you."

"Ah, but I was not speaking of my aunt." Mr. Darcy paused, and a slight grin came over his face. "But I suppose her choice in parsons could reveal some facts about my aunt to the careful observer.

"Back to our original discussion, however. In the time I have been visiting my aunt yearly, there have been three men who have had the honor of holding the living at Rosings, though I should state that the first had been there for what might have been decades. Of course, he was a timid sort of fellow, and though not as voluble as the estimable Mr. Collins, he also never dared to contradict my aunt. He died not long after my father, and though it is perhaps not the most charitable thing to say, I suspect my aunt simply wore him out."

Elizabeth laughed gaily at his portrayal of the great lady, prompting an indulgent smile from her companion. "That account does not reflect at all positively on your aunt, Mr. Darcy," admonished Elizabeth, but though she attempted to affect a stern countenance, she was well aware that it was ruined by the smile she could not quite suppress.

"My dear Miss Bennet—if you had ever met my aunt, you would undoubtedly understand." His look grew pensive for a moment, and he continued: "She truly is a product of her times and her upbringing. My uncle, the earl, though generally a kindly soul, can be overbearing himself at times, and his arrogance is quite beyond anything I have ever seen."

Privately, Elizabeth thought that Mr. Darcy had inherited that trait to a certain extent himself. He had shown himself to be much more amiable than she had thought, but she suspected that he still possessed a certain level of arrogance.

She put the thought from her mind immediately—no one was perfect, as Mr. Darcy had pointed out himself, and she was determined to think of him in a better light than she had before. And if his arrogance did make an appearance again, the thought of his more amiable qualities would no doubt make it seem much less important by comparison.

While she had thought on the matter, Mr. Darcy had continued speaking: "The second parson in Hunsford, Mr. Collins's predecessor, was also a humble man, and he fawned over my aunt, flattering her much as Mr. Collins has done, though I would say that he was not at all unintelligent. But Mr. Merryweather seemed to acquire a bit of a backbone after marrying his wife, a local woman. It was a matter of months before they both tired of the situation, and as soon as another one became available, they took the opportunity to move to a parish in which they were not . . . directed in everything they did. Mr. Collins, therefore, is new, and he has been employed by my aunt for less than half a year, as Mr. Merryweather was just preparing to leave when I last visited."

Laughing, Elizabeth regarded her partner playfully. "Well, I dare say that Mr. Collins will be content to sing Lady Catherine's praises as long as she deems him fit to perform the office. Or at least until he inherits my father's estate."

At this, Mr. Darcy turned to look at her fully. "Longbourn is entailed upon your cousin?"

"It is indeed," replied Elizabeth. "Had you never heard any mention of it?"

"No, I had not," said Mr. Darcy, though his manner was distracted. "You may have noticed that I am not the most loquacious of men. The matter could have been mentioned in my presence during my stay here, but I might not have been listening."

"We try not to speak of it much." Then Elizabeth let out a laugh which seemed, even to her own ears, to contain a certain nervous quality to it. "It occupies my mother constantly, as you might well imagine, though the rest of us avoid the subject wherever possible. It does no good to dwell upon it."

There it was. If Mr. Darcy was to be frightened away by anything, the news that expressing an interest in her might carry the responsibility for her silly mother and insipid younger sisters would do it faster than anything else Elizabeth could imagine.

"I can see how that would be worrisome," replied Mr. Darcy. Elizabeth was warmed by the smile on his face and the evidence of his regard in his eyes. He said nothing further on the subject, and they turned to other more mundane subjects for the next few moments.

But just when Elizabeth had started wondering where her father was, they were interrupted by a most unwelcome source. Mr. Collins came hurrying along the path, obviously searching for Elizabeth and her companion. When his eyes alighted on them, he peered at Elizabeth with suspicion before an expression of utmost servility replaced his mistrustful air when he espied Mr. Darcy. He hurried up the path toward them, all the while calling out to them.

"Mr. Darcy! Mr. Darcy!"

He hurried up to them, his puffing and sweating a testament to the exertions he had undertaken to find them as quickly as possible. It was difficult for her to suppress her laughter at the ludicrous picture he presented.

"I thought . . . I should relate . . . to you more of . . . the intelligence . . . I possess of your lovely . . . cousin, Anne, and her mother . . . Lady Catherine," wheezed the parson as he stumbled to a halt in front of them.

Elizabeth was certain he had been about to proclaim Anne de Bourgh as Mr. Darcy's betrothed, but he obviously remembered at the last moment the dressing-down that Mr. Darcy had given him the last time he had referred to her as such.

He was greeted with a faint look of annoyance by Mr. Darcy, who had apparently been as engrossed in conversation as Elizabeth had been herself. His stern glare revealed that he was not best pleased to be thus interrupted.

"That will be unnecessary, Mr. Collins," said he. "I received a letter from my cousin not five days ago, and so I have recent intelligence of them. You may relieve yourself of your stated duty without censure."

Though Elizabeth caught the sarcasm and the hint of impatience in Mr. Darcy's voice, Mr. Collins obviously did not. He bowed low and expressed that he was happy that Mr. Darcy was acquainted with the state of his beloved relations. But though Mr. Darcy obviously wished that the man would depart, he stubbornly stuck by their side, taking care to interject his rambling comments into whatever conversation Elizabeth managed to have with Mr. Darcy. Apparently, he had determined that he had best keep Elizabeth and Mr. Darcy apart, so as to protect his patroness's interest. Elizabeth would have laughed out loud at his ridiculous attempts at interference had the man not been so completely infuriating.

By that time, however, the moment for Mr. Darcy's departure had arrived, as Mr. Bennet appeared in the garden, wearing an overcoat and gloves for the short journey into Meryton.

"We should depart, Mr. Darcy, if we are to make any progress today."

Mr. Darcy bowed, but then he turned back to Mr. Collins. He frowned at the parson—and the normally oblivious man did not miss the glance, though he clearly had no understanding of why he should have been the subject of such a look—before glancing at Elizabeth with an appraising expression on his face.

"Mr. Collins," said he, "Mr. Bennet and I are to go into Meryton to take care of some business. Perhaps you would care to join us?"

Nonplussed by the invitation, Elizabeth stared at Mr. Darcy and was startled when he turned his head slightly and smiled at her. She nearly lost her composure at the sight and had to cough into her hand to cover the most unladylike snort which she could not quite suppress. Mr. Darcy, knowing what Mr. Collins was about, was clearly trying to spare her the odious man's pronouncements by inviting him along. Elizabeth could only hope that Mr. Collins would not ruin their endeavors.

Her father, however, clearly did not understand why Mr. Darcy would request the presence of a man who would only hinder them, after all. "Mr. Collins accompany us?" said he, his voice laced with skepticism.

"He is to be master of this estate eventually, is he not? Mr. Collins may eventually be party to similar doings—it would do him good to have a part in it."

Bemused, Mr. Bennet regarded the other man, clearly wondering what he was about. It was only a few moments before his eyes darted to Elizabeth—causing her to color in response—before he shook his head and chuckled under his breath.

"Indeed, you are correct Mr. Darcy. I wonder that I had not thought of it myself."

Mr. Collins, who had puffed himself up at their words, was soon ushered from the garden by Elizabeth's father, leaving Mr. Darcy with Elizabeth to say their goodbyes.

"I do not know whether I should thank you or question your sanity, Mr. Darcy," said Elizabeth with a wry smile. "I cannot think that Mr. Collins will be an asset to your cause."

"Perhaps not," agreed Mr. Darcy. "But I assure you that he will not be a detriment either. I dare say that he will do everything I tell him to do with alacrity."

Laughing, Elizabeth found that she could only agree with his assessment.

A moment later, Mr. Darcy bowed over her hand and bid her farewell. "I shall come again tomorrow, if you are agreeable," said he. "I do not know how long we will be gone today, but I doubt that we shall be back in time for tea. Tell your mother and sisters of Mr. Wickham, Miss Bennet. Let us pull his teeth before he even has a chance to stalk his prey."

And with that, Mr. Darcy was gone, leaving Elizabeth to reflect that all her beliefs were being overturned quite neatly by a man she had never even thought existed.

Chapter X

The men departed immediately, though Mr. Collins was clearly reluctant to be away from Longbourn. As Elizabeth was in no mood to listen to the man's pontifications, she was grateful to Mr. Darcy for ensuring that Mr. Collins would not be able continue importuning her. Or at least he would be prevented from doing so for the rest of that afternoon.

Elizabeth saw them off from the stables, and she found it necessary to stifle another round of giggles at the sight of Mr. Collins sitting on one of her father's horses like a sack of barley. The man had better find his seat soon—being comfortable on a horse was, after all, an integral part of being a gentleman unless he intended to walk for miles to visit his tenants. Elizabeth knew that *she* was certainly capable of such a feat, but the heavyset Mr. Collins would likely find it to be a trial.

Once she had been left alone, Elizabeth considered spending a little time in her room, organizing her thoughts about Mr. Darcy. Instead, however, she gathered her determination, squared her shoulders, and entered the parlor, intent upon sharing Mr. Darcy's intelligence regarding Mr. Wickham with her family. The women of the Bennet family were all still ensconced within the parlor, though Lydia and Kitty appeared to be bored and in need of some occupation. She could not have planned it any more perfectly.

"Lizzy," spoke up Mrs. Bennet, being the first to notice her entrance. "Has Mr. Darcy returned to Netherfield?"

Elizabeth was once again amused. Though her mother's voice still held a hint of distaste for the gentleman from Derbyshire, it also held a modicum of interest.

"Not to Netherfield, Mama," replied Elizabeth. "He has gone to Meryton, and Mr. Collins and my father have gone with him."

That piece of intelligence garnered the attention of everyone in the room, though it was likely due primarily to the fact that Mr. Bennet had so suddenly gone into Meryton.

"Gone to Meryton?" demanded Mrs. Bennet. "What business does your father have there? And for that matter, I cannot imagine that Mr. Darcy would have any business in the company of your father."

"You have been very mysterious lately, Lizzy," interjected Lydia. Both of her younger sisters, clearly remembering their conversation, were peering at her with some interest. "Perhaps their errand has something to do with Mr. Wickham?"

Elizabeth stared at her youngest sister. Was this truly Lydia? Selfish, thoughtless, oblivious Lydia? When had her sister become so perceptive?

"Come now, Lizzy," said Lydia with a huff when Elizabeth did not immediately respond. "I am not a simpleton. You told us of your suspicions about Mr. Wickham, then you have a long and private conversation with Mr. Darcy, and finally, proud, disagreeable Mr. Darcy shows up on our doorstep the very next morning and almost demands to speak with our father. Surely he must have some truly dreadful intelligence to impart concerning Mr. Wickham. Otherwise, why would he go to the trouble?"

Lydia's expression became sly, prompting no small measure of trepidation as to what Elizabeth's suddenly perceptive sister would say next. "Unless Mr. Darcy's purpose here was something entirely different from unmasking a villain or promoting a match between our eldest sister and his closest friend . . ."

"What do you mean?" demanded Mrs. Bennet before Elizabeth could say anything.

"I do have something to tell you all," said Elizabeth quickly. The best way to deflect her mother was to focus on what she had to say. Maybe she could quiet Lydia at the same time.

"Mr. Darcy has asked that I relate to you all what he has told me about Mr. Wickham. That way we may all be forewarned as to the kind of man he truly is."

"Mr. Darcy has something with which to accuse Mr. Wickham?" asked her mother.

"Indeed, he does," replied Elizabeth.

And so Elizabeth launched into the tale Mr. Darcy had told her the previous evening, taking great care to stick to the facts of what Mr. Darcy had told her rather than to any conjecture concerning the motives of the scoundrel himself. She told them of Mr. Wickham's debts and his inclination toward gambling, warning them to listen to nothing of the accusations Mr. Wickham made toward Mr. Darcy. She even obliquely referred to Mr. Wickham's attempted seduction of Mr. Darcy's acquaintance, though she was careful not to bring up any hint of her own conjecture about the girl's identity.

Typically, it was dear, sweet Jane who responded first. "Are we certain that there is no misunderstanding?"

"I cannot imagine how there could be any misunderstanding in such a tale," declared Mrs. Bennet. And though Elizabeth had not often had the opportunity to agree with her mother, she could only nod in this instance.

"Then I suppose we have no choice but to believe Mr. Darcy's account," said Jane with a sigh.

Unfortunately, Lydia, who was enraptured by any man wearing a red coat, was not quite ready to let go of her hope that Mr. Wickham was all that was amiable.

"But why should we consider Mr. Darcy's account to be any more trustworthy than that of Mr. Wickham?"

"Because of the impropriety of Mr. Wickham's communications," said Mary, speaking for the first time.

"But by the same token, are not Mr. Darcy's own words on the subject to also be treated with suspicion?" By this time, Lydia's voice had almost begun to take on the quality of her familiar whine. "We have not known Mr. Darcy much longer than we have Mr. Wickham, after all."

"That is true, Lydia," said Elizabeth. "But the circumstances are completely different. Mr. Wickham told his story without any provocation, and I can only assume that he was trying to play on my perceived dislike for Mr. Darcy."

"But Lizzy," said Kitty, "you *do* dislike Mr. Darcy."

Lydia let out a most unladylike snort. "If what I have seen the past two days is any indication, our Lizzy has warmed to Mr. Darcy." Elizabeth colored at her sister's words, but Lydia was not finished. "I am not certain why; Mr. Darcy slighted her, after all."

"I *have* warmed to Mr. Darcy," owned Elizabeth. "He not only apologized for that remark, but he has also shown me another side of his character."

"It behooves us all to take care not to pronounce adverse judgments on our fellow man," said Mary to no one in particular.

Elizabeth was forced to agree with her sister, though she looked at Mary strangely. Though the words were in keeping with most of Mary's usual comments, her tone lacked its usual pomposity.

Putting the matter from her mind, Elizabeth focused once again on her youngest sisters. "Mary is correct. As we discussed before, Mr. Wickham's story was completely improper. Not only was it the first time we had ever spoken more than a few words to each other, but it was also the sort of intelligence I would not feel comfortable sharing, even with an acquaintance of many years. In fact, Mr. Wickham expressly told me that he would never defame Mr. Darcy, even as he was doing it!

"As for Mr. Darcy, he responded to Mr. Wickham's accusations, and he did so out of concern, not only for his own reputation, but also for our family. He did not wish for Mr. Wickham to hurt us or the people of Meryton while he stood by and did nothing. Instead, he laid his private concerns bare for us to see, and that speaks well to his character. He could have done nothing, and he could not have been faulted for doing so."

"So what have Mr. Darcy and Papa gone to Meryton to do?" asked Kitty.

Elizabeth smiled at her younger sister. "It would not do the neighborhood much good if the Bennets were the only ones who were forewarned, now would it? If Mr. Wickham has misrepresented himself to *me*, then it is almost certain that he will do it to the people of Meryton as well."

"Is it truly prudent to provoke him this way?" fretted Jane. "It is possible that he has seen the error of his ways and wishes to reestablish his good character."

Elizabeth looked at her sister fondly, knowing that Jane was not so deficient as to think that no evil existed in the world. But Jane *was* disposed to think the best of people and to ascribe the best possible motivation to anyone she met. In the case of Mr. Wickham, Elizabeth knew Jane was not about to be taken in—the presence of Mr. Bingley in her life prevented that, even if Jane had not been the sort to engage in casual flirtation. But she would still persist in trying to discover some reason which would render *both* men blameless in their dispute.

"If that is so, Jane, then Mr. Darcy and Papa will find nothing in Meryton. But if history holds true, then Mr. Wickham has already beginning run up debts with the tradesmen, and that is something that we cannot countenance."

With that simple declaration, the conversation about Mr. Wickham ceased, and the sisters went their separate ways to engage in their own activities. Elizabeth was heartened; not only had her sisters accepted her words with very little disagreement, but even Kitty and Lydia appeared to be thinking about her words with more than their usual gravity. They had not turned into discerning and proper young women overnight, but Elizabeth was confident that now they had acquired a bit of forethought and would perhaps consider their actions in advance.

Mr. Bennet and Mr. Collins returned to Longbourn later that afternoon. But whereas Mr. Bennet's countenance contained a measure of hardness which was not in keeping with his normally sardonic outlook, Mr. Collins appeared to have acquired a startled air of confusion which made him appear to be more than usually absurd.

"Mr. Darcy has returned to Netherfield," said Elizabeth's father, apparently recognizing her interest in the whereabouts of the gentleman. "I invited him to join us for dinner, but he declined, citing the hour and the fact that Mr. Hurst was expecting him back."

Privately, Elizabeth was not inclined to believe such an excuse—Mr. Darcy had never shown much affinity for the gentleman's company, and they were as dissimilar as night and day. Only one short week before, Elizabeth would have ascribed Mr. Darcy's reticence to distaste for her family, but with his performance that morning, she rather suspected that he simply did not wish to impose on such short notice. Elizabeth felt in that moment no small amount of surprise at just how much her opinion had altered in such a short time.

"I must say that I have grown quite fond of Mr. Darcy," said Mr. Bennet, with no little humor. "He truly does not say much, but then again, sometimes the benefits of saying little while imparting much are very great indeed."

"Mr. Darcy is indeed a most gracious, condescending, and discerning individual," inserted Mr. Collins into the conversation. "Of course, I am convinced that anyone who is a member of my patroness's family must be so, as the traits which so distinguish Lady Catherine must breed true in all her family."

The parson's words were silly and in keeping with the man himself, and Elizabeth did not miss the fact that her father had been comparing the two men, though Mr. Collins obviously had. Father and daughter shared an amused look, and then Mr. Bennet spoke again, eyeing the females of his family with a little more gravity than was his normal wont.

"I suppose you are all waiting for the news of Mr. Wickham," said he.

"As well we should," cried Mrs. Bennet. "Is the young man guilty of the crimes Mr. Darcy has laid at his door?"

"Mr. Darcy is of such lineage and nobility that what he has told us must be true!" exclaimed Mr. Collins, affronted at the mere suggestion that Mr. Darcy's words were not trusted implicitly.

"Well, I dare say that we did not investigate *all* of those claims today," said Mr. Bennet, ignoring the parson's words. "But those that we were able to look into certainly proved Mr. Darcy's assertions most admirably."

Lydia and Kitty in particular gasped at their father's words. "Mr. Wickham has been leaving debts?" demanded Lydia.

"And imposing himself on young women?" echoed Kitty.

Turning a stern eye on his youngest daughters, Mr. Bennet said: "I shall thank you not to bring up such a subject so indiscriminately, Kitty. And as for you, Lydia, if you will allow me a moment, I shall tell you all."

When the younger girls appeared cowed by his words, Mr. Bennet glanced over all those present before he began to elaborate. "Though we could not bring up such a delicate subject with impunity, the shopkeepers and many of the landowners of the area were warned about the young man's proclivities. It seems as if this Wickham fellow is very charming and makes himself agreeable to all, but as yet, it appears that little other than some harmless flirting has occurred when it comes to his dealings with the young women of the area.

"The merchants were another matter. It appears that Wickham has begun to run up debts with almost every shopkeeper in town. Now, most are small debts—a few shillings here, a half a crown there—but the most concerning were two outstanding debts, one which is almost a full pound, while the other is more. And all of this activity is subtly done, with a word of flattery here and a charming smile there, and none of the shopkeepers had any idea that he owed to anyone other than themselves. Most of the merchants had not connected the fact that while they have extended credit to the officers, most of the other men, though they have been here longer, owe less or even nothing at all."

"And what is the total amount he owes?" asked Elizabeth.

"At this point, a little more than five pounds in total," replied Mr. Bennet.

There were several gasps heard around the room. "Five pounds?" screeched Mrs. Bennet.

"Indeed," was her husband's short reply. "I would never have imagined such an amount being accrued in such a short time, but there it is.

"As such, once we had gathered the evidence—which Mr. Darcy purchased, mind you, on the condition that the merchants do not extend any further credit to the inestimable Mr. Wickham—we approached Colonel Forster with what we had gathered."

"And his reaction?" asked Elizabeth.

"Much as could be expected," replied Mr. Bennet. "The colonel is a career soldier, and he is well aware of what an unscrupulous man may do to a regiment's reputation. The other officers were canvassed, and it was found that Mr. Wickham had already incurred a few debts of honor to the other officers. Our good Mr. Wickham has been quite busy since he arrived in our little community."

Elizabeth was surprised that the amounts had already reached such levels, but she was also highly gratified that Mr. Darcy's words had turned out to be true, though she had never doubted it for an instant. This knowledge would protect her sisters even more, she was certain. Of course, another part of her seethed anew at the blackguard for his attempt to draw her in and use her against Mr. Darcy. Such a thing was not to be forgiven!

"Mr. Wickham shall therefore be called in and informed that his pay is forfeit until he pays back all of his debts. Given what he must spend on his daily upkeep in the regiment, it will be some time before Mr. Wickham has repaid what he owes. Perhaps it will keep him out of trouble.

"And he is fortunate that his activities were discovered now rather than in several months, as he would be in real danger of debtors' prison had he continued in this manner. It is even more fortunate for the merchants that he was discovered at all."

"Did you see him?" asked Lydia.

"No. Colonel Forster thought it best that no mention of Mr. Darcy or I be made to the lieutenant. He will confront Wickham himself and inform him of these findings, though I do not doubt that Mr. Wickham will see Mr. Darcy's hand in the matter."

"No doubt he will," said Elizabeth quietly.

"I should not worry," said Mr. Bennet, and though he spoke to the whole room, Elizabeth was certain that his words were directed at her. "Mr. Darcy has been dealing with the scoundrel his entire life, and he knows what is to be done. I understand there is also a matter of some previous debts Mr. Wickham accrued, the receipts for which Mr. Darcy still holds. If the lieutenant steps out of line, I should think that a few threats to his freedom will bring him to an understanding of his true situation."

"I would expect that he might attempt to leave," replied Elizabeth. "He does not strike me as one who would put up with a bad situation such as this for long."

Mr. Bennet smiled. "In that opinion, you are joined by the colonel himself. And this time, Mr. Wickham may have overextended himself. One does not simply walk away from a commission in His Majesty's army, even if it is only a militia commission. He would need to leave the country, and at present, he does not have the funds to do so."

Mr. Bennet leaned forward in his seat, his expression as serious as Elizabeth had ever seen from him, and when he spoke, he spoke to the entire family with an air of authority which he had also rarely used.

"Girls, this man is a scoundrel of the worst sort. He has no scruples whatsoever, and he is not above taking advantage of young girls. I want you all to stay away from Mr. Wickham. Am I clear?"

Elizabeth and her sisters could only nod, though Kitty and Lydia appeared to be more than shocked by the whole affair, particularly since their father had forbidden them from speaking with the man. Mr. Bennet had rarely forbidden anyone in his family anything in the past, and the contrast only served to illustrate the danger that Mr. Wickham posed. Elizabeth hoped that Lydia and Kitty would pay heed to his words and not be taken in by any flattering words by the lieutenant.

"Very well, then," said Mr. Bennet. "Mr. Collins, shall we adjourn to my bookroom until dinner?"

Though the parson appeared as though he would rather stay in the parlor with the ladies—and even glanced at Elizabeth with narrowed eyes—he stood and followed Mr. Bennet from the room. While passing Elizabeth, Mr. Bennet winked at her, and she had to stifle a laugh in response. Clearly, he was trying to spare her Mr. Collins's presence, though whether he was doing it because Mr. Collins had said something specific or because he knew she found the man to be irksome, she was not certain. She was not about to question it, however. Both her father and Mr. Darcy had distracted Mr. Collins to her benefit, and she felt grateful to them both.

The ladies soon moved to other activities, and Elizabeth left to return to her room to think on the matter while Jane took up some needlepoint and Mary picked up one of the religious treatises she favored. As for Kitty and Lydia, they sat with Mrs. Bennet, speaking in low tones, no doubt on the matter of Mr. Wickham. Elizabeth hoped that her mother was reinforcing what her father had said on the matter. It must surely be the case—Mrs. Bennet would want nothing to stand in the way of her daughters' chances of making good marriages, after all.

Elizabeth had exited the room and had taken the first few stairs when she heard the voice of her closest sister behind her.

"Lizzy, are you well?"

Turning, Elizabeth smiled at Jane. "I am very well, Jane. I believe I simply need some time to digest everything we have discovered."

"I wanted you to know, Lizzy," blurted Jane, "that I like Mr. Darcy very well indeed. There is something pleasing about his attentions, and his way of expressing himself renders him uncommonly intelligent."

"Yes, it does, Jane," replied Elizabeth quietly.

"I am glad to know that you esteem the gentleman more than you did before. I believe he is well worth knowing."

With that, Jane retreated back into the parlor, and Elizabeth was left to climb the stairs and enter her room by herself. She had much on which to think. Although Jane was disposed to think well of everyone—or at least to ascribe the best possible motives to them—her words concerning Mr. Darcy resonated with Elizabeth. She was coming to the determination herself that Mr. Darcy was indeed well worth knowing.

Chapter XI

For all Elizabeth's thought on the matter, she was unable to come to a true resolution. Jane's words had truly impressed her, as she had come to believe that Mr. Darcy was indeed worth having as a friend. However, she could not forget his behavior when he and Mr. Bingley had first arrived in Hertfordshire. His apology for his words at the assembly had been heartfelt, and so they did not truly touch her any longer, and she was honest enough with herself to allow that those words had wounded her vanity, which was why she had responded the way she had. It appeared that years of being compared with Jane had affected her more than she had previously been willing to acknowledge.

Therefore, the question was: who was the *real* Mr. Darcy? Was he the proud and disagreeable man he had first showed himself to be, or was he the amiable savior of Jane's hopes and dreams? Was he the haughty man who only looked to see a blemish, or was he the sensible man who had spoken to her so kindly and complimented her so earnestly?

Elizabeth did not know—she had not as yet had enough time to determine what she believed—but she had the distinct impression that she would enjoy finding out.

And she was to be afforded every opportunity to do so, it would seem. Mr. Darcy visited again the next morning, and with the attentions he had been paying to Elizabeth, Mrs. Bennet was all too happy to see him in her company as much as possible, though the Bennet matron still acted a little cold and diffident toward him. Thus it was that Elizabeth found herself walking with the gentleman along with Jane the very next morning—Kitty and Lydia had gone to Meryton to shop for some baubles, while Mary was busy with some treatise or another with the ever-faithful Mr. Collins in attendance.

Now there was another situation Elizabeth could not quite figure out. Elizabeth had caught Mr. Collins looking at her at times, and she was certain that he wished to say something. But he did not speak up, and Elizabeth could only conjecture that Mr. Darcy had spoken to the man further on his supposed engagement with Anne de Bourgh and had told him in no uncertain terms that he should drop the subject.

Mr. Collins had turned his interest back to Mary, but as he often concentrated on Elizabeth, his attentions were scattered at best. And as for Mary, she received his attentions with what Elizabeth could only term as disinterest—she conversed with him and discussed their mutual interests, much as she ever had, but she did not appear to begrudge the frequent times when her suitor's thoughts were fixed on Elizabeth. It was a most curious way to conduct a courtship, but as Elizabeth had never truly understood her sister and did not wish to give Mr. Collins any hint of encouragement to resume his attentions to *her,* she determined to leave well enough alone.

"It is a beautiful day, is it not Miss Elizabeth?"

Elizabeth started and colored, realizing that she had been lost in her thoughts for some time and had consequently been poor company.

"Yes, it is, Mr. Darcy," replied she. And it was true. The weather had been cold and rainy before the ball, but as the clouds had cleared the day after the ball, milder weather, which she could only term as delightful, had also arrived.

"Have you heard from Mr. Bingley?" asked Elizabeth, though she spoke more from a need to fill the silence and atone for her inattention than from any expectation that Mr. Darcy had anything of substance to report.

Mr. Darcy seemed to recognize that fact, though he must also have noticed the way Jane seemed to perk up at the mention of her suitor.

"Nothing further than a short note to inform me that he had arrived," replied Mr. Darcy. "And I believe that I shall hear from him no further before his return. As we have previously discussed, Bingley is no great correspondent."

"Yes, but at least he has not left on a whim, never intending to return."

Mr. Darcy smiled at the reference to their conversation at Netherfield. "I seriously doubt that anything could keep him away. I believe you may consider Bingley to be quite settled at Netherfield for the foreseeable future."

Jane dropped off to the side of the path, ostensibly to examine some hardy plant or another which had caught her attention, though Elizabeth was not fooled. The talk of Mr. Bingley—and Mr. Darcy's assurance that he would return—had caused Jane to feel self-conscious, and she had fallen back to allow her color to return to normal.

Taking the opportunity which presented itself, Elizabeth turned Mr. Darcy. "I wished to thank you for your actions yesterday, sir. I shall rest easier knowing that my sisters shall not be taken unaware by Mr. Wickham."

Making a slight bow, Mr. Darcy responded: "It was nothing. Merely my responsibility as a gentleman."

Incredulous, Elizabeth peered at him. "How could Mr. Wickham be your responsibility?"

"Perhaps he is not *my* responsibility, as you correctly point out," said Mr. Darcy, "but as he was raised at Pemberley and educated due my father's regard for him, I do feel some responsibility for his actions. He has largely been formed by his relationship with me and my father's favor for him."

Elizabeth peered at Mr. Darcy, wondering how far she could go in expressing the questions which were running though her head.

"You seem to have a question, Miss Bennet," said Mr. Darcy, perceiving her hesitation. "Please feel free to ask anything at all."

Biting her lip, Elizabeth watched him, taking in his earnest expression, before she decided to take him at his word.

"My apologies for my impertinence, Mr. Darcy, but I am curious of something Mr. Wickham said. He attributed your dislike of him to jealousy of your father's love and attention, and I was wondering—"

She broke off when Mr. Darcy shook his head and laughed. "I believe I must attribute his words to an obstinate belief in what my father's regard actually meant. As I informed you earlier, my father would not have done more for Mr. Wickham had he been his natural son, which I assure you he was not.

"As for Mr. Wickham's claims concerning my father's regard, I can tell you that my father did indeed think fondly of him. Knowing of this, I chose not to illuminate him to Wickham's true character, though

I had thought to do so many times. As my father's health deteriorated, I determined that it would do no good except to remove some joy in the twilight of his life, which I would not do for anything.

"But I assure you, Miss Bennet, that my relationship with my father was as close as it could be — Mr. Wickham could not come between us, nor would he ever have attempted such a deed. He was well aware of the fact that it would have been to his detriment rather than to his benefit had he tried."

Feeling rather intimidated by Mr. Darcy's stern countenance, Elizabeth looked away for a few moments before she focused her attention on him once again, noting immediately that his expression had softened.

"I apologize for my impertinence, Mr. Darcy. But you did say that I could ask anything."

"That is why I enjoy our discussions so very much, Miss Bennet," said Mr. Darcy with a chuckle. "You are not afraid to speak your mind, and your opinions are intelligent and engaging. I find our discussions to be stimulating indeed."

"My courage always rises, Mr. Darcy," replied Elizabeth. "Any attempt to intimidate me — even with stern looks or false stories — only causes me to be even more obstinate."

Mr. Darcy smiled again, but then he turned to Elizabeth with his typical expression of gravity.

"And that is part of your appeal, I assure you. But Miss Bennet, I would urge you to take care and not give Mr. Wickham the opportunity to test your fortitude."

"But you have never known him to be violent, correct?" asked Elizabeth.

"I have not," confirmed Mr. Darcy. "However, I have never clipped his wings to this extent before either. And there is no telling what he may do since he has undoubtedly discerned my interest in you. I would urge you to never be found alone by Mr. Wickham. It is best to simply never allow him the chance to test what extent he is willing to go to hurt me."

Elizabeth murmured her consent, and they continued walking, speaking of inconsequential subjects as Jane followed behind. Had Elizabeth been able to give thought to such things, she would have noted how much like a courting couple with a chaperone trailing behind they appeared.

Later that day, Mr. Darcy had returned to Netherfield and Elizabeth was with her sisters in the parlor—Mr. Collins as thankfully absent, visiting with the parson of Longbourn church—when the first of two unexpected visitors made their appearance. As was her wont, Aunt Phillips bustled into the room, and after greeting the Bennet ladies in a hurried fashion, she proceeded to impart her gossip.

"Sister, you will never guess the news I bring today," said she in her excited manner. "It appears that Mr. Wickham has been found to have incurred dents with nearly every reputable tradesman in town. His credit has been revoked, and he has been ordered to surrender his pay until the debts have been cleared.

"And not only that, but Mr. Wickham has also begun to spread word of his ill-treatment at the hands of Mr. Darcy, claiming that Mr. Darcy is attempting to blacken his name and that he had always intended to repay his debts.

"Furthermore, there is some suggestion that Mr. Darcy has behaved improperly in the past, denying Mr. Wickham a bequest which was left to him by Mr. Darcy's father. Can you believe such a thing?"

"Not if it comes from the mouth of Mr. Wickham."

The women looked up and noted that Mr. Bennet had entered the room, apparently noting Aunt Phillips's arrival. He took his customary chair and peered at the women disinterestedly, though Elizabeth, who had always been able to read her father better than most, could tell that he was keenly interested in the conversation. Unless Elizabeth missed her guess, she suspected that her father had anticipated her aunt's visit and had responded accordingly.

"My dear Mrs. Phillips, Mr. Wickham has already shared this tale with our Lizzy previously, and he did so most improperly, I might add."

Mrs. Phillips turned her incredulous gaze on Elizabeth, almost as if she were a child who had been denied a favorite sweet. "Then why did you not say so before?"

Though Elizabeth loved her aunt, she was a simple woman, much like her sister. Mrs. Phillips delighted in gossip, and being denied such a tasty morsel to share with her friends and neighbors was something akin to a punishment.

"I did not share it because it was unsubstantiated," said Elizabeth. "I would not defame a good man on nothing more than the word of a man I had known for less than a full day."

Mrs. Phillips appeared a little chagrined. "Then you believe Mr. Wickham's tale to be false?"

"I have spoken with Mr. Darcy on the matter," replied Mr. Bennet.

"As the gentleman is a prominent member of society and has offered to provide proof of his claims, I have no choice but to believe him.

"And you must remember that Mr. Wickham has been most improper in relating these matters before all the neighborhood. In fact, I can only conjecture that it is *Mr. Wickham* who is attempting to defame another's character rather than the reverse. Mr. Darcy has done nothing more than to respond to Mr. Wickham's claims. You may take that as an established truth."

A gleam entered Mrs. Phillips's eye at the suggestion, and Elizabeth almost laughed. Her aunt now had something about which to gossip to her heart's content, no doubt exactly as Mr. Bennet had intended.

Mrs. Phillips was indeed a gossip. She had not the advantage of moving in genteel company and could be considered to be somewhat vulgar, but indeed she was a good and kind-hearted soul. It was quite the contrast, Elizabeth decided—her aunt was kind, but would never fit into polite society, while Mr. Wickham was everything which appeared good and proper on the surface, though he was the most black-hearted villain inside.

It was while Elizabeth was out walking in the gardens later that day when the second visitor arrived to disturb her peace. She had just completed her circuit of the grounds when one of the subjects of her ruminations suddenly appeared before her.

Though a little startled at the man's sudden appearance, Elizabeth quickly regained her wits and stared at him, wondering what he was about.

"Miss Bennet," greeted he.

"Mr. Wickham," replied Elizabeth in turn.

He did not immediately speak, and Elizabeth remained silent, determined to make him say what he wished without any encouragement from her. In fact, she was struck by how haughty and imperious he appeared—it reminded her greatly of her initial impression of Mr. Darcy, though she was certain neither man would appreciate the comparison.

"I should like to know why I have been betrayed in this infamous manner."

The question took Elizabeth by surprise—she had rather thought that he would begin to protest his innocence in a vehement manner. To open the way he did suggested ill use, and Elizabeth was struck by how manipulative Mr. Wickham could be.

"I am not aware of any betrayal, Mr. Wickham," said Elizabeth.

"You know *exactly* of what I speak," ground out Mr. Wickham in response. "I have you and Darcy to thank for the besmirching of my name. I would have expected it of him—his hatred of me is well known. But I can only conjecture that your actions are due to your hope that he will raise your state in life. A foolish hope, as it happens. Or perhaps you have not heard of his betrothal to his cousin."

Elizabeth laughed. "You truly are blinded by your own selfish concerns, Mr. Wickham. I have no hopes with regard to Mr. Darcy. Unlike you, I am sensible of my position in life."

"And what would you know of my position in life?" demanded Mr. Wickham.

"Nothing more than what you have told me yourself. But I must warn you, Mr. Wickham—I am not the only person in Meryton who is able to discern the impropriety of your words and actions. I suggest you ply your trade elsewhere."

Mr. Wickham threw his arms up in frustration. "Why is Darcy's account more believable than my own? And why must you share it with all and sundry?"

"You are mistaken, Mr. Wickham," replied Elizabeth. "I have not been to Meryton since the ball, and I have not shared anything I have learned with anyone in Meryton."

"I hardly think that likely," said Mr. Wickham with a sneer.

"It matters not a whit what you believe," snapped Elizabeth.

Her response appeared to truly anger him, but he was prevented from saying anything further by the sound of her father's voice.

"What is the meaning of this?"

Mr. Bennet hurried up and affixed a stern glare on Mr. Wickham. Longbourn's footman was following at a discreet distance, and though the man was a genial sort, Elizabeth knew that he could be menacing if he chose. "What do you do here, sir?"

"Merely exchanging a few words with Miss Bennet," said Mr. Wickham as he attempted to turn a charming smile on her father.

To say that it had no effect was a rather large understatement. "Perhaps you have not had the benefit of being raised in gentle society, sir, but at Longbourn, those wishing to speak with my daughters are expected to present themselves at the front door rather than skulking in through the gardens. And they are expected to do so during proper visiting hours."

Though Mr. Wickham's eyes gleamed with displeasure, his charming smile never faded. "I had a matter to discuss with Miss Bennet, and as I saw her on my way to the house, I decided not to bother you or your good wife."

"That does not excuse the impropriety of your being here," was Mr. Bennet's implacable response. "Furthermore, I must tell you, Mr. Wickham, that you are not welcome at Longbourn. You will leave my property immediately, and you will not return."

A long-suffering sigh emerged from Mr. Wickham's lips. "I see that Darcy has gotten to you, too."

"I need not explain myself to you, sir. I want you off my property, and I warn you that I will not have you importuning my girls. Do not address any of them again, Mr. Wickham, or I shall bring up this incident with your commanding officer."

Mr. Wickham bowed and turned on his heel, leaving the gardens immediately, though Elizabeth thought that she noticed a murderous glare on his face as he did so. Apparently, Mr. Bennet was not satisfied either, as he beckoned to the footman.

"Please ensure that Mr. Wickham has left the property. And when you have done so, please ask Mr. Hill to come and see me directly."

"Yes, sir," replied the footman before he left to follow Mr. Wickham away.

"Are you well, my dear?" asked Mr. Bennet as he turned to Elizabeth and grasped her hands.

"I am, Papa," said Elizabeth with a smile. "It appears that Mr. Wickham is so audacious as to expect that he can still flatter his way out of his predicament with nothing more than affected smiles and charming manners."

Her father chuckled. "I dare say you are correct. Given what Darcy has told me about the man, it seems like it is a shade in his character. One of many, I would surmise."

The light moment having passed, Mr. Bennet turned a serious look on Elizabeth. "My dear, I know that you love to walk outside, and with the commotion which is often present in the house, I do not blame you." Father and daughter shared a brief smile of commiseration. "But I must ask you to take great care. I do not trust this Mr. Wickham, and given what I have just seen, I do not think that he means to accept his lot quietly."

"I understand," said Elizabeth with a nod. "My long walks are largely curtailed due to the season, and when I walk in the gardens, I shall stay close to the house. If I should happen to see Mr. Wickham again, I shall return to the house directly."

"Good. I will tell the footman and Mr. Hill to watch out for you whenever you are out."

"And what of my sisters?" asked Elizabeth. "I should think that Lydia and Kitty are in more danger from Mr. Wickham than I."

"Due to their own silliness, perhaps, you could be correct. Of course, we shall be vigilant for all of your sakes, but Wickham seems to have singled you out, and that troubles me. I would not wish for you to be harmed by the man. Please indulge me in this."

"Of course, Papa," murmured Elizabeth.

They made their way back to the house, Elizabeth's hand in the crook of her father's arm, and she considered the warnings she had had from both Mr. Darcy and her father that day. In truth, Elizabeth did not know exactly what Mr. Wickham was capable of, but though she did not feel any great danger from the man, she decided she would take care. Better not to give the man an opportunity to hurt her than to be sorry that she had not taken precautions later.

Chapter XII

The business with Mr. Wickham was, in some respects, something of a blessing in disguise. Or it could be deemed that way from a certain perspective, given the fact that the man had not been able to harm the Bennets in any way.

Kitty and Lydia's situation was the easiest to discern, and Elizabeth, having given the matter considerable thought already, did not dwell on it over much. They were still not by any means proper young women, but Elizabeth thought that they had learned to think a little before they acted, which was certainly an improvement. Mary was as inscrutable as ever, and though Elizabeth could not state with certainty that Mary had changed to any great extent, she thought that Mary had at least lost a little of her former pomposity. As for Mr. Collins, well, he was a lost cause, but as he was not truly a member of the family—he was in fact more like an interloper to Elizabeth—she resolved not to think on the parson wherever possible. But the greatest change, perhaps, was that found in her father.

Now, it must be understood that Elizabeth had always been assured of her father's love for her and for her sisters. But it had never really been his love which was in question despite his regrettable habit of making sport with his children. Of more concern to Elizabeth had always been his commitment to the care and support of his family, both in molding her younger sisters into proper young women, and the circumstances of his family should he depart the world in an untimely fashion. He had always had a tendency to laugh things off, even those matters which Elizabeth considered to require his particular attention as head of the family.

But this matter with Mr. Wickham appeared to have spurred him to action as nothing Elizabeth had ever seen before. Suddenly, he was engaged in the family's concerns, intent upon protecting them from the immoral man who had recently been thrust into their midst. It reassured Elizabeth and spoke to his love for them all—he still was not perfect by any means, but when confronted with a situation which was a clear danger to his daughters, he was not inclined to sit back and allow events to unfold as they would.

Nothing further was heard from Mr. Wickham for those next few days—Elizabeth had learned through several sources that he was rarely seen in the village, which was probably for the best, as he was now looked on with suspicion rather than with smiling faces. He appeared to accept the colonel's restrictions, little though he appeared to like them.

Of Mr. Darcy, Elizabeth continued to see much, and the more she saw of the man, the more she began to understand him. Mr. Darcy could rarely be moved to speak of the situation regarding Mr. Wickham, tending to prefer to allow their discussions to proceed where whim took them. He was kind and solicitous and spirited in discussion, especially when it was a matter on which he possessed a strong opinion. He was always interested and eager to hear Elizabeth's opinions, and on the occasions where he did not agree—which were not a few, though they were less frequent than Elizabeth would have supposed—he listened carefully and responded with his own view while never disparaging hers.

In short, Mr. Darcy was a very agreeable suitor indeed. Of course, at this early juncture, he was not truly a suitor at all. He had not declared himself in any manner, though Elizabeth began to wonder if she did not wish him to declare himself. He was in fact an intelligent man, and Elizabeth was coming to the opinion that he would suit her very well. What she could not determine was the state of her heart, though she acknowledged to herself that if he continued on in this manner, that issue would be resolved swiftly.

Mr. Bingley had left on Wednesday, the day after the ball he had hosted at Netherfield, and the rest of the week proceeded agreeably, though Elizabeth was sensible of the fact that it might not have been so had it not been for Mr. Darcy's intervention. But Jane was reassured by Mr. Darcy's conviction that Mr. Bingley would return, and she was therefore quite content waiting. And while she waited, she took the opportunity to know Mr. Darcy better, though she was in no way in his company as much as Elizabeth was.

The one issue which arose between them was Mr. Darcy's reaction when he learned that Mr. Wickham had appeared at Longbourn. To say that he was displeased was a vast understatement.

"So the villain was here, was he?" said he, his countenance stony and displeased.

"He was indeed," replied Elizabeth, keeping her tone lighthearted. "He seemed to think—yet again, I might add—that he had been done a disservice and that his account should be believed implicitly, regardless of his obvious impropriety."

Mr. Darcy's expression was positively furious, and when he spoke, his tone was harsh. "I care not what he says or claims about *me*—I have dealt with him before. But I will not have him importuning *you*."

For perhaps the first time, Elizabeth realized Mr. Darcy's protectiveness toward those of his acquaintance, and she recognized that she was included in that sphere. It sent a little shiver up her spine to know that she was esteemed to the point where he would turn his considerable displeasure on another at even the hint of threatening behavior, and it was still a wonder to her, regardless of what she had learned at the ball and what his behavior had been since.

"It seems to me that perhaps Wickham has not learned his lesson," continued Mr. Darcy. "I believe some further *explaining* is required before it penetrates his thick head."

"Mr. Darcy," said Elizabeth quietly.

The man started and looked at her, almost as if he had forgotten her in his displeasure. His expression instantly softened, and he captured one of her gloved hands, bringing it to his mouth and bestowing a kiss on its back with tenderness. This time, the shiver was almost enough to cause Elizabeth's entire body to shake. But she focused on the man rather than the sensations he was causing and said:

"I am well, Mr. Darcy. My father was here to protect me, and even if he was not, I doubt that Mr. Wickham had any intention of harming me."

"Be that as it may, I cannot have him importuning you, Miss Bennet."

"And I shall beware of him and not give him the opportunity to do so. My walks are curtailed and limited to the gardens with the cold weather, and even if we should happen to be in company with one another, I shall stay away from him. He is being constrained for perhaps the first time in his life, Mr. Darcy, and such restrictions are causing him to lash out. Let us just leave him be so that we do not push him to any further desperation."

Mr. Darcy peered at her for a few moments before he sighed and smiled. "Very well. I shall not push this any further. But I wish you to be careful."

"Of course," replied Elizabeth, happy that he had listened to her and seen the sense of her words. He had been his own master for many years, and she was certain that he was used to following his own counsel and acting in a manner in which he saw fit. That he was willing to listen to her—a country miss of a mere twenty summers—boded very well indeed.

Of course, the mere thought shocked Elizabeth, though she was careful not to allow her reaction to show on her face. That she was willing to entertain such thoughts at all was surprising since she could not even name what she felt for him to herself, let alone others. It was something upon which she would need to think.

The week progressed apace, and the end of the week was to be looked on with anticipation, not only for the expected return of Mr. Bingley, but also due to Mr. Collins's imminent departure. Now, it must be said that Mr. Collins had not importuned Elizabeth further since day that he had accompanied Mr. Darcy and Mr. Bennet to Meryton to look into the matter of Mr. Wickham's debts. But Elizabeth had been easily able to detect his disapproval whenever he saw them together. He held his tongue and turned his attentions even more fervently on Mary, though she knew he wished to make his opinion known.

What Elizabeth was unable to determine was the state of her sister's feelings. Mary continued to accept the man's company and to allow him to give her his attentions, but though Elizabeth had always supposed that such attentions would bring a willing receiver much pleasure, she could detect no such reaction in her sister. In fact, as the week wore on, Elizabeth fancied that Mary was becoming even quieter than was her wont. But the reason for this taciturnity was beyond Elizabeth's ability to understand.

On Friday of that week, all was to become clear. Mr. Collins was to return to Kent on Saturday, as his leave was to expire, and Mr. Collins did not mean to return without obtaining a betrothed as his patroness had demanded. He had apparently resolved that Friday would be the day that he made his addresses and obtained the promise of Mary's hand. But unfortunately for the hapless parson, events did not proceed as he had hoped.

It came about after breakfast that morning. The day was fine, so Elizabeth had declared her intention to spend some time out of doors in the gardens, walking about the property. What she had not expected was that one of her sisters would insist upon coming with her.

"Lizzy, I believe I should like to accompany you," said Mary somewhat diffidently.

Though she was slightly puzzled at this behavior, Elizabeth smiled at her sister. "Of course, Mary. I would be pleased if you would walk with me."

Elizabeth had avowed her pleasure, but it was evident that there was one other in the house who was not pleased that Mary would leave the house. But Mr. Collins quickly recovered, however, and he announced his attention to attend the sisters on their walk, and Elizabeth, as she could not do otherwise and remain polite, agreed.

The first astonishing part of the coming outing came when Elizabeth and Mary were gathering their warm clothing. As soon as Mr. Collins was out of earshot, Mary turned to Elizabeth and whispered: "No matter what Mr. Collins says, please do not leave me, Lizzy!"

"Of course, Mary," replied Elizabeth through her surprise. "But I dare say that Mr. Collins is harmless."

Mary did not respond to her jest, as Mr. Collins had approached them—instead, she directed a pointed look at Elizabeth before turning to the parson, who had begun to speak.

"Shall we move outside, cousins?" said he in his normally obsequious tone. "It is wonderful to see such confidence between sisters. Indeed, with such loveliness before me, I believe I must consider myself to be the luckiest of men."

Having been looking in her sister's direction, Elizabeth managed to see Mary's reaction to the parson's speech, and she was thus shocked to see Mary actually roll her eyes. She was able to stifle a laugh by coughing into her hand, but the gesture made her begin to understand what Mary was about.

They spent some time out in the gardens, Elizabeth walking as she normally did while Mr. Collins and Mary generally walked together. Mr. Collins was at his most loquacious, making up for Elizabeth's silence and the fact that Mary said very little as well.

But even this seemed to wear on the parson after a while, as Elizabeth, sensing that Mary truly did not wish to return to the house, stayed out for longer than she otherwise would have. And the longer they stayed outside, the less Mr. Collins had to say. By the time they had been walking for forty-five minutes, the parson seemed to have exhausted even his almost limitless ability to speak.

When a further fifteen minutes had passed, he suddenly stopped and turned to the two sisters. "Though this activity is most pleasing indeed, is it not time to return to the house?"

"I believe that I am quite comfortable here, Mr. Collins," said Mary before Elizabeth could speak.

Mr. Collins's eyes widened comically at this response, but he gamely pressed his case. "But my young cousin," protested he, "I wish to have a most particular conversation with you, and I believe it is more comfortably had in one of Longbourn's well-appointed rooms than in the chill of the garden."

"But it is a fine day, is it not?" replied Mary. "I am very well right here. I believe that this conversation if yours will keep."

It was several minutes before Mr. Collins could respond to such a statement. Indeed, he did not know what to make of it at all. By now, Elizabeth was certain that Mary was trying to evade a proposal of marriage from the hapless parson. And though Elizabeth was well aware of the parson's ability to woo without a hint of encouragement, she would have thought that Mary's avoidance would have penetrated even his obliviousness. But unfortunately, it was not to be.

A few minutes later, Mr. Collins tried once again.

"Then perhaps, if my cousin Elizabeth will indulge me with a few moments of relative privacy, we can have our conversation here."

Elizabeth looked to her sister for direction, but Mary had turned her gaze toward the ground, and she appeared as if she was not about to look up any time soon. It became apparent at this point that regardless of Mary's wishes, Mr. Collins would have his say. It was best to allow him to do so as quickly as may be, and then Mary could refuse him if she was so inclined.

"Very well," said Elizabeth, noticing the way Mary's eyes left the ground to peer at her with equal parts confusion and betrayal. Elizabeth smiled at her and said carefully: "I believe, Mary, that it would be best if you allowed Mr. Collins to speak. Perhaps he has something to say which you would like to hear."

Mr. Collins smiled widely and almost appeared to preen at Elizabeth's words, and she was sure that he was excessively confident of his success. Elizabeth was not so certain, but she looked at Mary and could see that her sister had understood the thrust of her words and now appeared to be accepting of her fate. Elizabeth retreated a little in order to give them a little privacy, while staying close enough that she could be of use to her sister. Mary turned toward Mr. Collins with apparent trepidation, and as Mr. Collins began to speak, he made no attempt to moderate his tone, which allowed Elizabeth to hear every word that was spoken.

"My dear cousin Mary," began he, "if I was not already assured of your situation and need to make a good marriage, I might have suspected you of attempting to dissemble. Of course, I am also aware of the coquettishness of the fairer sex, and I know that you are known to use such devices in order to increase your suitors' love by suspense, regardless of your ultimate intention to accept when offered for. I must salute you, my dear cousin, for increasing the violence of my affections through your actions.

"But at some point, we must have a serious conversation about our futures, and as you are aware, I must return to Kent tomorrow. And as it is the particular advice of my excellent patroness that I marry immediately, I would not return to Kent without the ability to bear the news of my betrothal to her ladyship.

"As for my particular choice, I believe that all families should live in the harmony of mutual society and affection, and regardless of your father's offenses against my late, honored father, 'to forgive is divine,' after all."

Though the parson's words were offensive, Elizabeth knew that he was not intending them to be so—he was simply too oblivious, too wrapped up in his own selfish concerns to even truly understand the effect of his words. This was the only reason why Elizabeth kept her own counsel and did not interrupt Mr. Collins in his ramblings, much though she would have preferred to do just that. But though Mary said nothing, Elizabeth could see a tightening of her lips, and she knew that Mr. Collins was not recommending himself to her with his words. Unfortunately for the oblivious parson, his method of declaring himself would only become worse.

"Though you were not my first choice—indeed, I was quite captivated by your elder sisters' beauty when I first entered your father's house—I was forced to acknowledge that your piety, your adherence to the dictates of Fordyce, and your attention to the words of our Lord are pleasing indeed. In this matter, I flatter myself that to look for the finer attributes in a partner, rather than being blinded by beauty, is very commendable, and it will only increase your estimation for my person.

"Once we have been married, you will have a home in my very comfortable parsonage to call your own, and once your father has left this mortal life, you will find yourself established in an estate of your own. And while we live in Kent, you will enjoy the patronage of the honorable Lady Catherine de Bourgh, who is the very soul of condescension and who shall be instrumental, I am sure, in helping you to acclimate to your new situation. Indeed, I believe that it is a very fortunate situation for you, and I am assured that you feel likewise.

"My dearest Mary," continued he, a supercilious smile on his face. He was indeed very certain of himself and his being accepted. "I must conclude with an expression of how very much I esteem you and wish for you to become my bride. With your permission, I shall go to your father directly and obtain his consent for our engagement."

With those final words, the parson fell mercifully silent, and Elizabeth stared at him in shock. Elizabeth could not imagine a more insulting proposal. During the course of it, Mr. Collins had managed to insult Mary's beauty, her future prospects, and her family, not to mention he had placed the blame for the distance between his father and theirs upon Mr. Bennet. And to top it all off, he had made it very clear that she had *not* been his first choice, and he had not even gotten around to actually asking the question! Elizabeth could well imagine laughing in his face had the proposal been directed at *her*, but as it was Mary who had to answer to it, Elizabeth held her tongue and waited to hear the response.

At length, Mary was able to give the parson her reply, though it was not quite what Elizabeth was expecting. Mary took a deep breath, and she looked up at the parson, and in a clear voice, she said: "I am sorry, Mr. Collins, but I cannot accept your proposal."

Clearly, the parson was shocked that Mary had the audacity not only to refuse him, but also to do so without even a hint of explanation. His mouth worked with no sound issuing forth for several moments before he appeared to gather himself. He then turned an unctuous smile on her, though Elizabeth could tell that he was much less self-assured than he had been before.

"My dearest Mary," said he, "there is no further need to increase my love by suspense. I assure you that I am already completely besotted. "

"You certainly fooled me," snapped Mary.

Mr. Collins appeared perplexed at her words, but before he could say anything, Mary once again said: "I am not attempting to increase your love for me. I am simply refusing your proposal."

"This is unseemly," said Mr. Collins with considerable displeasure and a glower on his face. "I am assured that you have no other prospects, and you are not likely to have any in the near future. It would be foolish for you to reject my proposal. I suggest you do not try my patience."

"I am not trying your patience, sir," said Mary. "I simply will not marry you."

With a face like a thundercloud, Mr. Collins tried once more. "I shall speak with your father! He will make you see sense!"

"Do as you will," replied Mary with a dismissive wave. "My father will not even make my youngest sisters behave in company. I am assured he will not force me to marry against my will."

Mary turned to Elizabeth, motioning that she wished to leave—and that the parson was most definitely *not* invited—but she paused after a moment and turned back to Mr. Collins, who was still staring at her with an expression of utter stupefaction on his face.

"In the future, Mr. Collins, I suggest that should you have the opportunity to propose to some other young lady, you should do so with considerably fewer words, lest you offend her. Pointing out that a woman is *not* your first choice and that a woman has no other prospects is not the best way to go about inciting her acceptance of your suit."

Turning on her heel, Mary then marched away without a second glance back at the man. Elizabeth took one more look at him, noting the rising anger in his countenance and the way he regarded her retreating form with growing resentment, before she turned and hurried after Mary, who was retreating at a far greater pace than Elizabeth had ever seen exhibited by her sister before.

She followed Mary in silence, noting that Mary's gait could only be termed as stalking, and she was sure that the expression on Mary's face could have frozen a gorgon. Mary led them to the far end of the garden, where she suddenly stopped and flopped down on a nearby bench. Elizabeth's conjectures about Mary's state of mind held true, as Mary's face held an expression of displeasure which Elizabeth had rarely seen.

"The nerve of that man!" said Mary with a huff. "I dare say that he will have difficulty inducing *any woman* to accept him if he behaves in such a fashion."

Elizabeth agreed with her sister and sat down, looking at Mary carefully. "Surely you knew that he was not the most intellectually gifted man, Mary. Given what his pronouncements have been since his arrival, I am surprised that you would react in this manner."

Mary snorted. "I am not surprised in the slightest that he would botch his proposal. It was more the degree of idiocy to which the man descended that I find surprising."

Regarding her sister with some interest, Elizabeth said, "Come now, Mary, this cannot be your reason for refusing him. I know that you did not disfavor him when he suddenly shifted his affections from me to you. Surely there is something more to this than an insulting proposal from an insensible man."

Sighing, Mary lowered her head and looked at the ground. Elizabeth waited while her sister collected her thoughts, noting that Mary's anger seemed to have departed, only to be replaced by a certain melancholy. When Mary finally looked up at Elizabeth, it was with an expression of some pain, which took Elizabeth aback.

"I overheard your conversation with him," confessed Mary, and she immediately looked away.

"Overheard . . ." Elizabeth trailed off, thinking back to the previous few days. It soon became evident that the conversation to which Mary referred was the one which had occurred the morning after the ball, in which she had dissuaded Mr. Collins from returning his attentions back to her.

Chagrined, Elizabeth turned to her sister and said with some distress, "Oh, Mary. I hope you do not blame me for not telling you what he said."

"It does not matter," replied Mary dismissively. "I might not have given much credence to the matter had I not overheard it myself. I now understand why you should never eavesdrop—you never do hear anything good about yourself, do you?

"But regardless, hearing the way Mr. Collins was ready to transfer his affections back to you forced me to understand what sort of man he is. I realized that I would never be happy with him, and I resolved in that instant to refuse him should he ever condescend to ask."

"And he did condescend, indeed," said Elizabeth with a laugh.

Mary joined in, crying, "Indeed, he did! I have not been subject to much exposure on the subject, but I cannot imagine a worse proposal than the one to which Mr. Collins just subjected me!"

The sisters fell into each other's arms, their mirth at their ridiculous cousin flowing freely in their laughter. It was in fact somewhat of a new experience for Elizabeth, as she thought that she had not laughed with Mary in such a manner since they had been children. Even then she was certain that the times would have been relatively infrequent, as Mary had always been such a serious child.

When their mirth ran its course, Mary settled into her seat, and it seemed as if her melancholy had once again returned. She stayed silent for several moments before she turned to Elizabeth, and in a voice which seemed especially vulnerable, she said:

"Do you think Mr. Collins is right, Lizzy?"

"What do you mean?" asked Elizabeth, looking at her sister askance.

"That I won't ever have any other prospects for marriage." Mary looked at Elizabeth, a hint of a pleading expression on her countenance. "Have I just thrown away my only chance at matrimony?"

Elizabeth shifted closer to Mary and put her arm around her younger sister. "Mary, I would advise you to give Mr. Collins's words nary a second thought. He is senseless and unkind, and I do not doubt that there will be other opportunities for you . . . with men who are much more agreeable than William Collins."

Though appearing grateful at Elizabeth's words, Mary still looked anxious. "I know I'm not my mother's favorite child—"

"I could never claim to be so myself!" exclaimed Elizabeth.

Mary smiled and nodded. "I suppose not, as neither of us are beautiful enough or wild enough to lay claim to that honor. But Mama always . . . Well . . . She has never thought much of me, and I know that she considers me to be the most problematic when it comes to attracting a husband."

"Listen to what you are saying," replied Elizabeth in a firm and authoritative tone of voice. "Mama thinks of one thing only. I love her dearly, but in her way, she is as senseless as our cousin."

Still, Mary appeared unconvinced, so Elizabeth took her hands and gazed at her with affection. "Mary, you are not perfect—none of us are. There are perhaps some things that you could change to make yourself more attractive to a man."

"Such as?" prompted Mary.

Wondering how open she should be with her sister, Elizabeth considered the matter. The earnest look that Mary was giving her suggested that she wished Elizabeth to be honest with her, and after a moment's thought, Elizabeth decided that she could be honest but still be kind. Mary's view of herself appeared to be somewhat fragile, and it would not do to crush it.

"First," said Elizabeth, "I would suggest a change of the way you style your hair. I know that you believe that your bun shows you to be a demure young lady, but it does make you seem a little severe. We can change it and still keep it demure while showing you off to better advantage.

"Next, a little more flattering cut to your gowns would be beneficial."

Mary stared at Elizabeth with a steely glare. "You will not dress me up like Lydia."

"Actually, Mary, Lydia's dresses do not breach propriety," said Elizabeth. "I know that at times they are perhaps a little daring, but our mother will not allow any of her daughters to appear to any disadvantage, and that includes dressing us inappropriately. You prefer a more modest cut, which is fine. But there are ways to enhance your wardrobe without compromising your modesty."

Though she thought about it for a moment, Mary eventually nodded her agreement, and Elizabeth smiled at her. Mary was not merely plain—her lack of physical beauty was often remarked upon *in comparison to that of her sisters*. In fact, Mary's features were pleasant and could be enhanced if she would only take the trouble to dress to her best effect.

"Is there anything else?" asked Mary.

At that point, Elizabeth decided against bringing up Mary's devotion to Fordyce and her sometimes pompous pronouncements. Coaxing Mary out of her shell would almost certainly have the effect of lessening those, as Elizabeth was aware that they often came about due to her penchant for being alone. Instead, Elizabeth decided to focus on something else.

"I believe that the appearance of enjoyment in a ballroom would almost certainly encourage men to ask you to dance."

"I would enjoy a ballroom much better if I was not so frequently a spectator," muttered Mary.

Elizabeth smiled at her sister. "In that case, I believe that we should begin your transformation, so that you may dazzle the young men of Meryton. Come, Mary. Let us go to your room and try out a few new styles for your hair. I have some ideas which I think would suit you very well indeed."

They stood to return to the house, but Elizabeth, thinking on the matter a little further, stopped her sister and turned a serious look on her.

"Mary, I'm proud of you for standing up for yourself and refusing Mr. Collins—in our situation, it is not easy to refuse an objectionable suitor. But remember that life can be long, and if you choose your marriage partner unwisely, it can be very difficult indeed.

"I will not tell you who you should or should not marry, but I would advise you to take great care in making your choice. Do not compromise merely for the sake of security, I implore you."

"Thank you, Elizabeth," replied Mary. "I shall." Then Mary grasped her arm and pulled her along from the garden, exclaiming: "Now let us go to my room and try your ideas for my hair!"

Caught up in Mary's enthusiasm, Elizabeth smiled and allowed herself to be dragged back to the house. As they walked, Elizabeth reflected that much as Lydia and Kitty had turned out to be, Mary was actually a pleasant girl when she took the time to actually speak with her. This whole sequence of events was perhaps not easy for Elizabeth to take in, but it was leading toward closer relationships with her sisters, and that was something which could not be repined.

Chapter XIII

When Elizabeth and Mary returned to the house, it was to the sound of raised voices.

Within moments they could hear that the voices belonged to an obviously irate Mr. Collins and an equally angry Mr. Bennet. It was apparent that Mr. Collins, having been rejected by Mary, had instantly sought out Mr. Bennet and attempted to forward his suit with the father since the daughter could not be prevailed upon to accept him. Privately, Elizabeth wondered at the parson's senselessness—how could he actually want a bride who did not wish to be married to him? Was he so lost in Lady Catherine's edicts that he was desperate enough to attempt to force marriage on a young woman who neither wanted nor esteemed him? It appeared it was so.

They entered the house with the sound of male voices literally ringing throughout the halls, only to be accosted by Kitty and Lydia the moment they entered.

"It seems like Lizzy is not the only one to have caused a ruckus," said Lydia with a giggle as soon as she espied them.

"Mr. Collins is fit to be tied," added Kitty, watching as the servants took Mary's and Elizabeth's outer wear. "What did you do to anger him so?"

"Not now, Kitty," said Lydia with a sly look. "Mama wishes to see you in the parlor this very instant, Mary."

Mary's countenance paled at that news, and Elizabeth looked on with some sympathy. Though Elizabeth agreed with Mary's right to refuse Mr. Collins's proposal and knew that their father would support her, it was a simple fact that Mrs. Bennet would almost certainly *not* understand. Her mother had made it her mission in life to see her daughters married, and she would almost certainly not take well to one of her own daughters frustrating and delaying that desire.

"Lizzy, please stay with me," pleaded Mary.

"Of course, Mary," said Elizabeth with a nod and a smile.

This interplay appeared to confuse Kitty and Lydia, as they were not used to seeing Elizabeth and Mary in one another's confidence. Elizabeth decided to ignore that for the time being and began to shepherd an obviously anxious Mary into the room. In truth, Elizabeth had never intended for even an instant to leave her sister alone to face her mother. She was confident in her own ability to resist Mrs. Bennet's schemes and stand up for herself, but Mary's ability to do the same was very much in doubt.

"Mary!" rang out Mrs. Bennet's shrill voice. "Come in here this instant!"

"Oh, Lord!" exclaimed Mary, who appeared as if she would prefer to be almost anywhere than in the parlor facing her mother's inquisition.

Elizabeth, though surprised that Mary would actually use such language, steadied her and spoke into her ear as they walked. "Do not worry, Mary. I will be with you."

"But you know Mama," whispered Mary in return.

"Yes, I do, but I also know Mama is protective of her daughters. Perhaps word of how Mr. Collins attempted to return his attentions back to me will induce Mama to be more sympathetic."

Mary appeared to start for a moment before she turned and peered at Elizabeth. "Do you really think that would help?"

"I think that regardless of how thoughtless she can sometimes be, Mama does not take well to a slight against *any* of her daughters. I doubt that this instance will be different than when Mr. Darcy slighted me at the assembly. *I* am not our mother's favorite daughter, as you are well aware, yet she was quite offended."

This time, Mary said nothing in response, but it was clear from her demeanor that she had taken comfort from Elizabeth's words. For her part, Elizabeth knew that whatever fuss Mrs. Bennet made concerning the matter would ultimately mean nothing as long as Mary stood firm.

And certainly, as Mary had said, she was not her mother's favorite daughter, so it was not as if a withdrawal of Mrs. Bennet's favor was something to be feared.

They entered the parlor to the not unexpected sight of Mrs. Bennet's displeasure. Elizabeth, quite used to her mother's moods, was not affected in the slightest, but Mary, long accustomed to existing below her mother's notice, was clearly not as sanguine. Still, she showed admirable composure and marched into the room with her head held high, and if Mrs. Bennet's narrowed eyes were any indication, she was aware of the defiance which almost bled from Mary's very person.

"Mary!" exclaimed Mrs. Bennet as they approached. "What is this I hear about you refusing Mr. Collins?"

Lydia and Kitty, who had come in behind them, gasped in response—apparently, they had not known the reason for their mother's displeasure, though Elizabeth thought with some amusement that they might have guessed had they been paying more attention.

"A refused proposal!" exclaimed Lydia.

"What fun!" chimed in Kitty with a clap of her hands.

"Quiet, girls!" snapped Mrs. Bennet. She then turned her imperious glare back on Mary. "I am waiting, Mary."

If anything, her tone appeared to irk Mary, who responded in kind. "I *have* refused Mr. Collins, Mama. He was in no way suitable as a husband."

"Whatever can you mean? As Mr. Collins's wife, you would be the next mistress of this estate. How could he possibly be unsuitable?"

"He is in every way ridiculous," was Mary's reply. "His attentions are repugnant, and he is inconstant. I am convinced I would be miserable as his wife."

Mrs. Bennet's nostrils flared, and she turned on Elizabeth. "I suppose you had something to do with this? You told me that Mary would accept his addresses if I allowed him to shift his attentions."

"I said no such thing, Mama," replied Elizabeth in a stern tone. "I merely said that I thought Mary would be amenable to marrying Mr. Collins. Regardless, I do not believe that Mr. Collins has acquitted himself well as a suitor."

"Of what can you be speaking?" demanded her mother. She rounded on Mary. "You told me that you were not averse to Mr. Collins's attentions."

Her final words were spoken in an accusatory tone, but if anything, it only made Mary's countenance harden in response. "I have changed my mind, Mama. I was willing to accept his addresses until he proved himself unworthy of my regard by attempting to return his attentions back to Lizzy."

With a displeased expression, Mrs. Bennet regarded her daughters, who merely looked back at her placidly. A brief glance at Mary showed her to be calm, and Elizabeth immediately felt proud of her sister for the fortitude she was showing in the face of their mother's displeasure.

"Of what are you talking?" asked Mrs. Bennet after a brief pause.

"The day after the ball at Netherfield, Mr. Collins attempted to return his attentions to Lizzy," replied Mary.

"Is this true, Lizzy?"

It was easy to see that her mother's ire was quickly being directed from her middle daughter to the detested parson, though Elizabeth knew that she still needed convincing. But for the time being, she decided to keep her answer simple in order to engage her mother further in the matter.

"Yes, Mama."

"Why?" said Mrs. Bennet impatiently.

"I believe that he was concerned that I was encroaching on Miss de Bourgh's territory." Elizabeth could immediately see Mrs. Bennet's thoughts moving to her still somewhat nebulous relationship with Mr. Darcy. Elizabeth did not want this to become a discussion about Mr. Darcy, so she quickly added, "I told him that it was not proper for him to attempt to redirect his attention back to me when he had already excited Mary's expectations."

Mrs. Bennet looked at them with an air of injured exasperation. "Why was I not told of this?" demanded she. Glancing at Mary before fixing her gaze once more on Elizabeth, she continued in an accusing tone: "You told your sister of it. I should be notified of such things."

"I did not tell Mary, as I did not believe that it was my place to interfere. In fact, I did not know until this morning that Mary knew of the matter at all."

"I overheard them, Mama," interjected Mary.

"And what exactly did Mr. Collins say?"

Elizabeth related the account of her conversation with Mr. Collins and watched as her mother appeared to move from displeasure at her daughter's refusal of her suitor to annoyance that Mr. Collins would behave in such a manner—even Mrs. Bennet was not so blind to proper behavior as to miss the inconstancy of the parson's manners.

However, she obviously was still unable to reconcile this with her ever-present desire to have her girls married off as soon as may be, regardless of how repulsive that suitor should be. It was extremely diverting to watch as she struggled, and Elizabeth was not surprised when she decided to make one last attempt to salvage the situation and not lose Mr. Collins as a suitor.

"Surely you can overlook the matter," whined she.

"Would *you* wish to be married to such a man?" was Elizabeth's arch reply.

"I would be willing to put up with much to ensure the security of myself and my family."

"Perhaps so, but not everyone has the same opinion, Mama," said Elizabeth pointedly. "Some would prefer to be respectable in their marriages. Respectability would be difficult to obtain should one marry a man such as William Collins."

This reminder of their previous conversation was enough to deflate Mrs. Bennet's arguments quite neatly, and Elizabeth was able to have the satisfaction of knowing that she had scored a significant point.

"Well, it must be so, if you put it like that." She then became almost offended in her displeasure, though this time it was not directed at her daughters. "Mr. Collins is very much like his father, I dare say. Very ill-favored and entirely too full of himself."

Though amused at her mother's abrupt change of stance, Elizabeth was intrigued by her words. "I was not aware that you were at all acquainted with Mr. Collins's father."

"As much acquainted as I ever wished to be," said Mrs. Bennet with a derisive sniff. "He opposed my marriage to your father, you know. He was a man of the cloth himself, yet he acted like he was the Duke of Devonshire himself! A more pompous man I have never had the misfortune to meet—even Mr. Collins's airs are nothing to his father's, I assure you."

The five sisters looked at each other in surprise. "*That* was the genesis of Papa's disagreement with Mr. Collins's father?" asked Elizabeth.

"Indeed, it was," said Mrs. Bennet. And though Elizabeth was surprised by the intelligence of which she had never heard anything previously, she was also a little diverted by her mother's sudden change of heart. Gone was the almost manic desire to have one of her daughters married to the man, to be replaced by an affront at the man and his father, as if she had just remembered what had passed between them all those years ago.

"So you had met the younger Mr. Collins when he was still a boy?" asked Jane.

"I never laid eyes on him before he arrived at our door,"

contradicted Mrs. Bennet. "The elder Mr. Collins and your father had never truly been close, and Mr. Collins's parish was in Norfolk, making travel long and difficult. But when he heard of our engagement, he journeyed here, intent on making your father 'see sense,' as he referred to it." Mrs. Bennet's indelicate snort illuminated quite clearly what she thought of *that* particular concept. "As my father was an attorney — though the grandson of a gentleman himself — I suppose I was not good enough for Mr. Collins."

"Is that not the very essence of hubris?" queried Lydia with a frown. "Surely Mr. Collins, not being a gentleman himself, could have nothing to say concerning whom his cousin married."

"One would think." Mrs. Bennet sniffed with disdain. "Unfortunately, the apple does not fall far from the tree. Mr. Collins is much like his father in his unfortunate lack of sense."

The Bennet girls all snickered and exchanged amused glances. Not a one of them missed the irony in their mother's statement. It seemed that Mrs. Bennet was not to bemoan the loss of Mr. William Collins as a son-in-law as vociferously as she might otherwise have done.

But it was at that moment when the raised male voices, which could be heard in the background during the course of their discussion, suddenly became louder before ceasing entirely. They were replaced by the sound of rapidly approaching footsteps, and then Mr. Collins opened the door — none too gently — and entered the room. Displeasure could easily be seen in the dark scowl which adorned his face and the way he eschewed greeting them when he entered the room. Then, in a clipped tone, he turned his attention to Mary.

"My dear cousin Mary," said he, "it seems your father has seen fit to ignore his duty of talking some sense into you regarding my most eligible offer, so I have decided that I shall allow you some time to think about your future."

As he stared down his nose, as haughty as a prince, Elizabeth had to fight the urge to laugh in his face.

"I shall return to Kent and then arrange to visit again in one month's time. I suggest that you use the time I have afforded you to think very carefully of your future, for if you refuse me again, I shall not ask a third time."

"By my count I have already refused your suit three times, Mr. Collins," said Mary.

Elizabeth looked at her sister and silently applauded the evenness of her demeanor. She also suspected that Mary had responded so quickly because she did not wish her mother to entertain any notion of salvaging the situation.

"I was perfectly serious in my refusal, Mr. Collins. I beg you to refrain from inviting me to decline a fourth time."

If Elizabeth had thought that Mr. Collins was incensed before, it was nothing compared to the utter fury which suffused his features then. But for a moment, even the voluminous ability of Mr. Collins to speak was suppressed as he struggled for a way to respond to Mary's speech. Sadly, the moment was not to last.

"I cannot even begin to understand how a young lady of little accomplishment and no beauty could refuse my offer. Are you completely senseless?"

"You forget yourself, sir!" exclaimed Elizabeth. "If that is to be your behavior, I can only applaud Mary for refusing you."

Mr. Collins favored Elizabeth with a disdainful huff before he turned his displeasure on Mrs. Bennet. "And you, madam. First, you direct my choice from your eldest to your second daughter—who is perhaps the most impertinent and improper young lady I have ever had the misfortune to meet—and then you direct me toward your third and plainest daughter, all the while promising me that she will be amenable to the match. Will you not do your duty and prevail upon her to accept my suit, thereby ensuring your own security in the event of your husband's death?"

It was a powerful argument, Elizabeth knew, and for a moment, she almost thought that her mother would give in to the pressure exerted by the parson. But apparently her better nature and her protectiveness toward her daughters conquered her desired future security, and her expression darkened.

"I believe the audacity is all yours, Mr. Collins," replied she in a superior tone. Elizabeth almost thought it similar to the one Caroline Bingley had used so often. "After insulting my daughters so reprehensibly, you expect me to prevail against their wishes and make them marry you? And you did not think my Lizzy so very unsuitable when you beseeched her to allow you to direct your attentions on her after you had already bestowed them on Mary. I would not have my daughters marry you were you the very prince regent himself!"

His countenance mottled with anger, Mr. Collins turned on Elizabeth and said in a voice which was almost a bellow: "My cousin Elizabeth, this is most highly irregular! I am shocked to hear your mother say such. I would have expected a private conversation to remain private! How dare you proclaim it to all your family?"

"Perhaps you should take care to modulate the tone of your voice when you make such inappropriate statements, Mr. Collins," said Mary, holding her head high. "Elizabeth did not tell me of your conversation; you told me yourself."

Mr. Collins was truly taken aback by this intelligence, but he quickly recovered and favored Mary with a sneer. "It seems that you are as improper as your sisters. For shame, my cousin, to be listening to conversations meant to remain between others."

"That is enough, Mr. Collins!"

Mr. Bennet stepped into the room and moved to stand with his family. "I will not allow you to importune my wife or daughters any longer. Have done with this subject, or you shall leave my house forthwith."

A hard expression came over Mr. Collins's face, and his rage made him appear to even less advantage than ever. He glared at the entire Bennet family as though he had been insulted in the worst possible manner.

"I believe I understand what is happening here," growled he. "Your eldest believes that she shall soon capture a man of fortune, and even worse, you are actually encouraging your second daughter to attempt an entrapment of a man of the highest lineage. And with these supposed conquests, you have suddenly become too high and mighty for me."

"Mr. Collins," snapped Mr. Bennet, "I shall not tell you again. If you insult my daughters once more, I shall throw you from the house."

"I shall be very happy indeed to depart," said Mr. Collins. "Do not think that your designs shall ever succeed. Mr. Darcy shall not be importuned by the likes of you. I shall relate this matter in full to my patroness, and I assure you that she will know what is to be done. She will be most seriously displeased!"

And with that, Mr. Collins turned on his heel and marched from the room without a backward glance. Throwing an amused glance at Elizabeth, Mr. Bennet crossed the room and pulled on the cord to summon a servant. In a moment, Mr. Hill, the butler, entered the room.

"Mr. Collins has decided to leave us a day early," instructed Mr. Bennet. "Please see that he leaves the house directly. Once he leaves, he will not be welcomed back without explicit instruction from myself or Mrs. Bennet."

Mr. Hill acknowledged the directive with a word and a bow, and then he quit the room.

When the family had been left alone, Mr. Bennet turned his amused gaze back to his family. Kitty and Lydia were already giggling nearly uncontrollably at the spectacle they had just witnessed, and while Jane was every inch the serene young lady she had ever been, Elizabeth thought she detected a certain amusement in her sister's demeanor. Mary appeared a little shaken by the confrontation, prompting Elizabeth to stay close to her, while Mrs. Bennet appeared the most affronted by the parson's manner.

"Well, well," said Mr. Bennet in his normally playful tone, "I suppose that we have seen the last of Mr. Collins."

"And good riddance, I say," exclaimed Mrs. Bennet. "My first impression of him was entirely correct—he is as odious a man as I have ever met. Even his father never rose to such obnoxious levels."

"Although I am reluctant to contradict you, my dear Mrs. Bennet," said Mr. Bennet, "your statement is altogether untrue. Mr. William Collins is but a babe next to his father in his talent to render himself insufferable. You simply did not have the exposure to the elder Mr. Collins which would have allowed you to come to that conclusion."

Mrs. Bennet sniffed and sat in her chair rather primly. "I am sure I would like nothing better than to never lay see the man again."

"While I cannot promise that, Mrs. Bennet, I should rather doubt that we will see him here again as long as I live."

With that, Mr. Bennet turned to Mary, and approaching his middle daughter, he caught up her hand and squeezed it with some affection. "I commend your ability and foresight in refusing him, Mary. I would have allowed the engagement had you truly wished to marry him, but I believe you have made the correct decision. He is in no way suitable to be a husband to any of my girls."

Mary smiled wanly at her father. "I had come to that conclusion myself, Papa."

"Very well," said Mr. Bennet. "I believe we have had enough excitement for one day. Should anyone ask for me, I shall be in my library."

And with that, he left the room. The Bennet women did not remain in the parlor for long themselves after his departure. Lydia and Kitty left to go visit Mariah Lucas and share with her the inanities of the morning while Mary dragged Elizabeth, in the company of Jane, up to her room to begin to experiment with styling her hair.

Thus, when Mr. Collins left only a little later that morning, it was to the laughter of the three eldest daughters as they twisted Mary's hair this way and that, sculpting it into different styles and arrangements, some which looked utterly silly, while others looked very well indeed. It could only be conjectured what the parson's thoughts were at the time, but Elizabeth thought she could guess, even without being given the maid's description of his very sour look and his almost unseemly haste to quit the house.

No member of the Bennet family repined his departure. Indeed, each and every one wished for the next pleasure of his company to be postponed indefinitely, though, Mr. Bennet also looked upon the permanent absence of the man with a small degree of regret; his *was* a rather entertaining sort of inanity, after all.

Chapter XIV

"Truly, Mr. Darcy, there is no cause to be upset," said Elizabeth. Mr. Darcy turned an upraised eyebrow toward her and regarded her with seeming skepticism. "Do you not take offense to the accusations Mr. Collins laid at your feet?"

"I might if he were a sensible man, Mr. Darcy," replied Elizabeth, her gentle smile attempting to appease him and let him know that she took no offense. "You have met the man, Mr. Darcy, and I am sure you are aware of the fact that he has little room for thoughts in his head which have not issued from your aunt's mouth first. No, I am determined not to take offense. I know myself. His words mean nothing to me."

Halting, Mr. Darcy turned to her, favoring her with a warm smile which caused all sorts of fluttering to happen in her belly. "That is what I admire about you the most, Miss Bennet. Your independence and indomitable will to defend yourself and those you love is truly commendable. But more, it is your ability to overlook slights and barbs which are flung your way and laugh at them as if they were of no moment."

"They are not, Mr. Darcy," replied Elizabeth, though she was certain there was a flush to her cheeks. "I do not give them any credence because they are truly worthy of none."

"And I commend you for it."

Mr. Darcy was gazing at her with that earnest stare of his, which Elizabeth had at first found quite unnerving but now considered to be comforting. She fancied she could see his very heart in his eyes.

"I am afraid that I cannot claim the same," continued Mr. Darcy with a self-deprecating laugh. "I feel any and all slights far too keenly, I fear, and though I do not often strike back with my own, I remember them very well indeed." He smiled somewhat ruefully. "I was entirely correct in what I said in the Netherfield music room—my good opinion once lost is lost forever, and I am well aware it is a character failing.

"But even more, I tend to feel the slights to those I love even more keenly than the ones directed toward myself."

Elizabeth chose not to think of the ramifications of *that* statement and instead focused on her companion, favoring him with the seriousness with which he approached this conversation. "That is not a grievous failing, sir," said Elizabeth gently. "In fact, I may even say that in some respects, it might be a virtue. I can see from the way you talk of your sister, for example, that you are very protective of her. That I can only applaud."

"By all means, Miss Bennet—turn my failings into merits. I find the experience rather interesting, I assure you."

With cheeks blazing, Elizabeth continued to walk, and her companion fell silent. Mr. Darcy had arrived that morning a little late on account of having to handle a matter which had arisen among the Netherfield tenants. Of course, the creature of duty that was Mr. Darcy could not allow it to go unattended when he was available to resolve the matter. It showed his attention to duty and his willingness to help his friend when he himself was at leisure.

It was a side of Mr. Darcy that Elizabeth found fascinating, as growing up in her father's home and seeing his somewhat lackadaisical style had not prepared her to meet a landowner who was truly involved in all the concerns of his estate. It spoke highly to his character.

Thus, as Mr. Darcy had arrived toward the end of visiting hours rather than the beginning, he had missed the excitement of the morning, as Mr. Collins had departed almost an hour earlier. In truth, Elizabeth was happy that Mr. Darcy had missed the man's insults. Considering how protective as Mr. Darcy was, she could well imagine him taking Mr. Collins to task for what he had said, and though it would be amusing to see the parson set down, Elizabeth was happy that it had stayed a family matter.

Of course, that did not stop Mr. Darcy's protective nature from being aroused at hearing of what had occurred. While Mr. Collins's behavior had displeased him, he was particularly annoyed by the offenses Mr. Collins had laid at her door. Mr. Darcy was, as he said, even more protective toward those of his acquaintance, and his reaction had showed that very clearly indeed.

"Mr. Darcy," said Elizabeth, thinking on Mr. Collins's words. When the man turned to her, Elizabeth continued: "I was wondering something about your aunt, Lady Catherine de Bourgh. Mr. Collins said that his patroness would know what was to be done. Do you suppose that she might journey here on the basis of his words in order to confront my family?"

A grimace came over Mr. Darcy's face, and he looked away for a moment. "Unfortunately, I believe that is well within the realm of possibility. I have tried to tell her for years that Anne and I would not marry, but she refuses to listen. If she deems Mr. Collins's words to contain sufficient truth, then it is very possible that she may attempt to come here and dissuade you."

"Dissuade me?" queried Elizabeth with an arch smile. "I was not aware of the fact that *I* needed to be *dissuaded* of anything."

It was a challenge, Elizabeth knew, but a small part of her was curious as to how far Mr. Darcy was willing to go. He had all but declared himself the night of the ball, but since then, he had assiduously avoided the subject altogether. Though his motives were often difficult to discern, Elizabeth felt certain that it was not due to his own desires that he had not canvassed the subject any further, but rather, it was due to a concern for her feelings. But even though it had only been a few days since the ball, Elizabeth found that she was impatient to know his thoughts on the subject and to know whether he still intended to act on his words that night.

"I am not certain *you* need to be dissuaded about anything, Miss Bennet," replied Mr. Darcy with one of his serious looks. "Perhaps she had best direct her energies at *me*."

Coloring, Elizabeth dropped her gaze in the face of his scrutiny. But whereas before Mr. Darcy appeared to be content to give her the space she needed to adjust to her changing perception of him, this time he kept his gaze squarely upon her. As she fidgeted with the pleats in her gown, she could feel his eyes upon her, almost burning her with their intensity.

"Miss Bennet," said he, long before she was ready to hear him speak again. "I must own that this situation renders me somewhat uneasy."

Risking a glance at him, Elizabeth looked up and met his gaze, willing her courage to rise up when she needed it. "How so, Mr. Darcy?"

"I believe that whatever Mr. Collins tells my aunt, he will embellish upon it, and he will brand you as a brazen seductress who is intent upon capturing me and my fortune. Lady Catherine will be all too eager to believe the worst, I assure you. If she does take it upon herself to confront you, she will not be temperate in her remarks."

Elizabeth tilted her head to the side as she peered at him with some amusement. "And did we not just talk of my courage, Mr. Darcy? I will remind you that it rises with every attempt to intimidate me. I can deal with your aunt, especially when anything she says concerning me will be baseless hearsay."

"My dearest Miss Bennet," said Mr. Darcy, "I have no doubt whatsoever of your ability to handle my aunt. But I would do more to protect you, if I could." He paused and appeared to consider his words before he forged on ahead. "I know that I have been calling on you for but a short time, but if you are ready, I should like to formalize our relationship."

Pausing for a moment to ensure that she was composed, Elizabeth considered her response. He was turning out to be an acceptable suitor indeed. In fact, Elizabeth almost laughed at herself for having such thoughts—it was impossible to deny that he was an exceptional man and would fit all her desires in a future marriage partner. But though he had proven himself to be everything that was honorable, intelligent, interesting, and praiseworthy, she was not certain that she was ready yet to proceed. As a rational being, she was still hesitant, as it had not really been that long since her opinion of him had changed, after all.

"Mr. Darcy, is there a particular reason why you would wish to move forward? And may I ask exactly how far you wish to take this new understanding?"

"A formal courtship, Miss Bennet," said Mr. Darcy without hesitation. "And as for my reasons, I should think that they are self-explanatory. I feel for you a tender regard which has come nigh to overwhelming me. Your goodness and your strength of character, your knowledge and your compassion—all these things make it impossible for me not to feel an intense regard for you which would overwhelm any and all objections if such existed. But from a more practical standpoint, if you and I were formally courting, then I could become actively involved in your protection, not only from the likes of William Collins, but also from my own aunt."

"And you have no doubts concerning entering into a courtship with me?" asked Elizabeth. "I am sure you are aware, but I will remind you that a courtship is tantamount to an engagement. It will not be easy to back out of once entered into."

Mr. Darcy nodded. "I am well aware of that, Miss Bennet. I have given this much thought, and I have come to the conclusion that if you are willing, I will make you an offer. The timing alone remains to be decided, and that shall be decided by you. If you are ready, then we may enter into a courtship now—I have no doubt that I shall never repine such an offer. But if you still require more time, then you shall have it. I am entirely at your disposal."

As he made his declaration, Elizabeth was struck by the notion that she did not believe that she would ever repine the connection if she acceded to his desires then and there. Indeed, she was coming to esteem him above any other man of his acquaintance.

But whether it was the newness of the sensation or the fact that her opinion of him had been extremely low only a short time before, she found that she simply was not ready to take such a step. A part of her was furious with herself for not being able to agree to his proposal right then and there, but the greater part of her knew that she simply wished for more time in his company without the pressure of an official courtship.

But she knew that she needed to take care not to crush his hopes irrevocably. He was a confident man, but even the most confident of men required some encouragement to allow them to take a chance and declare themselves openly. She knew by this point that she did wish to hear these words spoken again, and she wanted to hear them from him. He simply needed to know this.

"Mr. Darcy, I am not averse to your declaration at all. What woman would scorn such honest sentiments from a man she esteemed and trusted? I assure you that your words are very flattering, and I am very sensible to the feeling behind them.

"But I find that I am simply not quite ready to hear them. It has not been so long ago, after all, that you and I had so completely misunderstood each other. I beg you for a little more time so that I might know my own heart."

A wry smile came over his face, and he grasped her hand and tucked it into the crook of his arm as he led them once again down the path. "I am not surprised to hear you respond thus, Miss Bennet. But since I have determined that you are the one I wish to say them to, I decided that in light of Mr. Collins's words and what he will tell my aunt, I could not stay silent.

"And I want you to know," continued Mr. Darcy as he halted and turned toward her, "that rather than discourage me, your words have actually heartened me considerably. If anyone should dare to suggest that you are after my fortune, *I* shall know without a doubt that it is not true."

"Then you are not offended?" asked Elizabeth with an impish grin. "I have not lost your good opinion forever?"

"I sincerely doubt that is even possible," said Mr. Darcy. He was silent for a moment, apparently deep in thought, before he turned to her again. "Was your opinion of me so very bad?"

"It was not good," replied Elizabeth with a sigh. "But I assure you that it is drastically different now and that my poor opinion was founded on misunderstanding. It is a distant memory, becoming even more distant by the day."

"Do not apologize, Miss Bennet. You had some provocation, and in my defense, I can only say that I was weighed down by some important matters when I arrived in Hertfordshire. I should have kept to myself whenever possible until I was able to work through them, regardless of Bingley's entreaties."

Elizabeth smiled at him. "I fully understand. Regardless, I believe that we understand one another much better now. Let us leave our past dealings in the past where they belong and focus on the future."

"Then I shall take the opportunity now to warn you that the future will include a repeat of what was said today. As I told you—I do not allow myself to be distracted when I have found what I want."

A little breathless, Elizabeth replied: "And I shall hold you to it, sir."

The day of Mr. Collins's departure was Friday, and the weekend passed in a pleasant fashion. Mr. Darcy visited again on Saturday, and both he and Mr. Hurst were invited to dinner on Sunday after church services. Monday, however, brought an excitement of a different kind.

When someone visited, the Bennet ladies—either a few or en masse—would cluster around the front window which overlooked the drive in order to see who was calling. That morning, however, Jane had dropped her embroidery needle on the floor, and the ladies were engaged in attempting to find it. They had only just resumed their seats when visitors were shown into the sitting room and announced.

"Mr. Darcy, Mr. Bingley, and Miss Bingley, ma'am," said Mrs. Hill as she led the men into the room. She then curtseyed and left the room.

"Mrs. Bennet," greeted Mr. Bingley with his usual effervescence as he stepped into the room, Mr. Darcy trailing close behind. Though Mr. Darcy was in no way as jovial as Mr. Bingley, he added his greetings with dignity before anyone else could speak into the silence. Of course, Caroline Bingley entered with an expression carefully devoid of any emotion. Elizabeth, who fancied herself a studier of characters, could immediately see in Miss Bingley's posture that she had no desire to be there whatsoever.

The guests entered the room to uncharacteristic silence, as the unexpected entrance of the Bingley siblings had caught them all by surprise. Their latest intelligence from Mr. Darcy—which had been given only the previous day—suggested that Mr. Bingley would be delayed a day or two. Thus, it was a moment before anyone was able to speak once again.

"Mr. Bingley!" exclaimed Mrs. Bennet, rising to greet her neighbor with a curtsey and a broad smile. "We had no idea that you had returned, sir. We were led to believe that you would be in town until Wednesday at the very least."

"And I had expected it to be thus," agreed the man with a beaming smile, "but I found that I simply could not stay away. I find Hertfordshire to be very much to my taste, and I cannot tell you how happy I am to be back."

Elizabeth did not miss the look that Mr. Bingley directed at Jane, and neither, it appeared, did Mrs. Bennet. For that matter, Miss Bingley seemed to notice it as well, as her pleasant smile became all that much more forced. All of this escaped Mrs. Bennet, of course—clucking happily, she monopolized the conversation for some time, which Mr. Bingley bore with composure and kindness, and as Elizabeth watched her mother, she was struck by the fact that it was difficult to determine who was happier with Mr. Bingley's return—Mrs. Bennet or her eldest daughter!

The pleasure on Jane's countenance was no less easy to detect, as she fairly radiated happiness and contentment at the sight of her beau's return, though as yet she had not had occasion to speak with him due to Mrs. Bennet's effusions. And though Elizabeth had known that Mr. Darcy's assertions were to be trusted—and she knew that Jane *had* trusted him—still, the knowledge of Mr. Bingley's prompt return, which he had attributed to the desire to see Jane, could only give further rise to her mood. Indeed, Elizabeth doubted that there was one person in the room who could not detect Jane's high spirits.

"Dear Jane!' exclaimed Miss Bingley while her brother spoke with Mrs. Bennet. "I have longed to see you through the course of our separation. You have been well, I can see."

"Yes, I have, Miss Bingley," said Jane in her usual self-effacing way. "I trust you had an agreeable journey to and from London?"

Miss Bingley's frowned slightly, as if she suspected Jane of throwing a barb in her direction. Elizabeth, who knew her sister better than anyone, was aware that Jane had done no such thing. Jane was much too good and gentle to ever attempt to bait Miss Bingley in such a way—her comment was no more and no less than what it appeared to be.

Apparently, Miss Bingley came to that conclusion—or else decided it did not signify—as she responded with apparent warmth:

"Traveling in the late autumn is always tiring and difficult with the cold, but we managed well enough. Louisa and I have been desolate without you. I believe we should like to have you to Netherfield again once we have become settled in."

In her normally gentle voice, Jane agreed in the scheme with alacrity, and the two women fell into conversation with one another. Elizabeth watched them with some exasperation. Miss Bingley was acting as if nothing had happened between them—as if she had not sent a letter with the intention of persuading Jane that Mr. Bingley would not return. Even if the tone of the letter had been all that was friendly, the intention to sever the acquaintance had been evident in every word, and Jane would have been devastated had Mr. Darcy not intervened.

And yet Miss Bingley would stoop to such arts, declaring that she had longed to see Jane and that she wished to further their acquaintance, when it was clear to anyone with wit to see that she wanted nothing more than to take her brother away forever. Elizabeth was filled with indignation toward the supercilious woman, and she wished to share with her exactly what she thought, though she was well aware that Miss Bingley did not care for her opinion in the slightest. It was only for Jane's sake that she held her tongue. Due to the assistance of Mr. Darcy and the constancy of Mr. Bingley, Miss Bingley's schemes had been foiled, and Elizabeth decided that that was enough.

They sat speaking for some time. Mrs. Bennet had ordered a tea service moments after their guests had arrived, and even if the conversation sometimes became stilted—especially between Miss Bingley and any of the Bennets, save Jane—for the most part, the atmosphere remained agreeable. Even Mr. Bennet emerged from his library and drew both Mr. Darcy and Mr. Bingley into conversation, thereby rescuing the latter from Mrs. Bennet.

Once the appropriate time for a morning visit had elapsed — not that any of the Bennets wanted their guests to go away — Miss Bingley turned a significant eye on her brother.

"Charles, I believe the polite time for a visit has passed. Perhaps we should return to Netherfield. I have some tasks which must be accomplished after our return from town."

"I was thinking that we should walk out for a short time," said Mr. Bingley in response, his cheerfulness at odds with his sister's sudden displeasure. "It is a fine day, after all, and Darcy tells me that he has handled the estate business in my absence."

"Oh, what a marvelous idea!" cried Mrs. Bennet. "I am sure the girls would be vastly pleased to accompany you and show you the best parts of our park."

The scheme was readily agreed upon by all the participants — though Miss Bingley did not appear to be amused at all. But she was caught by her own words as to the necessity of returning to Netherfield, and she presently took her leave with all the appearance of civility and departed, promising to send the carriage back for the men.

Soon, the party had left the house, dressed in their winter wear, and Kitty and Lydia took the lead, talking and laughing among themselves, with Mary keeping a close watch on them. Elizabeth walked behind next to Mr. Darcy, while Jane and Mr. Bingley brought up the rear, seemingly content to allow the rest of the party to outstrip them. It was only a moment before Elizabeth turned a mock-accusatory glare on her companion and said in an arch tone:

"You are a sly thing, Mr. Darcy. You did not drop even a hint that Mr. Bingley was to return when you were here yesterday. In fact, you told us the opposite!"

"That is because I had no knowledge of the matter until Bingley returned late yesterday afternoon," replied Mr. Darcy with a complaisant smile. "What Bingley said about himself that day at Netherfield was completely true — he truly is impulsive, and he makes up his mind in an instant. He had no desire to be in town, and as such, he hurried his business along as quickly as he was able."

Then Mr. Darcy chuckled and shook his head in amusement. "To hear Bingley say it, he sent his sisters into a tizzy yesterday when he announced that he was ready to return to Hertfordshire. Not only had they expected to have an additional two days with which to persuade him to stay, but he caught them completely off guard when he told them that they would either be ready to accompany him, or he would leave them behind in London. It was amusing to hear his account of the matter, particularly his story of Miss Bingley's annoyance when she was just able to step into the carriage before the footman shut the door on her."

Laughing merrily, Elizabeth exclaimed: "I cannot imagine she appreciated that! It would be quite beneath her dignity to be seen scampering toward the carriage in an attempt to get in before the door closed!"

Mr. Darcy joined in the laughter, and they walked on for several moments before Elizabeth turned to him.

"Let me express my gratitude to you again, Mr. Darcy," said she. "If you had not given Jane your assurance, I am certain she would have found reason to suppose that he had returned for some other purpose. Thank you again for sparing her."

"Miss Bennet," returned Mr. Darcy, "though I appreciate your thanks, I assure you that I have only acted in a manner which seemed right."

A sudden grin suffused his face. "But if your thanks is an indication of your increasing regard, then I am very happy to accept."

There was nothing Elizabeth could say to that, so she opted simply to continue walking by his side. She had no doubt as to his meaning, and she was well aware that the outcome for which he hoped was coming closer by the minute.

The day could not have been any more perfect had it been planned in advance, which the final event of the day proved without any doubt. While walking in the garden with Mr. Darcy, Elizabeth shared a great deal of conversation with the gentleman, most of it lighthearted and playful. They quite lost track of their walking companions, so engrossed were they.

Elizabeth first noticed that some time had passed when she had an opportunity to glance around and noticed none of her sisters were nearby. She did not think much on the matter, however, as propriety was satisfied by the simple fact that she and Mr. Darcy were well within sight of the house, and she shrugged and turned back to her conversation.

A few moments later, her attention was caught by the sight of Lydia and Kitty running toward them, calling her name.

"Lizzy! Lizzy!"

Wondering what was causing all the fuss, Elizabeth turned to face her sisters, noting that even Mary, who was following behind, appeared to have an uncharacteristic excitement evident in her manner.

"You shall never guess what we just saw!" cried Kitty as they breathlessly ran up to Darcy and Elizabeth.

"Mr. Bingley and Jane were in the copse," said Lydia in just as much excitement as her sister. "And he was down on one knee in front of her!"

"A proposal!" squealed Kitty, clapping her hands with delight.

"I feel as if we intruded on a very private moment," said Mary much more sedately as she strode up behind her sisters.

"Oh, stop it, Mary!" exclaimed Lydia. "Jane will not mind. She will be far too happy that Mr. Bingley has come to the point to worry about having an audience."

"Only because I pulled you away before you could make a scene," said Mary.

Elizabeth was far too excited to listen to her sisters' bickering. Rather, she turned an upraised eyebrow at Mr. Darcy, who gazed back at her with his normal inscrutable look.

"You appear to have a guilty countenance, sir."

"Guilty? What reason have I to be guilty?"

The younger girls stopped their quarreling and turned to Mr. Darcy almost as one.

"You are Mr. Bingley's closest friend!" exclaimed Kitty. "He must have told you something of his intentions."

"Though I am Bingley's closest friend," said Darcy rather placidly, "I assure you he has not taken me into his confidence in this instance."

Upon seeing the girls' disappointment at this statement, Mr. Darcy amended with a smile: "But I will own that I have never seen Bingley appear so ebullient as he did this morning, though he *is* a rather cheerful sort. I did suspect something, though again I will stress that he did not actually tell me anything."

That seemed to satisfy Kitty and Lydia, and they once again began chattering with one another excitedly. It was a big event in the Bennet household—not only was Jane to be the first one of them betrothed, but with the specter of the entailment hanging over the entire family, it would also mean a measure of relief for the entire family. And unless Elizabeth missed her guess, she imagined that every one of her sisters was secretly hoping that their mother's nerves would be calmed due to the prospect of future security.

"Am I forgiven, Miss Bennet?"

Turning at the sound of his quiet voice in her ear, Elizabeth smiled up at the gentleman. "I suppose so, Mr. Darcy. *If* Mr. Bingley did not tell you of his plans explicitly."

"Ah, then I thank you for my reprieve from the gallows."

Elizabeth gazed back at him with mock affront. "We are not so uncivilized here at Longbourn, sir. You would have received lashes — nothing more."

At that, Mr. Darcy laughed merrily. "In that case, I thank you nonetheless. I doubt I could have endured lashes with any degree of equanimity. I shall count on your forbearance."

Any reply Elizabeth would have made was lost at the sudden appearance of the now supposedly acknowledged lovers. Elizabeth favored Mr. Darcy with one more impish smile before she started forward toward her favorite sister. The smile on Jane's face, coupled with the exuberance of her general demeanor, told Elizabeth all she needed to know, and she stepped up to her elder sister and engulfed her in a fierce embrace.

"Oh, Lizzy!" cried Jane. "I am so happy!"

"And I am happy for you!" said Elizabeth, tears in her eyes. "You deserve it. No one is as good as you."

"I believe you are, Lizzy," replied Jane. "And if I am not very much mistaken, you shall be enjoying your own happiness very soon indeed."

Though she did not let go of her sister, Elizabeth chanced a glance back at where the gentlemen stood and saw Mr. Darcy congratulating his friend with a hearty handshake. But though he was speaking to Mr. Bingley, Elizabeth noted the fact that his attention was firmly on *her* as he favored her with his typical concentration.

Blushing, Elizabeth turned back to Jane and shared a few more words with her while Mary, Lydia, and Kitty all clustered around eand offered their own congratulations and wishes for Jane's felicity. And Jane, dear soul that she was, accepted their wishes with a grace and dignity matched by few. And Elizabeth was content. Mr. Bingley, with the help of his friend, had shown a constancy which was much to be desired in a marriage partner, and Elizabeth was convinced that Jane would be happy.

And for herself, Elizabeth knew that Mr. Darcy was quickly rising in her estimation. It would not be long, she felt, before she was ready to give him the answer he desired.

Chapter XV

After the engagement between Mr. Bingley and Longbourn's eldest young lady was finalized in the garden of the estate, Jane's ardent lover quickly removed himself to the master's study in order to obtain Mr. Bennet's blessing. Though that blessing was quickly granted and the engagement duly announced to the inhabitants of the home — Mrs. Bennet being the only one who was not already apprised of the situation — Mr. Bingley appeared to be a little glassy-eyed upon emerging from Mr. Bennet's bookroom. Elizabeth was not the only one to notice his look.

"Do you think Bingley's manner is due solely to his engagement?"

Elizabeth turned to Mr. Darcy and noted his fond smile at his friend. "Not solely," replied she. "I do not doubt that my father took the opportunity to sport with your friend — it is a pleasure I doubt he could suppress given Mr. Bingley's character and his errand."

Mr. Darcy laughed, but then he affixed her with his typical intense look. "Should I expect the same treatment when I approach your father for his consent to marry one of his other daughters?"

Blushing immediately at the implication of his words, Elizabeth nevertheless answered gamely: "I think he would consider himself to be honor bound to make the experience memorable for any young man who possessed the temerity to make such a request."

"I will take that under advisement, then," replied Mr. Darcy. "I shall attempt not to be intimidated by the prospect."

Privately, Elizabeth doubted that Mr. Darcy would be intimidated by anything her father had to say, but she contented herself with a laugh and a nod, and they continued to speak of other matters.

As the days slipped by, Mr. Darcy and Mr. Bingley continued to be regular visitors to Longbourn. Though Mr. Darcy had respected her wishes and remained silent regarding his intentions, the fact that he looked on Elizabeth with admiration was about the worst-kept secret at Longbourn. In fact, though there were few engagements to be had during those days, tales of Mr. Darcy's particular visits to Longbourn appeared to be well known to the entire neighborhood. For a change, Elizabeth was certain that her mother was not the author of these tales—rather, it appeared that Kitty and Lydia had carried the stories to Lucas Lodge, and from there, Lady Lucas had taken over. Of course, Aunt Phillips was involved as well, Elizabeth suspected. She surely would not be able to keep silent, especially after being denied the initial gossip concerning Mr. Wickham.

Mr. Darcy bore it well, Elizabeth decided. He was a private man and was not prone to idle conversation, especially that which contained little substance. But he was also an intelligent man, and he was certainly disposed to speak when the conversation was a challenge to his faculties. It was true that there were relatively few sources of such interesting conversation in their small neighborhood, but he performed his social duties with grace, dignity, and kindness—behavior which he had certainly not shown when he had first arrived in the area.

The one thing Elizabeth witnessed over those days which she found heartening was the rapport which appeared to develop between her father and Mr. Darcy. While they were very different in some ways, they were similar enough in their tendency to avoid social situations and in their love for the written word—and also, a small part of her suggested, in their love for her—that a friendship quickly sprang up between them. Mr. Darcy was most often to be found in the company of Elizabeth when at Longbourn, but on those occasions when her attention was commandeered by her mother in her never-ending discussions about weddings, apparel, and other fripperies, he would often be found with Mr. Bennet, engaged in a game of chess or a discussion of books, politics, and a multitude of other subjects. Given the fact that she was rapidly approaching the point where he would become much more intimately connected with her family, it was gratifying that he was taking so well to her father.

Unfortunately, during a time when the gentlemen from Netherfield were not present at Longbourn, an event occurred which was long expected yet unwelcome. On this unlucky day, Longbourn was invaded by several visitors of varying degrees of respectability.

It happened during the late afternoon hours close to the time when the family would be retiring to the dining room for the evening repast. The gentlemen were engaged to eat dinner at Longbourn, as were Miss Bingley and the Hursts—which was undoubtedly the work of Mr. Hurst, who would never miss an engagement to dine despite the Bingley sisters' obvious reluctance—and they were all expected to arrive shortly. In fact, it was because of the expected arrival of the party from Netherfield that the noise of an approaching carriage did not raise much of a commotion from the inhabitants of the estate; Lydia had been the only one to approach the window, and she reported nothing more than the fact that a large carriage had arrived. It was understandable that she would not see more than that, as the light was waning due to the lateness of the season.

The ladies of the house were waiting in the parlor for the visitors to be announced—Mr. Bennet was in his study taking care of some business—when the sound of voices could be heard from the entrance hall. In particular, it sounded as if a rather demanding and somewhat deep female voice was doing most of the talking, though Mrs. Hill's voice and that of a man could also be heard. Mrs. Bennet had just exchanged perplexed glances with her daughters and risen from her chair to see what the fuss was about when the door opened and a tall, rather imperious looking lady entered the room. Hard upon her heels was a young woman of a rather sallow complexion and a familiar simpering man. Lady Catherine had come to Longbourn, and the only surprise was the fact that she had brought her parson along with her.

Her ladyship's nose turned up in apparent disgust as she entered the room, though it was not clear whether the inhabitants or the locale was the cause. With a haughty gait, she crossed the room, almost brushing past Mrs. Bennet in a blatant show of ill manners, before she sat on the chair which the Bennet matron had just vacated. Following closely in her footsteps, the young lady—who must be Anne de Bourgh—sat in a nearby chair, though she appeared to be very ill at ease. The parson, for his part, merely took up his station behind his patroness. He attempted to emulate his patroness's glare of contempt, but it only came off as comical from such an ineffectual man.

"So these are your cousins, Mr. Collins," said the great lady after she spent some moments looking down her nose at the Bennets.

"Yes, your Ladyship," replied Mr. Collins, though his tone was filled with distaste.

"And which is the one who refused you?"

Mr. Collins indicated Mary, who was situated by Elizabeth's side. "My cousin Mary was the one who refused my offer of marriage, though her elder sister, Elizabeth, played some role in the affair."

Lady Catherine sniffed with disdain. "I suppose there is no reason to bring up how foolish it was for a young lady of little dowry and with no brother for protection to refuse any offer of marriage."

"Perhaps she did not feel it was wise to accept the suit of a man she did not esteem," said Elizabeth, unwilling to allow Lady Catherine and her odious parson to insult her sister.

Eyeing her with more than a little annoyance, Lady Catherine replied: "Esteem plays very little into matters of marriage and future security. Considering her refusal, do you think your cousin will be inclined to charity when your father leaves this life?"

"I should think that my eldest's upcoming marriage will ensure our future security," interjected Mrs. Bennet. Elizabeth was surprised by her mother's frosty and challenging tone; she would rather have imagined her mother being quite overwhelmed to be hosting a woman of Lady Catherine's rank in her parlor.

"Perhaps so," said Lady Catherine. "But it was poorly done, regardless, and it will undoubtedly put more of a burden on your new son," said she, speaking this last with a curled lip, "when he and his wife are required to look after you and your unmarried daughters after your husband's death."

"It may be as your ladyship says," replied Mrs. Bennet, "but as you are completely unconnected with us, I cannot imagine it would concern you in the slightest."

"However unwilling the connection, my parson is your cousin, and as a result, my concern for the situation does exist."

"I am sorry, Lady Catherine, but did you come here with a specific purpose?" asked Mrs. Bennet. Her tone was short and almost unfriendly, deservedly so, as Lady Catherine had done nothing to deserve respect, let alone friendship.

Lady Catherine glared as Mrs. Bennet, as if she was the one behaving in a churlish manner. "I believe that your daughter should be given the opportunity to reconsider her refusal. In light of what I have said, I can only imagine that she would now wish to accept Mr. Collins's suit with alacrity."

"And you would suppose incorrectly," said Mary with her head held high. "I cannot imagine any consideration which would tempt me to accept my cousin. Furthermore, I might wonder why he is so intent upon having a wife who has already refused him *four* times!"

His eyes appearing as though they would pop out of their sockets, Mr. Collins stared at Mary as if she had muttered some blasphemy. But no sound was forthcoming, which Elizabeth believed to be quite fortunate.

"I believe you have done your duty, Mr. Collins," said Lady Catherine to her parson. "And I believe it for the best that you do not become more closely connected to this . . . family than you already are. Once Mr. Bennet is dead, you may safely turn the rest of the family out as soon as may be."

"Indeed, I shall," said Mr. Collins, finally finding his voice. "As always, your advice is wise and just."

"Did you come here with the sole purpose of insulting us, Lady Catherine?" asked Mrs. Bennet. "For if you have, then I believe that I must ask you to leave."

"I shall leave when I am ready to leave," said Lady Catherine. "To promote a match between Mr. Collins and your daughter is nothing more than a minor consideration. I thought to test you to see if you would be reasonable. It is unfortunate that you are determined to be so intractable. More is the pity.

"What I must have is an audience with your second eldest," continued the lady as she rose from her chair. "You will follow me out into the garden where we may speak in private."

"So that you may insult her there away from my hearing?" demanded Elizabeth's mother.

"Whatever I say to your daughter is not your concern," said Lady Catherine. "Come, Miss Elizabeth."

Knowing that there was nothing to be said to gainsay Lady Catherine and that it would become a much bigger scene should she not be obliged, Elizabeth motioned to her mother. "I am willing to hear Lady Catherine, Mama. I shall only be gone a few moments."

While it was evident that this did not appease Mrs. Bennet to any great degree, Lady Catherine nodded to Elizabeth as if her capitulation were a foregone conclusion. She then turned back to Mr. Collins. "You will watch over Anne, Mr. Collins. I would prefer that she was not forced to remain in such . . . company while I speak with Miss Bennet, but I cannot have her take a chill while waiting in the carriage."

Though Elizabeth was amused by that little morsel of inanity—

Anne de Bourgh had just spent the entire day in the confines of a carriage! — Elizabeth held her tongue. She was surprised to witness Anne turning her head in response to Lady Catherine's words, and she thought the glimpsed the woman roll her eyes.

Mr. Collins, however, seemed to see nothing amiss. On the contrary, he puffed himself up as though he had been given the task of guarding the Crown Jewels themselves and positioned himself behind Miss de Bourgh's chair.

Taking heart in the fact that Mr. Darcy was indeed expected very soon, Elizabeth grabbed her pelisse and gloves from a waiting maid before following her ladyship from the house. The late afternoon air was bracing, and Elizabeth shivered slightly, though she was not at all certain that it was the chill in the air which caused it. Lady Catherine took no notice of her whatsoever as she walked out the door and into the garden, and Elizabeth wondered if she was normally so imperious and disagreeable, or if this was a show to remind Elizabeth of her inferiority.

When at last they had arrived at the garden, Lady Catherine stopped abruptly and turned to face Elizabeth. Elizabeth would have expected the grand dame to immediately begin berating her for her temerity, but Lady Catherine simply stood there regarding her as if she was some sort of wild and infectious animal. And when she finally spoke, her words were insulting beyond belief.

"I suppose this shall not be terribly difficult after all."

Confused, Elizabeth regarded the other woman with a healthy sense of wariness. "I beg your pardon?"

"Separating you from my nephew," clarified the lady in an offhand manner. "I was prepared for the worst after what my parson told me. But I know my nephew, and he could never be taken in for long by a woman without fortune, connections, or even a modicum of beauty to tempt him.

"It has always been my concern," continued Lady Catherine, "that he would succumb to the allurement of some well-dowered and well-connected young lady and that I should be forced to give way. If his choice is you, however, then I can be assured that I shall carry my point. A grasping, artful sort of fortune-hunting girl such as yourself could never hold his interest for long. It shall be the work of a moment to remind him of his duty."

Elizabeth was affronted and more than a little disdainful of this meddling termagant. "I might wonder what you might feel you have to gain by insulting me so in my own home."

"It was no insult—it was nothing more than the truth, I assure you."

"Very well," replied Elizabeth. "In that case, if you are finished, I believe it is time for me to return to the house."

"Not so hasty, Miss Bennet," said Lady Catherine. The woman actually had the audacity to extend her walking cane in front of Elizabeth to forestall her departure. "Regardless of the truth of the matter behind Mr. Collins's rambling, I will have your assurance that you will cease in this attempt to ensnare my nephew. You will oblige me."

"I know of no inducement whatsoever that would persuade me in anything you should deign to ask," said Elizabeth. "Your behavior has been so rude and insulting that I doubt any civilized person could fail to take offense."

Lady Catherine glared balefully at her. "So you *do* have designs on him. How typical of the lower classes, never content to stay within the sphere in which you were brought up."

"I cannot imagine what you are talking about, Lady Catherine. Mr. Darcy is a gentleman. I am a gentleman's daughter. The disparity about which you speak simply does not exist."

The elderly lady's eyes bored into her, and she tapped her cane on the grass with annoyance. For a moment, Elizabeth almost thought the woman would raise it against her. The moment passed, and Lady Catherine's glare intensified. She spoke thus:

"You are witless if you do not understand the vast chasm which exists between the two of you, rendering the mere thought of an alliance an anathema to all. You are a simple country girl, and as such, you can have no understanding of the world in which you can have no part. You are in no way an equal to Mr. Darcy—you are far and away his inferior in every respect."

So intent were the combatants upon each other that neither had noticed the spectator to their argument until a gasp was heard at Lady Catherine's last insult. Elizabeth stepped back, surprised, and with a sinking feeling, she watched as her mother stepped forward to confront Lady Catherine, her eyes blazing with anger. All possibility of keeping this situation from escalating would now be gone now that her mother was interfering.

"How dare you?" said Mrs. Bennet as she put herself face to face with Lady Catherine and in front of Elizabeth. "My daughter is every bit the lady, and I resent the implication that she is not good enough for your nephew."

"Of course you would feel that way, Mrs. Bennet," said Lady Catherine with a sneer of contempt. "Your upbringing and lack of breeding make you as witless as your impertinent daughter."

"Coming from you, I need not view that last as an insult!" retorted Mrs. Bennet.

For the first time during the confrontation, Lady Catherine's countenance darkened in anger. Elizabeth supposed that she had been so confident in her superiority over the Bennets that she had no notion of the fact that they might not simply agree with whatever she decreed.

"Do you not know who I am?" demanded Lady Catherine.

"You are a loud and obnoxious woman who has invaded my house, insulted my daughters, and made outrageous demands upon my family. If I was not already certain of your connection to Mr. Darcy, then I would not have believed you could be related. He has been everything that is good and amiable, whereas you are perhaps the most disagreeable person I have ever laid eyes upon!"

"How dare you?" raged Lady Catherine. "Never in my life have I been subjected to such impertinence!"

"I highly doubt that," replied Mrs. Bennet scornfully. "With such rudeness as this, it is a wonder you receive anyone's notice at all."

Though Lady Catherine appeared to be on the verge of apoplexy, she mastered herself with a visible effort. Armed once again with her disdainful and imperious glare, she addressed Elizabeth and her mother again:

"Though you have taken leave of whatever reason and decorum you might have possessed, I shall not do the same." She turned her attention directly upon Elizabeth and continued: "You! Girl! Has my nephew made an offer of marriage to you?"

"He has not officially proposed," said Elizabeth, though she would have liked to disabuse Lady Catherine of the notion that she would ever bend Mr. Darcy to her will. "But I expect it to occur in the very near future."

"You expect incorrectly," snapped Lady Catherine. "I shall ensure that he never makes an offer to you. But regardless, I must have your solemn promise that should he ever do so, you shall reject him forthwith."

"Elizabeth will make no promise of the kind!" interjected Mrs. Bennet.

Elizabeth could not miss the irony inherent in the fact that Mrs. Bennet was now defending Mr. Darcy's right to make an offer to her when only days ago the sight of him incited a sense of scornful outrage. But the murderous expression which suffused Lady Catherine's face all but drove such thoughts from her mind. Elizabeth was not certain how far the lady would go to see her designs come to pass, but she heartily wished that Mr. Darcy would arrive and put an end to this farce.

"Yes, she will!" cried the lady. "She must! Mr. Darcy is engaged to Anne by the will of her mother, his mother, and every member of their family. This shall not be prevented by the machinations of an upstart family without honor or connections. How dare you presume to rise above your station!"

"It seems to me that your purpose is faulty, Lady Catherine," said Elizabeth. "Mr. Darcy declaimed all obligation to your daughter in front of every member of my family. I hardly think that he would suddenly change his mind and agree to marry your daughter, even if I should refuse him."

"Darcy knows his duty!"

"Apparently, his opinion of his duty and yours are separated by a vast chasm."

"It matters not!" interrupted Mrs. Bennet shrilly. "I shall not have you importuned an instant longer by this woman. Come, Elizabeth. Let us return to the house."

Mrs. Bennet turned away, grasping Elizabeth by the arm and making to depart. But Lady Catherine was not to be dissuaded.

"What shall it cost to ensure your compliance?"

Aghast, Elizabeth turned to the elderly woman. "Do you think that you can bribe me to refuse Mr. Darcy's offer?" asked she incredulously.

"Of course I can," snapped Lady Catherine. "Greed is the hallmark of the lower classes."

"If I am so consumed by greed, then the lure of Mr. Darcy's ten thousand a year must be a greater inducement than anything you can offer. Why do you think I would desist?"

"Because I shall see to the utter ruin of your family if you do not oblige me."

"That is enough!" boomed a powerful male voice.

Surprised, Elizabeth turned and beheld her suitor approaching them from the house. His countenance was suffused with a thunderous glare which was directed at the person of his aunt, and he appeared to be as furious as Elizabeth had ever seen him. He stopped at Elizabeth's side on his way to confront his aunt, and his eyes took in her countenance, his rage giving way to anxious concern.

"Miss Bennet, you are unharmed?"

"I am well, Mr. Darcy." Elizabeth turned an unfriendly glare on his aunt, who was watching their interaction with fury. "I am a little affronted, but it is nothing that time and distance will not heal."

Grasping her hand in his own, Mr. Darcy grazed the back with a feather-light kiss and regarded her with affection. "I shall do my best to see that you get that time."

"Darcy!" cried Lady Catherine. "Get away from that woman!"

"That woman is Miss Elizabeth Bennet, in case you did not bother to inquire," said Mr. Darcy.

"I know her name," said Lady Catherine with obvious impatience. "She will be nothing but the ruin of you if you will not stop this unseemly behavior immediately."

"Rather, she will be the making of me, Aunt."

"This is not to be borne!" cried Lady Catherine.

But Mr. Darcy took no notice. "Mrs. Bennet, Miss Bennet, I must speak with my aunt. If you would be so kind as to return to the house, I believe that it should be done in private. I shall come to you directly when my aunt has departed."

Though Elizabeth would have preferred to stay and offer her support while he confronted his aunt, something in his expression told her that it would be better should she depart and take her mother with her. And given the insults which had already flown between the three ladies, she could only agree with his request. So she left as he asked, guiding her mother away and listening for only a few moments more to the argument which had resumed between Mr. Darcy and his aunt.

Elizabeth might have been concerned had he been any other man. She was convinced, after all, that her happiness was tied up with his, and she knew that her disappointment would know no bounds should he withdraw his attentions at this late date. But this was Mr. Darcy, and whatever she had thought about him previously, she had always known that he knew his own mind and was not about to allow anyone to intimidate him away from his chosen course. She was confident that he would not be persuaded. It was a comforting thought, given the circumstances.

Chapter XVI

*I*t was fortunate that the parlor in which the Bennets entertained their guests was situated away from the back garden, as Elizabeth was able to hear Lady Catherine's shrieks from well into the house. It was perhaps not a charitable thought, but Elizabeth wondered how Mr. Darcy could be related to such a woman. Even when her opinion of him had been at its lowest, she had never thought his manners could in any way be compared with the display his aunt was making.

Of Lady Catherine's dire predictions for her future, Elizabeth spared not a thought. Not only was she convinced that she would be very happy with Mr. Darcy should they ever come to an understanding, but she was well aware that though there would undoubtedly be some who would look down on her, most of them would only pay attention to her until the next scandal caught their attention.

It was a quiet and subdued parlor to which Elizabeth returned, her mother having left her in the hall after they had entered the house. Mr. Collins was still standing behind Anne de Bourgh like some sort of knight errant protector—though the mere thought of considering him in such terms almost caused Elizabeth to giggle uncontrollably. Elizabeth's sisters were present, of course, and the three younger ones were quietly speaking among themselves while Jane sat with Mr. Bingley. Mr. Hurst sat with a glass of port near Elizabeth's father, who was ostensibly speaking with the gentleman, though Elizabeth suspected he was in truth anxiously waiting for her entrance. As for Mr. Bingley's sisters, they sat in close conference with one another. As Elizabeth stepped into the room, Miss Bingley shot her a supercilious look, but it appeared to be half-hearted at best; Elizabeth suspected that the other woman was aware of the reason for Lady Catherine's appearance and was pondering this unexpected impediment to her own ambitions with regard to Mr. Darcy.

Mr. Bennet rose and approached Elizabeth with an expression of concern. "Elizabeth, are you quite well?"

"I am, Papa," replied Elizabeth. "I dare say it would take more than Lady Catherine to discompose me."

Mr. Bennet smiled affectionately. "I do not doubt it. I was more concerned for her behavior, knowing what I do about her."

"There is no need to worry. Mama assisted me, and Mr. Darcy is handling the situation now."

A raised eyebrow met her statement. "Your mother helped, did she? You will have to share that story with me, my child.

"You know, I was rather surprised at the tenacity of your young man. I discovered Lady Catherine's presence at about the same time as Mr. Darcy arrived. I had thought to come and remove her from the premises myself, but your beau convinced me that he should deal with his aunt. He shows a rather impressive tenacity and a sense of duty which I can only applaud."

Though she blushed at her father's reference to Mr. Darcy as her "beau," Elizabeth's attention was caught by her mother's entrance into the room. Mrs. Bennet took one step into the room, frowned, and then retreated, returning only moments later. She next approached Anne de Bourgh and addressed her thus:

"Miss de Bourgh, you must be exhausted, you poor dear. I have sent for some tea to help revive you. Or perhaps you would prefer to retire to a room to rest?"

But she was not given a chance to reply, as Mr. Collins answered for her in his typically oily fashion:

"My patroness has decreed that her daughter should have no contact with you and your family, madam. Indeed, I cannot but agree with her. Miss de Bourgh is in no way accustomed to interacting with such . . . coarse persons as the Bennets, and furthermore—"

"Oh, do be silent, Mr. Collins," interrupted Mrs. Bennet testily. "No one wants your sermons here."

Mr. Collins's countenance appeared not unlike that of a beached fish, and he struggled to form a response, finally settling for a high-pitched: "My patroness will not be pleased with such willful disregarding of her orders. I must insist that you do not attempt to talk with Miss de Bourgh any further."

Fixing him with a steely glare, Mrs. Bennet warned: "If you do not be silent, Mr. Collins, I shall have my husband remove you from the house."

A quick glance revealed Mr. Bennet's bemusement at his wife's uncharacteristic words, but he readily supported his wife in his own particular style. "I suggest you desist, Mr. Collins. My wife has determined that your patroness's daughter is in need of a little mothering, and I suspect that she shall not be deterred. Take a seat."

Though he clearly wanted to object further, Mr. Collins seemed to recognize the fact that he was not in friendly company, and his next act was perhaps the most sensible that Elizabeth had ever seen from the man—he sat down on a chair, near enough that in his own mind he was still protecting Miss de Bourgh, yet far enough that he was not hovering any longer. He did not do it without muttering imprecations under his breath, but he at least subsided for the moment.

When Mr. Collins had been thus disposed of, Mrs. Bennet turned back to Miss de Bourgh with a kindly smile. "Shall we show you to a chamber where you may rest?"

For the first time since she had entered the room, Miss de Bourgh responded with a tired smile. "I do not need a room, Mrs. Bennet, though I thank you for the offer. A little tea, however, would be heavenly."

"Of course," Mrs. Bennet said. "I shall see to it directly."

The tea service arrived soon afterward, and Mrs. Bennet, with the assistance of Jane and Elizabeth, saw that it was distributed to everyone in the room, taking care to serve Miss de Bourgh herself. Even the unwanted Mr. Collins was given a cup of tea, little though he seemed to appreciate it.

"There," clucked Mrs. Bennet once she had seen Miss de Bourgh settled, with herself in close attendance, "I dare say you shall feel better with a little refreshment."

"I thank you, Mrs. Bennet," replied Miss de Bourgh. Then she appeared to gather her courage, and she addressed Elizabeth, who sat in a nearby chair. "I apologize for my mother's words, Miss Elizabeth. I cannot imagine that she moderated any of the sentiments she spoke to me throughout our journey here."

"Miss de Bourgh," began Mr. Collins in his normal obsequious tone, "surely you cannot mean to censure your lady mother thus. Perhaps you have been in the company of my cousin's family too much already."

Miss de Bourgh's response was nothing more than a quelling glare which Elizabeth fancied resembled Lady Catherine's, though their features were not generally similar. The effect on Mr. Collins, however, was much as it would have been had it been Lady Catherine herself who had delivered it—he subsided his protests rather quickly, though his resentful glares around the room did not cease.

"Do not concern yourself, Miss de Bourgh," said Elizabeth. "She said nothing that I had not expected. I am well aware of the fact that your cousin does not share your mother's opinions. I emerged from the experience quite unscathed, I assure you."

A shadow of a smile appeared on Miss de Bourgh's face, and Elizabeth fancied that she could understand the other woman a little, and she was certain that Anne de Bourgh seldom had reason to smile. At that moment, she determined that should she and Darcy ever marry, she would make it her mission to ensure that his cousin experienced some joy in her life.

Leaning closer to Elizabeth, Miss de Bourgh said in a low tone: "Regardless of what my mother says, Darcy and I have never desired to marry."

A strangled sound from Mr. Collins attracted her attention, but another glare quelled his outburst before it could leave his mouth. Satisfied that he was silenced for the moment, Miss de Bourgh turned back to Elizabeth and said: "Darcy is rather. . . imposing, is he not? Far too imposing for me, though he certainly has his amiable moments. To be honest, I rather suspect that you might be able to handle him quite well indeed."

Mr. Collins once again gasped, but no one paid him any mind. A quick glance at her mother showed a calculating gaze, but for once, Mrs. Bennet held her tongue. With that little bit of improper conversation out of the way, the discourse turned to much more benign matters, with Elizabeth and Miss de Bourgh chatting amiably one to another. Mrs. Bennet interjected from time to time, inquiring about Rosings and how their journey had been, but for the most part, she seemed to be content to allow the two younger ladies to carry the conversation.

So it continued for some time, as those in the room engaged in

166 %b Jann Rowland

desultory conversation, though the thoughts of most were likely out in the garden with Mr. Darcy and his aunt. The fact that they had not been called in to dinner yet suggested that Mrs. Bennet had given instructions to the kitchen staff that they hold dinner at least until their visitors had left. It was an unexpected bit of civility on Mrs. Bennet's part, as Elizabeth knew that she was vindictive enough to have treated Lady Catherine and her daughter as naught more than interlopers and ordered dinner for no other reason than to prove a point.

When perhaps no more than ten minutes had passed since Elizabeth and her mother had left Mr. Darcy to the company of his aunt, voices were once again heard in the hallway approaching the drawing room, and it seemed as if Lady Catherine was making no more attempt to moderate her tone than she had previously. Their final words were clear as they approached.

"I will speak to my brother," said she in a high and shrill tone which spoke to her perturbation of mind.

Mr. Darcy's voice, though certainly not as loud, also carried through the closed door. "You may, but even if my uncle should attempt to impose upon me as you have done, he will have no more success. I am my own man and am beholden to no one. I shall act as I see fit and in accordance to my own conscience."

The door opened, and Mr. Darcy stalked into the room, though when he saw Elizabeth and her mother sitting close to Anne, he directed a tight smile at them. Lady Catherine was following closely on his heels, still haranguing him about this supposed engagement to Miss de Bourgh. Mr. Darcy, however, was paying her no more heed than he had before.

The next absurdity made itself known in the person of Mr. Collins, as might well be expected. The clergyman rose to his feet and stepped toward Mr. Darcy, his manner a ridiculous mix of pomposity and exaggerated deference for Mr. Darcy and—more likely—Lady Catherine.

"Mr. Darcy," said he with a low bow, "I must concur with my lady patroness about this most unseemly display. It is the duty of the younger generation to look up to and respect their elders and to acquiesce with grace and dignity to the agreements made by their parents, which must, of a certainty, be for the very best of intentions and means of promoting the happiness of their children. My cousin, though a gentlewoman, is so far beneath you that any alliance with her must be considered to be the most reprehensible of connections, for she can in no way make any pretense toward inhabiting your sphere with the grace and ability that your dear cousin must, by the simple fact of her birth and upbringing, have been born to.

"If you have concern over the thought of my cousin's reputation being harmfully affected because of your level of attention, I shall readily offer myself up as a replacement in your stead, as you shall, therefore, be free of all obligations toward her."

This last was said with a leer toward Elizabeth which made her shudder in revulsion. And though Mr. Darcy's lips tightened in anger, and Lady Catherine's countenance brightened slightly—Elizabeth was certain that Lady Catherine was not happy with the idea of her marrying Mr. Collins, but rather thought it infinitely preferable to Elizabeth's *stealing* Mr. Darcy—the first right of response fell to another.

"Mr. Collins," interjected Mr. Bennet, "before you offer yourself up to Elizabeth—or indeed any of my other daughters—you should perhaps remember that with the exception of my eldest, who is thankfully already betrothed, my permission would be required before an engagement could be entered into with any of them. And furthermore, given your display here tonight, I would be hard pressed to agree to any proposal you might make, particularly since your intentions seem to shift with the wind."

"But Mr. Bennet," said Mr. Collins in an affronted tone, "my position as a clergyman and as heir to this estate highly recommend my suit and render it—"

"Most absurd," inserted Mr. Bennet. "Even disregarding the impropriety of your sentiments and your offer, I highly doubt you could make any of them happy."

"Is it happiness to infringe upon a previous agreement?" demanded Lady Catherine. "Or do you encourage your daughters to hunt for the highest prey possible in order to grasp for the most they can get?"

"I simply encourage them to act with regard to their own happiness," was Mr. Bennet's pointed reply. "I certainly would not suggest that they act in deference to the wishes of someone who, after all, is in no way connected to them."

The lady's face had by this point turned so red that Elizabeth was afraid that Lady Catherine was about to suffer some apoplexy. Her ladyship was obviously not accustomed to having her will opposed, and the fact that it was in so near a concern to the lady was certain to make it even more difficult for her to bear.

"I am shocked, Mr. Bennet," she fairly screeched. "I would have thought that a gentlemen would understand these things and not seek to raise his children up beyond the sphere in which they have been raised. I am determined to carry my point, sir, and I assure you that I shall."

"Perhaps you may, madam, but you shall do so in another location. I believe it is time for you to depart. You have insulted my family quite enough."

"I believe that is most sensible," said Mr. Darcy. Then he turned to Mr. Bingley and said: "Might I have your permission to conduct my aunt and my cousin to Netherfield to stay the night?"

"Of course, Darcy," replied Mr. Bingley.

A glance at Mr. Bingley's sisters showed Elizabeth that *they*, at least, would prefer anything but to have such a woman stay with them for the night regardless of Caroline's pretensions toward higher circles. Obviously, they were both intelligent enough to understand that Lady Catherine would be no friend to their ambitions.

"Nonsense!" objected Lady Catherine. "Anne and I shall return to London immediately. We shall spend the night at my brother's house—I have business with him, after all."

Glancing out the window, Mr. Darcy turned a dubious eye on his aunt. "It is rather too late to be starting for London, Aunt. It would be better—and safer—if you would stay the night."

The full force of Lady Catherine's sneer of disdain was unleashed upon Mr. Bingley and his relations. "Stay the night in the house of a tradesman? You might feel it acceptable to debase yourself in such a fashion, but I certainly do not. I have a comfortable carriage and capable drivers—we shall be very well indeed."

"Perhaps that is for the best, Lady Catherine," said Miss Bingley, her tone credibly disinterested. "We would not wish for you to stay where you would not be comfortable."

Elizabeth happened to be looking at Mr. Darcy, and though he seemed as if he had to suppress a smile at Miss Bingley's sentiments, it was clear that was still worried, which was more likely for his cousin's sake than his aunt's. He was prevented from replying, however, when Lady Catherine once again made her opinion known.

"Your scruples do you credit, I am certain," said Lady Catherine, and though her words were benign, her tone fairly oozed superiority. "Despite your low origins, it is apparent that you at least understand a little of such things."

Miss Bingley sniffed in disdain, but Mr. Darcy interjected before any other comment could be made. "Aunt, my cousin does not appear to be well. Surely you can stay the night?"

"I will be well," said Miss de Bourgh. "I am not as frail as you think."

Mr. Darcy regarded her dubiously, but she did not give him any further opportunity to argue. Instead, she stood and approached Elizabeth, saying: "Congratulations, Miss Bennet." She smiled a little and continued: "I do not know if you understand what you are taking on with my dour cousin, but I do hope you are able to inject a little levity into his manner."

"Anne!" snapped Lady Catherine. "You must stop speaking such nonsense! You know that your betrothal with Darcy is a decided fact. I will brook no more argument on this subject."

Though Elizabeth was surprised, Miss de Bourgh's eyes narrowed with displeasure. Her mother would not have seen it given the fact that the daughter was facing away from her, but the action occurred nonetheless.

"I believe that this conversation is one best continued in privacy, Mother," said Anne.

Everyone, even those who did not know Miss de Bourgh well, looked at her with some surprise. She did not appear to be the sort of lady who would speak in such a forthright manner and with such a stern tone of voice, especially to a mother known to be as assertive and dominating as was Lady Catherine. But there was no mistaking the air of command in her words; even Lady Catherine appeared to notice how Anne had addressed her, though Elizabeth would not have called her the most perceptive of women.

"I am not accustomed to such language, Anne," said Lady Catherine in a rather frosty tone.

Miss de Bourgh merely turned to Mr. Darcy. "Cousin, will you assist my mother to the carriage please? I believe there have been enough unseemly displays concerning our family's affairs for one night."

Mr. Darcy readily agreed, and the trio—followed by an obviously bewildered Mr. Collins—left the room, though not before Miss de Bourgh bid the company a warm farewell, directing most of her attention at Elizabeth and Mrs. Bennet. For her part, Elizabeth wondered at the other woman's behavior. Given what she had been told by Mr. Collins and her own first impressions of Miss de Bourgh, Elizabeth would not have thought that the woman possessed the reserves of strength necessary to contradict her mother in such a fashion.

Regardless, it did not affect Elizabeth's determination. She recognized that Mr. Darcy's proposal would occur in a matter of time which was largely to be determined by Elizabeth herself and that she would one day be mistress of his estates. She did not know Miss de Bourgh well enough to be certain what the other woman wanted from life, but Elizabeth could not countenance her living in so obvious a lack of cheer as she did currently. She would do her best in the future to ensure that Miss de Bourgh was afforded some measure of joy in the Darcy homes.

The company sat conversing quietly for several moments, waiting for Mr. Darcy to join them. Elizabeth was sensible to the fact that her mother had once again spoken with Mrs. Hill to delay their dinner, and she could only wonder at this behavior. Perhaps Mrs. Bennet was thawing a little to Mr. Darcy, and Elizabeth could only be glad of that fact. Even more so, Elizabeth was happy that her mother's gradually improving opinion was keeping her tongue in check.

At length, the gentleman did return, and Mrs. Bennet invited the entire company into the dining room for the overdue repast. The seating was rather fortunate, as Mrs. Bennet usually did not stand on ceremony, and only the barest attention was paid to the proper rank when the company took their chairs. As a result, Mr. Darcy, as the highest ranking man present, not only escorted Mrs. Bennet in to dinner, but he also escorted Elizabeth on his other arm, thereby ensuring that he was situated to Mrs. Bennet's right at the foot of the table and that Elizabeth was situated to his left. And given the fact that Mr. Bingley had sat to Mrs. Bennet's left, with Jane by his side, Mrs. Bennet appeared to be holding court with the highest-ranking members of the party. Mr. Bennet appeared to be bemused at the loss of his eldest daughters—his normal dinner companions—but he merely smiled a little ruefully and turned his attention to the Bingley sisters, who had ended up at his end of the table.

But Elizabeth had no opportunity to witness the interaction between her father and those nearby, as keeping her mother from exposing herself in front of Mr. Darcy became her primary concern. It was therefore a surprise when Mrs. Bennet showed herself to be much more subdued than Elizabeth had ever seen her. For the most part, Mr. Bingley and Jane carried the conversation, though Mr. Darcy was doing his best to be civil and attentive. Elizabeth herself did not speak as much as she normally would, for she was feeling somewhat reflective. But while Mrs. Bennet would in any other circumstance have monopolized the conversation, she seemed to have relatively little to say. In fact, her attention was focused on Mr. Darcy, unless Elizabeth missed her guess.

It was later after dinner when it all became clear, though Elizabeth never could have imagined what her mother was thinking. The gentlemen joined Mr. Bennet in remaining in the dining room for port, but it was not long before they made their way to the parlor where the ladies awaited.

For some time after coffee and tea were delivered, the conversation flowed effortlessly, and conversation partners were somewhat fluid. Mrs. Bennet left briefly to look after some matter of the servants, and when she returned, she espied Mr. Darcy, who was approaching Elizabeth. Seeing this, she intercepted Mr. Darcy before he could achieve his objective.

"Mr. Darcy," said the Bennet matron, "I would speak with you for a moment."

Though obviously surprised, Mr. Darcy stopped and turned to his hostess. "Of course, madam. How may I assist you?"

Elizabeth could not imagine what her mother's intent could be, but she looked around briefly as she felt a stab of unease. Fortunately, only Miss Bingley appeared to be close enough to hear what they were saying; furthermore, Mrs. Bennet, for once, appeared to be keeping her voice quiet. Yet Elizabeth could not help but notice that Miss Bingley appeared to be quite fixated upon the discussion despite the fact that she was ostensibly engaged in conversation with Jane and Mr. Bingley.

"I merely wish to understand your intentions toward my daughter, Mr. Darcy."

It was all Elizabeth could do not to gasp; such direct questioning was not done! And it was *certainly not* done in a drawing room where anyone could overhear! A quick glance at Miss Bingley showed an understated but definitive sneer for Mrs. Bennet's indelicate question. But Miss Bingley's distaste did not make her any less eager for Mr. Darcy's answer, if the way she leaned in their direction was any indication.

"You certainly did not consider her worthy of your attention upon first acquaintance, and your behavior until recently was not obliging. I have often had difficulty understanding Elizabeth, Mr. Darcy, but that does not make her any less dear to me. I would not have her hurt."

Finally, Mr. Darcy seemed to find his voice. He smiled at Mrs. Bennet and said: "I believe that I can completely agree with you on that point, Mrs. Bennet. I assure you that my intentions are completely honorable.

"And while we are speaking frankly, I would like to take this opportunity to apologize for my behavior that night at the assembly which I am certain must be on your mind. I told Miss Elizabeth that I would not like to give excuses, and there is none for such incivility, except to say that I was weighed down by some pressing concerns and should not have come out into society that night."

Mrs. Bennet waved him off impatiently. "Yes, yes, Mr. Darcy, your behavior that night was unfortunate. I am more concerned with my daughter."

"I assure you, madam, that there is no cause for concern."

"And how far do you mean to take your attentions?"

"To their natural conclusion." was Mr. Darcy's serious reply.

A slow nod met his declaration, though Elizabeth would have expected her mother to erupt in a fit of hysterics. Judging by the look of anticipation on her face, Miss Bingley expected a similar reaction. Yet the expression quickly turned to disappointment as Mrs. Bennet did nothing more than curtsey and return to her seat, allowing Mr. Darcy to take his place beside Elizabeth again. With his return, Elizabeth fixed her attention back on him, leaving Miss Bingley to her dark looks and anger.

"Thank you, Mr. Darcy," said Elizabeth. "I believe you may have won her over to your side."

"It was my pleasure, Miss Elizabeth. And much to my benefit, I assure you."

At her quizzical expression, he smiled teasingly and said: "Now that your mother is aware of my intentions, I do not doubt that she will be an enthusiastic supporter of my suit. I dare say that she would be unhappy if my offer, when I make it, is not accepted with alacrity."

Elizabeth looked at the teasing man with mock indignation. "For shame, Mr. Darcy. Turning my mother against me constitutes a betrayal of the most acute kind."

Mr. Darcy chuckled and looked back at her, his affection evident in the depths of his eyes. "You well know that the choice shall be yours. But another person supporting my designs is very welcome, I assure you."

There was truly nothing further to stay to that, and Elizabeth felt her world once again spinning. Mr. Darcy was getting much closer to obtaining the answer he desired, and she knew that he was well aware of that fact. But for some reason, Elizabeth could not repine the power the man was quickly gaining over her.

The reprieve from Mrs. Bennet's raptures was short-lived indeed.

Elizabeth went to bed that evening, her head full of thoughts of Mr. Darcy and the esteem she was rapidly gaining for him. But to Mrs. Bennet, he represented another step in her designs to wed her daughters off and thereby ensure their—and consequently, her own—security. With Jane engaged to Mr. Bingley and Elizabeth's anticipated betrothal to Mr. Darcy, Mrs. Bennet would never have to fear for her security after her husband's death. And that was a cause for her nerves, which had been curiously absent the past several days, to once again make an appearance.

"Elizabeth!"

Startled from her sleep, Elizabeth sat up straight and peered about wildly.

"Shall Mr. Darcy visit you again today?"

Recognizing the note of hysteria in her mother's voice, Elizabeth shook her head to herself, partly with regret for the end of the welcome interlude and partly from exasperation.

"He calls most days, Mama," responded Elizabeth with a yawn. She looked out the window to see that although it was somewhat later than she could usually be found abed, it was decidedly earlier than usual for her mother to be up and about.

"Yes, I suppose he does at that," said Mrs. Bennet. "It is a shame that you did not see fit to tell me of Mr. Darcy's intentions before. I could have seen to it that his favorite dishes were served at dinner. At the very least, you must let me know what they are so that I may see to it that they are served for luncheon. Surely the gentlemen will consent to stay for luncheon."

"I do not know, Mama," said Elizabeth through a suppressed sigh. "And I cannot tell you what Mr. Darcy's favorite foods are, for I do not believe it has ever come up in conversation."

Mrs. Bennet clucked her tongue in disapproval. "You must pay more attention to these things, Lizzy. A man will not bestow his attentions on a woman without some encouragement, you know. You must use every opportunity to make yourself indispensable to Mr. Darcy so that he will be induced to propose as soon as may be."

Sighing, Elizabeth attempted to burrow down even further under her blankets, reflecting that Mr. Darcy had been moving along quite charmingly without Mrs. Bennet's encouragement.

But further sleep was not to be. It did not matter that Elizabeth would have preferred to sleep more that morning or that it was still some time before the gentlemen could politely visit. Now that Elizabeth had caught the attention of a man of means, she had to be shown off to her best advantage.

So for the next hour, Elizabeth was fussed over, with her mother presiding over every detail of her appearance. Nothing was beneath her notice; from her hair to her dress to her slippers, everything was fretted over and agonized over until Elizabeth felt sure that she was ready to pull her hair out. When it was all done, her mother stood in front of her, critically examining her work.

"Well, I suppose it shall have to do. It is at times like this that I wish you were as beautiful as your sister, but *you do* look very well, I must say."

Accustomed as she was to her mother's ways, Elizabeth did not take affront to the lukewarm compliment. Rather, she fixed her mother with a steady gaze. "Mama, I really do not think that I am required to do anything more with my appearance than I have previously. I am certain that since Mr. Darcy has developed an interest in me, he did so regardless of whatever physical imperfections I may possess."

"And it is to his credit, I am sure," said Mrs. Bennet. "But there is no harm in helping things along now, is there?"

She then turned and left the room, fussing all the way, leaving Elizabeth to her amused thoughts. Mrs. Bennet would obviously never change, so Elizabeth decided that she would not concern herself with the matter. It was now later than her usual time to break her fast, and Mr. Darcy would soon arrive. She was confident in the constancy of his feelings, but she still wished to be on hand to greet him.

Chapter XVII

Mr. Darcy and Mr. Bingley were prompt in visiting, and the appreciative expression on Mr. Darcy's countenance when he saw her made her rather incongruously grateful for her mother's attentions that morning. Of course, as soon as the thought struck, she remembered that he always seemed to have that expression when he looked at her, regardless of her apparel.

The morning was spent in good company, and the gentlemen were indeed persuaded to join the family for luncheon. They left soon afterward, however, citing a previous engagement for that evening. The Bennets themselves were also engaged for the evening to dine with the Gouldings, but Elizabeth felt strangely bereft, as it had been some time since they had been occupied at different locations on the same evening.

Discounting it as the silly musings of a love-sick girl, Elizabeth determined that she would enjoy the evening regardless.

In addition to the Bennets, there were several of the other families of the area who had been engaged to dine. An invitation to the militia had also been tendered, as the society of the officers was still a sought after addition to the dinner parties of the area. Now, it must be said that though Mr. Wickham had not been excluded from recent events—it was difficult to single out one officer among many—he was treated with far more caution than he had been when he had first arrived in Meryton. Elizabeth had seen him once since he had accosted her in Longbourn's gardens, but he had not attempted to speak to her or importune her any further. Due to his awareness that Elizabeth had seen through his prevarications and understood his character, she would have expected that he would give her wide berth. But discretion, it seemed, was not a character trait he possessed to any great measure.

The evening began innocuously enough. The Bennets were welcomed into the Gouldings' home with the typical pleasantries and conversations which were exchanged between families of longstanding acquaintance. The before-dinner conversation was polite and engaging—though Elizabeth again lamented Mr. Darcy's absence—and the dinner was everything Elizabeth would have expected from a night at the Gouldings' home. It was after dinner when Mr. Wickham finally shed his uncharacteristic reticence and approached Elizabeth.

Now, it must not be supposed that Mrs. Bennet would in any way be able to hold her tongue about her daughters' suitors. Within moments of the arrival of the Bennets, she was crowing about the good fortune of not only her eldest, but also her second eldest. Of course, the fact that Elizabeth's relationship with Mr. Darcy had not as of yet been settled was not something upon which her mother gave much thought. As the man had declared his attentions to be honorable, it was already a decided fact in Mrs. Bennet's mind.

Mr. Wickham had spent most of the evening apart from the rest of the diners, speaking only infrequently, and when he did say something, he spoke almost exclusively with his fellow officers and those few people with whom he was still friendly. Therefore, it appeared to be some time before he had occasion to become acquainted with Mrs. Bennet's hopes and expectations regarding Elizabeth's future. In fact, in an almost perverse twist of fate, Elizabeth was witness to the instant when he became aware of Mrs. Bennet's words.

It happened some time after the dinner hour. Elizabeth had been speaking with Mrs. Goulding some ways apart from where Mrs. Bennet was standing with Lady Lucas and some of the other ladies of the area, and Mr. Wickhams was standing almost directly behind the small group. And as Elizabeth could hear every word which issued forth from her mother's mouth, it was clear that Mr. Wickham could as well.

"I am so pleased for my girls, Lady Lucas," said Mrs. Bennet in her usually excited tone of voice.

Lady Lucas's words were lost in the general murmur of conversation in the room, her voice being much lower in volume.

"Oh, I never doubted for an instant that my Jane would be able to attract a man of good fortune. She is so beautiful and obliging that I knew that Mr. Bingley would be able to see her worth.

"But I must allow that I was shocked when Mr. Darcy—who we all thought of as high and mighty and above his company—told me of his intentions toward Lizzy. I cannot begin to tell you how surprised I was!"

It was almost comical the way Mr. Wickham's head whipped around, his incredulous gaze falling upon first Mrs. Bennet and then Elizabeth. It was not long, however, before his astonished gaze turned to one of displeasure and then one of calculation. Elizabeth felt discomfited by his frank appraisal of her person and the slightly knowing smirk he directed at her. If she had not already understood exactly what type of man he was, that expression by itself would have informed her.

Mrs. Bennet had continued speaking in the interim. "I suppose that Mr. Darcy is not so high and mighty as we all thought. He shows great discernment in preferring my Lizzy over the many high-born ladies of his acquaintance in society."

Again, there was a pause while one of the other ladies spoke, and then Mrs. Bennet's voice could be heard again. "When he first arrived in Meryton, he *was* as you describe him, to be certain. But since the ball at Netherfield, he has been nothing less than obliging to my family, I assure you. He visits nearly every day, and he always has some compliment to leave with us, to say nothing of the attention he has been paying Lizzy. I tell you, we shall be hearing wedding bells ere long!

"He even gave us a very important warning," continued Mrs. Bennet in a confiding tone, though the volume of her voice had not been lowered appreciably. "I dare say that we would never have known about the . . . the *viper* in our midst if he had kept the matter to himself."

A round of agreement—coupled with several knowing glances in the direction of Mr. Wickham—could be heard. Mr. Wickham, for his part, appeared to affect nonchalance and an insensibility to their conversation, but Elizabeth was not fooled. She was certain he had been listening very closely to everything which had been said.

The ladies' conversation moved on to other topics at that point, leaving Elizabeth wishing that her mother had kept the glimmer of sense she had shown in the past few days and refrained from speaking of sensitive topics in such a loud tone of voice. Mr. Wickham appeared to be thoughtful, though Elizabeth could only conjecture that he was considering how to use his newly acquired intelligence in the most advantageous manner. She resolved to avoid the man and deny him the opportunity to say anything to her.

But her resolution turned out to be in vain, though it was some time before he was presented with an opportunity to importune her on the subject. As the company began to break up and return to their homes near the end of the evening, she became distracted enough to allow him the chance to approach her. Elizabeth had just moments before said farewell to some acquaintances, and she was distracted by their leave-taking, as was most of the room. Knowing that her father would soon wish for his family to also take their leave, Elizabeth began to think about gathering her things for their departure when she felt a presence at her side.

She turned with some surprise, only to see Mr. Wickham's unpleasant smirk up close. "I understand that you have made quite the conquest, Miss Bennet," said he.

Though his tone fairly oozed insincerity and faintly suggested intimidation, Elizabeth refused to allow herself to be cowed by this man. "You should not believe everything you hear, Mr. Wickham."

"Even if I hear it from your own mother?" His tone was disbelieving and held just a hint of mockery. "I was surprised," continued he in a conversational tone. "I did not think Darcy had it in him. He has always been such a cold fish, especially when it comes to the fairer sex. Although I must own that I would find the inducement inspiring myself."

This last was said with a leer which made Elizabeth feel as though he was attempting to see through her dress. Given what she knew of the man, Elizabeth was certain that this impression was not far from the truth.

"Did you have something particular you wished to say, Mr. Wickham?" demanded Elizabeth. She wished for nothing more than to be out of this odious man's presence.

"Merely to congratulate you, Miss Bennet," replied Mr. Wickham with an elaborate bow. "I am certain that such a triumph as to ensnare the great Fitzwilliam Darcy is something quite out of the ordinary way. I believe that I underestimated you—you certainly understand the benefit of focusing your attention on one who can afford to woo you. It makes me wish that I possessed an income sufficient to please you."

At this, Elizabeth actually laughed at him, ignoring his responding dark look. "You truly are one of the most amusing men of my acquaintance, Mr. Wickham. I believe that your words reveal your second great weakness, one which is beyond those more obvious faults of character and basic decency. Not only do you expect people to believe you based on nothing more than your pretty, affected manners, but you expect that everyone else is ruled by their selfish desires and avarice. I thank you for this amusing insight into your character."

Though Elizabeth could tell that she had affronted him greatly, he held the temper she knew was simmering under the surface of his pretty manners, and he addressed her thus:

"I would advise you to take great care, Miss Bennet. This good fortune of yours may not last. Not only do I expect the great Darcy pride to make a swift reappearance, but in your attempts to procure a rich husband, you have forgotten that he may have other obligations which are expected of him. You may *think* that you have managed to secure his affections, but he would never go against his sense of duty and the claims of his family."

"And I have no reason to think he would," replied Elizabeth in a flippant tone. She was aware that Mr. Wickham was referring to Anne de Bourgh, but since he could not know of Lady Catherine's visit, his assertions were amusing in the extreme.

"Then you *do* have the measure of him," said Mr. Wickham with a knowing smile. "Now that you are about to achieve your greatest desire, perhaps it would behoove you to correct an injustice done to another. It would be a shame if your designs were prevented by some unfortunate happenstance and through no fault of your own."

"I am sure I do not know to what you refer, Mr. Wickham," replied Elizabeth, though his words instantly put her on her guard. Mr. Darcy had told her that Mr. Wickham would do almost anything to hurt his enemy, and his words sounded like a veiled threat, though she could not decide just exactly to what he was referring.

"I mean simply that fate will sometimes intervene and punish those who unjustly accuse another. A few words in town will help counteract the damage you have done to my reputation, slandering me when I did not deserve it."

"I believe our discussion has almost come to an end, Mr. Wickham," said Elizabeth, noting that her father was now looking for her. "But let me correct your perceptions concerning two matters. First, though I doubt my word would mean anything to you, I have never said anything to anyone in Meryton concerning you.

"Furthermore, I must remind you that if anyone has uttered slanderous words about another, it was most certainly done by *you*, sir. Mr. Darcy has done nothing but respond to your words, and if the truth lies with one of you, then I am certain that the matter will become clear over time. I must also remind you that you were the one who started this war of words.

"Thus, I must ask you again to keep your opinions to yourself. Perhaps if you attempt to deal with all fairly and without avarice or deception, your character will speak for itself. As for myself, I have nothing further to say to you on this or any other subject."

Mr. Wickham's eyes fairly glittered with his displeasure, though he kept an affable expression firmly fixed on his face. She had to acknowledge to herself that the man was very practiced, and if she had not been looking for his inconsistencies, she might have been completely taken in by his manners and speeches.

But their tête-à-tête was now at an end, as her father had approached them. He looked at Mr. Wickham rather severely, the expression one which appeared to come to him much more naturally in recent days than it ever had before.

"And what are you doing here, Mr. Wickham?"

"Merely speaking with your daughter, Mr. Bennet," said Mr. Wickham.

Mr. Bennet looked at him, his hard look becoming even flintier by the moment. "Elizabeth, your mother and sisters are preparing to leave. Please join them while I have a word with Mr. Wickham."

"Of course, Papa," replied Elizabeth, and with the barest hint of a curtsey and no verbal farewell, she turned and left.

On the carriage ride home, Mr. Bennet spoke of the matter of Mr. Wickham to all of his family.

"Girls, I know you all understand just what manner of man this Mr. Wickham is. Mr. Darcy's communications cannot be misunderstood." He fixed his gaze upon Kitty and Lydia particularly before he continued to speak. "The man is a libertine of the worst sort, and he has no scruples at all where young ladies are concerned. Your portions are unfortunately small, but you must understand that this will not be a deterrent to a man such as Wickham. He will ruin you, and he will not spare the matter a second thought if you give him even the smallest opening to do so.

"He approached our Lizzy again tonight, and though I do not know the subject of their conversation, I cannot imagine that his discourse was at all what I would wish my daughters to engage in. Is that not correct, Lizzy?"

Elizabeth nodded and addressed her sisters, all of whom were attending to the conversation. "He dons his cloak of respectability with a practiced ease, but though his manners are as they ever were and his speech is all that is pleasing, he speaks in innuendos and makes veiled threats."

"As I suspected," said Mr. Bennet. "I have instructed Mr. Wickham that he should not speak to any of you or even acknowledge your presence. I expect that he will ignore my directive whenever it should suit his purpose, so I shall be having a conversation with his commanding officer yet again. But I shall also put it to all of you—should Mr. Wickham even give you a glance across a crowded room which makes you uneasy, I wish to know of it immediately. And should he actually speak with you, you are to excuse yourself and refuse to talk to the man. Am I very clear?"

A chorus of acknowledgements met Mr. Bennet's demand, though the moods of the sisters were obviously different. Jane was as placid as ever, while Mary was unconcerned and gave her assurance readily. Kitty and Lydia were different than Elizabeth would have expected—whereas Kitty solemnly gave her assurance of her compliance, Lydia appeared thoughtful and would not look up from the floor of the carriage, which suggested to Elizabeth that she had still hoped that some measure of redeeming quality could be found within the handsome young man. Some part of Elizabeth mourned the passing of her sisters' youthful innocence, though the greater part of her was well aware of the benefit such knowledge would be to them.

The remainder of the journey back to Longbourn passed largely in silence, as even Mrs. Bennet and the youngest Bennets appeared to be in an introspective frame of mind. For Elizabeth, her mind was on the morrow and the fact that she would see Mr. Darcy once again. She found herself greatly anticipating the pleasure and wondering just how close he was to a declaration, though she was aware all the while that it depended entirely upon her. She found that she was not of a mind to make him wait much longer.

Chapter XVIII

Unfortunately for Elizabeth, the following morning did not proceed according to her design, though the events that did occur were very much to the benefit of her entire family. The previous evening had ended quietly, with the family retiring soon after their return from the Gouldings' dinner party. The true surprise was that on the following morning, Lydia had also risen early and could be found in the dining room even before Elizabeth and her father, who were always early risers, had arrived.

When Elizabeth entered the room, Lydia looked up at her with a hopeful expression. Lydia appeared as if she wished to speak, but she ultimately said nothing other than the banal platitudes which might be expected during breakfast. The entrance of their father put an end even to the appearance of wishing to speak, as she seemed distinctly uncomfortable at his entrance.

For his part, Mr. Bennet was no less surprised than Elizabeth had been upon seeing Lydia in the breakfast room so early in the day. "Good morning, girls," said he as he sat down to a plate of light fare typical of a morning after a night out. "Lydia, I must own that I am a little surprised at seeing you here at this hour."

Lydia mumbled something about being hungry, though it felt much like an empty excuse. Mr. Bennet, however, did not push the matter, though he did regard his youngest for some time with a quizzical expression on his face before shrugging and turning to his breakfast. Elizabeth, however, was still curious, as she had the sense that Lydia was uncomfortable about something. She resolved to watch her sister and make certain that she was available should Lydia wish to speak. Her resolution turned out to be unnecessary, as Lydia was not inclined to leave her sister's presence.

"Lizzy," began Lydia once Elizabeth had finished her breakfast.

Elizabeth looked up. Though Lydia had addressed her, she did not immediately speak, and her manner bespoke an indifference which was completely uncharacteristic of the usually fearless girl. In fact, Elizabeth had the impression that Lydia had finished eating some time earlier and had been waiting for her to leave the room.

"Where . . . What . . ." Lydia tried, and after stammering for a moment longer, she took a deep breath and looked Elizabeth in the eye. "Do you intend to walk out today?"

"No further than the garden," said Elizabeth with a smile. "It has become a little cold for a walk of any length, and there is . . . company in the area whom I would not wish to come upon alone."

Lydia seemed to understand to whom Elizabeth was referring, and she blushed slightly at the reminder. Elizabeth's suspicions were aroused as to the source of Lydia's disquiet, though at that moment she was not certain exactly what about Mr. Wickham had resulted in Lydia's obvious unease.

"May I . . . May I accompany you?"

"Of course you may, Lydia," said Elizabeth, trying to put her sister at ease, though she was afire with curiosity. "You do not even need to ask."

Smiling, albeit somewhat tremulously, Lydia accompanied Elizabeth to the vestibule, where they donned their winter gear and stepped out into a fine, though somewhat cold, winter day. There was very little conversation between the sisters—Elizabeth was content to simply enjoy the fineness of the day, and Lydia appeared caught up in her thoughts.

Finally, about the time when Elizabeth was ready to go back inside, Lydia turned to her, and in a shy voice, said: "Lizzy, can I speak to you for a moment?"

"Of course, Lydia."

Elizabeth directed her sister toward a bench—ironically, it was the same bench they had occupied when Elizabeth had shared her suspicions about Mr. Wickham—and they sat together. But though

Lydia had indicated her desire to speak and sat facing Elizabeth, she kept her eyes averted. Some part of Elizabeth began to be concerned — this was not the brash and fearless sister to whom she was accustomed.

After a silence of several moments in which Lydia fidgeted with her gloves, Elizabeth finally prompted her: "Lydia, you wished to speak with me?"

"I am afraid that you will be cross with me," confessed Lydia as she dared a hesitant glance at Elizabeth.

"That depends on what you think you have done wrong," said Elizabeth. "Is it something which cannot be undone?"

Lydia's expression grew contemplative. "I am not certain. At least, I think it can be undone."

"Then you have no cause to concern yourself," replied Elizabeth gently. "Lydia, you must tell me what is bothering you."

Though she let out a sigh of resignation, Lydia began to speak immediately, but her words did not give Elizabeth any comfort. "You have to understand, Lizzy, that he is so very handsome, and he spoke such pretty words of admiration. I simply could not help myself."

"Who, Lydia?" asked Elizabeth in a quiet voice, though she had a sinking feeling that she knew exactly of whom Lydia was speaking.

"Mr. Wickham," mumbled Lydia, confirming Elizabeth's conjecture.

"What of Mr. Wickham?" asked Elizabeth. Though she was anxious of what Lydia had to say and had to fight to keep from demanding answers, Elizabeth forced herself to stay calm and present the image of a confessor rather than an inquisitor.

"He asked me to elope with him, Lizzy. I very nearly agreed with him."

Mind awhirl, Elizabeth gazed at her sister, completely aghast at what she was being told. But then the more rational part of her mind reasserted itself; Lydia obviously had not agreed to elope with him, or she would not be here having this halting conversation. And if her activities with Mr. Wickham were nothing more than harmless flirtation or even a few stolen kisses, then the damage would not be irreparable. Hopefully, it was nothing more serious than that . . .

"I believe, Lydia, that you had best tell me exactly what you have done with Mr. Wickham. Do not leave anything out."

"It is nothing, really," said Lydia, and though she was not precisely dissembling, she was also not as of yet being completely open with Elizabeth. "It began after you told us of Mr. Darcy's accusations toward

Mr. Wickham. I met him on the street in Meryton, and he flattered me, telling me that I was the most beautiful of my sisters." She gazed at Elizabeth with a plaintive air. "You do not know how difficult it is being the youngest, especially when my mother speaks incessantly of Jane's beauty. I was quite charmed by his words."

This was one instance in which Elizabeth could commiserate with her youngest sister wholeheartedly. How often had she felt exactly the same way? Though Jane was the dearest creature in the world, Mrs. Bennet did not make sisterly affection easy with her constant pronouncements, not only of Jane's beauty, but also of Lydia's vivacity. But now was not the time for such thoughts, so Elizabeth listened to Lydia with growing anxiety.

"It was not much longer before he met me on the road from Longbourn to Meryton, and his attentions became even more pronounced." Lydia paused and chuckled, though her laugh had a definite self-deprecating quality. "You know that I have always wished to be the first of my sisters to marry. I thought I might have the chance with Mr. Wickham."

"You would consider it even after all Mr. Darcy shared with us to warn us of this man?" cried Elizabeth. "Lydia, I cannot believe that you could be this senseless!"

"But his words seemed to ring so true," wailed Lydia. "He claimed that Mr. Darcy was only believed because of his money and that his enmity was due to nothing more than jealousy!"

"Come now, Lydia. Of what could Mr. Darcy have to be jealous?"

"His father's love," said Lydia. "He said that Mr. Darcy hated him because Mr. Darcy's father loved Wickham better than his own son."

It was certainly a story that a gullible girl such as Lydia might have found plausible. The idea of being romanced would have been nigh irresistible to such a young and impressionable girl, though Elizabeth knew that Lydia's selfish desires were what had blinded her to what she had been told about the man.

"What else happened, Lydia?" asked Elizabeth, focusing in the immediate issue at hand.

"Two days ago, he met me again and asked me to elope with him."

"And what did you say?" pressed Elizabeth.

"I was excited, but something told me to be cautious. He pressed for my answer, but I told him I would need to think on the matter."

"And when were you to give it?"

"There is no set timetable," mumbled Lydia. "He asked me to think about it and reply as soon as I am ready."

"No doubt he expects that his charming manners and gentlemanly countenance will convince you of his sincerity," spat Elizabeth. "I doubt he could even conceive of the notion that you would inform me of his actions."

"He now has no more hope of a favorable answer," said Lydia. "I shall be certain to let him know of that fact when next I see him."

"I believe that would be unwise," said Elizabeth, directing a cautionary look at her sister. "I do not doubt that Mr. Wickham would have no trouble taking matters into his own hands should you give him an opportunity."

Gasping, Lydia gazed upon Elizabeth with an expression akin to one of horror. "You think he would . . . would . . . compromise me?"

"I cannot claim to understand the mind of one such as Mr. Wickham, but I would not put it past him."

"He did not importune me because he loves me, did he?" asked Lydia in a small voice.

Elizabeth regarded her sister with compassion. For perhaps the first time, her eyes were truly being opened, and unlike the previous week in which Elizabeth had been attempting to induce her to see sense, now Lydia was being forced to grow up, recognizing herself as the victim in a manner which she could not fail to understand. It would no doubt be a painful experience for Lydia; not only would Mr. Bennet take a dim view of Lydia's improprieties, but Lydia would also come to understand her own vulnerability. Should Mr. Wickham have the chance, he would almost certainly have no scruples in letting her know exactly how foolish she had been. After all, he had done it before.

But while this would ultimately turn out to be a good learning experience for Lydia, Elizabeth was determined to spare her feelings. Lydia needed to learn, yes. Yet she did *not* need to have her confidence shattered by this event.

"I am afraid not, Liddy," said Elizabeth, using the family's pet name for Lydia in order to set her a little at ease. "I am not certain that Mr. Wickham has the capacity for feeling love for anyone other than himself."

"Then what do we do?" asked Lydia in a small voice.

"That will be up to my father to decide," replied Elizabeth while rising to her feet. The sooner her father knew of this matter, the sooner he could take action to prevent Mr. Wickham from obtaining his revenge.

"Oh, I cannot tell Papa!" squeaked Lydia, her eyes wide with fright. "He will be ever so angry. Could we not just keep it between ourselves? If I do not give any notice to Mr. Wickham, he will surely give up."

"Lydia," chided Elizabeth, "Mr. Wickham is not the kind of man to simply allow this matter to rest. Papa must know of what has occurred so that he may take steps to protect us all.

"And you must consider," continued she in a comforting tone, "the fact that you have chosen to bring this to me rather than to run off with Mr. Wickham speaks very highly in your favor. Papa will certainly take that into consideration when he learns of this matter."

Elizabeth could see that Lydia was still unconvinced, so she continued in a much firmer tone: "We do not have a choice. We must inform Papa."

"Please stay with me, Lizzy," cried Lydia, attaching herself to one of Elizabeth's arms. "I will be less frightened if you are with me."

"Of course, Lydia," said Elizabeth with a smile of compassion. "Let us go."

As Elizabeth had predicted, Mr. Bennet, while angry, saw the courage Lydia had mustered to speak to Elizabeth concerning the matter. The greater part of his anger was reserved for Mr. Wickham, the author of the Bennet family's current distress. Mr. Bennet was not a man given to overt displays of emotion, but Elizabeth, who knew him better than almost anyone else in the world, could see his anger quite clearly. That, of course, did not prevent him from stating his displeasure to his obviously cowed daughter in a manner which she would never forget.

"I thank you, Lydia," said he. "Today you have confirmed my belief that I have, in fact, sired the silliest young woman in all England. What possessed you to speak with this man in such a manner, even after all you had been told of his behavior?"

Lydia stayed silent, which was likely for the best; her first attempt to justify her actions to her father—by stating that Mr. Wickham was so very handsome and that she had thought he was in love with her—had produced an effect opposite of that which she intended. Considering the events of the day, however, perhaps there was some hope for her after all.

"I trust that perhaps this episode will induce you to think a little more before you allow your fancy to take hold of you?"

Lydia's only response was a glum nod. Elizabeth watched her sister with compassion—she was a flighty and headstrong girl, but she was not a bad one. And in her defense, though Elizabeth and Jane had received the guidance of their aunt and uncle in addition to the attention their father had given them before the gaggle of females in his house became too much for him to bear, Lydia and Kitty particularly had received no such guidance, and by the time Elizabeth and Jane had been old enough to provide it, Lydia's excesses were largely ingrained and, more importantly, supported by her mother.

"Well, it appears that we must deal with the brigand," said Mr. Bennet. "I believe that Mr. Darcy should be arriving soon?"

Elizabeth nodded. Though she thought that she had avoided blushing rather credibly at the mention of her suitor, Mr. Bennet was not fooled, and he looked on her with a fond eye. "In that case, I believe that his assistance and expertise in working on Mr. Wickham would be invaluable."

Mr. Bennet then turned a flinty glare upon his youngest. "Lydia, this episode has reinforced exactly how negligent I have been in instilling in you the proper manners of good society. From this point forward, you are forbidden to walk to Meryton by yourself, and you must stand up with your sisters should you wish to attend a ball."

Tears were glistening in her eyes, but Lydia had the sense not to protest her father's restrictions. Taking compassion on her, Mr. Bennet smiled and said: "I dare say it will not be so terrible. And if you can convince me that you are able to spend ten minutes every day in a rational manner, I may just be persuaded to relax the restrictions I have placed on you."

Though Lydia did not appear to be comforted much by his assurances, she nodded her head and replied in a small voice that she would take greater care next time. Elizabeth saw her father's lips twitch in amusement, and she knew that he was on the point of telling her that there *would not be* another time, but he kept such observations to himself. With the state she was in, Lydia was not likely to appreciate his humor.

When Mr. Darcy arrived, his presence in Mr. Bennet's study was quickly requested, and the knowledge of Mr. Wickham's latest perfidy was related. Given the number of times the man had insinuated himself in Mr. Darcy's life, Elizabeth was not exactly surprised when his lips tightened in response. It was to his credit that his outward reaction was no more severe than that.

"I believe, Mr. Bennet, that the time has come to ensure that Mr. Wickham never again has the power to impose himself in my life or the lives of your daughters."

Mr. Bennet gazed at him with some speculation. "You have

something in mind?"

"I do," confirmed Mr. Darcy. "But first I believe that I should write to my cousin. Not only is he a colonel in the regulars, but he is also aware of every particular of my dealings with Wickham. His assistance will be invaluable."

"Then by all means, Mr. Darcy," said Mr. Bennet, gesturing toward his desk. "I am as eager to have Mr. Wickham gone as you appear to be."

The letter was written and quickly dispatched, and Mr. Darcy spent the next hour in the study speaking with Elizabeth's father concerning how exactly they would deal with Mr. Wickham. Elizabeth left in the company of her sister and returned Lydia to her room, where she undertook the task of explaining gently the reasons for the rules of propriety and the damage any breach could do to her reputation and the reputations of her sisters. It was a very subdued Lydia who was left to think on the consequences her behavior might have brought upon them all.

The decision had been made to keep the knowledge of Lydia's indiscretion from the rest of the family. It would serve no purpose, after all—Mary's behavior was not a problem, Jane was Jane, and Kitty would largely follow wherever Lydia led, so improved behavior by the one sister would undoubtedly lead to an improvement of the other. And as for Mrs. Bennet, they decided to keep exactly what happened from her and limit the communication to a vague explanation that Lydia had done something to anger her father and was being punished accordingly.

Once their plans had been laid, Mr. Darcy left Mr. Bennet in his study, and he soon found Elizabeth in the garden. For her part, Elizabeth had wished to avoid Mr. Darcy while she thought about what had occurred that day. Mr. Darcy had been focused on Mr. Wickham since his arrival at Longbourn, but though he had made no specific complaint, Elizabeth could not but think that for such a scrupulously proper man as Mr. Darcy, this proof of her sister's improper behavior could only be a blow. Elizabeth was proud that he had been so single-minded and determined to make certain Mr. Wickham did not succeed in his plans. Yet she was also ashamed that he had to involve himself at all, for the man had done him much wrong, and it was unfortunate that Mr. Darcy should have to be further involved in Mr. Wickham's affairs.

"Miss Bennet," said Mr. Darcy, as he approached her.

Elizabeth had been so lost in thought that she had not noticed his approach, and she started. She smiled at him warmly, but she did not speak, and he seemed to catch her pensive mood. He sat beside her and for some time, neither spoke.

For Elizabeth, the time spent sitting on the bench in his company was not filled with the easy conversation which had characterized their interactions during the past several days, nor was it the comfortable silence they had sometimes indulged in. No, this was a silence filled with tension due to Elizabeth's nerves, which were frayed by the actions of her sister. Would Mr. Darcy decide that her charms were not worth being related to such a troublesome family? Would he take his leave after the situation with Lydia was resolved? She was well aware that his sense of responsibility would never allow him to depart as long as Mr. Wickham was still free to prey upon the local populace.

She had just made a desperate resolution to speak with him when his voice once again startled her.

"Miss Bennet, you need not be distressed. I shall deal with Mr. Wickham, and I swear to you that he shall never importune your family again."

Elizabeth regarded him with some surprise. "I am sure you shall, Mr. Darcy. I never doubted you for a moment."

"Then this . . . reticence is not due to your concern over Mr. Wickham?" asked Mr. Darcy slowly, a frown of concentration upon his face.

"No. Yes. Oh, I do not know," said Elizabeth, not very coherently. She took a deep breath and looked away. "It is all of this and more, Mr. Darcy. I must own that the revelations of the morning have disturbed me. Even though I never doubted your account for an instant, I had also never thought Mr. Wickham to be capable of . . . of . . . *this*." Elizabeth punctuated her word with an aimless wave of her hand.

"The worst of it all is . . . Well, that is to say." Sighing, Elizabeth turned and gazed into his soulful eyes, half afraid of what she would find. Unfortunately his countenance was expressionless, and his eyes almost appeared to be shuttered. "I am aware that you have had some reservations concerning the behavior of my youngest sisters, Mr. Darcy. Today's . . . adventure with Lydia must provoke second thoughts concerning your attentions to me."

Voicing her fears seemed to almost make them real. Elizabeth regarded her suitor, her insides all aflutter, though she felt that she managed to hide her apprehension admirably. Mr. Darcy initially made no response, his inscrutable mask still firmly in place, and for a long and awful moment, he remained silent. Then his expression softened, and he gazed at her with that heart-felt expression he so often wore when with her, causing her own heart to flutter most alarmingly.

"Perhaps I should tell you a story, Miss Bennet. Then you may judge for yourself what I think of Miss Lydia's actions."

Caught by surprise due to his seeming non sequitur, Elizabeth could only nod for him to continue.

"You are aware that my sister, Georgiana, is many years my junior, correct?" At Elizabeth's nod, Mr. Darcy continued. "After my father passed on, Georgiana was left to the guardianship of myself and my cousin, Colonel Fitzwilliam, who will, I hope, be joining us very soon. Perhaps two young bachelors are not best suited to be guardians for a young girl, but it was done, and we have attempted to do our best in guiding her. She has had the best masters and attended the best schools, and we have given her every advantage that we possibly could.

"In the past year, Colonel Fitzwilliam and I decided that it was time for Georgiana to prepare to go into society. Her formal schooling ended, and she was put into the care of a Mrs. Younge, who acted as her personal companion. We vetted Mrs. Younge carefully, but in the end, we discovered that her references were forged, and she was, in fact, a confederate of none other than the author of your family's current woes, George Wickham."

Elizabeth gasped, now understanding where exactly Mr. Darcy was going with this recitation. She thought to stop him for a moment, but as he continued, she noted that he was speaking more easily of the trials he and his sister had undergone, and she realized that this confession was having a cathartic effect on Mr. Darcy. So she allowed him to proceed without interruption.

"All seemed well for some time," said Mr. Darcy, "and when Mrs. Younge suggested a holiday for my sister at Ramsgate, my cousin and I thought nothing of the matter. Permission was granted, and my sister and her companion were soon installed in a house there.

"By design, Mr. Wickham soon repaired to Ramsgate himself, though he presented it as a chance meeting to my sister. During the course of a fortnight, he was able to ingratiate himself into Georgiana's affections, persuading her that he was in love with her and gaining her consent to an elopement. You will be shocked, of course, to know that at the time, my sister was only fifteen years of age."

Mr. Darcy paused and appeared to gather himself—this last revelation having provoked a measure of anger which she suspected he did not wish to show to her. When he had mastered himself, he continued, though his words and tone were somewhat mechanical, as if another were speaking through his mouth.

"I arrived in Ramsgate for a surprise visit to my sister, though I had not initially intended to visit at all. Imagine my surprise when Georgiana expressed her joy at the prospect of her approaching nuptials.

"Mr. Wickham arrived soon afterward for what I learned was a prearranged visit to discuss the exact details of their proposed journey to Gretna Green. As soon as he was made aware of my presence, he knew that his plot had been foiled, but he continued to play the part he had set for himself. We adjourned to the study in the house I had rented for my sister's use, and there, Mr. Wickham attempted to extort more money from me, using Georgiana's indiscretion as a weapon against me. I told him then that should Georgiana's reputation suffer due to *his* efforts, I would see him in prison."

Mr. Darcy hung his head and continued: "I should have kept him away from her, but knowing that she was now safe, I made the error of not ensuring that she was not beyond the reach of his contempt before escorting him from the premises. It was then that he did as I had previously stated—he told her most emphatically that the only reason that he had pursued her was for her fortune and that any other man who did likewise in the future would undoubtedly have the same purpose.

"I hope you will forgive me, Miss Bennet, for what happened next." Mr. Darcy chuckled, though mirthlessly, and confessed: "I grasped him by his shoulders and threw him into the dust of the street where he belonged. I told him that if he ever came near my sister, I would ensure that he would never be able to show his face in polite society again."

"I dare say that such a fate was the least of what he deserved, Mr. Darcy," said Elizabeth, speaking for the first time. "What an abominable, reprehensible man Mr. Wickham is."

Mr. Darcy nodded. "That he is, indeed. Though I did not realize it at the time, his behavior even as a child foretold the kind of man he was destined to become. But I never could have dreamed he would have descended to such malicious revenge. My sister is the daughter of the man he claimed to love and esteem. I cannot ever forgive him for what he has done."

"How is Miss Darcy now?" asked Elizabeth, knowing what the answer would likely be.

Sighing, Mr. Darcy turned back to her. "She has always been of a quiet and withdrawn temperament, Miss Bennet. This episode with

Mr. Wickham has almost destroyed her self confidence, and it has caused her to draw further within herself. Even now, months after the event, despite the combined efforts of her relations and despite the fact that she is in the care of a very capable and compassionate woman, her spirits continue to be low.

"But of particular import to this conversation is the similarity to be found in the situations of my sister and yours. They were both taken in by a practiced deceiver and made to believe that Mr. Wickham had honorable intentions. Their differences in fortune are substantial, but there is one common thread between them—they were both specifically targeted by Wickham due to his desire to revenge himself upon me.

"Thus, to hold your sister's behavior against her when it has been so similar to *my sister's behavior* would be hypocritical of me, would you not agree?"

There were some truths in his words, but Elizabeth could not quite agree with him yet. "But my sister was particularly warned against any association with Mr. Wickham. I assume your sister had no such information. Am I correct?"

"No, she did not," agreed Mr. Darcy. "More the fool am I, but I chose not to enlighten her as to his bad conduct, feeling that there was little reason to do so. As I said before, I underestimated him."

"Then their behavior cannot be compared. Lydia acted against specific warnings that she had been given, while your sister responded to a man she thought she could trust."

"Ah, but Georgiana has been taught proper behavior from the time she was a little girl. She should not have agreed to an elopement at all, and certainly she should never have agreed to any arrangement with a man which did not have my blessing, especially since she is not even out."

"But Lydia has been wild and willful her entire life. She will not listen to anyone and exposes herself to ridicule at every opportunity."

By this time, the corners of Mr. Darcy's lips were creeping up in the beginnings of a smile, to which Elizabeth felt herself responding. The irony of him arguing for her sister while she argued for his was lost on neither of them.

"But she showed courage and repentance in approaching you to confess and rectify her mistake."

"As did your sister, Mr. Darcy."

Grinning broadly, Mr. Darcy replied: "Touché, Miss Bennet. Touché."

He then turned to her, and taking her hands in his, he looked her in the eye and said gently: "I cannot blame your sister for falling victim to Mr. Wickham because her experience is so similar to my own sister's. It *is* unfortunate, but I prefer to look on this matter as an opportunity for learning. It is painful, to be certain, but as I once told you, I do not believe that your sisters are so far gone that a little guidance will not correct them.

"And I will reiterate that only you can send me away. I will not retreat unless it is by *your* specific desire."

"And I do not desire it," whispered Elizabeth. "I am sorry, Mr. Darcy, for having so little faith in your constancy."

"Your concerns were natural and understandable," said Mr. Darcy, "and I do not fault you for them. But let us speak of this no more. I have summoned Colonel Fitzwilliam, and with his help and that of your father, we shall ensure that Mr. Wickham is not allowed to continue to prey upon innocents such as our sisters. This, I promise you."

Their conversation now moved to other matters, though little of substance was discussed. But it left much for Elizabeth to ponder, and her feelings, growing as they were, seemed close to bursting. She was proud of him—a lesser man might have fled upon learning of such weakness of character as Lydia had betrayed, regardless of how his own relations had behaved. Mr. Darcy's attentions were pleasing indeed, and she knew without any doubt that he was as moral and upright as any man she had ever known. And he was the perfect man for her. Of that, she had no doubt.

Chapter XIX

The next day was Jane's engagement party with Mr. Bingley. As Longbourn had been deemed too small to hold such an affair, Netherfield had been offered as an alternate location, an offer which was, no doubt, a part of Mrs. Bennet's design. Therefore, to Netherfield they were to go.

Of course, such an event—particularly one as significant for the family as this—could not be attended without a flurry of activity aimed at making Mrs. Bennet's daughters appear to best advantage. There were preparations to make and dresses to be pressed, hair to be tied back and final details to be worked out, and such was the frenzy of the household that even those of the family with the most tolerance for Mrs. Bennet's ways felt more than a little relieved when the Bennet carriage finally left Longbourn bound for Netherfield. Those possessing the least patience were considering the merits of a quick flight to the continent.

When the Bennet party arrived at Netherfield, they were greeted by the master of the estate himself in the company of his good friend, and hardly had Elizabeth alighted from the carriage than she found her hand resting upon Mr. Darcy's arm, his smile warm upon her. But to her surprise, though he greeted the Bennets with friendly yet reserved comments, the other young lady he chose to escort into the house was none other than the youngest Miss Bennet.

"How do you do, Miss Lydia?" said he as he smiled and offered her his arm.

Lydia, though puzzled and more than a little reticent due to her experience the day before, nevertheless quickly recovered, and with a hesitant smile, she accepted his arm and said: "Very well, Mr. Darcy."

In this fashion, they advanced into the large sitting room where the diners would gather to await the coming dinner. "I am very glad to see you all," continued Mr. Darcy, more for Lydia's benefit than for anyone else. "I believe that my friend Bingley's cook has outdone herself tonight. It should be an excellent repast with pleasant company indeed."

Elizabeth looked on Mr. Darcy with a slight grin at his changed manners—this was certainly not the forbidding man who had first graced their neighborhood and refused to stand up with any of the local ladies.

"You seem rather ebullient tonight, Mr. Darcy," said an amused Elizabeth. "One would almost think that you have grown accustomed to our little gatherings."

"Indeed, I have, Miss Bennet," said Mr. Darcy. "I find that I have all I need here—the company of my very good friend, the relaxed atmosphere of the country, and the delights of new and welcome acquaintances."

The way he gazed steadily at her as he spoke left no doubt as to the meaning of his words—or perhaps more precisely, the person at whom he had directed them. Lydia, showing a flash of her old self, giggled at the sight, and then with a hasty curtsey, she left them to go and speak with Maria Lucas.

"You will leave me in a state of constant embarrassment if you continue to speak so, Mr. Darcy," said Elizabeth, challenging him to respond.

"Then by all means, I must continue," replied he with an amused smile. "I find that I rather enjoy the effects of your embarrassment on your countenance."

"Mr. Darcy, there you are!"

Turning toward the sound of the voice, Elizabeth noted the approach of none other than Miss Bingley. Elizabeth had not seen much of the woman of late, as she had not visited Longbourn and the gentlemen had largely confined their courting to locations where Mr. Bingley's sisters were not present. It was obvious by the way Miss Bingley spoke so animatedly to Mr. Darcy that she had by no means given up in her quest to secure him for herself. In fact, as she approached, Elizabeth thought for a moment that she would actually be so forward as to grasp his arm. Miss Bingley managed to control herself, however, and she contented herself with some flattering words for her guest, though she all but ignored Elizabeth's presence.

"Miss Bingley," greeted Mr. Darcy when he was finally able to insert a word into her monologue.

The lady smiled at him in a coquettish fashion. "I have been looking for you for some time, sir. I am sure that you prefer a more refined company than you will generally find here, so I thought to offer my services."

A flick of Miss Bingley's eyes informed Elizabeth—had she not already known—of the fact that Elizabeth was not viewed as refined or even agreeable. Elizabeth, however, knowing what the other woman was about, merely smiled and greeted her hostess.

"Oh, Miss Eliza," exclaimed Miss Bingley, feigning surprise. "I am afraid that I did not see you there, hiding behind Mr. Darcy. I see that you have graced us with your presence."

"Thank you for your kind welcome, Miss Bingley," said Elizabeth. "Of course I would not miss this for the world. I am very happy for Jane—as happy as you are for your dear brother, I am sure."

Miss Bingley's smile became brittle and somewhat forced. "I am happy for dear Charles indeed. Jane is such a sweet girl—I am certain that they shall be quite . . . content together."

Miss Bingley's outward affection for Jane had never been in question, though Elizabeth had always considered it to be as insincere as everything else about this woman. But as Miss Bingley always treated Jane with affability—regardless of how forced it sometimes appeared—Elizabeth was willing to respond with perfect respect. She was under no illusion as to what Miss Bingley thought of the entire Bennet family, though it truly mattered little. Elizabeth was not marrying into the Bingley family, and as such, her contact with them would be more limited than Jane's.

Ignoring Elizabeth once again, Miss Bingley turned her attention back to Mr. Darcy. "Shall we sit, Mr. Darcy? I believe I should like some conversation."

"I agree," said Mr. Darcy in response. But though Miss Bingley might have hoped that he would escort her to the nearby sofa, he merely turned and gestured for Elizabeth to precede him, and he followed her, sitting himself beside her, leaving no room for Miss Bingley other than a nearby chair. The lady appeared to be quite put out by his behavior, but she assumed a superior air and sat, proceeding to monopolize the conversation.

Thus began a most frustrating night for all concerned. Though Elizabeth and Mr. Darcy might both have preferred the opportunity to converse with each other on a more intimate basis, they were thwarted at every turn by the ever-vigilant mistress of Netherfield, who attempted to gain Mr. Darcy's attention for herself. Miss Bingley appeared to be just as frustrated as the two lovers, for Mr. Darcy would listen to her politely when she spoke and then turn his attention back to Elizabeth as soon as she had finished.

Luckily for the two still unacknowledged lovers, dinner was one forum in which Miss Bingley could not control matters, as her seat was determined by the simple fact of her position as mistress of Netherfield. Mr. Darcy, as the highest-ranking man present, was to escort the mistress into the dining room, but he avoided paying her specific attention by also extending his free arm to Elizabeth and escorting her into the room as well. Once he had seen Miss Bingley seated in her position, he guided Elizabeth down the table to where Bingley was sitting with Jane, taking the chair on the other side and sitting Elizabeth next to him. Miss Bingley, by the expression on her face, was about as pleased with this as she was by most of what had already occurred that evening. Unfortunately for Miss Bingley, she could do nothing about it.

"Are you quite comfortable, Miss Bennet?" asked Mr. Darcy once Elizabeth was seated.

Elizabeth smiled. "I am indeed, Mr. Darcy."

Down toward the other end of the table, she could see that Miss Bingley was regarding her with an expression which could only be termed poisonous. Mr. Darcy noticed Elizabeth's slight frown, and he leaned toward her with a vague air of concern.

"Is Miss Bingley bothering you, Miss Bennet?"

With a wry grin, Elizabeth replied: "Not at all, Mr. Darcy. I understand what she is about and why she dislikes me so. But it is she who has set me up as a rival. I cannot control her feelings, and she does not intimidate me, so I ignore the worst of her behavior."

"She is delusional if she considers herself a rival," muttered Darcy, but his voice was not low enough to escape Elizabeth's hearing, and she had to stifle a giggle at his slightly improper words.

"I had thought that perhaps you were less than enthused at her . . . subtle overtures."

Mr. Darcy snorted, and then he looked over at Mr. Bingley, who was engaged in a deep conversation with Jane and did not appear to have realized they were talking about his sister. He turned back to Elizabeth and leaned toward her, saying in a low voice:

"No, I have never encouraged her, even to the slightest degree." He paused and then continued in a thoughtful manner, "Although, to be fair to Miss Bingley, she has not always acted thus."

At Elizabeth's quizzical expression, he clarified his statement. "I met Bingley in his first year at Cambridge, which was, coincidentally, my last. We became friends quickly, but it was not until two years later that we became the confidantes we are today. My father died soon after my final year at Cambridge, and I was not at liberty to spend much of my time with friends until after I became more comfortable with the management of Pemberley. "

Elizabeth nodded and gave him a fond smile, thinking that his adherence to duty was one of the things she admired the most about him.

"I was first introduced to Bingley's sister after I had reentered society. I will not prevaricate — she has always been attracted to higher society and the privileges inherent with that lifestyle. But when first I met her, Miss Bingley was not as . . . overtly ambitious as she is now. She has always been alert for potential conquests, but she was not so focused upon *me*."

"Then how do you account for her current behavior?"

Mr. Darcy smiled, and after directing another surreptitious glance at Mr. Bingley, he responded: "I suspect that the fact that she has remained unattached has caused her to fear staying that way. It has only been in the last year that she has begun to concentrate on me."

"Oh, come now, Darcy," said Mr. Bingley suddenly in a quiet voice, though he was still easily heard by Elizabeth, "you know exactly what has prompted this change of heart. She has realized that her pretensions of joining the first circles are exactly that, and as you and I are such close friends, she has attached herself to you as the only one from among your circle with whom she has the slightest hint of a chance."

Mr. Darcy appeared shamefaced at this frank assessment of Miss Bingley, and he hastened to say: "I apologize, Bingley. I should not have spoken of your sister in such a manner."

Watching, Elizabeth sympathized with the man, though Jane appeared to be surprised and almost scandalized. Tempering it, however, was likely the realization that his words were almost certainly true. Jane at least was no longer under the impression that

Caroline possessed any true feelings of friendship toward her, and Elizabeth knew that her sister accepted that fact and the fact of her future sister's character, little though she liked to acknowledge such an acceptance.

For his part, Mr. Bingley just sighed. "That is why you are such a good friend, Darcy. I appreciate your tolerance of her pretensions due to your friendship for me. It speaks very highly of your character indeed.

"But I am not blind to my sister's faults, though I do hope that once a certain . . . happy development is announced," he paused and regarded both Elizabeth and Mr. Darcy with a knowing grin, "she will learn to redirect her attentions in a more appropriate and welcome direction."

Elizabeth colored, but Mr. Bingley only regarded her with pleasure while Jane looked on with a hint of contentment. "I assure you, Miss Elizabeth, that I welcome your effect on my dour friend here. He could do with a little livening up."

With a raised eyebrow, Elizabeth regarded him. "He is lively enough given the right inducement," said she with a hint of impertinence.

Mr. Bingley chortled at Elizabeth's words and, perhaps more specifically, at Mr. Darcy's rather smug look. "You had better keep her, Darcy. *And* marry her before she *truly* comes to understand your foibles."

"Oh, I intend to, I assure you," said Mr. Darcy, his gaze once again fixed on Elizabeth in that intent way of his. Elizabeth, of course, blushed once again under his steadfast gaze, but she would not allow him to intimidate her, so she raised her eyes to his once again and returned his stare in a challenging fashion.

Mr. Bingley regarded them both with fond amusement. "I always suspected that you would meet your match one day, Darcy; I just never expected it to be the sister of the woman I would marry. I must consider it to be a matter of divine providence that we shall one day be brothers. I am the most blessed of men."

"I believe that I rank up there with you, my friend," replied Darcy.

The dinner continued after that, and the conversation continued in this lively manner. It was later that evening near the end of dinner when the discussion once again turned to the events of the past days and what would come in the near future.

"Have you heard from your cousin, Mr. Darcy?" Elizabeth ventured to ask.

"I have indeed," replied Mr. Darcy. "Colonel Fitzwilliam will arrive tomorrow. We shall then take matters in hand and ensure Mr. Wickham is neutralized once and for all."

Elizabeth nodded; she was well aware of the determination Mr. Darcy had with respect to Mr. Wickham. But she trusted Mr. Darcy, so she turned the topic back to his cousin.

"What manner of man is the colonel?" asked she.

"He is more like a brother to me than a cousin," replied Mr. Darcy with a fond smile. "In some ways, he is much like Bingley — he is happy and garrulous and at ease in any social situation. I have always felt that I was blessed to have the friendship and support of such a man, especially when it comes to the guardianship of my sister."

This was a matter which intrigued Elizabeth, as she wondered why his sister had not been left to his sole guardianship.

When she said as much to Mr. Darcy, he smiled and said: "As I was yet a young man when my father passed away, I was grateful for my father's foresight in appointing Fitzwilliam to the position he holds. His insight and support have been most welcome, I assure you."

Smiling, Elizabeth replied to the effect that she was happy he had such a confidante. As Mr. Darcy was such a confident and capable individual, Elizabeth had supposed that he would be able to handle any situation which life threw in his direction. And though he was supremely competent, he also obviously understood that there were instances in which every man required assistance from others. Elizabeth began to feel that to Mr. Darcy, she would never be merely an adornment for his arm. She anticipated the prospect of being a partner in a loving relationship.

After dinner had been completed, they returned to the interference of Miss Bingley, though Elizabeth wondered at the woman's willful obtuseness. Mr. Darcy's attentions were so pointed that it seemed incomprehensible that Miss Bingley, who Elizabeth acknowledged was quite intelligent, could not recognize they were so.

But Elizabeth decided it did not affect her — let Miss Bingley attempt to commandeer his attention in such forums. Elizabeth knew exactly where she stood with Mr. Darcy, and she was well aware that Miss Bingley, for all her pretensions, would not be the one who would receive a proposal from the man.

The morning after the engagement dinner at Netherfield brought new developments in the intrigue with Mr. Wickham. Elizabeth was sitting in the parlor with Jane and Mrs. Bennet when Lydia entered the room and, after a slight hesitation, came and sat directly beside Elizabeth. It did not take long for Elizabeth to realize that something was amiss, for Lydia, though she had never been the calmest or most sanguine of girls, was quite jittery.

"Lizzy, can I speak to you for a moment?" asked Lydia when she noticed Elizabeth's attention upon her.

Nodding, Elizabeth stood and led Lydia from the parlor, instinctively understanding that Lydia would wish to keep whatever she had to say private. Elizabeth only hoped that there was nothing wrong which had prompted Lydia's agitated manner.

When they had left the house and entered the garden, Elizabeth turned to her sister with a raised eyebrow, but she did not need to attempt to drag an explanation from Lydia, as her sister turned to her, blurting:

"I just agreed to elope with Mr. Wickham!"

With some difficulty, Elizabeth managed to avoid saying any of the censorious things which crossed her mind in that moment. Lydia would hardly have said anything concerning the matter had she intended to steal away with the scoundrel.

"Of what are you speaking, Lydia?"

Lydia blushed, belatedly recognizing how her impromptu confession must have sounded. "I do not truly intend to elope, Lizzy."

"Then what do you mean to say?"

"I just met Mr. Wickham out at the edge of the park."

"At the edge of the park?" exclaimed Elizabeth. "The man's audacity knows no bounds!"

"Yes, yes, Lizzy," replied Lydia impatiently. "He has ignored Papa's strictures once again. But I am no longer surprised at his daring, and that is not the material point in any case."

Knowing her sister to be correct, Elizabeth inclined her head and waited for Lydia to continue, which she did with alacrity.

"He was most insistent that he was in love with me and that I must agree to leave for Gretna Green so we might be married."

Lydia paused and fidgeted a little, and Elizabeth could see a slight trembling in her hands. She reached forward to grasp her youngest sister's hands between her own, noting their cold and clammy feel.

"What is it, Liddy?"

"I felt . . . I felt almost . . . afraid of him, Lizzy," managed Lydia finally. "It was almost as if he . . . well, as if he would not allow me to refuse."

"Did he threaten you?" asked Elizabeth through barely controlled fury.

"No," replied Lydia, though Elizabeth had to acknowledge that her manner was a far cry from her normally fearless self. "It was more the intensity with which he importuned me and the look in his eyes when he beseeched me. I had a feeling that he would spirit me off right there if I gainsaid him, so I gave him my agreement."

She peered at Elizabeth, an expression akin to desperation alive on her features. "Do you think he would have been capable of such a thing?"

"I do not know what Mr. Wickham is capable of, Lydia. But I believe that you were correct to avoid testing his resolve."

Wringing her hands, Lydia's looked to Elizabeth, pleading with her for an answer to the dilemma. "But whatever shall we do?"

"Do about what?" interrupted another voice, and Elizabeth looked up to see the smiling visage of her suitor.

The congenial expression soon turned hard when he took in Lydia's nearly frantic countenance. "What has happened?"

With a sigh, Elizabeth rose to her feet and coaxed her sister up with her. "I believe that this is a matter we should take up with my father, Mr. Darcy."

His eyes searched hers, and then he gave a tight nod, perhaps instinctively understanding that Lydia's involvement — and her noticeable distress — suggested that Mr. Wickham was likewise involved. He gestured toward the house and said: "Shall we? I had just arrived with my cousin to see your father about certain matters."

Nodding her agreement, Elizabeth joined him, and they walked toward the house, though Lydia was obviously reluctant.

"Do you think Papa will be very angry with me?" whispered Lydia.

"I cannot imagine he would be," replied Elizabeth in kind. "It is not as if you can choose to be importuned or not. Papa will understand that."

Though Lydia was still visibly concerned, Elizabeth was heartened by the fact that she straightened her shoulders and came along willingly.

They entered the house and went straight to her father's study, and upon entering the bookroom, they were introduced to Mr. Darcy's cousin. Colonel Fitzwilliam was in word and behavior every inch the gentleman, genial, intelligent, and possessed of happy manners and a pleasant countenance. He was made more attractive by his manners than by his looks, Elizabeth quickly decided, though she wondered if she would consider him more handsome had the example of his cousin not been before her.

To her credit, Lydia did not make anything of the fact that the good colonel was dressed in his regimentals. The introductions were completed in a quick fashion, after which Colonel Fitzwilliam turned to Elizabeth and addressed her thus:

"I am very pleased to finally make your acquaintance, Miss Bennet. I have heard much about you, and none of the praise appears to have been exaggerated."

Elizabeth favored him with an arch look and replied: "And I have heard much about *you*. But I shall refrain from repeating your cousin's words in your hearing."

Turning to Mr. Darcy, the colonel said: "Have you been telling the lady tales of me, Darcy?"

Far from being offended, Colonel Fitzwilliam appeared to be amused, and Mr. Darcy returned his words in like fashion. "Nothing more than the truth, Fitzwilliam."

"In that case, you must allow me to tell you something of my cousin, Miss Elizabeth," said the colonel, turning back to her. "There are some very interesting stories about his youth which will amuse and delight you, I am sure."

"Do not listen to anything he says," responded Mr. Darcy in a stage whisper. "I was an angel as a child. The only time I was in trouble was by *his* instigation."

The colonel guffawed and exclaimed: "I own that there is a certain amount of truth to that."

Mr. Darcy smiled, clearly at ease with his cousin. He then turned a little more serious eye upon Lydia, who had been watching the greetings with something akin to anxiety. "But perhaps we should focus on the matter at hand."

A look of distaste came over Colonel Fitzwilliam's face. "Wickham!" spat he, almost as if the name were a curse. He turned to Elizabeth and Lydia and eyed them with some concern.

"Since Darcy is in the room and speaking so companionably with you all, I am certain that you have not given Wickham's words any credence."

"Miss Bennet saw through his words instantly, Fitzwilliam," said Mr. Darcy, smiling at Elizabeth with something akin to pride.

"Not instantly," refuted Elizabeth, feeling the color rising in her cheeks. "It was not until he contradicted his words that I began to suspect him of dishonorable intentions."

"And that is more than most people are able to discern," replied the colonel. "I must attribute some greatness of mind to you, Miss Bennet. Even my uncle, Darcy's father, was fooled by Wickham's affected manners, and he was an intelligent and astute man."

Blushing, Elizabeth turned to Lydia determined to remove the focus from herself before she fairly glowed red. "There has been a development to what you have previously heard."

Until this point, Mr. Bennet had been silent, observing the conversation with amusement, but at Elizabeth's words, he leaned forward and pierced his youngest daughter with a suspicious glare. "Have you been having further conversations with Mr. Wickham, Lydia?"

Desperation filled Lydia's features, and she clung to Elizabeth for support.

"Not by choice, Papa," said Elizabeth.

She then proceeded to relate all that Lydia had told her earlier. Incongruously, the expressions on the faces of the visiting gentlemen became darker as she spoke, while her father's own became lighter. When she was finished, there was silence for several moments before Mr. Bennet addressed Lydia.

"It seems that you were put upon improperly, my child. There is no blame attached to this, and I commend you for being sensible enough not to tempt the scoundrel's resolve."

"Thank you, Papa," replied Lydia in a very quiet tone.

"Does this man truly think that he can charm so easily?" continued Mr. Bennet, addressing the cousins. "He displays a remarkable level of arrogant confidence, the likes of which I have never before seen."

Mr. Darcy and Colonel Fitzwilliam shared a look.

"I suspect that Wickham feels that he can get whatever he chooses by the force of his smile," replied Colonel Fitzwilliam. "He likely has no doubt that he has been completely successful in inducing your daughter to elope with him."

"And that gives us the advantage," added Mr. Darcy. His expression, pensive only a moment before, had been overset with a grin the likes of which Elizabeth had never seen him wear. In comparison, she could only imagine a cat who had managed to get into the cream.

"It seems to me that you have something in mind, cousin," said the colonel as he watched Mr. Darcy with some amusement.

"Indeed, I do. In fact, if it works, Mr. Wickham could be out of our lives forever."

"Excellent!" exclaimed the colonel. "Do share. I have a great desire to see George Wickham pay for his many indiscretions against our families."

Chapter XX

*L*ate that night, all was still and calm in Longbourn manor, most of the inhabitants asleep without a care. The night was fair, but the early December chill was present in the air, a sign of the coming months of drab days and inclement weather.

One of the doors on the upper floor of the manor opened, creaking slightly as it moved on its hinges. An indistinct figure paused, waiting for any hint that the sound had been detected by the other occupants of the house. When the silence remained undisturbed, she nodded to herself and continued through the open door, closing it behind her as quietly as she was able.

The stairs were navigated without incident, and the front door opened to allow her passage to the outside world. As she departed from the house, she turned for one last look back at the place where she had been raised. It was dark and undisturbed, but as she remembered the joyful times she had spent in its confines, a sense of happiness stole over her—she had led a truly blessed life, and though it would soon be seen as a place she visited rather than as her home, she would always remember with fondness the times she had spent there. Her father would almost certainly be upset with what she was about to do, but she was convinced it was for the best.

Turning resolutely away, she hurried away from the door and down the drive, moving through Longbourn village, a shadow passing through hazy streets and by shrouded doorways. She reached the edge of the tiny hamlet quickly and hurried out into the fields and groves beyond. It was only a moment before she had reached the appointed place, and she stopped there, holding her small satchel to her tightly. All around, she could feel eyes upon her, and she glanced upward, thankful at once the sky was not only clear, but that the moon was only a sliver, giving off little light. She would not be easily seen this night.

As it was still a few minutes before the appointed time, she was not surprised that she was still alone. Patiently, she waited, knowing that the inducement was such that he would not have been able to resist, even had the night's adventure not been his proposal in the first place. She needed only wait a moment longer, and then he would arrive.

Almost on cue, she noticed a movement from the direction of Meryton, and a horse and rider began to take shape in the gloom. Situated as she was half-facing toward Longbourn—completely by design—she feigned ignorance of his presence, willing him to come a little closer.

"Lydia!" sounded his voice. It was a soft call in keeping with his desire to avoid discovery, but she also fancied she could hear a hint of almost hysterical desperation.

Again, she acted as though she had not heard him call, hoping he would come closer.

With a sigh of exasperation, the man dismounted from his horse and approached, his footsteps heavy against the gravel beneath his feet.

"Lydia!" called he as he strode forward, leading his horse by the reins.

Knowing he was approaching to the point she desired, she calmly turned and watched his approach, seeing his indistinct features in the darkness. In them, she could see an indication of the attractive features that had entranced her at the beginning of their acquaintance.

She smiled as he approached and beckoned him forward with her hand while keeping her face still hidden by her bonnet. He perhaps should have realized that something was amiss, but he was so caught up in his arrogance and his belief in his own power of persuasion that it was clear that he could not fathom anyone not falling for his affected manners and silver-tongued promises.

When she judged that he was close enough, she lifted her head and peered at him, saying: "Mr. Wickham."

Mr. Wickham started and stared at her with consternation. An incredulous "Miss Elizabeth?" escaped his lips.

But he was quick on his feet, Elizabeth had to acknowledge, as his expression of shock quickly turned to a leer. "This is a surprise, though not an unwelcome one. I must own that I am at a loss to understand how you have arranged to take your sister's place."

Elizabeth shook her head with a smile. "When Mr. Darcy first came to Meryton, I erroneously thought that he was overly prideful. It has become abundantly clear, however, that if anyone has been steeped in arrogance, it is *you*."

Before Mr. Wickham could respond to her statement, however, shouts erupted, and several figures on horseback emerged from the surrounding woods and quickly converged upon them. Elizabeth, uncertain as to how Mr. Wickham would react to the overthrowing of his plans, backed away from him quickly. One of the figures made directly for her, and she heard the voice of her beloved saying:

"Elizabeth! How came you to be here?"

"Mr. Darcy," returned she with a laugh. "I am most happy to see you too, sir!"

To say that he was unimpressed with her lighthearted reply would be an understatement. While they were speaking, Colonel Fitzwilliam and several of the officers from Colonel Forster's regiment had approached Mr. Wickham and taken him into custody. The trapped man appeared to be furious, but he wisely kept his own counsel, settling instead for glaring at all and sundry, particularly Mr. Darcy and Elizabeth herself.

After assuring that Mr. Wickham was indeed under the control of Colonel Forster's men, Mr. Darcy turned his severe gaze upon Elizabeth, and he was joined in his disapproval by the stern personage of her father, who had followed Mr. Darcy from the nearby woods. It was Mr. Bennet who spoke next.

"I believe that Mr. Darcy asked you a question, Lizzy."

"It seems to me that the reason for my presence here is obvious," replied Elizabeth. "I was providing the bait to ensure that Mr. Wickham would not be tempted to run if not one was here to meet him."

The two men exchanged a look, and Mr. Darcy glanced over at the prisoner, who was glaring at her with daggers in his eyes.

"You nearly gave us away," grumbled Mr. Bennet, and though Elizabeth could tell that he was somewhat cross with her, he also looked on her with affection and respect. He *had* been the one to encourage her inquisitive nature and her decisiveness. "We thought at first that Lydia had decided to try to elope after all."

"I counted on your confidence that Mr. Wickham would be caught easily," explained Elizabeth. "I was certain you would wait until he appeared before confronting me. And, I did not wish him to keep himself hidden until Lydia appeared, and then slink off to freedom when it became evident that would not be joining him.

"Besides," continued she with a hard look at Wickham, "this libertine importuned *my* sister. I wanted to make certain that he would never attempt to ply his trade with any other young woman."

"Perhaps you are simply jealous that I turned my attention to your sister," called Mr. Wickham, a most unpleasant sneer affixed to his face. "*She* is more comely in face and figure, and your sharp tongue would certainly be a trial."

"Be silent, cur!" spat Colonel Fitzwilliam as he cuffed Wickham on the side of his head. "You are already in deep enough trouble. I suggest that you do not make it any more difficult for yourself."

Mr. Wickham glared at the colonel, but he kept silent. Mr. Darcy, however, looked at his erstwhile friend and seemed to regard him pensively. "I suppose that we might as well discuss Mr. Wickham's future now and set him on his way."

"I agree, Mr. Darcy," said Colonel Forster as he glared at his officer. "Wickham, you are a disgrace to the uniform! If I had my way, I would see you in Marshalsea!"

It appeared that Mr. Wickham was not foolish enough to return his commanding officer's words in like fashion, and when he was silent, Colonel Forster grunted and said: "Your tongue appears to have lost some of its glibness. Pity. In that case, I will turn you over to these gentlemen so that they may inform you of your next assignment."

At that, Mr. Wickham turned a sardonic smirk upon Mr. Darcy. "Well, Darcy, it appears you once again hold my future in your hands. Are you willing now to treat me as your father's will instructs?"

Mr. Darcy shook his head. "Apparently, you have not lost your glibness after all. No, Wickham, you will not be a clergyman under my authority or under any other, if I have any say in the matter."

"Then what shall it be?"

"Spain," said Mr. Darcy. "Fitzwilliam has arranged for your immediate transfer to a regiment in Spain."

Mr. Wickham laughed, a harsh, mocking tone coloring his voice. "I have never known you to have a sense of humor, Darcy, and I think you would be better served to avoid attempting to develop one at this point in your life. What makes you think that I would accept such a posting?"

"It seems to me that you do not really have much room to bargain," was Mr. Darcy's implacable reply. "Attempting to desert? With a gentleman's daughter no less? It appears to me that you have finally taken a step which is beyond your ability to talk your way out of."

"So, you *were* here to run away with me?" jibed Mr. Wickham. "And I thought you preferred your men silent and proud."

There truly was no response to be made, so Elizabeth held her tongue, settling instead for just a shake of her head.

But Mr. Darcy was not nearly so lenient. "I suggest you do not dig your hole any deeper, Wickham."

Mr. Wickham snorted. "What hole? You know as well as I do that you cannot accuse me of attempting to abscond with Miss Elizabeth here. Not if she wishes to maintain her reputation in polite society."

"No, you are correct there," agreed Mr. Darcy with a pleasant smile which, unaccountably, appeared to put Mr. Wickham on his guard. "But what of your attempted desertion?"

"Do not insult my intelligence, Darcy," growled Mr. Wickham. "You have nothing on me."

"You are out here tonight with one of the regiment's horses, are you not?"

"I merely came out for a night-time tryst," replied Mr. Wickham with a salacious leer at Elizabeth. "Even *you* must own that the inducement is well worth it—I am surprised that you have not thought to attempt something similar yourself."

Colonel Fitzwilliam cuffed Mr. Wickham on the back of the head. "It seems to me that your glib tongue is once again running ahead of your discretion."

"It does not signify," said Mr. Wickham with a glare at his tormentor. "With such flimsy evidence, a week in the stockade would be the most that they would do to me. And I would resign my commission before I would accept a transfer to the regulars."

He appeared to be supremely confident, but Elizabeth though she detected more than a hint of anxiety under his bluster. She glanced over at Mr. Darcy and noted the slightly sardonic grin with which he regarded Mr. Wickham.

"You always were a little too impressed with your own cleverness," said Mr. Darcy.

"If you would give me my due, I would not have to survive on my cleverness."

Mr. Darcy shook his head. "Oh, I will give you your due, Wickham.

Of that, you may be assured.

"You seem to have forgotten that I hold your debts from Cambridge and Lambton." At this reminder, the sneer fell away from Wickham's face, and he glared at Mr. Darcy. "In addition, you were engaged in your usual tricks here before we curbed your activities. The amount in Meryton alone is enough to see your pay docked and your resignation refused until it has been repaid. If I were to call the earlier amounts due, I dare say that you would never again see the light of day."

A truly ugly expression came over Mr. Wickham's face, and he began to curse Mr. Darcy, his language fouler than Elizabeth had ever heard before. It was abruptly brought to a halt when the officers guarding him tightened their grip on him and Colonel Fitzwilliam once again forced him to silence. Mr. Wickham's glower never once subsided, and Elizabeth was startled to see how it transformed his pleasing features into ugliness. This was truly a side of Wickham which he rarely allowed others to see.

"As I was saying," continued Mr. Darcy with exaggerated patience, "I have the means to make your life very unpleasant for a very long time."

"It is nothing you have not done ever since your father passed away," spat Wickham.

Mr. Darcy only shook his head, a sadness of which Mr. Wickham was undeserving settling over him like a mantle. "It is obvious that you will never be convinced, so there is little point in attempting to persuade you. I will not, however, allow you to continue to prey on the good people of towns such as Meryton. Personally, I would prefer to have you transported, but the army takes a very dim view of attempted desertions, and as they are involved, they have insisted that your punishment must contain further service time."

"Do not look so glum, Wickham!" interjected Colonel Fitzwilliam with a jovial slap on Mr. Wickham's back. Of course, he might have used a little too much force, as the blow staggered the lieutenant. "Consider this a chance for you to finally make something of your life."

Mr. Wickham's acid look was again turned to the colonel, but it was met by nothing more than a wide grin, which soured the beleaguered man even further.

"I suppose you will require my rank to be reduced to that of a common soldier?"

"No," replied Mr. Darcy, "but you cannot expect me to allow you to maintain the same rank you have possessed up until now, Ensign Wickham."

"Nor would the army allow it," said Colonel Forster.

"So there you have your choice," continued Mr. Darcy. "You can accept the transfer to Spain, or I will have you in debtor's prison."

"And what of when the war ends?" demanded Mr. Wickham. "Am I always to have those accursed debts hanging over my head?"

Mr. Darcy affixed a stern glare on the unfortunate man. "I have no interest in your ruin, Wickham. If you would conduct yourself in a proper manner, then you would not have your debts 'hanging over your head.' The fact of the matter is that you have brought your misfortunes upon yourself.

"But I shall give you one final boon, if you desire it."

Despite looking somewhat skeptical — something completely unwarranted in Elizabeth's mind, given what she knew of Mr. Darcy's honorable nature — Mr. Wickham also appeared to be hopeful. "And what is that?" asked he, suspicion lacing his voice.

"If you serve with distinction in Spain and do not incur any more debt, then when you return to England, you may seek me out again. At that time, I will provide you with a ticket away from England to a destination of your choice and a little money to get you started in a new land. In addition, I will give you all the debt receipts the moment you depart on a ship away from England's shores."

Mr. Wickham appeared to mull that over in his mind, allowing Elizabeth to think on the discussion between the two men. Particularly, Elizabeth watched Mr. Darcy, and though he was outwardly stern and unyielding, she thought that she sensed a sadness in him which he could not completely hide. After all Mr. Wickham had done to him and his family, the fact that he could still feel sorrow for an erstwhile companion who had strayed so far truly spoke to his character. And his offer to Mr. Wickham to forgive the debts and see him started in a new land was truly far more than the man deserved. It bespoke an uncommon generosity of spirit which Elizabeth had never before seen.

"Very well then, Darcy," replied Mr. Wickham at length. "It appears that I have no choice. I accept your terms. But I will hold you to them."

It was laughable, Elizabeth decided, that a man such as Mr. Wickham would use such stern language toward Mr. Darcy. But it was much less audacious than she knew the man could be. Regardless, though it was laughable, Elizabeth knew it was no laughing matter.

Mr. Darcy and Mr. Wickham shook on their agreement, and shortly, Mr. Wickham was led away from the road to be returned to the camp. Knowing how efficient Mr. Darcy was and how implacable his will was once he had decided on a course of action, Elizabeth suspected that Mr.

Wickham would be on his way to the peninsula at the earliest opportunity. His departure also marked the departure of the officers after Colonel Forster had shaken hands with Colonel Fitzwilliam, Mr. Darcy, and Elizabeth's father. Soon, she was left on the road with the three men.

Freed from the distracting presence of Mr. Wickham, Mr. Darcy turned back and looked sternly at Elizabeth, though she thought she could detect a hint of amusement in his stoic gaze.

"And as for you, Miss Bennet," said he, "while I commend you for your bravery and determination, I find I must question your judgment."

"How so, Mr. Darcy?" asked Elizabeth. On the one hand, knowing his feelings for her, she was aware that he was concerned for her welfare and wished to ensure that she was safe. On the other hand, he was not her father and should not be speaking to her thus. A single glance at Mr. Bennet told her that she would get no help from that quarter; her father was watching her with a stern glower, clearly content to allow Mr. Darcy to lead the discussion.

"You are fearless, too," interjected Colonel Fitzwilliam. He was a contrast to the other two men—clearly, though he liked Elizabeth based on their short acquaintance, he had not known her long enough to form a strong emotional connection with her, and he thus did not have as much fear for her personal safety as her father and her suitor possessed.

Mr. Darcy scowled at his cousin. "Do not make this any more difficult than it already needs to be. Wickham is not the only one in possession of a glib tongue."

The only response Mr. Darcy was to receive from his cousin was a snicker. But Mr. Darcy had already turned back to Elizabeth.

"I assure you that I was in no danger," said Elizabeth, and though she had not intended it, even she could detect a hint of primness in her voice. "I knew that nothing would go wrong."

"*Nothing?*" was Mr. Darcy's incredulous reply. "Surely you do not understand the gravity of the situation, madam. You could have been waylaid or come to some accident between Longbourn and here, which is not to mention the damage you could have done to your reputation."

"I am truly sorry I worried you," replied Elizabeth, directing her words at all three men. "I simply wanted to make certain that Mr. Wickham would not slip through your fingers."

"And you knew that we would not agree, so you did not tell us what you planned," said Mr. Bennet with a rueful smile and shake of his head.

"Would you have allowed it?" asked Elizabeth with a saucy grin.

"Certainly not!" exclaimed Mr. Darcy.

"Then I am glad I did not tell you," replied Elizabeth.

Mr. Darcy watched her from behind a stony countenance for several moments before he turned to Elizabeth's father. "Mr. Bennet, I presume that you will be returning your daughter to her room now?"

With a grunt, Mr. Bennet replied: "Assuming we can get her into the house and to her room without alerting her mother to her nighttime . . . adventure. I hate to think of what a commotion my wife would cause should she know of Elizabeth's activities tonight."

"In that case, would you allow my cousin and I to escort you to Longbourn? And might I be able to have a word with Miss Bennet in private as we walk?"

It was clear that Mr. Bennet, in his own sardonic way, found amusement in the situation. "You do realize that this is wholly improper at such an hour, Mr. Darcy."

"I do," said he. "But given the situation, I doubt that anything could be more proper than a walk chaperoned by her own father."

"Well said, young man!" replied Mr. Bennet in a jovial tone. "In that case, Colonel Fitzwilliam and I shall go on ahead, and you may follow us to the house. Please refrain from loitering about too long, as I doubt my old heart is strong enough for the frenzy which would erupt should we need to dispatch search parties to find you."

And with that, Mr. Bennet and Colonel Fitzwilliam—the latter looking vastly amused by the situation—began walking down the path back toward Longbourn. In keeping with Mr. Bennet's instructions to stay close, Mr. Darcy gestured toward the path and began to follow them, though at a slower pace. Soon, the other two men were some distance ahead of them, though they could still be easily discerned. Mr. Bennet looked back at them from time to time, keeping a close watch on them, and Elizabeth knew that Mr. Darcy would not take advantage of the situation. It was well that he was so honorable—Elizabeth was by this time uncertain that she would be able to deny him anything he should ask.

They walked in silence for several moments, Mr. Darcy obviously trying to decide what to say as he attempted to stay in control of his pique. Elizabeth, for her part, was content to simply walk by his side and allow him to make his case. She was well enough acquainted with her own character—and honest enough with herself!—to know that while she had most assuredly taken action to ensure that Mr. Wickham did not escape justice, she had also acted as she had because she had felt compelled to be a part of the man's undoing.

"Miss Bennet," said Mr. Darcy, startling her out of her thoughts. "Though you are probably expecting to hear recriminating words from me, I find that I am unable to summon them. I *do* think that you have behaved somewhat recklessly tonight; I also have the highest respect for your intelligence, your resolve, and your loyalty toward those you love. I might have wished that you would have allowed us to deal with Wickham in the manner we saw fit, but I also understand that you are not content to be a mere bystander when great events are taking place. Though perhaps I should condemn this trait, I find that it enhances your charms most disconcertingly. I rejoice in the fact that should I be successful in my suit, I shall be gaining a life partner, one who will walk the road of life by my side rather than be content to follow."

Elizabeth smiled. "By all means, you must take my faults and make them into virtues. I find that I quite enjoy the experience."

Smiling, Mr. Darcy placed his free hand over her hand which held his arm. "You know, Miss Bingley once said that your behavior betrays an abominable sort of conceited independence. I suppose that this trait is one of those which attracted me to you from the very beginning."

"So you agree with Miss Bingley about me?" demanded Elizabeth, feigning affront. "I do not know if I am willing to accept the hand of a man who means to be as critical about me as the amiable Mr. Bingley's sister!"

"You know that I suggest no such thing," replied Mr. Darcy, and though his tone was serious, his attitude was all complacence. "I merely stated that you are a much livelier companion than most others could boast. You must own that Miss Bingley was not far from the truth."

Elizabeth arched an eyebrow at him, which caused his smile to become even wider. "She may have something, I will grudgingly confess. However, I really must take issue with the word 'conceited.' *I* would certainly never use such a word to describe myself—what person, who had the good fortune to have Jane as a sister, could ever become conceited?"

"Do not make light of your charms, Miss Bennet," said Mr. Darcy. "It is true that your sister is a very beautiful woman, but I, most strenuously, take exception to the suggestion that you are in any way deficient in appearance when compared to her. You are a beautiful woman in your own right, and I will not hear anything to the contrary!"

A heat spread over Elizabeth's cheeks, and she knew that she was blushing fiercely at his praise. She was gratified that he should think so highly of her charms, but incongruously, she was also grateful that the darkness hid her response from him. Drawing on all her willpower, she forced herself to attend to their conversation, and she was soon able to reply:

"I certainly thank you, Mr. Darcy. But 'conceited' is not the proper word. Mayhap 'determined' or 'indomitable' would be a better choice?"

"I cannot disagree with that," said Mr. Darcy, and then he lapsed into silence.

For her part, Elizabeth was thrilled with the path the conversation had taken. She had actually expected that he would have much more to say about her "conceited independence" than he had taken the opportunity to express. The fact that he admired this trait about her spoke well to her future felicity with him. Should he ever get around to proposing, that was. It could not be long now. At least, she hoped that was the case.

"When did Miss Bingley make this . . . insightful observation?" asked Elizabeth, more to fill the silence than anything else.

"The first evening of your stay at Netherfield to tend to your sister," said Mr. Darcy. "You had supped with us and then left to return to your sister's side. Miss Bingley waxed eloquent on the deficiencies of your character and behavior, I assure you."

"I can well believe it, Mr. Darcy. But surely you must have had the same thoughts yourself."

Mr. Darcy turned his head away from her, a little uncomfortably, she thought. "I will own that I said a phrase or two that I should never have uttered, and I now regret it most heartily."

"Do not feel ashamed," said Elizabeth, smiling brightly. "It was more than likely no less than I deserved—and certainly no less than what I once said of you."

"You do not indeed deserve such censure," replied Mr. Darcy as he turned to look at her again. "Though perhaps most ladies of high society would not have done as you did, the fact that you walked from Longbourn to Netherfield due to nothing more than a sincere concern for your sister speaks very highly of you. I assure you that whatever I said was half-hearted at best."

Then Mr. Darcy grinned, and he said with a slightly mischievous air: "And I managed to defend you to Miss Bingley in a manner which left her in no doubt as to *my* feelings, though she still attempts to deny it to this day."

Intrigued, Elizabeth asked him to explain himself, which he readily did:

"I had previously confessed to Miss Bingley that I find your eyes particularly fine."

"I can hardly credit it!" said Elizabeth with a laugh. "But if it is so, then it is no wonder she disapproves of me with such determination!"

"I assure you that I did," replied Mr. Darcy. "It was most impolitic of me, but she caught me at an unguarded moment, and once I had said too much, she was determined to pull it all from me, willingly or no.

"In the instance where she referred to your independence, she said something to the effect that your little . . . escapade had almost certainly served to dampen my admiration of your fine eyes. Of course, not being able to dismiss such a challenge, I responded, saying 'Not at all. They were brightened by the exercise.'"

Throwing her head back, Elizabeth laughed gaily, to which Mr. Darcy responded by joining in.

"I am sure she could not have accepted such a statement from *you* with any equanimity."

"It silenced her for a brief moment, I assure you. But then she and her sister attempted to lessen your appeal by enumerating all the disadvantages of your situation, including your fortune and connections. It was easy enough to ignore them, considering the fact that Miss Bingley, for all her airs, is in actuality the daughter of a tradesman, little though she would wish to recall the connection."

Still chuckling, Elizabeth left all thoughts of Mr. Bingley's sisters behind—she did not wish to think of *them* at such a time, after all. She looked around, and even in the dark, the landscape was familiar. She knew that it would not be much longer before they would arrive at the gates to her home and be separated once again for the night. Such thoughts caused a melancholy to settle over her, and she wondered when he would declare himself again. She almost wished that she had simply encouraged him the last time he had brought it up! Then she would not have to endure this uncertainty, though she supposed that in all honesty, there was not anything unsure in the slightest about his intentions.

She turned back to him and noted that he was now watching her intently, following her profile as they walked through the darkened landscape. Elizabeth's breath caught in her throat at the thought that this might finally be the moment when he would declare himself.

"Miss Bennet," said he, addressing her as she gazed back at him. "I must say that our discussion tonight, though essentially similar to the conversations we have had in the past, has given me hope that your own thoughts and feelings have been clarified these past few days. Tell me, am I mistaken?"

Feeling her heart beating with a wild cadence in her chest, Elizabeth looked at him and said: "No, sir. You are not mistaken."

Mr. Darcy stopped in the middle of the road and turned so that he was facing her directly. "In that case, there is no need for me to wait any longer. I have long been certain of my own feelings, and I assure you that my comments about your appearance earlier were only a small part of what I feel for you.

"Miss Bennet, you are a jewel among women. You are beautiful and lively, witty and charming, gracious and elegant, and I believe that I could search the length and breadth of Britain for the rest of my life and never find another who enchanted me as much as you have with so little effort. I had not been here a week before you began to intrigue me, two before I found myself caught by your vivacity and *joie de vivre*, and a month before I was hopelessly in love and completely content with the web in which I was caught. I have come to feel for you a passionate love and regard that I have never before experienced, and I hope that you feel the same for me."

Elizabeth, feeling tears flowing down her cheeks, could muster no more response than a nod to his unspoken question, and the heartfelt expression of delight which brightened his face made him more than uncommonly handsome. If this was the response she could provoke in him, then she felt that she would very much enjoy a lifetime of sharing such adoring looks with this man.

"I love you with all of my being, *Elizabeth*," continued he, and she gasped at the intimacy of hearing nothing more than her Christian name on his tongue for the first time. "I beg you to accept my hand and consent to be my wife."

Overpowered by the emotions which were raging within her breast, Elizabeth flung her arms around his neck and whispered over and over again: "I will. I will."

Mr. Darcy's arms settled around her, and Elizabeth felt more secure and safe than she ever had in her life. She was where she belonged.

A cough sounded from behind her, and Elizabeth stepped away from Mr. Darcy, her cheeks once again blazing. Mr. Darcy gazed down tenderly at her for a moment before he squared his shoulders and looked up toward where her father and Colonel Fitzwilliam were watching them. While it was difficult to make out their expressions, Elizabeth fancied that she could see nothing more than amusement in their demeanors, though she thought that her father's countenance was a little sad as well. She immediately understood—she had been his companion for years, and he would of course feel a little reluctant to let her go.

"I believe I shall speak to your father now, Elizabeth," said he in a quiet tone.

"By all means, William," responded Elizabeth. "I long for our new understanding to be acknowledged to the world."

Mr. Darcy reached down and grasped her hand, lifting it to his lips and bestowing a tender kiss upon its back. "I find myself similarly impatient."

And with that, he strode away, boldly asking for a moment of Mr. Bennet's time. The colonel moved toward her to give the two men a little privacy, but his beaming smile told her how he felt about the events of the past few moments.

"I must commend you, Miss Bennet," said he after they had walked together for a few moments. In truth, Elizabeth had a difficult time forcing her attention away from her newly betrothed, but she would not be rude to his closest cousin, so she turned to hear what he was saying.

"I have rarely seen Darcy so . . . carefree and open. I have long despaired that he would ever be this way with anyone outside our close family circle. And yet somehow you have managed to affect him to this great degree—and in so short a time."

"Then you approve of me?" questioned Elizabeth, though she already knew the answer.

"For this alone, I would approve of you," said Colonel Fitzwilliam. "The fact that I do like you very well indeed regardless of our short acquaintance is merely more of a confirmation that you will suit my cousin very well. I thank you for bringing a little joy into his life. Other than his sister, Georgiana, joy has been in short supply in the life of Fitzwilliam Darcy for far too long."

"Then I shall do my best to ensure that he has an abundance of joy for as long as I can."

The colonel smiled at her. "I am sure you will."

And with that, they fell into a companionable silence as they continued to follow Mr. Bennet and Mr. Darcy, who were now in earnest conversation.

At length, they reached the edge of Longbourn village. The two men stopped, and Mr. Bennet held out his hand, which Mr. Darcy clasped and shook heartily. Mr. Bennet turned and beckoned for Elizabeth to draw closer.

"Well, this is perhaps the least surprising revelation in the county, my dear, but Mr. Darcy has asked for my permission to marry you, which I have granted with alacrity."

"Thank you, Papa," said Elizabeth, stepping forward to kiss her father on the cheek.

"I believe that Mr. Darcy shall make you happy. I certainly could not have parted with you to anyone less worthy of you. Yes, you shall be very happy indeed."

"I shall," was Elizabeth's quiet response. Her heart was so full that she thought that it might burst, but she would have it no other way.

"Well, well, I believe that it has all transpired for the best," continued her father in a cheerful tone. "However, I will caution you again, sir—the exact timing of your proposal should be kept from the local populace. As such, if you arrive early tomorrow morning, I shall see to it that you and Elizabeth are afforded an opportunity to reach an understanding in the morning. After that, you may join me in my study, thereby escaping the incessant talk of feminine fripperies and wedding details to which I am subjected daily. I am very much in your debt for allowing me a respite, brief though it will be; however, you will still owe me for now ensuring that talk of weddings, wedding breakfasts, lace, and other such nonsense will increase the noise level in my house most substantially."

"Oh, Papa!" said Elizabeth with affection. "You should enjoy it now while you can. Eventually, *all* of your daughters will leave, and I dare say when we are gone, you will miss the noise and bustle of the house."

It might have been a trick of the light, but Elizabeth almost fancied that she could see a little moisture appear in the corner of her normally stoic father's eyes.

"Right you are, my dearest Lizzy. Now, I believe it is time for us to part. You may have a moment to bid your young man farewell."

And with that, Mr. Bennet turned and walked toward the house once again. Colonel Fitzwilliam also withdrew a short distance, but not before he congratulated Elizabeth again in a most enthusiastic way. And for a moment, she and Mr. Darcy were once again left to their own devices.

"I thank you for accepting me and for allowing me the opportunity to show you who I truly am," said Mr. Darcy after a moment. "I will cherish this time and promise you now that you will never have reason to repine the choice you have made here today."

"I am certain I never shall, William," replied Elizabeth. "And since I have not said so before, I would like to assure you that I do love you very much. Nothing will make me happier than to be your wife."

Seemingly overcome with emotion, Mr. Darcy drew her to him, and she laid her head against his chest, overcome by the sensation of being so close to him. It was right, she decided, to accept this man. She could only be grateful that she had possessed the presence of mind to question Mr. Wickham's account of his former dealings with Mr. Darcy. If she had not, she was certain she would have continued in the bitterness of spirit, believing him to be the worst of all men and showing him that she was not worthy of him

For now, however, she knew that she was at home. She would never leave his side again.

Chapter XXI

*I*n later years, the circumstances surrounding the engagement of Fitzwilliam Darcy and Elizabeth Bennet became somewhat of a legend for those of their family who knew exactly how it had taken place. Some members, of course, remained uninformed, as the story had the potential to cause considerable embarrassment and call into question the reputations of those involved. But those members of the family who could be trusted to keep it in confidence eventually learned of it, and it was with some amusement that the story was embellished until Elizabeth felt that it contained less truth than fantasy.

Nevertheless, she would not have changed anything which had happened for the world, for though it had undoubtedly been unorthodox and slightly improper, still Elizabeth had received her heart's desire. In addition to this, she received several lessons in the bargain, the least which was not the necessity of reserving judgment.

But before the principles can be settled, it would, perhaps, be best to consider those around them, for their stories were many and varied. In particular, the story of the villain, Mr. Wickham, ended in a rather surprising fashion which no one who was at all familiar with the man in question could have predicted.

Mr. Wickham was indeed shipped off to the Iberian Peninsula as Mr. Darcy had promised, and since the army kept a close watch on him in case he should decide to try to desert, he spent the next two years in the midst of the fighting in Spain. When he finally returned in the spring of 1815, he was a changed man, soft-spoken and with the look in his eye of a man who had seen much death and had not remained unaffected by it. Upon arriving in London, where Mr. Darcy and Elizabeth had been attending the events of the season, he had sought out Mr. Darcy, and after a conversation, he had received the receipts of his debts as promised in addition to the money and the ticket away from England.

Mr. Darcy never told Elizabeth much about that meeting, but what she was able to infer gave her hope that the man would be able to make something of his life. Regardless, he sailed away from the shores of England toward the new world less than a fortnight later, and he was never heard from again. Elizabeth liked to think that he had reformed and had managed to start a new life for himself in the Americas, but she was well aware that regardless of his experiences, it was possible that he had once again succumbed to the lure of his previous ways and been left in a position as dire as the one which had led to his service in the regulars in the first place.

Somewhat less villainous, though still distasteful, was the person of her cousin, Mr. Collins. That young man had, of course, been forced to leave Longbourn without a bride, and though he never established contact with the Bennets again, Elizabeth did have a reliable source of information concerning him in the person of Mr. Darcy's cousin, Anne de Bourgh. Mr. Collins eventually ended up marrying the daughter of one of the tenants of Rosings Park, and though Elizabeth never met the woman, she heard that she was nearly as silly and vapid as her husband.

Anne de Bourgh herself never married, as she had always intended, and while Lady Catherine eventually came to understand her daughter's choice, she never reconciled herself to her nephew's, leading to a permanent estrangement. The lady died many years later, survived by her daughter, who, though in chronic poor health, still managed to live a respectable and enjoyable life. In Anne, Elizabeth eventually found a friendly woman who was herself a studier of character. Of course, their intimacy did not occur until after Lady Catherine's death, as the lady remained as violently opposed to Elizabeth at the end as she had been from the beginning.

As for Rosings itself, it was eventually left to the stewardship of Colonel Fitzwilliam in Anne's will, though he did not inherit it until later in his life. The colonel married a woman of good fortune for whom he developed an affection, though it was perhaps not quite as happy or close as the one the Darcys shared. Still, he was content with his life and with his family, not to mention the ability to pass Rosings down to his eldest son.

As for the Bennet sisters, they all eventually married, though by some twist of fate, it was Kitty and Lydia who both married pastors, Lydia settling in Kympton under the patronage of her elder sister's husband while Kitty settled in nearby Nottinghamshire, no more than thirty miles from her sisters. Mary wedded a young master of an estate near York, and though the estate was small, it was prosperous and industriously managed by her husband. He was a man for whom Elizabeth always had the highest respect, though he was a garrulous and open fellow, which meant he contrasted greatly with the staid and serious Mary. It was a shock to them all that she had managed to find herself such a man.

Jane, of course, married Mr. Bingley, eventually purchasing an estate within twenty miles of Pemberley and completing the exodus of the Bennet daughters to the north of England. There, she and Mr. Bingley settled down to raise a gaggle of children, all as mild and obliging as both their parents.

In the matter of Mr. Darcy's attentions to Elizabeth, however, the younger of the Bingley sisters, at least, was far from accepting of *that* particular turn of events. However, some credit for intelligence was to be given to Miss Bingley regarding the way in which she conducted herself. She knew that Mr. Darcy would not appreciate any overt attempts to disparage Elizabeth, nor would he be prevailed upon to marry her by any underhanded means, so she confined herself to merely trying to make herself appear to greater advantage than Elizabeth, though her attempts did contain a hint of desperation.

Sadly for Miss Bingley, it was not to be. Very quickly—perhaps more quickly than was to be expected, considering her single-minded pursuit—she determined the lay of the land and, deciding that it was better to keep the connection which could still help her greatly in town, she graciously—though perhaps a little frostily—capitulated. Eventually, Miss Bingley ended up marrying the proprietor of a large estate in Shropshire. There, she was happy, as she realized that she had discovered a man for whom she actually possessed some affection.

In due time, Elizabeth became acquainted with Mr. Darcy's sister, and she found Georgiana Darcy to be a quiet and shy girl, much as Mr. Darcy had intimated. Through Elizabeth's gentle tutelage, Georgiana was able to acquire a measure of confidence and was finally able to put her experiences with Mr. Wickham in the past. In this endeavor Elizabeth was assisted by Lydia, though it might be more correct to state that the two girls assisted one another in their paths to maturity and adulthood. It seemed like their shared experiences with Mr. Wickham bound them together, and they were forever close confidantes and friends.

Finally, Elizabeth found great pleasure in her season of courtship, eventually arriving at the altar not long after her elder sister. Mr. and Mrs. Darcy forever after shared a strong and loving marriage, and Elizabeth was happy throughout all the rest of her days, for though it was impossible for two such intelligent and strong-willed people to go through life without disagreement, their quarrels were always of short duration, and their reconciliations all the sweeter. She often thought of those days in which her opinion of her husband had been changed, considering the fact that while moving from dislike to love in a single day was far too much, the journey could be quite satisfactorily completed in less than a month. It was obvious that he was a man who met all of her requirements in a husband, and he was one whom she could both love and respect. She could only be thankful that she had been able to see through Mr. Wickham's words and accept those spoken by the man who would become her husband. Truly, her eyes had been opened.

THE END

ALSO BY ONE GOOD SONNET PUBLISHING

Acting on Faith
Though Darcy has no assurances of Elizabeth's regard after her rejection of him, he nonetheless moves forward in his quest to secure her hand. Unfortunately, neither Caroline Bingley nor Elizabeth's childhood friend Samuel Lucas intends to make it easy for him.

Waiting for an Echo, Volume I: Words in the Darkness
When Mr. Darcy comes to Hertfordshire to decide between two prospective brides, he has no idea that his eye will be irrevocably caught by someone so much lower in consequence than him as Elizabeth Bennet.

Waiting for an Echo, Volume II: Echoes at Dawn
When Elizabeth travels to Kent to stay with her newly married sister, she meets Mr. Darcy's two prospective brides and is forced to deal with the consequences of a pair of tragic events. Can her feelings for Mr. Darcy conquer even the villainous machinations of a former love interest?

For more details, visit
http://rowlandandeye.com/

About The Author

Jann Rowland was born in Regina, Saskatchewan, Canada. He enjoys reading, sports, and he also dabbles a little in music, taking pleasure in singing and playing the piano.

Though Jann did not start writing until his mid-twenties, writing has grown from a hobby to an all-consuming passion. His interest in Jane Austen stems from his university days when he took a class in which *Pride and Prejudice* was required reading. *Acting on Faith* is his first published novel, but he envisions many more in the coming years, both within the *Pride and Prejudice* universe and without.

He now lives in Alberta, with his wife of almost twenty years, and his three children.

Printed in Great Britain
by Amazon.co.uk, Ltd.,
Marston Gate.